# DO I MAKE MYSELF CLEAR?

It felt comforting, Nathaniel's jacket against her shoulders, with the heat of his muscled body beneath. She leaned into him. If he were as real as he claimed, would he disappear into thin air at the author's whim, leaving her to sprawl on the ground? He didn't. In fact, he pulled her the slightest bit tighter with what felt like an absolutely there arm.

He lowered her onto a stone bench and stepped back. Candlelight spilled from tall windows behind him, illuminating the pale color of his breeches and the blackness of his hair. Cold began to seep through the thin fabric of her dress, startling her senses into a nervous clarity. "What would I be *doing* here?" she asked, more of herself than him.

"You are a minor character."

Given an opening, annoyance slipped right past consternation to claim the upper hand. "I am a lot of things, but never minor."

# HERO
# WORSHIP

Dawn Calvert

**ZEBRA BOOKS**
Kensington Publishing Corp.
www.kensingtonbooks.com

ZEBRA BOOKS are published by

Kensington Publishing Corp.
850 Third Avenue
New York, NY 10022

All Kensington titles, imprints and distributed lines are
available at special quantity discounts for bulk purchases for
sales promotion, premiums, fund-raising, educational or
institutional use.

Special book excerpts or customized printings can also be created to fit specific needs. For details, write or phone the office
of the Kensington Special Sales Manager: Attn. Special Sales
Department. Kensington Publishing Corp., 850 Third Avenue,
New York, NY 10022. Phone: 1-800-221-2647.


Zebra and the Z logo Reg. U.S. Pat. & TM Off.

First Printing: December 2006
10 9 8 7 6 5 4 3 2 1

Printed in the United States of America

*For my sister Sue.*

# Chapter One

In the lonely hours of a Saturday night, with worn pink bunny slippers on her feet and a musty nineteenth-century book clutched in her hands, Andi found the man of her dreams.

True, Nathaniel Chamberlain, the hero of *Wedgfeld Hall*, existed only in fiction written almost two centuries in the past. But he beat every man she'd ever dated by a long shot.

She closed her eyes, picturing him. Nathaniel, standing with his arms crossed, snowy white cravat a stark contrast to his thick black hair and the deep blue of the sky behind him; breeches straining against well-honed, powerful leg muscles; dark eyes with flecks of green that locked a woman in their commanding gaze, flickering with just a hint of vulnerability.

Just the idea, the thought of him, caused Andi's heart to skip a beat. The men she knew not only paled in comparison, they disappeared altogether.

But he wasn't real. And she, gripping the book's fragile pages until her knuckles whitened, was losing faith she'd ever find a living, breathing man who could come close to the fictional Nathaniel.

But that couldn't be true . . . could it? She believed everyone had a soul mate, a perfect match. Somewhere. Waiting. Without the kind of love that would set her heart on fire, the world would be an ugly place. With it, there was hope for a life that really, truly mattered.

So if she believed so passionately in its possibilities, why in the hell did a loving, committed relationship fly past her like light rail running two hours late?

Heaving a sigh, Andi reached for another tissue, blowing her nose with a honk that made her cat blink with annoyance. It had to be a leftover reaction from *Romeo and Juliet*. She shouldn't have watched that video again. It always made her cry.

She ran a reverent finger down the cover of the book. It had been a find. An 1810 first edition that had joined Andi's fledgling rare book collection last week. So far, it had been worth every cent. In fantasy, if nothing else.

She stretched her body the full length of the couch and pulled the book onto her chest. Two chapters into the book and she already wanted nothing more than for Nathaniel Chamberlain, with eyes that smoldered with promise and a heart that beat with the strength of beliefs fiercely held, to materialize in person, sweep her into his arms, and spirit her far away.

A gentleman. Thrown into a desperate situation by the order of his birth and a responsibility he would not turn away from. Determined to do the right thing, no matter what it cost him. Ancestral home and family above all else. Throw in manners, noble breeding, the hint of a rakish past, and a barely contained sexuality that leapt from the page, and Andi's heart was lost.

Her mother's voice crept unbidden into her head. *There you go, overdramatizing again, Alexandra. Any minute now you'll take your bow and wait for the applause.*

She punched a pillow and stuffed it behind her head. Right. Just like she'd "overdramatized" when Tristan, the man of her *mother's* dreams, left Andi, gowned in a Vera Wang to-die-for dress, standing at the altar after he'd whispered in her ear. And left. The pungent smell of roses still made her nauseous.

*Quiet, mother.* With a long, cleansing breath, Andi cleared all thoughts of that day from her mind and turned to the beginning of the third chapter.

*When his eyes landed upon her, Catherine knew she should cast her own demurely down, but her gaze remained steadily upon him. He began to move toward her, weaving his way through ball guests with little regard for the meaningless courtesies required. Whispers followed him, though he turned not. He moved with a confidence she envied. At last, he stood rigidly before her, his proud chin defiantly high.*

*In that moment, she wanted very much to know if the rumors swirling about Mr. Chamberlain were true. Should they be proved accurate, she would be wise to disregard the thoroughly pleasing look of his face and the grave formality with which he bowed upon introduction to her. Much, it seemed, could drive even a reluctant man to make the offer she sensed hovering at his lips. Yet much could drive a woman, most particularly one in her position, to accept.*

*As if a woman would even have to think about it.* Andi mentally elbowed the book's heroine aside to imagine herself standing before Nathaniel, casting a seductive glance that would cause his eyes to widen and all thoughts of Catherine Havington to disappear.

She flung an arm across the back of the couch, her fingers brushing a small object on the table. Tearing her eyes from the page, she picked it up, examining its opaque sheen by the light of the lamp. A wishing stone, the dealer had called it. He had thrown it in with the price of the book, admitting that he didn't know what else to do with it.

A wishing stone. Just what every truly frustrated woman needed.

It felt smooth, except for one rough spot, which she rubbed against the tender side of her thumb as she turned back to read further. Nathaniel Chamberlain was being introduced to other guests.

*"Mrs. Lofton-Hale," Horatio Havington said, "and her daughter Alexandra."*

Mrs. Lofton—and her daughter Alexan—Andi froze, staring at the page as the significance of the names began to sink in. Then she gasped and bolted upright. She read the words twice, and then three times. The black print blurred as she strained to read it again. It couldn't be.

But there it was, her name. Alexandra Lofton-Hale. In a book written some 200 years ago. She laid her fingertips across her forehead, pressing hard.

She'd stayed up too long. Fantasized too much, until she could no longer separate reality from fiction. That had to be it. She looked sidelong at her watch. Midnight. She'd drifted half off to sleep and her imagination had taken over. Again.

She inhaled, sucking air through her nose until it stung, and stared at the page again.

> *"Mrs. Lofton-Hale," Horatio Havington said, "and her daughter Alexandra."*

"Aahgggh!" Despite the empty wineglass next to her, she wasn't anywhere near sleep. Maybe that was the problem. Her name, right there. Strange, really strange.

No, scratch strange. It was bizarre. Freakish.

Andi juggled the book between her hands before flinging both it and the stone to the other end of the couch. They hit the wooden arm, landing with a thud and then a ping.

"Coincidence," she announced. "Happens all the time." Blinking hard, she launched into the relaxation breathing she'd learned last year when she'd been called to the principal's office for veering from the established high school English curriculum to have her students read *Wuthering Heights*. The breathing exercises hadn't worked, but there was always a first time.

In. Count to four. Out. Count to four.

Her cat, Mr. Rochester, raised his head and blinked a question, while making it clear he didn't care to know the answer. The clock in the kitchen ticked out a steady beat, and outside, a siren wailed in the distance. After minutes that went on forever, Andi felt her heartbeat slow to a pace somewhere near normal. "Nothing to get worked up about." She narrowed her eyes and, after a minute, snapped her fingers. "My mother!"

Hattie Hale, for as long as Andi could remember, had complained about the name birth and marriage had stuck her with. "Sounds like a woman with a single-wide and a washboard," she'd say. "I made sure my daughter didn't have the same problem."

Her mother could have read *Wedgfeld Hall* before Andi's birth and decided that Alexandra Lofton-Hale sounded like a magnificent name. Of course, she'd never seen her mother, whose attention could barely be held by a short magazine article, pick up any novel, much less one from Jane Austen's era. But nothing else made sense.

Andi sat down again, crossing and uncrossing her arms and tapping her toe, until, unable to stand it any longer, she made a grab for the book.

As she did, a piece of paper slipped from the back and fluttered to the floor. She picked it up, the touch of her hand on the thin surface revealing it was likely as old as the book. She caught her breath in anticipation, remembering the century-old love letter she'd found in the back of another of her rare finds. With great care, she turned the paper over and read, *The sport of wishing* in a precise, sloped handwriting. *A guide for those so disposed.*

If wishing were a sport, she'd take the gold medal. When Andi wished, she did it from the hair Joaquin cut to trendy perfection every month to the Pink Tanqini polish on her toes. No point in going halfway. All or nothing kept dreams alive.

The paper listed instructions. She threw her body

across the couch, scooped up the stone, and held it in the center of her right palm, as instructed. *Next, it said, form a wish.*

Could she ever.

Following the steps written in faded handwriting, she began to rub the stone with her left forefinger, in a circular motion, repeating the words *a posse ad esse* over and over again. Even though it seemed silly, a pinprick of hope began to push upward. She shook her head, trying to suppress it. It was a game, that's all. *But wouldn't it be amazing if it actually could . . .*

She'd begun formulating the wish deep into the first few pages of *Wedgfeld Hall*, even before she could give it words. *Please. Let me meet a man like this, one I can love with every piece of my heart and soul. One who will love me back.*

She rubbed harder.

Glancing down, she read the next step, which told her to voice her wish aloud and close her eyes when the stone began to heat. No problem there. This wish was coming from deep in her wounded heart, with all the passion of the awkward, bookish fifteen-year-old she'd once been and the woman she wasn't sure she'd ever become.

She could only hope that, when she'd given voice to the words and the stone again went cold in her hand, the letdown, irrational as it was, wouldn't send a bad night spiraling downward. Her mother had told her twice today there was no sadder sight than a woman her age with no grandchildren. The eyes of Andi's male students had glazed over during her discussion of *Pride and Prejudice*, and she'd had to stop pretending they were actually reading the book and not finding summaries on the Internet.

And her blind date for the evening, not that she'd ever speak to that friend again, had shown up late, bored and expecting her to drool over him and his Lexus. Not exactly Prince Charming.

She closed her eyes and lifted her chin, saying the words again, *a posse ad esse,* this time in a singsong chant. "I wish," she said aloud, with all the projection and articulation she'd been taught by her high school drama teacher, "to become Alexandra Lofton-Hale in the book *Wedgfeld Hall.* To, for once in my life, meet a man like Nathaniel Chamberlain." Then she held her breath.

Nothing. The sound of muffled voices in the hallway, a door closing; but in her apartment, nothing but the familiar ache of disappointment. She let go of her breath, squeezed her eyes tight, and forced her eyes open, where they landed on the stack of ungraded papers she'd been ignoring all evening. Come on. Even *she* knew better than to pin her hopes on something called a wishing stone.

In the next instant, a loud pop sounded on her right, accompanied by a deafening, whirring rush of air. Her head jerked backward. A second later, she was knocked off the couch and sent flying through the air, feet first. Darkness, streaked with razors of light, surrounded her. She couldn't see, couldn't move, couldn't breathe.

Earthquake? End of the world? The rush of noise knotted her stomach in fear and panic shot through her with a fury as she hurtled into the blackness. She tried to stretch her arms to find something to hang on to, anything that could stop the missile her body had turned into, but they remained glued to her side, as helpless as every other part of her. Once again, her eyes closed.

And then, just as suddenly, it was quiet, followed by the silvery strain of music in her ears. Her body righted itself. She heard people's voices. Not frightened, not worried, but . . . conversational. Feminine, against a background of . . . violins?

She was standing, her feet pinched, as though they were shoved into shoes a size too small. Andi opened one eye slowly, carefully, terrified of what she might see. Her apartment in shambles? An alien demanding to be taken to her master?

Ummm . . . not quite. Instead, voices, strings playing, and the swish of elegant fabrics surrounding her in a dimly lit room. She opened the other eye. Candles everywhere, warm and glowing, their wicks leaping with flame.

*This isn't happening, isn't real. You're dreaming, Andi.*

Her eyes widened at the sight of the man standing before her. Tall. Muscular. Thick black hair with a hint of a wave. A gaze so heart-stoppingly sensual, she'd know him anywhere. Nathaniel Chamberlain.

Right then, she was pretty certain, her heart did stop. Or at least stumbled and skipped a few beats.

"Miss Lofton-Hale, are you unwell?" he asked in the most formal of clipped tones.

*Unwell?* Her chin dropped and her shoulders pulled themselves into a hunched, submissive position. "Not at all, sir. Thank you." The words weren't hers, but they came from her mouth, spoken straight to the floor.

She wanted to fawn wordlessly all over him, to drape her arms across him and revel in how much she loved this dream, but her tightly held body seemed to prevent any such movement. Not only that, but where had those words come from? *Not at all, sir?* Spoken with an accent that didn't come from growing up in the Northwest.

Heat rose in her cheeks. With difficulty, Andi raised a hand to touch her face and felt a tendril of hair curling against it. But her hair, stick straight from birth, didn't curl. Not even the time Joaquin had tried his hardest to give her a Sarah Jessica Parker look. This soft, apparently obedient hair didn't belong on her head. She gave the tendril a yank, which turned out to be a mistake when her scalp reacted in pain and her head flew up.

"Miss Lofton-Hale?" Nathaniel leaned in.

His voice. Low and utterly masculine. Each syllable perfectly placed. Yes. This was a dream to hold on to. With any luck, she'd sleep right through the sound of the morning paperboy and keep on going.

"One moment, sir." Again with the accent. She raised a forefinger to ask for his patience while she worked up the courage to glance down. She wore a dress of gold, made of silk, so long that it draped in folds from her body to sweep the floor. Cut so high that it flowed from under her breasts, but so low it left her cleavage clearly visible. A graceful, elegant gown, just as she imagined herself wearing every night she became so immersed in a Regency-era book that she lost all track of time. Hold on. Something wasn't quite right. Cleavage? This dress must come with a Wonderbra.

Her eyes moved to the gloves covering her elbows. Like the smoothest of suede, but lighter. Wrapping her arms in gentle softness, they made her feel delicate, dainty, as though she were a lady of refinement, a—

The subtle clearing of a masculine throat interrupted her thoughts. Her eyes darted back up to Nathaniel and then to her right, where she met the clearly displeased gaze of an older woman. "Alexandra," the woman said, dragging the last syllable between clenched teeth.

"Please," Andi said, "forgive me. I fear I did feel a bit unwell, for a moment." Her face smiled all by itself, though she could feel the corners of her mouth twitching nervously. If this kept up, she might collapse in a heap at Nathaniel's feet, which wouldn't be the best way to make a first impression.

Unless, of course . . . he knew CPR.

In. Count to four. Out. Count to five. No, four. Um . . . five. So much for the breathing.

Whose words kept falling out of her mouth? And there went her shoulders again, drawn in so tight that her breath began to come in gasps. Much more of this and she'd have a permanent hunch.

"Perhaps you wish to be seated." Sensuously full lips parted to show white, even teeth. Those details hadn't been mentioned in the book, at least so far. She must be adding them in as the dream progressed. And doing a fairly good job of it.

"No need. Thank you, sir," she whispered. *Interesting response,* Andi thought, as though observing from a distance. *Now when do I get to talk?*

The woman at her side piped in. "My daughter has not yet had the chance to dance, sir. It would most assuredly be a welcome diversion."

*Daughter?* Andi's head whipped around in surprise. How odd that she would dream a different mother for herself. Hattie had her moments, but she was at least a known quantity. She stared at the woman, who quirked an eyebrow at her in some unknown, but seemingly obvious, signal. Andi tried to frown, but her face wouldn't cooperate.

Well, that's how it goes with dreams, she decided. No control. And she was bound to wake up again soon, this great fantasy fading into her unconsciousness, the details frustratingly unreachable by day. She turned back to the man, straining with every part of her being to throw him the innocent but mischievous gaze that had first caught the attention of Carlos, the espresso-stand barista with the beautiful eyes.

Of course, Carlos had turned out to be gay, dashing that hope. About the luck she had when she tried to get dates on her own, which was something Carlos loved to tease her about every time he'd seen her since.

After some effort and an exorcist-like battle with her face muscles, she succeeded in throwing him *some* kind of gaze.

Nathaniel Chamberlain's skeptical expression began to fade, replaced by a slow smile that more than hinted at interest.

*Now we're getting somewhere.* Anticipation began rippling up Andi's spine.

Then he froze in place.

The music stopped, dancers halting midstep and all conversation grinding to a stop. Andi wrenched her gaze from Nathaniel to lift an eyebrow at the woman claiming to be her mother. "Again," the woman said in a low voice, rolling her eyes.

"What's happening?" Andi whispered. She pulled

her shoulders up straight, relief flowing through her body as her muscles unlocked.

Nathaniel shot her a look. "She is wrapped in thought."

*She.* He said it as though she should know. Andi allowed a beat to pass before venturing, "Who?"

"Louisa," he said with an edge to his voice. "We must remain quiet."

"Quiet," Andi repeated. Everyone appeared to be obeying that dictate, though she thought she heard a toe or two tap against the floor. From across the dance floor, someone coughed. *This Louisa must carry a lot of weight,* she thought. Louisa? Wait a minute. Did he mean . . . ?

"Louisa Rawlings?" she hissed. *The author of* Wedgfeld Hall? Now she wasn't speaking with a British accent and her facial muscles had relaxed. She tried smiling, just to be sure. Much better.

Instead of answering, he raised one hand in the air in a signal everyone seemed to understand, even before he spoke. "She has closed her desk." Heads nodded all around. "Until tomorrow, then."

"Tomorrow?" Andi's voice came out with a squeak. This dream looked like it might be ending. Not without her okay, thank you very much. One hand shot up to jam itself on her hip as she prepared to demand an explanation. From the woman, though, not Nathaniel, whose very presence, so close to her, had her stomach doing somersaults.

"When she resumes her writing." His hand reached out to touch Andi's gloved arm, his gaze intrigued, as though she were a puzzle he couldn't quite figure out. "Then we shall see what events transpire."

She struggled for a response, as hurtling herself

into his strong arms did not seem entirely appropriate under the circumstances. What would that body of his feel like with her legs wrapped around his waist, what would those lips feel like on her . . .

Eyes glued to his face, she watched as amusement played around his mouth. Then he dropped his hand back to his side and turned away.

The brush of his fingers on her arm had been so quick, not even skin to skin. Yet, it set off a reaction that had every one of her nerve endings standing up and paying attention. She flushed with embarrassment, right before fear shot through her that he might be leaving her dream. For good. "Wait!" She couldn't let him get away.

He had already begun to stride across the hall. The woman at Andi's side laid a firm hand on her elbow, pulling her back. "Come. We must retire to our rooms." She pointed across the emptying ballroom. "Our bedchambers are in this wing."

"But I—he—" She broke off, taking in the woman's arched brow and the cool steel of her expression. A warm, motherly type she wasn't. All right. So Andi would play along for now, but just until she could make a break for it and finish this dream up right.

The woman gave a small jerk of her chin and moved away, clearly expecting Andi to follow. After a moment, she did so, her chin high, dress swishing pleasantly around her ankles. People who had been dancing only moments ago spoke quietly to each other as they put on wraps and disappeared through the hallways. Plates of food were whisked away by servants, their heads bowed. In a corner of the vast room, musicians put away their instruments.

An invisible curtain had dropped in the middle of a scene, to a silent theater. And no one appeared to think it at all strange. Through an open door, she could hear the whinnying of horses and the sound of carriage wheels crunching on a road. The chill of night air floated in from a doorway, sending goosebumps up the exposed parts of her arms.

The woman led her through the door and down a darkened corridor before walking quickly up a flight of stairs. Andi had to grab a fistful of dress to lift the hem high enough that she could follow. On they went, through a series of twists and turns. Just when Andi decided she should have grabbed some bread to scatter crumbs, the woman stopped, midway down a narrow hall. "This is where you shall sleep," she announced, pointing at a wooden door.

Enough, already. She didn't even let her real mother order her around. Well, most of the time, anyway. "Who *are* you?" Andi longed to wrap her arms around Nathaniel, instead of wasting valuable dream time on a mom wannabe.

The woman frowned. "Annabelle Lofton-Hale. Your mother."

"Right." Annabelle was a fairly melodic name for someone who looked as though she spent her spare time sucking lemons.

"Be certain you have your rest," Annabelle advised. "Tomorrow may be most tiring."

Tomorrow. Interesting concept. Andi drew her brows together. "Why?"

"She writes extraordinarily fast in the mornings. Or that has been my experience previously. It can be quite taxing to keep up." She shook her head.

"And the changes." Eyes turning heavenward, she added, "They can come just as quickly."

"I see." She didn't. But hey, it was a dream. "Guess I'll just"—she pointed at the door—"get some rest, then."

The woman nodded approval and turned away, moving down the hall with a grace that defied her rigid bearing. She disappeared around a turn without even a glance back.

Alone. Andi turned her gaze to the floor, the door, and then down the hallway. She had only one thing to do: find Nathaniel Chamberlain. Just once before she left this dream, she wanted that man to kiss her. In a heart-stopping embrace that would tell her there was nothing wrong with holding out for a man who would make her toes curl. That such a man really could exist. If she had to end up an old lady surrounded by cats, she wanted a memory, even one she invented herself, to hang on to.

Of course, it might not actually be a dream. There was that wishing stone. She *had* made a wish. A big one. What if that stone really could . . .

Who was she kidding. Even she wouldn't be so dramatic as to think something called a wishing stone could transport her back some 200 years, dropping her in the middle of the story of a relatively obscure author.

Drama, she knew. Tragedy, she had at least a passing acquaintance with. Fantasy that smacked of science fiction? Not so much.

# Chapter Two

Andi pulled off the annoying, too-small shoes and darted glances in both directions before creeping down the hall on her tiptoes. Annabelle might appear again, with that pinched look, to whisk her back to her assigned wooden door. A person only had so much time in a dream, and Andi wasn't about to waste any of it twiddling her thumbs in a bedroom.

She took two wrong turns in the stillness, wondering what it would be like to live in a house so large that a map would be considered practical, before she finally found the stairway. From somewhere below, she heard a masculine voice. She leaned over the rail to listen closer. Though muffled, the voice sounded a lot like Nathaniel's. Funny she should know his voice after hearing him say only a couple of sentences, but then it had sounded just as she had imagined it would, rumbling through to speak straight to her heart.

This could be it. Her big chance to make sure she awakened on a high note, filled with hope that no sane person should have to live her life settling for a guy who thought that all that romance literature embodied was a waste of any real man's time. No matter how much her mother urged her to give up and marry someone with money. "Love drifts away," Hattie was fond of telling her, "but stocks, bonds, and children last."

Careful not to make a sound, Andi moved down the stairs, pausing for a moment to peer over the banister at yet another stairway. At the sudden pleased expression of a man standing two flights below, she straightened abruptly, dropping her chin in one quick motion to glance down at the bodice of her dress. She'd probably given that stranger an eyeful, she realized, her cheeks flushed.

A dress cut this low would take some getting used to, not to mention becoming accustomed to the fact that she now actually had something to reveal. She tugged at the top of the dress, cleared her throat, and continued down the stairs.

When she reached the bottom, she tiptoed to the ballroom's partially open doors and wrapped her fingertips around the edge of one, peeking around to see Nathaniel talking with another man. They faced each other, their profiles to Andi. With his casual, yet commanding, stance and classic features, Nathaniel was even more handsome than she had first glimpsed. Was that stubble along his chin? Oh, dear God, yes.

She caught her breath and then exhaled in a sigh that went all the way to her toes. No doubt about it, she picked her fantasy men well.

"Indeed, sir," Nathaniel said, "I would be most honored if you would do me the privilege of joining me in a shoot at Wedgfeld Hall. The game is among the best to be found."

The man standing opposite him, his white hair impeccably groomed and face deeply lined, nodded in one sharp motion. "I will surely do so, sir," he said. "And I thank you for the invitation."

"Your daughter, of course, would be most welcome in accompanying you on such a visit."

The daughter would have to be Catherine, the one destined to save Nathaniel's family estate, Wedgfeld Hall, Andi thought with a sniff. Catherine, who needed her reputation salvaged in return. A practical exchange for this time and place, and not at all unusual, but it seemed a little too neatly wrapped.

She hadn't read past chapter three of the book yet. Maybe it wouldn't happen. Louisa could and should have something better in mind, like a heroine with, for instance . . . brand new cleavage. A sad story, to make her sympathetic? No problem. How about being left at the altar? She winced. Too close to the truth. Something else, then. She poked her head inside a little farther.

"I appreciate your kindness, sir," the older man answered in an imperious voice that carried across the ballroom. "My daughter, I am certain, would be pleased to accompany me."

"Very good, then." Nathaniel gave a small courtly bow. "It appears as though this thoroughly enjoyable evening has unfortunately come to an end and I must take my leave. My carriage waits." He dipped his head. The other man dipped his in answer and Nathaniel turned away, moving across the ballroom with easy, powerful strides.

He was halfway to the doorway at the other end before Andi managed to propel herself into action.

"Hold it!" The words echoed, bouncing back at her from each corner. He stopped to partially turn toward her, surprise on his face. It was all the invitation she needed.

She scampered across the polished floor, her feet alternately gliding and skidding. The weight of her hair bobbed back and forth, tendrils slapping against her cheeks. So, possibly the frantic edge to her voice was a little less than alluring, not to mention the fact that this dress was hell to manage. Why did the hem insist on wrapping itself around her ankles? She grabbed it with both hands.

By the time she reached him, her nearly exposed chest was heaving. Her hair surged forward when she pulled to an abrupt stop. She put up a hand to push it back and felt something satin-like against the hair. Ribbons. She'd always wanted to wear ribbons in her hair. Not the style in twenty-first-century Seattle.

Nathaniel tipped his head to one side. "Miss Lofton-Hale?"

How could she have even noticed her hair, let her attention wander for one second, when Nathaniel Chamberlain was standing before her, a living, breathing man.

"Yes." Andi took a deep breath and smiled her brightest, hoping she still had on the "first midnight kiss" lipstick she'd purchased yesterday, only to reject the idea of ever allowing her blind date to come within a foot of her mouth.

"Miss Lofton-Hale." Catherine's father was the one saying her name this time, from the other side of the room. The man knew how to project. He started toward her.

"Everything's fine," she said to him, smiling brightly. "I just need to . . . converse with Mr. Chamberlain for a moment."

The older man stopped, glaring at her. Andi tossed him a look of deliberate politeness and turned her back to him. "I was thinking we should talk," she said to Nathaniel. "Could I possibly walk outside with you?"

She hoped he would take her up on that request only if absolutely necessary. By now, he should have folded her into his arms, all the world subsiding as those lips brushed hers and the new lipstick melted into a distant memory. Her heartbeat sped up. There wasn't all that much time; the alarm clock would go off any minute.

Forget the white-haired guy with the loud voice. Forget everyone else in this dream. She wanted only Nathaniel.

His brow furrowed. "Miss Lofton-Hale, you appear to have adopted a most distinctive manner of speech."

"Well, yes." She blinked, hoping he wouldn't spend much time dwelling on something she didn't herself understand. "I don't really know what's going on there, but nothing about this dream makes any sense." She drew up to her full height, gestured toward the door, and tried a more formal mode of speaking. "May I walk with you, sir?"

He hesitated and then bowed slightly, making it clear he considered himself to be humoring her. "I am at your command." With a sweep of his hand, he indicated for her to walk ahead of him.

Andi paused long enough to flash him a winning smile, though she noticed her lips were trembling. There was a great deal riding on this man. What if the longed-for kiss turned out to be a crushing disappointment? She'd never be able to believe in love, to . . . *Be quiet, Mother. I am not being dramatic.*

It was her dream, after all.

Before she could lead the way out of the ballroom, Catherine's father suddenly appeared next to them, the hard edges of his face tight with displeasure. "You will allow Mr. Chamberlain to take his leave, Miss Lofton-Hale." He jerked his chin impatiently. "All others have retired to their rooms."

"I realize that," she answered, trying to suppress her annoyance with a sweetness that sounded forced, even to her ears. He meant all the other women. "But I have very quick business to discuss with Mr. Chamberlain." *Like it's any business of yours?* "I won't keep him long, I promise."

She inclined her head in the direction of the door, leading the way out of the ballroom and down yet another staggering staircase, darting one quick look back to see if Nathaniel had followed. He had, but remained behind her as they descended.

Andi's hand hovered above the banister, her fingertips dancing on the gleaming wood even as her heart pounded nearly out of her chest. With her other hand, she lifted the skirt of the dress, willing herself not to trip over it. Sprawling downstairs to whack her head on the landing would suck the romance right out of this situation.

She reached the bottom of the stairs, walking briskly across the polished floor, through the doors of the front entrance, and into crisp, cool night air that washed over her overheated skin. She hugged herself tightly and breathed in deep, trying to still her racing pulse.

"I fear you will catch a chill." Nathaniel's voice came from her side.

He feared for her. She loved it. "I'd rather you call me by my first name. Alexandra." For once, the formality of her name seemed to fit.

"As you wish."

If he only knew what she'd wished. She tried to aim a look at him that mixed haughty with inviting; but as her face contorted, she realized she didn't quite know how to achieve it. Her repertoire was the tiniest bit lacking in seductive gazes.

He took a step back, his forehead puckering. "The hour grows late."

Late or not, she had something to discuss. A matter of sweeping her off her feet and exactly when it would happen. But how best to approach it? She could hardly demand that he wrap her in his arms and carry her to a place far, far away. She settled for commenting on the obvious, until she had time to think. "You're far from Wedgfeld Hall."

"It is true."

"Me too." At his puzzled expression, she added, "Far from home, I mean."

"I understood your relations to reside just over that hill." He waved a hand to his left.

Should have thought of that. "Of course." She leaned in closer and dropped her voice to the level of a conspirator. "Just exactly *who* is my family?"

He didn't show the smallest sign of amusement. "Miss Lofton-Hale, if you will pardon me, your family is not a matter of my concern."

Only in this era could she be dismissed quite so formally while being asked for her pardon. She tried again, this time with a flirtatious smile. "It's not a lot to ask for some backstory."

Eyes narrowed, he watched her for a moment before proclaiming, "I must return." He dipped his head and began to walk away.

She couldn't let him.

"Wait!" In one quick movement she closed the distance between them. Standing on her tiptoes, she held on to the lapels of his jacket with both hands and, lifting herself up, landed a kiss on his cheek. Beneath her lips, his skin felt warm and sandpapery rough. *Nathaniel's whiskers.* Inhaling, she drank in the indefinable, yet thoroughly masculine, scent of him.

As she dropped down, trying to decide whether she should feel mortified or exhilarated, she surreptitiously ran her tongue across her upper lip, savoring the slightly salty taste of his skin. He hadn't drawn away from her. She'd felt his body stiffen and then start to lean toward her. She was sure of it.

Andi stole a look at him through her lashes. "I want you to know" she said, her voice soft, "that I believe you to be a most honorable, and indeed desirable, man." Even if she couldn't quite muster a British accent, she could use this language for all it was worth. Say things that should be said. She drew a shaky breath.

For what seemed at least two lifetimes, she waited for his reply. As she did, she wondered what he would do if she were to fling her arms around his neck and hold on for dear life, combing fingers through that thick hair and closing her mouth over one that was now half open in seeming bewilderment. Tristan be damned. With a real man, one who prized honor above all else, things would be different.

Finally, taking a step back, he spoke, "I wager this is not a turn of events Louisa has planned."

He didn't sound happy about it. That face, so close; those eyes, melting her into a puddle at his feet. "Louisa?" she asked, her senses blurring. "What does she have to do with—?" Her knees sagged as her legs seemed to surrender all ability to keep her upright.

Nathaniel exhaled, placing his hands on the sides of her shoulders, his firm grip keeping her from falling. "Has Louisa given you to believe that you are to play a significant role in the story? I must confess I do not think it possible."

That name had become unbelievably annoying. The man had turned her, an educated, by all accounts reasonably intelligent, woman into a pool of jelly, ready to do whatever he wished, and he brought up someone else's name? Twice.

Any self-respecting hero should know better.

Andi raised her hands to her hips, clearing her throat with a small sound. The fog that had enveloped her began to lift. "Let's focus on the moment," she said. "I'm here. And Louisa isn't."

Nathaniel regarded her solemnly. "Her health is precarious. All must proceed just as she wishes, without disruption."

Andi could tell Louisa a thing or two about wishes. Hers had almost come true. He'd possibly, probably, maybe been close to making a move. Or letting her make . . . um, another one. "I'm sorry to hear she's ill," she said carefully. "But that does not preclude our spending time with each other." Her voice rose with hope on the last word.

His mouth twitched; only a little, but she didn't miss it. "I must bid you a good evening." He paused as though he wanted to say more, but apparently thought better of the idea. With a nod so curt it should have injured his neck, he strode toward the house.

Andi tapped one bare set of toes, watching, her breathing still uneven. "Well," she sighed, fanning her burning cheeks with one hand. "At least I kissed him."

Even without Nathaniel's participation, the brief touch of his skin on hers had outdone any romantic encounters she'd had recently. Just as a for-instance, there was Michael, an attorney, with a beautifully appointed office in a downtown high-rise. He'd proved to be six feet four inches of arrogance, bragging all evening about the court cases he'd won and the judges who hated him for it. Hadn't taken long for Andi to see why.

When she couldn't stifle her yawns any longer, she'd begged off dinner, inventing an early morning. Michael brought her home, insisting on a lip-locking, wench-claiming kiss at the door that had seemed to leave him confident of his prowess, but startled her into punching him in the stomach. An attorney should be better at reading body language.

He'd kissed her with the cocky confidence of someone administering to the romantically needy. She'd been *there* before. And she wasn't going back.

Nathaniel had reacted to the touch of her mouth on his cheek. She'd heard the intake of air, felt the beginning of a move toward her. If her luck held out and she was able to continue this dream beyond the morning newspaper's thump against her door, Nathaniel Chamberlain might come to realize the passionate, waiting-to-be-unleashed heart that beat so hard inside her scantily covered chest.

Andi cast her gaze at the ground, spread a protective hand across the newly acquired cleavage, and turned to walk back inside. Her steps were slow and deliberate, and she'd only taken two before she saw legs, clad in black, squarely blocking her way. With a small gasp, she dragged her eyes upward to meet the furious ones of Catherine's father.

"You will explain yourself," he demanded, through lips drawn so tight they had all but disappeared. "I have never before had the misfortune to witness such appalling behavior."

Instinctively, she took a step back, putting a hand up. "I don't know what you're talking about." Appalling behavior? Whose?

"Mr. Chamberlain is to wed my daughter. Your actions betray my family, and indeed your own."

Hurtling straight from rejection to accusation in less than five minutes? Not happening. Hands on her hips, Andi leaned toward him with the same expression she directed at students who tried to tell her their dogs, cats, guinea pigs, brothers, aunts, or faulty alarm clocks were responsible for missed homework. "I'll say it again. I don't know what you're talking about. Even if I did, how I choose to behave is my business. And while my behavior is sometimes unexpected, it is almost never appalling." She made a sweeping motion with her hand. "Please step aside and allow me to pass."

His nostrils flared and his eyes flashed. "Their intent to wed shall be announced shortly. And the behavior you have had the unfortunate judgment to demonstrate shall not be tolerated." He took a step toward her. Andi drew back, now struck speechless by the force with which he delivered the words.

"Were it not for the fact that your father was a gentleman and, indeed, a man I considered to be a friend, I should have you dismissed from here immediately."

Hold on. Her father? This man didn't know her father. He couldn't. She opened her mouth, trying to work up to a response that might at least approach self-defense, hating as she did that this man could back her into such a corner, she couldn't even seem to fight for herself. Before she could deliver a response, Catherine's father turned on his heel and strode away, apparently having decided she had been adequately warned. Behind him, the door banged shut.

Digging her fingers into the bare flesh of her arms, she contemplated the new picture of herself as wanton woman, capable of throwing herself at someone else's fiancé. This dream was so confusing. Her subconscious must be finding entertainment in throwing Catherine's father into the dream. Now how did she kick him out?

She shivered in the still night, feeling very alone and far from home, even though she knew that, on some level, she had to be lying on her bed.

As she trudged back into the house and up the first staircase, she fought a sense of disappointment nearly as strong as her confusion. Couldn't win a decent guy, even in her own dream, where she supposedly called the shots. Maybe she should give it up, after all, and form a support group called An Unfortunate Destiny that would meet in one of the library's empty meeting rooms. Make it a book club and they'd be good to go.

Of course, she might end up being the only member.

She hugged herself tightly, her eyes landing on an upholstered couch. Letting her weary body sink onto it, she laid her head down, feeling, as she shifted, the scratch of brocade beneath her cheek.

Andi awoke to find herself standing in the ballroom and wearing the same gold dress, though it appeared none the worse after a night scrunched beneath her on the rock-hard couch. Stabbing pain said the shoes were back on her feet. Great. Didn't anyone think to take foot measurements around here?

All around her, activity buzzed, the ballroom once again lit with the glow of candles and filled with people elaborately dressed. In the corner, discreetly shrouded by shrubbery, musicians played a lilting, upbeat song. Dancers skipped across the room, the women with tiny, mincing steps, their gloved arms extended in the air. Black-jacketed men countered with broad, snapping steps and courtly bows.

*I've been here before.* In the next instant, Andi sank in on herself, shoulders curling. Her breathing became shallow and her heartbeat erratic as her chin dipped, focusing her gaze on the polished floor.

With difficulty, she forced her eyes to the right.

Annabelle was again at her side, her consternation visible. "You must be introduced to him," Annabelle said, speaking from one corner of her mouth. "I hear his fortune is substantial. Six thousand pounds a year. Or more."

"Ma-ma?" Andi winced as the word came out of her mouth, high-pitched and quivering. What? Was she six years old?

"He is the second son," Annabelle continued, "but it appears as though the elder brother has vanished, which will quite tidily leave the estate to this one. The brother had only a daughter." She paused to flash an on-and-off smile at a passing couple.

"Six thousand pounds a year," Andi repeated in that odd, high-pitched voice.

"There is rumor here and there about the present state of the family fortune, but I have decided that we are to pay them no heed. It was only Mrs. Buckingham who offered such an opinion, and I find her observations are not to be trusted. One look is adequate to establish Mr. Chamberlain is a gentleman of means. And that, my dear, will be quite good enough for you."

Different time period, different manner of speech, but the motherly sentiment had a certain common theme to it that Andi didn't appreciate. Her mouth, however, would not open to allow her to say so.

Following Annabelle's gaze, she saw it riveted on Nathaniel Chamberlain. He stood several feet away, talking with a woman whose entire being seemed elegantly swept upward, from the shimmering lines of her dress to her high pink cheekbones and the pale blond hair fastened with a glittering clip.

"He is, of course, obligated to converse with Catherine Havington," the voice next to her commented.

Catherine, Andi thought, looking with interest at the woman facing Nathaniel. The heroine of Louisa Rawlings's book. Raised in wealth and privilege, emotionally scarred by a quiet, tragic love gone wrong. Kind, but sad. Strong, but duty-bound. And according to what she'd read of the book, slated to marry Nathaniel.

In other words, competition.

"Oh, this will not do," Annabelle said in her ear. "Will not do at all. There goes Miranda Dolson, with that horse-faced daughter of hers, begging Horatio Havington for an introduction. We shall see about that." The woman's chin bobbed up and down in indignation. "We have not as yet had *our* proper introduction."

Horatio Havington, Catherine's father. Trapped by the dictates of good manners, he smiled grimly as Mrs. Dolson and her daughter closed in on him. Didn't anyone else know he considered Nathaniel Chamberlain off-limits to anyone but his daughter? Word must not have circulated yet. *Taking your life in your hands, Mrs. Dolson,* Andi wanted to shout.

"Ma-ma, I am beginning to feel most unwell." The words spilled out of her mouth, tripping their way over her tongue. Andi was beginning to feel like an interested observer, both fascinated and repelled by what she would say next. "Perhaps we should not attempt an introduction."

"Nonsense." Narrow fingers closed on her arm. "How would you propose to find a husband without an introduction to those eligible?" Her mother's eyes stared at her, demanding an answer. "You are a most handsome girl, if only you would deign to hold your head high."

"Yes, ma-ma." Again, the squeaking voice. *This is ridiculous,* thought Andi. *I'm the same person who kissed that man last night, in the moonlight, surprising the hell out of both of us.* She stopped. *Or am I?* Suddenly, she didn't know anymore. The room, the people around her, seemed to be blurring around the edges, colors flowing into each other. The music rose, its chords increasingly strident.

*Concentrate,* she told herself. *Don't lose your grip on*—well, not exactly reality.

"Come," said Annabelle.

Andi's feet, paying no attention to her growing sense of distress, seemed to be carrying her dutifully behind the woman who claimed to be her mother. Annabelle simpered up to Horatio Havington, subtly elbowing aside the Dolson daughter, who stood with her shoulders curved in seeming defeat. Andi recognized the stance. It mimicked her own.

Nathaniel, who had broken away from the group of milling people, led Catherine to the dance floor. Andi's shoulders relaxed enough to allow her to watch him. She'd read enough of the book to know the idea was for him to heal the woman's heart, not to mention her wounded reputation. Noble. And so Nathaniel. But it didn't help Andi's cause any.

He strode across the floor, each of his movements practiced and smooth, his lean body distinguished by the simple, flattering cut of his clothing. As the dance continued, he moved closer to where Andi stood. She saw the corners of his mouth turn up, toward Catherine, in a smile no doubt intended to mesmerize. Was it just Andi's wishful thinking, she wondered, or did that smile not reach his eyes?

They sailed past, close enough for Andi to see Catherine sweep her long lashes down and then up, bestowing a seemingly shy smile on Nathaniel. He held her gloved hand in his as they danced.

It was all wrong, Andi thought, narrowing her eyes. She didn't have long to claim the embrace, the kiss, of Nathaniel Chamberlain. Her only chance to experience the touch that would allow her to build warm, wonderful fantasies for less-than-satisfying nights. Catherine could take a short break, couldn't she? She had him for the rest of the book.

As the dance ended, the couples in the center of the floor dispersed, heading back to join others along the edge of the ballroom, some laughing and some looking down long noses in well-practiced snobbishness. It was the era for it. "Shall I accompany you to supper?" Andi heard a young man ask. The woman at his side giggled her agreement.

Once again, without warning, the invisible grip on Andi tightened. Her chin dropped as though a string holding her neck had snapped.

"Head up, child," Annabelle whispered fiercely in her ear. "Such an opportunity does not often present itself." She lifted Andi's chin with her hand and grasped her elbow, steering her into a solemn procession led by a grim-faced Horatio Havington. On they trooped to the corner of the room where Nathaniel now stood alone.

Introductions were given, Andi assumed, though the rushing in her head didn't allow her to hear clearly. He was close to her again. So close.

Andi's mouth opened to speak. "A pleasure to meet you, sir." Again, that silly, girlish voice, with a British accent. *No,* she raged inwardly. *I am not a twit. And I won't act like one.*

She forced her arms to press tightly across her waist, struggling to find her voice. The words seemed to gurgle in her throat before she could make them come out. "I believe—" The sheer effort caused her to gasp for air. Not. Giving. Up. Now. "Believe we have . . . already met, sir."

"You are mistaken, Miss Lofton-Hale," Nathaniel replied. His jaw tightened and his eyes carried some kind of a warning. He couldn't have forgotten the moment in the moonlight so quickly? He couldn't have.

"Yes, sir. My daughter is indeed mistaken," murmured her mother. "We have not yet been so fortunate as to make your acquaintance."

Horatio Havington stared.

"We have met, sir," Andi plowed on, forcing a thick tongue to form each syllable. "It left an impression upon me I could not easily forget." She wrenched her shoulders free and drew herself up straight. Let Nathaniel have a good look at that cleavage. That ought to jog his memory a little.

He was still for a moment, his eyes sweeping over her in apparent contemplation. Of course he remembered. She could see the amusement that he looked to be fighting twinkling in his eyes. His mouth opened, teeth gleaming white in the candlelight. As the beginnings of a smile played at his mouth, his eyes locked with hers in a gaze that stopped her heart. It was as if a movie camera had zoomed in for a close-up of the two of them, with all of the people in the background fading into a blur of color.

"It may indeed be so," he began to say, his voice rumbling with what sounded like a suppressed chuckle. "You, I believe, had taken me by the—"

Everything stopped—the dancing, the music, the conversation.

Silence.

Someone groaned. In distress or frustration, Andi couldn't tell.

Nathaniel went rigid, the smile disappearing from his face. He held up a finger. "Quiet, please."

"Again," Annabelle murmured, casting her gaze at the floor. "Why must this be so difficult?"

Nathaniel let his hand fall to his side. "It seems that one of us," he said in an undertone Andi could barely hear, "is proposing to complicate matters." He looked straight at her.

Biting her bottom lip, she looked to her left and then to her right, hoping someone would back up her right to say what she pleased. Anyone. Speak right up.

No takers.

Faces turned to her, one by one; Horatio Havington's white-hot gaze needed a warning label. She was reminded, uncomfortably, of the day she'd accidentally spilled red cranberry juice on the snow white dress of the prettiest girl in first grade. A ring of popular girl faces had instantly surrounded her with much the same looks.

That, she'd been able to fix with a giant bag of M&Ms the next day. This situation might take a little more. And Nathaniel, it seemed, possessed the nerve to think she would actually forget the touch of his skin on hers.

"We are at a pause," he said, turning to address all in the assembled room. "Louisa has closed her desk and undertaken a stroll." Then he turned to Andi, reaching out to grasp her elbow, his hand both warm and impatient. "And you and I, Miss Lofton-Hale, are about to follow suit."

# Chapter Three

With his grasp firmly on her, Nathaniel steered Andi out of the ballroom. Heads continued to turn. Let people stare. Things were not going at all as planned. Or rather, as wished. Every time she got close to him, something happened.

It was the *something* she couldn't quite figure out. Except that she knew it had to do with Louisa.

"Is there a problem with me saying what I think?" she asked tightly. Nathaniel propelled her down the stairway and through the front doors, releasing his hold only when they emerged into the night air. Then he put his hands on her shoulders, spinning her toward him. "Miss Lofton-Hale," he began.

Andi pressed fingertips to her head. "Please," she said, "at least call me Alexandra."

"Since a thousand eyes are most certainly looking askance at our having removed ourselves, I hardly think that appropriate." Dropping his hands to his side, he took a deep breath and blew it out, his expression stern. "You must allow the author to continue without your intervention."

The author. Andi shook her head. This whole thing was beginning to take on an *Alice in Wonderland* quality. Starting and stopping and words coming out of her mouth that she didn't put there. Things she would never say. This was not helping her campaign to get him to kiss her.

She sighed, wishing he would look at her with longing, instead of irritation. But if anything, his eyes were becoming colder.

"Look," she said, "maybe I dreamt you up because it's slightly possible I have a problem with . . . relationships . . . that I'm trying to work out." She rolled her eyes. "My mother would say that, anyway, but she's not right that often. And she only wants to see me married, at any cost, to a man with a lot of money and membership to the country club. I just want to . . . forget it. Even if you don't understand, I would think you could at least *cooperate*."

His lips parted and he leaned closer, brows knit. "It is quite true I do not understand. Pray, enlighten me."

She crossed her arms in front of her, pulling hard on her gloves. "If I have to bare my soul on this . . ." Drawing a deep breath, she continued, "I believe in real and true love. In falling, at first sight, for the one you're destined to be with. Without going over his tax return. And staying with that person forever. Growing old together. Still having your heart hammer nearly out of your chest when he walks into a room." She paused, and then added, "Is that so strange? So much to ask?"

Nathaniel blinked, making a sound that came out somewhere between a stutter and a cough.

"In your case, it was first read, instead of first sight,"

Andi said, averting her eyes as a sudden shyness stole over her at the admission. She cleared her throat. "I know, this is starting to sound like a TV show where they would flash words underneath my face that read something like"—she raised both hands to form an invisible frame—"Mother says she's the worst kind of drama queen. Or . . . afraid she'll die alone, with forty cats and a dog named Fred."

"Fred?"

She began to pace back and forth as her voice made the shift from nervous to earnest. "When I read about you, I *knew* I had been right to continue wishing for something better, something more. I"—she waved her hands in the air, searching for the right words—"am meant to be with someone who has principles, someone who will fight for what he believes in. Because it's more important than what people *expect* him to believe in. I want to be with a man who will desire me for my intellect, my heart and soul, for something other than—" She paused, hands in midgesture, thinking about what she'd said. "Not that that part of things won't be *amazing*, because when you're with the one you love—" Here, she stopped, watching as Nathaniel cocked his head to one side.

"Think Cathy and Heathcliff. Romeo and Juliet. Cary and Deborah." Her voice rose with the mention of each love-crossed pair.

Still, he didn't react. In fact, he looked even more perplexed.

She tried again. "Someone who wants to know my middle name before he wants to know if I'll sleep with him!"

At that, Nathaniel stepped away, boots crunching

hard on the path, hands clasped behind him. Andi ran through a familiar routine of self-recrimination for not editing the side of her that wanted to spill all. *When you lay all your cards on the table, Andi,* her father had once told her, *you only succeed in helping someone else win the game.*

And how, she wondered, was it really fair to say what she had when she herself had been consumed with the idea of Nathaniel's powerful body wrapped around hers from the first moment she'd seen him?

He stopped pacing and turned back. "Louisa has devoted days, indeed months, to her characters. To assembling our story in such a manner that the book will create pleasure for those who read it. And all of us"—he made a sweeping gesture that included her and the people inside—"shall be allowed to continue on with a life most beneficial once the book concludes. Pray, tell me why you would be so occupied in preventing such a happy outcome."

Straightforward seemed the only way to go. "My dream. *I* should be the heroine."

Apparently taken aback, he opened his mouth, then closed it. Confusion again flashed across his features.

"I would be a good one," she added because he hadn't.

"With such a manner of speech I can only assume you to be the heroine of another story, Miss Lofton-Hale. Perhaps one that is to come." He drew himself up straight and continued, "However, it is not to be this one. I must assure you that this story shall continue as Louisa sets forth."

"That may be true for you, although I wonder if

you really believe it. But since I'm not actually here, the rules are different."

"Not here?" He repeated the words with care, as if they were foreign to him.

"Neither are you. Except on paper."

Head down, he resumed his pacing before stopping to sweep his eyes over her once again. "You are gravely mistaken, Miss Lofton-Hale. You are very much here."

"Not possible." She lifted her chin. "I'm dreaming you. And I'll be waking up as soon as the alarm clock goes off or the paperboy throws a ninety-eight-mile-an-hour fastball at my front door."

"Dreaming."

"So you can see we don't have much time." Andi tried a flirtatious smile, but wasn't quite sure she had it right. Parts of her face seemed to be moving in the wrong directions. She ignored that, plunging ahead. "It should be enough to know that any other man is going to have a really hard time living up to the idea of you. For the rest of my life."

He didn't respond, his face registering a range of reaction, from skepticism to cautious interest.

"I'll be waking up any minute." Her voice took on a note of desperation she didn't want to think too hard about. "Better take your chance while it's here. I'm pretty sure I mentioned 'amazing,' didn't I?" She began pinching her arm.

"Miss Lofton-Hale," he began, putting up a hand at her protest. "As you wish. Alexandra."

She nodded, continuing to pinch. Her arm ached as much as the sting of rejection. Happened even in her dreams. There was an irony in that. One she didn't like at all.

"I will acknowledge that many of us began as a dream that occurred during a writer's slumber," he said, more gently now. "However, once she succumbs to bestowing life upon us . . ." He paused, gesturing as though Andi should be able to fill in the rest.

"Anyone knows fiction is just that. Fiction. The characters do not exist." Even she knew that and she *lived* through books. He was making it sound like he actually believed that he . . . as though he thought that he . . . had actually taken on some sort of existence. Impossible. Frustrated, she pulled the gloves off her arms and threw them to the ground. She didn't need to have her hands and arms encased in fabric any more than she needed shoes a size too small. Reaching down, she pulled them off too, throwing them one at a time to skitter across the path.

Bestowing life on characters, he said. Should she be expecting to see Elizabeth Bennet walking gracefully down the road next, followed by Emma Woodhouse coming to call? Crazy. Impossible. She'd always thought, though, that she and Emma could be fast friends. They had the same—Enough!

He looked from her to the shoes and back again. "Upon what facts do you base your opinion?"

Opinion. As though it were a topic open for debate. Flustered, she stumbled through the words. "Because it's only her imagination. And mine. You couldn't actually . . ."

He took a step forward, standing only inches from her. She shivered as shock waves ran up her arms and took a deep breath, looking up at him. How could he jump to life, talk and dance, have eyes that drew her in and breath that smelled of peppermint?

"Pay close heed, Alexandra. An author who brings characters to life, in a way utterly believable to the reader, is able to do so only because they quite absolutely exist. Though their lives are accessible only to her until the book is completed and she shares those lives with others."

Exist? Lives? Maybe she'd had some kind of terrible accident and descended straight to drama-queen hell. Her mother had often threatened consequences for Andi's Olympic-level skill at conclusion jumping. Nice to know *now* what they were.

She began pinching again. With each renewed stab of pain, she squeezed harder. Nothing.

"It is an entirely tolerable life. And we must believe that Louisa will allow a most satisfying conclusion." He paused. "For all concerned."

The still, nearly black air around her began to close in, clutching at her throat. A wave of dizziness swept over her, causing her head to dip and bob and her knees to give way. "But, how?" she began, the words cut off by the thudding of her heart as she remembered, clearly, the *how*. Take one wishing stone, add a longing so desperate it occupied every square inch of her soul, and you get . . . here.

In one swift motion, Nathaniel's arm closed in around her shoulders, holding her upright and half walking, half dragging her down the path. Sharp, tiny rocks stung her feet each time her tender soles pressed down.

It felt comforting, his jacket against her shoulders, with the heat of his muscled body beneath. She leaned into him. If he were as real as he claimed, would he disappear into thin air at the author's whim, leaving her to sprawl on the ground? He didn't. In fact, he pulled her the slightest bit tighter with what felt like an absolutely there arm.

He lowered her onto a stone bench and stepped back. Candlelight spilled from tall windows behind him, illuminating the pale color of his breeches and the blackness of his hair as he appeared to chew over what he wanted to say. But he didn't speak.

Cold began to seep through the thin fabric of her dress, startling her senses into a nervous clarity. "What would I be *doing* here?" she asked, more of herself than him.

"You are a minor character."

Given an opening, annoyance slipped right past consternation to claim the upper hand. "I am a lot of things, but never minor."

"Of that, I am entirely certain."

"I was in my apartment, reading the book *Wedgfeld Hall*," she said softly. "It came with a wishing stone."

A glimmer of light seemed to dawn in his eyes. "A wishing stone. There are such things, of course. I have heard reports they may even accomplish what is promised." He nodded. "Perhaps that is the source of your confusion. Your wish appears to have come true."

The first time she could remember a wish coming true and it had to be this. Nothing like starting big. She gave a short laugh that evolved into a less-than-seductive snort.

"It is of little consequence how you came to be a part of the tale," he said. "It is, however, of great consequence that you appear utterly determined to set your own course."

Not the first time she'd heard that. The trouble seemed to start when she let someone *else* set her course.

"It presents Louisa with a most difficult situation."

In the distance, a horse whinnied. The smell of trees, fresh dirt, and flowers filled her nostrils. Gone was the ever-present sound of sirens that seemed to punctuate city life. A different world.

Slowly, carefully, Andi rose from the bench to stand before him, searching his face. Could what she wanted so badly be right in front of her? Looking back at her with dark, lazily sensual eyes that melted the frozen places in her heart?

If she *had* wished herself right into a story in progress, she had one chance to get it all, to live a life she'd only ever read about in books. Instead of the lonely one that tied her into knots of longing so tight it was hard to breathe some nights.

To wear the clothing she had imagined herself in so many times. To learn to play a pianoforte, to embroider peacefully in an actual drawing room, which couldn't be found in America anywhere, let alone her condo. To leave a calling card, for God's sake. She'd always wanted to. An e-mail wasn't the same.

And the words. Speaking them in everyday conversation. Hearing them, feeling them roll off her tongue in a setting other than the front of her classroom, where she awoke from the near-dreamlike trance of Regency-era dialogue to find her students staring at her, unimpressed and unappreciative.

She laid her hands on Nathaniel's jacket, feeling the uneven rise and fall of his chest.

His eyes washed over her with an unmistakable curiosity. "I confess," he said, "you have a most interesting way with words. Quite unlike any I have ever—" He stopped.

She could show him a few things that were quite unlike any he'd ever . . . A woman who wouldn't settle for a preselected destiny, for one. Who would speak her mind, for two. Who would mix pleasure with the business of courting, for three. Come to think of it, a twenty-first-century woman could have some kind of fun in a Regency novel.

"You must allow Louisa to write the story she intends," he said, his voice dropping, a huskiness edging it that tempered the directive. "If you do not, if you continue to refuse . . ." He bit off the words as Andi's hand skated upward, toward his neck.

She watched as his eyes clouded. "If I am to stay here, sir," she whispered, "there may be things we wish to explore." *Oh-kay!* The words rolled from her tongue with ease, as though she had been born to speak them. Clearly that switched-at-birth issue. Maybe at last she'd returned to the place she belonged. Where the men were courtly, dashing. Principled.

He drew his brows together. "If the story does not move as the author intends . . ." A warning hung in the air.

"Stories change. Every writer, any writer, will surely speak to that."

His expression turned ominous.

"Would you have me believe, sir, that should we displease the author, we disappear in a puff of smoke?" Ouch. It would be very, very good for him to say no to that.

A flicker of something that looked like pain crossed his face, just for an instant. She watched him withdraw, as clearly as if he had taken a step away. "I will escort you inside to your mother."

Her words had hit a nerve. "I am not ready to go inside."

"There is nothing further to say."

"It is not necessary to talk."

"Then pray tell me what you propose."

"We could simply enjoy each other's company." Wrong. She had something entirely different in mind. Something that could earn her a spot on reality TV in the twenty-first century, but brand her the worst kind of social outcast in Regency England.

His voice came from deep in his throat, a rumble dangerously close to a growl. "Louisa directs such activity."

"Of course she does," Andi repeated, her eyes drifting half closed with the last syllable as she imagined what those lips would feel like on hers.

He bolted upright, his entire body stiffening. Andi's eyes flew open, following his gaze as he stared off into the distance.

"She has returned to her desk," Nathaniel said. "Come."

"No," Andi screeched. "Let her sit. We don't have to obey her every—"

"She is Louisa Rawlings, author of *Wedgfeld Hall*. She controls the destiny of each person." Impatience dragged through his voice as the authoritative presence once again took over. He glanced toward the door and then back at her. "Make haste. We must return."

"No! I said I am not ready." She put her hands on her hips. This was going to take some figuring out. "You're the hero. You must have the power to—?" She sputtered helplessly, wishing she knew how to finish the sentence.

His dark lashes swept down and then up. "My dear," he said, "I most decidedly have power." His voice dropped. "The secret lies in how that power is used."

She shook her head as dizziness once again began to tumble over her.

"If Louisa finds the story she has wrought a satisfying one," he continued, "we shall continue on after its close." He reached over to tip her chin up toward him, his eyes darkening. "There is, however, danger in a lack of cooperation. Recalcitrant characters are often eliminated from the story."

Recalcitrant? So . . . she might have been called that a time or two. Usually by the principal of her school.

"Come," Nathaniel said. He crooked his arm toward her, making it clear she had no option in taking it. "We must remove to the ballroom. Kindly take my words to heart and address your actions appropriately."

He was refusing to acknowledge the electricity that had passed between them? With enough voltage to light the entire city of Portland? Her eyes widened, her breath coming in furious spurts.

"While it was a request a moment ago, it is now a command." Nathaniel grasped her elbow, moving her forward.

She didn't have time to protest. As he hurried them up the stairs and back into the ballroom, she held on to his arm to keep from falling. The hem of her dress assaulted her ankles, making it impossible to get up the stairs without stumbling over it. Finally, she grabbed a hunk of the fabric, throwing it over her arm and exposing her knees. If Nathaniel noticed, he didn't say anything.

When they reached the doors to the ballroom, she let the dress fall back into place. No point in shocking *everyone*. Any more than she already had, anyway.

As they entered, faces turned expectantly.

"Forgive us," Nathaniel said, his voice raised. Andi wondered whether the apology was meant for the assembled people or the author. Heads nodded and voices bubbled in what sounded like relief.

Once again, they were in their places. Nathaniel stood before her. The people behind him sailed into a gracious dance, and the music played as though it had never been interrupted. Andi felt her shoulders hunch, drawing her inward, her heart fluttering like the wings of a small bird.

Again, the murmured introductions. "How do you do, sir," she heard herself say in a formal British accent. This time she did not fight it, but let her mouth open and the words spill out.

Annabelle jabbed her in the side. "Head up," she whispered in a furious breath, all the while bestowing a pleased smile on Nathaniel. "Mr. Chamberlain, my daughter and I are most honored to make your acquaintance."

"Madam, the pleasure is all mine," he responded.

Andi watched as his gaze flickered back in the direction of Catherine.

Miranda Dolson and her daughter bore down on the small group, the older woman clearly on a mission. "Oh, Mr. Havington," she cried in a shrill voice, "such a lovely ball, so very fine."

Horatio Havington nodded, acknowledging the compliment, and Mrs. Dolson blinked her eyes innocently in Nathaniel's direction. "My daughter Amelia will most certainly become quite exhausted from all the dancing. She is so light on her feet, you know, and the young men frequently choose her for a dancing partner." Mrs. Dolson fanned herself with one hand. "I fear I do not know how she keeps up with all of it."

Andi peered at Amelia. The young woman's eyes were glued to the floor, a flush staining her cheeks, her hands locked in a death grip in front of her. She took a tentative step backward, as if hoping her mother would allow a retreat.

While Andi knew women in this time were commonly offered up to the highest bidder, for sheer survival, the situation became that much more heart-wrenching when it happened to someone who stood before her, the young woman's fragile emotional state laid bare. Amelia would likely end up forced into marriage with a man twice her age, or no one at all. Unless . . . Andi struggled to straighten her shoulders, to no avail. Annabelle shot her a warning look from the corner of her eye.

"My daughter Amelia, Mr. Chamberlain," Mrs. Dolson was saying.

"An honor," he replied, nodding. "Now, if you will excuse me." He dipped his head in what seemed to pass for a bow and left before they could answer, moving with an easy grace across the crowded floor.

Andi felt her body relax, freedom flooding back into her limbs. She sighed with relief and shook her arms to loosen them up.

"You should have met his eyes squarely on," Annabelle reprimanded Andi. "A gentleman likes that, you know. Perhaps if you had done so, he would have remained long enough for conversation."

"He did not ask my Amelia to dance," huffed Mrs. Dolson. "Quite incomprehensible." She turned to Annabelle. "She is most popular as a dance partner, you know, Mrs. Lofton-Hale. I confess I cannot keep up with the number of young men who ask her." Mrs. Dolson shook with the injustice of Nathaniel's perceived slight as her daughter's cheeks turned redder.

"Perhaps if she had once raised her head to the gentleman," Annabelle commented, her eyes narrowed in judgment.

Mrs. Dolson sucked in a breath, tucking her chin into the folds of her neck. Amelia looked as though she wanted the floor to swallow her whole.

Andi had to do something. No matter what Nathaniel said, she *had* to. Like a Jane Austen heroine, she would have to do it within the confines of the circumstances.

"I believe," she said, "that Mr. Chamberlain may only have been deferring to the pitiful looks of the gentleman in the corner, who has been fixing his gaze quite longingly upon Miss Dolson."

Mrs. Dolson's lips formed a stunned circle. "Upon my Amelia?" she whispered.

Amelia's eyes grew wide.

Annabelle looked at Andi as though she'd taken a dive off the edge of sanity.

Andi raised a finger and pointed. "Do you not see him there?"

Mrs. Dolson's head whipped around, her curls bobbing.

Andi examined her hand. She hadn't noticed the gloves again appear, but there they were.

"That gentleman?" Mrs. Dolson asked, whispering louder now. "Who stands quite alone?"

Amelia turned to peek from behind gloved fingers. She couldn't do that to the poor guy she'd first pointed at. He looked too nice to be hunted as prey. "Actually, no. The gentleman in question is standing with that group." Andi waved and stepped away, hoping to fade into the background before Mrs. Dolson descended on the huddle in the corner. She hadn't meant to sacrifice them, but Amelia had silently screamed the need for rescue. Andi had been in the same spot enough times herself to recognize the signs of a sister soul drowning in humiliation.

With the women's attention diverted, she could lose herself in the crowd without anyone noticing, which could give her time to think about the exciting, baffling, and actually frightening picture Nathaniel had painted. Leave it to Andi to get into trouble with a wishing stone. She'd claim it wasn't possible, but knew too well that it apparently was. Placing her hands behind her back, she made her way through the people standing in noisy groups.

Laughter rang out every few moments. This ball didn't look all that different from the last faculty Christmas party. Different clothes and accents, but the people seemed almost familiar. Dressed in their best and trying to impress. The paunch-bellied man letting his eyes roam over the young thing standing, unaware, next to him. His sharp-nosed wife frowning. The slightly drunk man in the corner, laughing too loud, his cheeks bright red.

Andi drew up short. Nathaniel stood not far away, his gaze fixed on Catherine.

Lifting the hem of her dress, Andi moved closer. She glanced down as she walked, hoping she wasn't falling out of the top. It was a new and different experience to have this nicely stacked body, but she was pretty sure there wasn't any double-stick tape holding her in.

She stopped a few feet from the couple and picked up a glass, absently holding it to her lips. What did Catherine really have, anyway, except money?

From the first portion of the book, she knew Nathaniel needed the money that Catherine had, or would inherit. His older brother had disappeared under mysterious circumstances, shortly after running the family fortune into the ground. There wasn't much money to keep the large estate going, and worse, there were rumors that Nathaniel's brother was dead.

That made the problem Nathaniel's to solve. He was too much of a man to turn away from the estate that had been in his family's hands forever.

Granted, Wedgfeld Hall was in bad straits, but there had to be a better way than marrying a stick of wood like Catherine. The woman's carefully composed features didn't seem to ever change, even when she was engaged in conversation. If it were the twenty-first, instead of the early nine-teenth century, Andi would have sworn the woman had overdosed on plastic surgery, which would ac-count for the masklike quality of her face. True, in the book, Louisa had seemed sympathetic toward her, but so far, Andi hadn't seen much depth there.

Looking down at Catherine, Nathaniel's mouth curved into a smile, his eyes bathing her face with cool appraisal. Andi leaned closer. In a moment, she could swear, he was going to pick up the woman's hand and kiss it.

A small ball of fury took shape in Andi's stomach. One hand jammed onto her hip while the other tightened its hold on her glass. Let Catherine get her own hero. She was making tracks all over Andi's.

She tried to move forward, but her feet remained rooted to the ground. Busted, apparently, by Louisa, wherever she was. There went the shoulders again, folding in on their own, pulling her head down.

She would not go along with this. Absolutely not. If she opened her mouth to talk, something wimpy would come out of it, albeit with precise British dic-tion. And she'd had just about enough of Louisa's invisible control.

*This* Alexandra Lofton-Hale didn't sit pretty and smile. Ask anyone at Willamette High School.

Fighting to free her body, she leaned forward at a forty-five-degree angle, one arm flailing, the other holding the glass upright as the liquid in it sloshed. To one side, she heard a feminine gasp. She gritted her teeth. *I am not a twit,* she repeated to herself. *I am not a twit.*

A sudden release broke her free. Before she could savor the victory, she fell headlong toward an unsus-

pecting Catherine. On the way down, Andi watched
the liquid from her glass splash out and onto the
shimmering, delicate, and obviously expensive folds
of Catherine's dress. The glass meanwhile left her
hand, flying straight toward Nathaniel's legs.

When at last she hit the floor, she closed her eyes
and debated whether to stay there or slink away,
inch by inch, until she could hide under the musicians' shrubbery. Silence rang in her ears as she lay
paralyzed by indecision. Finally, she opened one
eye, letting it travel upward along the path of liquid
dripping from Catherine's dress.

First grade all over again.

Nathaniel's glare held venom. And as for Catherine . . . Well, Andi had been wrong about the woman's
face. Catherine's smoothly perfect features creased in
sympathy as she extended a small white hand.

"Oh, but this is too terrible," Catherine said in a
voice spun from sugar. "Have you injured yourself?"
She turned to Nathaniel. "But pray, why do you
stand there so, Mr. Chamberlain? We must help her."

Definitely a heroine Andi could grow to hate.

# Chapter Four

When Nathaniel's strong arms lifted her effort-lessly from the floor, Andi's hopes surged, only to be squashed by the realization that his grip conveyed a distinct irritation, rather than a concern for her well-being. Dropping her into a chair, he growled, "I must assist Miss Havington. You will excuse me." She barely had time to swallow the thanks bubbling in the back of her throat before he dipped his chin with a sharpness that straddled the line of civility and walked away.

He was, of course, returning to Catherine, the innocent victim of Andi's clumsiness. She looked down at her hands, folded in her lap. All eyes in the room had to be staring at her now, wondering why she, a "minor character," would do such a thing. Everyone except, she suspected, Horatio Havington, who was likely deciding to toss her out on her ear, friendship with her dearly departed fictional father no longer a good enough argument for hospitality.

Only one person's opinion mattered. And he hadn't hesitated to make it known.

She worked her thumbs back and forth, inwardly cursing the heat she could feel beginning to creep into her cheeks.

Taking a deep breath, she balled her hands into fists. As though she had *meant* to spill her drink on Catherine. He actually thought she would . . . Well, maybe she would, but she hadn't. He had no right to be angry with her. Not to mention wasting her time with this blustering display of male ego. She raised her eyes to bore them into his back. If he didn't watch it, he might just lose man-of-her-dreams status.

She watched as he strode toward Catherine, who protested that she was quite well, thank you, fluttering her fingers toward Andi as if to suggest it was the other woman who needed assistance.

Gag. She would have to be that nice.

Miss Havington, he called her. *Having him* is more like it, Andi decided with a spurt of nastiness she didn't try to suppress. A very small part of her deep inside began to lose hope. What would a man like Nathaniel see in Andi Lofton-Hale from Portland, who might as well be signing her name with the tag line "perennially unlucky in love."

Cue the houseful of cats.

And then, as if a switch had flipped, the music began and the dancers picked up where they had left off, swirling and gliding across the floor, smiles on their faces, soft-spoken words on their lips. The smell of candle wax permeated the air, mixed with perspiration that had to be coming from the man a few feet away who was mopping his forehead with a cloth. Andi pressed her back to the wall, relieved that attention would be directed elsewhere. The story had picked up once again, right where it had left off.

She was beginning to understand that the position of her body, and the words that seemed to come from nowhere, signaled Louisa's control over her . . . character.

Suddenly, it felt hard to breathe, her throat tightening as she struggled for composure, and air. She sat up straight, putting a hand to her throat and then across her forehead. Her glove came away damp.

It made no sense. And all the sense in the world. As a reader, she became so enraptured with a book's characters, why would it be difficult to believe they, once created, actually did exist on one level or another?

A writer, after all, carried a mysterious command over a universe Andi had spent her college years and now the beginnings of a teaching career attempting to decipher. Before, she'd thought it encompassed only a firm hold on a reader's emotions. Now, she realized, it went much further, to a reality few, if any, really knew existed.

This high school English teacher had the opportunity of a lifetime. Not only to teach the literature of the era, but to speak and actually *live* the words. The Jane Austen action figure she kept in the corner of her classroom would quietly approve.

And she had an advantage no one else here did. A wishing stone that represented her ticket back. Any time she wanted to use it. In other words, nothing to lose, everything to gain.

To borrow from a less than literary but totally appropriate song, *Hell, yeah.*

Her gaze scanned the room, taking in the dancers, the candlelight, the rise and fall of conversation around her. An actively writing Louisa had resumed command of the scene, with Alexandra Lofton-Hale relegated to the background.

Andi sat quietly, sliding her shoes back and forth along the floor. Her gaze followed Catherine's exit to the other side of the room, amid several clucking tongues, where a maid knelt at her side to dab at the dress with a cloth. Great. Make one little mistake and that's what Louisa decides to include in the story. Maybe she thought it added to Catherine's warmth and humanity, endearing the reader to the semitragic figure even more. Terrific. Now Andi was helping to write the story, in the wrong direction.

Why should Catherine get to claim all the sympathy? Andi had seen her share of romantic tragedy, after all. Two minutes, or better yet, three hours with the author's ear and she could tell her a few things, or fifty, about a search for true love. Her history in that area would fill a book all by itself.

Okay. *Enough.* Self-pity only went so far. There was such a thing as making a fresh start, and she knew just the potential heroine to do it. *Audition time.*

Taking a deep breath, she lifted her chin in time to see Amelia heading toward her. With her pale cheeks flushed and head held high, Amelia was a different-looking woman than the one Andi had rescued a short time ago. This story was going better already. Once it was done, Louisa might actually have to thank her. Aha. An idea for a book jacket. Author and character shaking hands. Odd no one had explored it as yet.

She was going a little crazy now.

Amelia sat beside Andi, spreading the skirt of her dress with tiny, precise motions. "I have done it, Miss Lofton-Hale," Amelia whispered with an asthmatic breath, staring straight ahead at the dancers.

Andi gave herself a moment to wonder, before she spoke, just what would come out of her mouth. "Done what, Miss Dolson?" she asked. No accent. Excellent sign. Louisa must be busy elsewhere. Keep the language century-appropriate and Andi might not get caught until it was too late.

"I have danced." Wonder filled Amelia's voice.

"And you . . . do not often dance?"

"Before this night, I danced only with gentlemen who were most carefully instructed to invite me. Never with one who asked me purely of his own will."

Andi made a sympathetic face and considered the woman next to her. Amelia wasn't unattractive, though she had a long, angular face and stocky eyebrows. Her best feature seemed to be strikingly deep green eyes, at least when she held her chin high enough for them to be seen.

They turned toward Andi now. "It is quite true, though it gives me unconscionable pain to admit it." A smile quivered at her lips.

"May I inquire who invited you to dance?"

"The gentleman whose attentions you pointed out, of course."

"Oh . . ." Andi nodded her head. An invented truth, but at least it hadn't backfired. "And your mother had noth—not a . . . no influence over the gentleman's request?"

The blush on Amelia's cheeks deepened. "No, Miss Lofton-Hale. I at last decided that I would no longer allow my mother to do such a thing."

"So, he . . ." Andi gestured for Amelia to go on.

"It is dreadfully difficult to believe, even for me." She ducked her head. "I must confess that I found the courage to approach him myself."

Andi's face came as close to breaking out in a smile as it could when the muscles felt as though they hadn't been used in a very long time. "That is wonderful, Amelia. I may call you Amelia?"

"Oh, most certainly." Amelia's head bobbed up and down vigorously. "I fear I nearly fainted with the boldness of it, but I could not bear for my mother to again announce how very popular I am as a dancing partner." She closed her eyes and gave a sigh that took over her body. "It is only her wish, not the truth of the matter."

"She is somewhat fervent in her assertion," Andi agreed. "How were you able to approach him without your mother seeing?"

Amelia covered her mouth with her hand before giving a short, nervous laugh. "I told her I had overheard Mr. Poole speaking favorably of her this evening." For the first time, Amelia's eyes sparkled with life.

Andi lifted one brow. "Mr. Poole?"

"He is a gentleman of some means. My mother is widowed, which is not a state she cares to continue. She is *most* interested in any attentions Mr. Poole would deign to pay her. Were she to believe that he carried a favorable opinion of her . . ."

The smile on Andi's face broadened. "And she now believes that?"

Amelia nodded, her eyes wide.

"Even though he did not ever . . ." Andi again gestured, encouraging Amelia to fill in the details.

"The conversation in question unfortunately did not occur, though who is to say it would not." Amelia smoothed her dress again, her long, gloved fingers trembling. "But the very thought of it, once expressed, succeeded in capturing my mother's attention."

"Nicely done." Andi chuckled.

Amelia gave her a curious look. "You give the impression of being American, but I must confess your speech is at times difficult to follow, though I have made the acquaintance of other Americans."

Andi's tentative feeling of comfort skidded to a halt. She'd been doing pretty well, but had to remember not to go back and forth. She put fingers to her mouth, promising herself she would think before she spoke. "I am certain it must . . . sound a little different," she acknowledged, turning her palms up. "I am from a part of America where we speak a little differently. An accent, or simply a way of phrasing."

"What part of America?"

"Oreg—" Wrong. It didn't even exist. "It is of little consequence. Not a place you will have heard of."

"Your mother is not American." Amelia gave a little shake of her head. "It seems most odd that Louisa would have given you such a background."

Oh, please. Louisa had nothing to do with her "background." If someone actually *were* scripting her life, her love life would be a heck of a lot more interesting. Andi took in a short breath and blinked, smiling with what she hoped looked like reassurance. "As I said, it matters not. Of greater importance is what you did tonight."

"He has a most pleasing way of holding me as we dance." As soon as the words were out of Amelia's mouth, she colored, snapping her mouth closed.

Andi grinned and leaned over to whisper. "It is fortunate he has the ability to please you."

"If my mother were to know that I could give voice to such a thought . . ."

"It is only I, Amelia, who hear you say it, and I shall not tell another." Andi's gaze swept over the dancers, searching for the man whose touch *she* craved. Chances were good he would have a pleasing way with just about any way he wanted to hold her. In that moment, she forgave his single-minded focus on the dutiful Catherine, wanting nothing more than to dance with him, to feel the strength contained in his body. To lose herself in his embrace.

He was, after all, only doing what he thought necessary to continue the story. It would be up to Andi to convince him things could be otherwise. Horatio Havington's glowering face made a brief appearance before her mind's eye, but she shoved it away as quickly as it had intruded.

A sigh, long and deep, escaped her. She might as well be a part of the wall behind her, for all the good wishing did her when Louisa had taken the reins of the story. Of course . . . Louisa had to get tired sometime and totter off to bed.

Andi looked over at the woman next to her, placing a speculative finger on her chin. "Amelia," she said slowly, "how well are you acquainted with Catherine?"

"Miss Havington? Not well, I fear."

"But you could easily become better acquainted with her." Andi paused. "As could I."

"Would Louisa wish it to be—"

"Forget Louisa!" Seeing Amelia flinch, Andi reached out an apologetic hand. "My sincere apology. Please. Do not give my words another thought. They were most ill-advised." The way Louisa was revered around this place, Andi would have to approach this differently. You'd think the woman ran the world. Of course, she sort of *did* run this peculiar world.

Amelia's lips parted. Andi interrupted before she could speak. "Surely we are able to pursue the acquaintance and companionship of others during our . . ." She paused, searching for the right term. "Leisure."

"Leisure?"

"The periods when Louisa is not writing the story. When she takes to her bed or is otherwise engaged."

Amelia tipped her head, as if to indicate she hadn't thought about that before.

"Fully developing her characters will only add richness and depth to the story," Andi continued. "Indeed, we can be of aid by spending time with one another when she is not putting pen to paper. The story is bound to proceed more smoothly if we allow events to occur even as she slumbers." *Agree,* she silently instructed Amelia. *Just agree.*

The other woman shook her head very slightly. "I do not believe Louisa would allow such—"

"I cannot believe she would object!" Andi proclaimed, with all the spirit and confidence she could muster, though it didn't feel like much. "We must do all we can to assist her, particularly given her precarious health."

"Miss Lofton-Hale—"

"Call me Alexandra."

"Alexandra. You do not understand what danger can lie in—"

"I have heard much about the danger." She allowed herself to add, under her breath, "Too much, in fact." Then, in a normal voice, she said, "I confess I do not see the truth in it."

Amelia leaned closer. "But you must," she said in an urgent whisper.

Andi stood her ground. "She gave life to characters who live and breathe, who feel sorrow, joy, and indeed, love. Of course we must speak to each other at every opportunity and build upon the tale she weaves, to ease her pen in writing the words. It is the only *compassionate* thing to do."

"That is true, I suppose," Amelia said slowly.

"Spoken by the person who invented Mr. Poole's good opinion of your mother." Andi grinned. "Unless I am gravely mistaken and it was Louisa who did so?"

Amelia dipped her head, a flush once again staining her cheeks with impressive speed.

"As I thought," Andi said gently. "You were able to find your courage because Louisa endowed you with the ability to do so. She was at your side, though she wrote not a word of your actions."

A shy smile spread across the other woman's face.

"And there is much yet ahead." First on the

agenda, make friends with Catherine and gain her confidence. Find out where she was vulnerable to competition. After that . . . Well, she'd figure it out.

Andi's eyes riveted on Nathaniel, in the midst of the dancers, his hand locked with Catherine's fragile, gloved fingers. How the man could so easily participate in such a formal, mincing style of dance while radiating the very embodiment of raw masculinity, she didn't know. He moved easily, as though it cost him no effort.

But Andi knew what it cost Nathaniel to be here with Catherine, courting her, hoping she would agree to marry him. It was the only hope he had of saving Wedgfeld Hall, after his brother had driven the family fortune into the ground.

Nathaniel now bore the future existence of the family estate on his broad, strong shoulders and had already shown he was willing to sacrifice his own happiness to save it. A small sigh of longing escaped Andi's lips. This man contained more character and ethics in his little finger than the men she'd dated, or almost married, put together.

The dance was drawing to a close. Andi watched Nathaniel move closer to Catherine, a lock of black hair falling carelessly across his forehead as he held her in his gaze. An instant later, he stopped in his tracks. So did Catherine. Surrounding conversation seemed to melt into the background. Once again that eerie silence, the sense of waiting.

Andi held her breath. She wanted it to be her. *Her* with Nathaniel. She, who had studied, analyzed, and lived vicariously through fictional heroines for as long as she could remember, deserved at least a chance. She'd be spirited, likable, sympathetic—everything an author could ask for. Yet the story was moving ahead. Without her. She had to get Louisa's attention.

Breathe out. Two, three, four. In— What? How many counts?

And then, as though invisible puppet strings had been released, everyone relaxed. Nathaniel gave Catherine an easy smile and brought her hand to his mouth, brushing it with his lips. He swept his gaze around the assembled guests to proclaim, "A most pleasantly productive day."

Relief bubbled forth from the crowd, conversation resuming as people began to say their goodbyes. Andi rose from her seat. Nathaniel held Catherine's hand still, his eyes half closed in what appeared to be an expression of affection. He talked with her, in a voice so low Andi could not hear the words.

It should be her bathed in the intimacy of those words.

She turned to Amelia, trying to temper the words that fought to spill out as a demand for information. *Keep things casual.* "Is Miss Havington likely to stay for a time?"

"She will retire to her chambers, Miss Lof—" She tried again. "Alexandra."

Andi glanced across the room, watching as Nathaniel dipped his head in courtesy bows to the guests who passed before him. Catherine stood alone, an elegantly gowned, solitary figure, looking after him.

This wasn't a time to hesitate. Andi turned back to Amelia, reaching to grab the woman's hand. "Miss Havington," she said, "is desperately in need of our companionship. This is her home, though she appears to know few of those gathered here."

"Alexandra!" Amelia's shocked voice echoed the warning already sounding in Andi's head. Approaching Catherine Havington in such a manner would be unusual, to say the least. It must be done with care, but it must be done.

Were Catherine to react coldly to her, it could well expose a flaw in the heroine that would be difficult for Louisa to surmount. That alone made it worth it. "Please," she urged Amelia as she took a step forward. "We cannot delay. I believe she needs a friend."

Catherine appeared confused when two potential friends presented themselves for duty, one on a mission and the other too speechless to protest.

"Miss Havington," Andi began, "or perhaps I may address you as Catherine?"

Catherine hesitated and then nodded. "By all means, Miss . . . ?"

"Alexandra Lofton-Hale," Andi pronounced. "You may call me An—" She glanced at Amelia, whose chin had dropped straight down. Any further and it would be attached to her neck. "Please call me Alexandra."

"Ah, yes," Catherine murmured. "My father has mentioned your family."

"Please forgive the unfortunate accident with your dress. I fear I have not been blessed with a natural grace."

The smile that Catherine trained on Andi was well-bred, gracious, and hardest of all to take, genuine. "Do not trouble yourself. I am often prone to such accidents myself."

Andi had a little trouble with that picture. With her every hair in place, every movement perfectly choreographed, it would be difficult to buy into the idea of a clumsy Catherine. She plunged ahead. "I am relieved it does not appear to have caused permanent stain."

Catherine shook her head, setting off a tinkling sound that had to come from the expensive earrings adorning her small, sculpted ears. Of course Nathaniel would want to marry her. Her jewelry alone could likely keep his estate going well for several years. *But that doesn't amount to love,* Andi resisted the urge to shout.

Louisa Rawlings obviously needed help here. And Andi needed Nathaniel. Just for a bit. She'd give him back. If she had to. "You have danced all evening," she said to Catherine. "It must be fatiguing, yet you appear none the worse." Were those the beginnings of shadows under her eyes?

"It has been a most full evening." Catherine straightened her shoulders, a so-happy-to-have-met-you smile beginning to take shape on her face.

"Amelia and I have decided to venture out for a stroll in the morning," Andi interrupted before Catherine could say anything further. Amelia's head rose in surprise. "And we would be so pleased if you would consent to join us. Would you not think it entertaining to discuss the events of the evening, admire the dresses, the food . . . ?" She searched for an appropriate way to add "the men," but couldn't come up with one fast enough.

From the looks she received in return, Andi had

to guess she hadn't managed to make a chick chat sound appealing enough to nineteenth-century women. Lines of concern wreathed Catherine's forehead, while Amelia's uncertain expression now seemed frozen into place.

After a moment of awkward silence, Amelia whispered, "Alexandra, it is best that we—"

"Morning exercise is exhilarating," Andi broke in. "It clears one's mind so. Whenever I feel somewhat muddled, a leisurely stroll makes all the difference."

"Morning exercise," Catherine repeated, her voice faint.

"The estate's grounds are beautiful. I *must* see more." She looked from the face of one woman to the other. "And while I hesitate to confess the loneliness of being an only child, I must admit I crave the companionship of others nearer my own age." At least she hoped she was an only child.

Amelia swayed. Andi reached out to grab her arm. "Are you feeling ill?"

"I must take my leave," Amelia said below her breath. "My mother awaits." She gestured toward the door, her hand trembling.

Andi flashed her a "nice try, but I need you" look. Amelia opened her mouth, but no words came out.

"Surely Mrs. Dolson will allow you a moment longer," Andi said. "I believe she may be detained, speaking with Mr. Poole?" Amelia's head whipped around, toward the dispersing crowd.

Turning back to Catherine, Andi said, "Will you show us the grounds in the morning, Miss Havington?" She heard the desperation in her voice. The confidence she'd felt a moment ago was quickly subsiding.

"I am not certain I . . ." A frown puckered the woman's forehead as she searched for an answer.

"I often wish I had sisters," Andi said softly. "If only to discuss those things another female would understand."

Amelia started to pull away. Andi pulled her back.

Catherine drew in a breath, blinking slowly. Then she raised her eyes to meet Andi's. "I have also regretted a lack of sisters, for just such a reason." Her words were slow and deliberate. "A stroll. I shall think it the very thing to do." She turned to Amelia. "And surely your mother will release you? Our grounds are indeed quite lovely in the morning. I am certain I shall find a walk invigorating."

# Chapter Five

By the early hours of morning, Andi would have signed away the rights to her firstborn child for a grande nonfat vanilla. Each time she closed her eyes, she hoped to see a familiar green-and-white mermaid sign when she opened them again. Beckoning her to caffeinated pleasures.

No such luck.

She stood before the Havington home, gazing into the distance. For what appeared to be miles ahead, all she saw were the lush, gently rolling hills of the estate, bathed in the gentle rays of morning light, with a winding dirt road the only mar on the serene landscape. Blue sky, dotted with cotton-candy wisps of white cloud. No electric poles, cell towers, cars.

And everything so much . . . bigger. Quieter. Life was harder in this era, particularly for a woman, who had fewer choices and less control over her future. But it also would be more relaxing, in a number of ways. Worrying over dresses, hair, social class, and finding a husband. Instead of how to afford a good apartment and something of a social life. Impressing her principal so she would be offered a contract next year. Getting her mother to let her live her own life.

She allowed herself half a smile. So one thing was consistent between the centuries.

Surprisingly, she hadn't missed her cell or her palm at all. Only her espresso. Sure, she wouldn't want to live like this full-time, forever. But as a needed break from real life, a way to capture the reality of the era and infuse her lectures with the ring of authority that would have her students rapt with attention, and best of all, enable her to live out a fantasy she'd held close in her heart since her early teens.

A creak from the front door interrupted her thoughts. Catherine, looking a vision of precisely groomed perfection in butter yellow, stepped outside, breaking into a hesitant smile at the sight of Andi's hand, lifted in greeting.

"Good morning, Catherine." Andi smoothed her skirt and raised self-conscious fingers to her hair. She hadn't quite been able to figure out what to do with it this morning, so she'd used the weapon-sized hairpins in her room to pin it up and back. It now looked, she was sure, a haphazard mess that would label her a complete hair klutz.

Catherine, not a hair on her head daring to veer out of place, hesitated, her mouth working as though she wanted to say something. A tiny frown puckered her forehead.

"Is something amiss?" Smile fading, Andi was afraid to hear the answer.

"Forgive me, Alexandra, but did your maid not awaken this morning to assist you?"

It was that obvious, then. Andi rubbed a finger across her aching forehead, spirits plummeting even as she wondered why she hadn't thought to find and waken the maid most certainly assigned to her. A maid. Her mother would be proud. "I awakened unconscionably early," she said, "and allowed her to sleep."

"That was most generous of you." Catherine sounded baffled.

"The occasion is rare when she is allowed to do so."

Catherine cocked a delicate eyebrow. "Of course."

*Mental note: Find maid as soon as I get back. Don't step outside the bedroom door without her help again.*

Andi turned away to scan the road, shading her eyes with her hand. "I *had* thought we would see Amelia by now." As soon as the words were out of her mouth, she spied a carriage in the distance, coming closer, moving at a roaring speed of at least twenty-five miles an hour. She squinted and then pointed. "Could that be her?"

"It is indeed."

The two women watched in silence as the carriage approached. Andi darted a glance at Catherine, who waited serenely for Amelia's arrival, her only movement the slow blinking of her lashes. With any luck, a frustrated woman beset by turmoil lurked beneath, Andi mused, waiting only for a chance to run screaming for her independence. She let that mental picture drag across her thoughts before deciding that Louisa wouldn't be accommodating enough to give Andi that much to work with.

So she'd have to make it happen herself. She flashed Catherine a sweet smile, which the woman

returned in kind. "Did you sleep well?" Andi
inquired politely.

"Quite well, thank you."

"A ball can be exhausting, particularly one so
large, with all of the details to be seen to."

Andi received only a nod as reply. One thing appeared clear about Catherine—she wouldn't talk a
person's ear off.

"Still, I hope you were able to enjoy yourself. It
was so lovely. And Mr. Chamberlain appears to be a
fine dancer?"

A few seconds passed, long enough for Andi to
register the other woman's brief hesitation, before
Catherine replied, "Indeed, he is." No hint of a sigh
or giggle as she remembered, no fingers traveling
surreptitiously up her arms to indicate she remembered being held in his. No glint in her eyes saying
she thought about more than his dancing.

Either the woman had the best poker face in all of
England, or Louisa had not yet been able to instill
any deep feelings for Nathaniel. She forced her attention to the carriage as it pulled to a halt in front
of them in a clatter of hooves, reins, and dust. A
footman leapt down to open the door and Amelia
descended, her feet landing on the ground with a
thump while her rigid spine remained straight,
hands clutched in front of her. From the set of her
mouth, Andi gathered Amelia was close to terrified
at the idea of a morning stroll.

Andi cleared her throat and stepped forward.
"Amelia," she said. "I am so happy you have arrived.
We shall have such fun this morning."

"My mother granted her permission, though she

cautions I must take care. My health is often thought to be delicate."

Andi fought back a grin. Amelia, reed-thin but sturdy, looked anything but delicate. Mrs. Dolson must think a fragile girl would be more attractive to eligible males. "Of course," she said, grasping Amelia's arm to pull her along, "we will not venture far. You have my word." She cast a look over her shoulder at Catherine, who hesitated and then began to follow, chin high and posture firmly upright.

Good. They were walking. Together. First order of business, get to know Catherine. That could give her the key to unlock the innermost characteristics of a Louisa Rawlings heroine. And help her turn herself into one, however briefly.

"It is a lovely morning," she remarked, hoping her tone sounded casual. "The sun's warmth is welcome, indeed." She lifted her face upward, wincing as a pounding head protested the motion. She *knew* it hadn't been a good idea to stay hooked on a grande latte every single morning, but she did live in Portland, after all, where it was close to criminal *not* to be addicted to caffeine. "And there are no grounds more beautiful to be found anywhere."

"I have always loved them." Catherine looked down, seeming mildly distressed as the hem of her skirt swept the tops of the rocks. Daintily, she lifted it from the ground. "Although on most occasions I stroll only to the stables." She gave a wistful smile. "I do so love to ride."

Andi nodded, encouraging her to continue. "And do you have a favorite horse?"

"Ah, yes." Warmth spread over Catherine's features. "Since I was but a girl."

Not much more than a girl now, Andi thought, but thought better of saying so.

"He is called Thunder," Catherine added shyly.

"You must enjoy many hours of pleasure riding him in such a place." Andi's wave took in the surrounding property.

Catherine's gaze followed the direction of Andi's gesture. "The grounds gave my mother much joy, I am told. It was she who determined which flowers should be planted. My father tells me she lingered over them many long hours, tending to the smallest detail."

Andi looked around, nodding her head in appreciation. Flowers bloomed in an artfully arranged pattern of color, bordered by immaculately tended shrubs. No self-respecting weed would come anywhere close. "Her care is evident." She paused for a respectful moment, then plunged ahead. "Did she die when you were very young?"

"A mere few days following my birth."

Silence fell. "I am sorry," Andi said at last. The words seemed inadequate. Much as her own mother made her want to tear her hair out, she couldn't imagine having grown up without her. She took a deep breath. "Does your father often host balls? Perhaps it helps him to forget?" As she mentioned the man, she suppressed a shudder, remembering, all too clearly, his furious face in the moonlight.

"No, my father does not usually care for such events." Catherine looked up at her and then down at the ground again. "But this one is not without purpose. He has arranged that I—" She broke off.

Andi waited, but not for long. "That you . . . ?"

she asked. Gently, she hoped. Abruptly, she was pretty sure. She tried not to sound too eager to pump an unwitting Catherine for information, though she wanted to shake the woman until it tumbled out of her. It would be easier than this polite dancing around questions that needed to be asked.

Color began to rise in Catherine's cheeks. Andi slowed her steps. "He's arranged that you . . . ?" she prompted again.

"Be introduced to a husband," Amelia interjected, finishing the sentence Catherine didn't seem to be able to. Catherine's cheeks flushed.

"Ah, a husband."

Catherine averted her face, looking off into the distance.

Andi looked from one woman to the other. "I cannot imagine that you would not have the fervent attentions of most, if not all, gentlemen of the county." She hesitated. "Do you not find this particular suitor . . ." How to say appealing, sexy, amazing . . . She couldn't believe she'd even have to ask the question of Catherine. "Intriguing?" It was too much to hope, but of course, possible. A sprig of hope began to churn in her stomach. If Catherine, deep in her heart, didn't click with Nathaniel, Louisa would have a difficult time getting them together and making it believable.

All three women stopped walking. Catherine turned, directing her words to Andi. "He is admirably solicitous. And most handsome. Best of all, he is kind." Her eyes, appearing troubled, belied the softly spoken words.

"Mr. Chamberlain?" Andi asked, just to get the confirmation officially out in the open.

Catherine nodded.

Amelia offered, "Such a match would appear an excellent one. Every woman in the county would be the picture of envy."

"All the mothers at the ball appeared intent on attracting his attentions for their daughters," Andi said. "But you alone, Catherine, held his interest." She paused. "How very flattering."

Catherine began walking again. This time each step beat out a rhythm of determination. "I *am* a fortunate woman to have a father who cares for me so. Whose only wish is to see me firmly and well established."

Her words carried on the breeze as the other two hurried to follow her. "It is fortunate to be well looked after," Amelia agreed. "And to have the meeting happen in a manner so arranged has much to be said for it."

Now Andi stopped, placing her hands on her hips. Different era, yes. One with few choices. But romance was romance, and Louisa wasn't writing it very well if the most these two women could talk about was the security that Nathaniel offered. As though that was ever a guarantee. He deserved so much more. She wanted to scream at the writer, scream at Catherine, scream at someone. Before she knew it, she'd stomped her foot on the dusty path. Both faces turned toward her in surprise.

"Well looked after?" she asked, palms lifted to the heavens. "Marriage, choosing to spend your *life* with someone, should be something more than tolerable. Wouldn't you agree?"

The other two women also stopped, near a grove of trees offering thin fingers of shadow as respite from the morning sun. Two pairs of eyes trained on Andi.

"There is so much more to life than being taken care of," she said, her grip on the language of the day disappearing as fast as her voice rose. "If that was all there was to it, I could have picked ten men who would have done just that. Yes, it would have made paying the bills easier, a *lot* easier, and they were all good-looking and reasonably intelligent, but where would I have been? Not in love, that's where. Just existing day to day. Settling for what was easy and hoping for better, but knowing it wouldn't come." Never mind that the one she had settled for had decided *he* hoped for better. "Who wants to live like that?"

Andi spread her arms for emphasis, her heart pounding with the injustice of it all. All she'd ever wanted was a passionate, knee-crumpling love. Sure, she hadn't found it, but these two women didn't know enough to even hope for it. That had to be worse. "What about loving another person with your whole heart and soul?" Her words resonated in the morning silence.

Catherine and Amelia stared at each other, seeming to make a silent pact. Andi saw their footsteps moving south, even under the long skirts. "My mother, I believe—" Amelia began to say in a voice so faint she could barely be heard.

"Yes," Catherine interrupted. "I must return as well."

Andi took a deep, gulping breath. This would be a tough era to introduce the idea of female independence. She stepped forward and placed a hand on each woman's arm. "Please," she asked, "forgive my outburst. My mother does despair of me at times, knowing I have an unfortunate inclination to speak what is on my mind without the slightest thought." True enough.

Polite nods answered her apology, though the women looked doubtful.

"I meant to inquire whether you thought it possible to have both an envious match and a husband who makes your heart . . . ?" Andi patted the area of hers to indicate a fluttering.

Amelia burst into startled laughter, while Catherine's eyebrows lifted nearly to her hairline. Another shy smile quickly followed.

Andi began to walk again, silently praying the others would follow. After a brief hesitation, they did. She adjusted her steps so they could catch up, biting her bottom lip to keep from coming out with something else that would set her cause back.

At last, she remarked, with only the mildest interest, "He *is* very handsome."

A pause. "The kindest of men, with a face most pleasant."

Kindness appeared to be a theme for Catherine. Not surprising, given her father. "But he doesn't do it for you." So much for her attempt at subtlety. Yet again, Andi's mouth defied her, the statement coming out flat and more than slightly accusing. She stole a sideways glance at Catherine to see consternation cross her placid features.

Finally, the other woman said, "Never again would I dare to protest the wishes of my father."

Both Andi's and Amelia's heads popped up, but it was Amelia who eagerly asked, "Again?"

Catherine's cheeks stained a delicate pink as she raised a hand to tuck a nonexistent stray hair behind her ear. She shook her head. "I fear I have misspoken. Please do not allow my words the smallest consideration."

"You are among friends," Andi said quietly. "We determined last evening to be the sisters each of us never had. Sisters do not ever fear misspeaking." Her top lip now also joined the struggle to rein in words fighting to get out. Go slow, easy, she told herself. Apparently, she wasn't listening. "Please. Tell us," she urged. "We must know if we are to be the confidantes of your heart. And you of ours. Amelia?" Andi poked the other woman in the arm, making her eyes wide in a plea for her to join in.

"I myself—went quite against my own mother's wishes only last evening." Amelia gave her head a helpless shake, as if to ask if that was what Andi sought from her.

Catherine brightened. "I spoke with your mother," she said with a tiny smile. "I imagine that going against her wishes might well meet with resounding disapproval."

"It is true that few would dare cross her!" Andi agreed. "Please do go on, Amelia." She gestured. "Tell us more." The last was more a command than a plea.

Amelia nodded uncertainly. Message received. "My mother most incorrectly imagined that I should be presented to Mr. Chamberlain, thinking he was seeking such introductions."

"I believe this . . . agreement of my father's is not

commonly known," Catherine said. "The assumption would not be illogical on your mother's part."

"But, Amelia," Andi urged, "pray tell Catherine what you did."

Amelia, whose rigid posture had briefly relaxed, quickly drew herself up again. "I should not have," she mumbled. "It was decidedly wrong."

Catherine and Andi exchanged amused looks. "That cannot be," Catherine said. "I could have no belief that you, Amelia, would wrong your mother."

Amelia stared at the ground, her hand clenching and unclenching. Andi felt a stab of regret at having urged the woman to spill a secret she had confided only to Andi. It must have taken courage to do what Amelia had done, and that was a trait the woman didn't seem to have in Costco-size bulk.

Suddenly, though not for the first time, Andi was struck by the fervent wish that she really had a sister. Or even a really close friend to stick with through thick and thin, kindergarten and beyond. It might have made it easier to know when not to step all over someone.

Instead, she'd grown up with her head, and thoughts, wrapped in books, lamenting what she assumed to be the tragic switch at birth that had taken her from the moors of England to land her ungracefully in Portland, Oregon. That conviction hadn't exactly helped her form fast friendships. When she thought of the looks she'd received the few times she'd tried to share that some female child on the moors was living her life—

"Forgive me, Amelia," she said now, trying to rectify things, "I have no wish to—" She searched her brain for the Regency equivalent of "make you uncomfortable." The other woman, staring straight ahead, appeared not to have heard.

"I distracted my mother with the unlikely possibility that Mr. Poole held a favorable opinion of her," Amelia said slowly, deliberately. "And I then presented myself to a man I wished to dance with." She snapped her mouth closed and squeezed her eyes shut, as though expecting to be struck dead by lightening.

Catherine gave a cry of admiration. "Why, Amelia," she said, "what a very brave thing to do!"

With a small frown puckering her forehead, Amelia turned toward Andi and Catherine. Her face relaxed visibly when she saw theirs. "It was wrong," she repeated, but this time, she sounded cautiously cheerful about it.

Andi patted her shoulder. "I pronounce it a wonderful, and indeed charitable, thing to do. Your mother is pleased by the prospect of Mr. Poole's high opinion, and you were able to dance with a partner you chose. A fine turn of events." She stopped herself an instant before she asked if Amelia had given her dance partner her number. Switching between two worlds was, at times, difficult. These women couldn't imagine a telephone, let alone a cell and that vital tool of dating, caller ID.

Catherine let out a sigh so loud it could have come close to injuring her.

Andi hesitated before offering, "You could do the same, Catherine. Perhaps you could tell your father—"

The woman pulled to an abrupt halt in her petite tracks. "I could not."

"If you have no wish to wed the gentleman? But of course you could. Should, in fact." Andi's heart sped up. "Tell your father you cannot marry Mr. Chamberlain. As simple as that." Her words spilled over each other. "What is he to do? Turn you out of your home? It is not possible he would so. You are his daughter. His only wish will be to see you happy." At least, she hoped so. From the little she knew of Horatio Havington, she'd bet a generous heart wasn't high on his list of character traits.

Catherine shook her head slowly, looking at Andi with trepidation. "Louisa."

*Again with Louisa.* She should have known. "The author created you to have a will of your own, did she not?"

Emphatic shakes of the head from both women.

"It cannot be . . . enjoyable for her to have you behave only as she dictates. She has devoted much time and thought to your story. If the liaison she proposes is not the one most desirable, you must help her with finding the one that is. Ensuring a happy ending for all." *Especially me.*

"You do not understand." Catherine's words were so soft; Andi had to slow her steps and lean closer to hear.

She dropped her voice to match the other woman's. "What do I not understand?"

"Louisa saved me from a most improper relationship."

Now Andi shook her head. "But do you not see, Catherine? If that is the truth, she was the one who devised the improper relationship."

"No." The word was sharply spoken. "There is no excuse but my own willfulness. The author had no such intention." Catherine stopped walking and closed her eyes. Andi watched a tear in the corner of one eye, poised to trickle down the flawless ivory skin. She glanced over at a wide-eyed Amelia. All three stood in an uncomfortable silent circle, beneath the morning sun. Somewhere nearby, a bird called.

"Catherine," Andi ventured, "there can be no shame in a relationship that occurs because of feelings you cannot deny." Of course, there could be a lot of other reasons. Defiance of an overbearing father, rebellion against the requirement to come into an arranged marriage pure and virginal, the plain and simple allure of something that could be described as an "improper" relationship, just to name a few. Okay, so those would be reason enough for Andi. As far as the delicate Catherine was concerned . . . Andi scanned her memory furiously. Louisa had written very little about Catherine's past in the opening chapters, only enough to hint that the woman needed to be rescued from scandal by a heroic Nathaniel.

Catherine's nod was so slight Andi almost missed it. "Does your heart continue to belong with another?" she asked.

The woman's eyes flew open at that. Brushing at her eyes with a furtive hand, she replied, "That would be impossible." Her voice wobbled on the last word.

"*Possible* rarely enters into matters of the heart." Take Andi's current situation, for one. Fall for a fictional hero, end up in the story. She looked at Amelia for support, but the other woman quickly shook her head, as if to plead, "Don't ask me."

"My father was quite right to take action," Catherine said, her chin held high, "forcing me to recover my good sense."

"I would sooner hear that observation," Andi observed, "from your father."

Catherine whirled on her. "That is *not* for you to question, Miss Lofton-Hale."

"I see," Andi replied, feeling verbally smacked into her place. She had gone too far. Again. "Please forgive me."

"I must return. Thank you for the stroll. It proved quite refreshing." Turning on her heel, Catherine set off in the direction of the house. After several steps, she stopped, a lone figure standing in the middle of the path, as though torn between whether to go or stay.

Andi lifted her head, watching, but Catherine did not turn around, and after a moment, she resumed her determined pace. A wave of sympathy washed through Andi, but she pushed it away. The improper relationship might be nothing more than one with a man who didn't have half the money Catherine's father had. It would do Andi no good to feel sorry for the heroine she longed to replace. Still . . . If anyone knew the tragedy of love gone wrong through no fault of her own, it would be her. She heaved a sigh.

"It feels most unpleasant to have upset her so," Amelia ventured after a moment.

"Truly, it does," Andi agreed. "However"—she turned to wag a finger at first Catherine, now a small figure in the distance, and then at Amelia— "we have now learned Catherine's heart is held fast by another. It is our task to determine who that is and help the two to see it is proper to once again be together, as Catherine clearly wishes."

She dipped her head, pleased with the way she

had summed up the situation. The hope that had materialized as a ping-pong ball inside her now began to pick up speed. "It is only right, after all, for Catherine to be with the one she is meant to be with, leaving Nathaniel Chamberlain . . . free. For the person he is meant to be with." She smiled blissfully at how clear it all seemed.

The horrified look on Amelia's face should have been enough to warn her.

# Chapter Six

Andi nearly had to drag Amelia to her waiting carriage. The woman was so overcome by the idea that Andi would attempt to alter the course of Louisa's story, she couldn't move or speak for several minutes.

"You— You cannot—" she choked out.

Andi huffed and puffed as she half pushed, half pulled Amelia toward the waiting carriage. If the woman's mother described her as delicate, she hadn't tried moving her any time recently. "Do not worry so, Amelia. I am convinced this author is seeking our help, though she does not say so."

"Oh!" Now Amelia swayed to the left, overcome by the drama of it all.

Andi darted a look upward at the carriage's driver, who seemed to be suppressing a smile. "Your mother will no doubt be missing you," Andi said, struggling to make her voice sound reassuring as she bundled her new faux sister up the step and into the seat in a tangled confusion of skirt and parasol. "As soon as I have decided how we are to proceed in this venture, I shall tell you." Then, throwing her shoulders back and thrusting her chin up, she tried to make it clear that objections were useless. Not only would she have a plan, she wouldn't be afraid to use it.

"B-b-but," Amelia stuttered in response. "One can—not—" Again, her throat seemed to tighten with the gravity of it all, leaving her cheeks pink and her eyes like saucers.

"Why the hell not?" Andi muttered. She slammed the door shut. "All will be well, Amelia." Not necessary to add that *well* could be a matter of definition. She patted the door and motioned to the driver, whose expression had lost all traces of amusement. She gestured again, impatiently this time. He cast a glance at the footman, who joined him in directing a mutual glare at Andi.

Yes, she knew they weren't accustomed to receiving their instructions from women who swore when the situation warranted it. But she didn't always behave according to society's norms in her *own* time. And she was on a mission here.

The footman resumed his position with an offended grunt. A slap of the reins and command to the horses followed.

The wheels crunched along the road, carrying a shell-shocked Amelia back to the refuge of her home. Andi turned back toward the Havington house, her eyes sweeping up its broad stone exterior. An elegant country manor, with three floors of tall, narrow windows and steep roof lines that managed to appear at once both welcoming and forbidding. No doubt it still existed, with little change, in modern-day England. It might even have a little gift

shop now, for Americans to spend their money
while they trooped in and out on supervised visits.

Andi would be thrilled to visit the estate under
those circumstances, closing her eyes to imagine
herself sweeping through its halls in another time,
on the arm of Nathaniel. In a dress like this one,
though she would have picked a different color.
Maybe something in apple green. Or sky blue. Even
if she wouldn't have thought to add the cleavage,
she was all for that idea now.

But that visit would have been firmly anchored in
the safety of the real world. Not exactly the situation she found herself in now. Before she returned
inside, she needed time to herself. To think and to
formulate her plan. She glanced first to her right,
then to her left and back again. No one about, not
a sound to be heard. This might be her only chance
to find that alone time.

She left the walkway that led to the main door,
choosing one that meandered toward a grove of
trees to one side of the house. Around her, birds
trilled as her feet beat out a steady rhythm in the
stillness. The shoes weren't exactly made for walking, but they did the job with only minor discom-
fort. The narrow dirt path led her through a maze
of sturdy oaks until she spotted another, winding
away from the house and down to a much smaller
stone building in the distance. She heard the faint
sound of a horse's whinny coming from that direction. The stables?

Catherine's favorite stroll, Andi remembered.
Maybe it would also do her good. The idea of being
able to murmur her troubles into the patient ear of
a horse had always held a strong appeal. She loved

the romantic idea of a windswept ride along the moors, her long hair floating in graceful slow motion against her back, the horse's proud head held high and black tail sailing behind. The two of them together, wild and fast.

They were, she understood, gentle, intelligent creatures, able to establish powerful bonds of loyalty with humans. She'd often thought she'd been supposed to have one. What a team they would have made, she and her horse, examining the world with lofty confidence. People would admire the animal's beauty and her regal, almost royal, bearing on him. Her. She never had been able to decide which.

Didn't matter. Since there weren't stables in the city, she'd never met a horse, let alone learned to ride one. She sighed at the thought. Another reason to believe that her city birth and upbringing had been something of a cosmic accident.

Along with her new chest measurement, she might have acquired the skills of a horsewoman. At this point, she was ready to believe nearly anything.

She stood for another few moments, gazing in the direction of the stables, before she began to follow the path that led to them. It was a beautiful morning, the sunlight streaming in gold ribbons through the trees and all around her a serene, almost-eerie silence. Shading her eyes with her hand, she spied the stables ahead, flanked by cobblestones, at the bottom of the path, which wound downward in a descent suited for a workman's rough boots. She didn't have any handy, so the flimsy shoes she wore would have to do.

She picked her way carefully, taking care not to

catch her feet in the many ruts. The grounds of the Havington estate were immaculately kept, so it must be that she had chosen a back way not often used. Still, she persevered.

Nearby, the horse whinnied once again, this time in a long, lonesome sound that seemed to cut straight through to Andi's heart. She raised her head to whisper, "I'm coming." Maybe as the sunset wrapped its rays around the stables, Nathaniel would appear, his lean, muscular body silhouetted by the waning light . . .

At the thought, she closed her eyes, letting her mind drift to what would happen next as his arms stretched out to her. That brief moment of inattention was all it took for her to catch her foot on a dip in the path and begin to stumble. As one leg flew out from under her and the other began to fold, Andi's eyes opened in surprise. But in that same instant, right before she hit the ground, she felt strong arms catch her from behind.

Her heart leapt first in gratitude and then in anticipation, but only until she realized in the next second that the smell of the unwashed body that held her could not possibly be coming from Nathaniel. This person was shorter, stockier, and as she looked down at the hands that held her, had dirt-smudged fingers browned by the sun and edged with grimy black nails. Her nose wrinkled in dismay.

"Got you, I did," a low voice said in her ear, managing to sound both teasing and menacing. And way too close. He was pressing himself into her back, holding her tight, well past the time she'd needed to regain her balance. A low, skanky criminal, lying in wait to take her money, hit her on the

head, and leave her gasping for life on the ground.
Probably just got out of the . . . What? Joint.
Omigod, omigod.

Wait. She didn't have a purse. In fact, hold on a
minute, what was that all about? She couldn't be expected to function without her debit card and her
Visa. Who the hell was she relying on for money?
Annoyance shot through her, until she heard a
chuckle in her ear and smelled the man's potent
breath tickling her hair. There were other things a
criminal, someone with nothing to lose, could do
to her. She froze at the thought and then struggled
to suppress the bile rising in her throat.

He spoke again, "Lucky, it was, you comin' down
here. The master, he wanted me to be havin' a talk
with you."

A talk? The master? Every warning her mother
had ever sounded about strangers began to peal in
her ears. Andi shook her head in a failed attempt
to still the alarm bells and tried to pull away from
the man. He responded by sliding his hands downward and moving them to clasp her wrists in a grip
that sent pain shooting up her arms.

Her breath was coming shorter now. She'd seen
no one around. Not one person who could help
even if she screamed. But she was a city girl who
could scream loud enough to be heard twenty blocks
away. And she hadn't wandered that far from the
house; someone would have to hear her. Wouldn't
they?

But even as she opened her mouth to pierce the
man's eardrums with a blood-curdling scream, she
realized that the resulting scandal would only add
one more travail to her fledgling reputation as a

troublemaker. Havington really would kick her out of here. And if he didn't do it on his own, Louisa would take care of it.

If by any stretch of the imagination, and it would have to be a giant stretch, this wasn't a dream and Nathaniel had been right about characters who were written out, she could end up floating in cyberspace somewhere for eternity, tantalized by the smell of fresh ink on paper and unable to find her way back into her life. No chance for love, no chance for a happily ever after, no chance for anything.

Screaming was out, then. She'd have to handle this one on her own. At least the guy was short. Leverage might work in her favor. She tried propelling her body forward so she could bend at the waist, to no avail. He only held her tighter. "Let me go," she demanded as fiercely as her racing pulse would allow.

"We could be havin' some fun, you and me," the man said, the hint of laughter edging his vile voice. "And I could be paid handsomely for it, I could."

*Fun?* Oh God, no. No. It was too appalling, too frightening to even think about. A blinding anger rose within Andi, spreading throughout her body until she could feel even her fingertips take on renewed strength. "You will not," she bit out, "have your way with me, you filthy coward."

Then with a throaty growl that had to come straight from the childhood memory of mimicking her mother's German shepherd, she mustered every bit of her strength to spin her body halfway around until she was at last in a position to deliver a solid kick to the man's groin. The cry of pain she let out at the grip he tightened on her wrists was, she noted with vengeful satisfaction, nothing compared with his agonized yelp when the toe of her shoe made contact with its unsuspecting target.

The rough hands holding her released.

"Ohhhh!" He doubled over, gasping for air. It took a few minutes for him to manage to say, "I was just havin' some fun."

"You were not just having some fun," Andi countered in a voice that, despite her best efforts, trembled. Adrenaline coursed through her, weakening her knees. She blinked hard, her chest heaving with the force of breathing and her wrists screaming. "And you have two seconds, maybe less, to explain yourself."

"Nahh . . ."

On closer examination, she saw that the man may not have been much older than his twenties, though his face was creased with venom and half his teeth were missing. His clothes hung on him and looked as though they hadn't seen washing in weeks. Under normal circumstances, she'd probably feel sorry for him, like the bums on the street she gave what she thought of as "God dollars," under the theory that God made them come back to her eventually. "Why'd ya do that?" he protested. "Not much appropriate for a lady."

"And what you had in mind for me was?" Andi's voice rose until it nearly squeaked. "You will tell me, right now, why you grabbed hold of me like that and what you meant by your master wanting you to talk to me." She took a gulp of air and waited.

Still bent over and his fists clenching and unclenching as he apparently, to his credit, tried hard not to grab his crotch, he looked at her in disgust and shook his head.

"Tell me!"

He dropped his chin.

She took a step toward him, lifting her skirt far enough for him to see her shoe. "Do I have to—?" Her foot lifted from the ground in a clear threat.

He turned his head and spat before looking up at her again, his eyes defiant, as if to say he wasn't afraid. Still, his hands moved from a hovering position to face her, palms out. "The master, he wanted me to tell you to keep away from the gentleman."

The gentleman. "Mr. Chamberlain?"

The man jerked his head in assent. "Always where you don't belong, the master says. You're not to be talkin' with him. And I'm to see to it." He straightened slowly, deliberately, and said the last proudly, though still grimacing from the effects of Andi's well-placed shoe.

"Are you kidding me?" Who was Horatio Havington to tell her who she could and could not talk with? The sheer nerve of the man, not to mention the gall. He had tried to intimidate Alexandra Lofton-Hale into staying away from Nathaniel. Andi was so angry she couldn't even finish the offended sentences her mind formed. She had never been so insulted in her life, not even when the math department chair had laughed at her outspoken opinion in a faculty meeting and referred to her as their "token romantic."

She took another step toward the man. This time she pointed a finger in his face, wincing from the smell of his body and the aroma issuing from his partially opened mouth. "Now you listen and listen

good. No one, but *no one* tells me who I can talk to."
She stopped, pulling her mouth tight and giving a
sharp shake of her head. "With."

He cocked his head with insolence and narrowed
his eyes, which were little more than slits in the first
place.

Now Andi showed him the palm of *her* hand, holding it in front of his face to make sure he didn't miss
the message. "You're lucky I didn't kick you harder,
because I could have and not even felt a thing. You,
though, wouldn't be making children any time soon,
or ever, which would be a good thing for the women
around here. I can't believe you put even so much as
a little finger on me. You tell your master that—"

He reacted then, moving swiftly to close the
space between them. Clamping one arm around
her in a viselike grip, he used the other to hold a
filthy hand over her mouth.

Andi struggled, pushing against him in desperation, panic rising at the stocky man's strength and
her own seeming lack of it. Her scream was stifled,
and try as she might, she could not move her teeth
far enough apart to bite him. Her heart raced at
full speed now, at a rate that scared her almost as
much as the man's apparently evil intent. She
might have to hope for a heart attack. It would be
a better fate than what he had in mind.

He turned her in one quick movement, his hand
still over her mouth and his arm locking her solidly,
while his other hand began to travel up toward her
breasts, cupping one to give it a painful squeeze.
"The master, he says I got free rein," he whispered
in her ear with a low chuckle. "The gentleman, nor
no other, is going to want you then, now is they?"

Andi squeezed her eyes shut, summoning every muscle in her body to force a scream through the leathery palm that held her powerless. She tried kicking blindly at him, anywhere she could make contact, but succeeded only in stumbling, the sound of the scattering rocks sounding very far away. He pushed her harder against him, as though she were a rag doll.

"If you're not goin' to listen to the master, I'll have to see to it that you do," he said, voice fierce. She was lifted from the ground, her feet kicking uselessly in the air. The fear surging through her every vein seemed to drain any power from her body, leaving her with a sickening feeling that quickly turned to nausea.

This couldn't be happening. Would it all end like this, with her thrust to the ground, broken in spirit and body? Her mind swirled and raced, buzzing with a frantic alarm. She continued to struggle, but he only held her tighter, seemingly without effort.

*Please. Do. Not. Let. This. Happen. Louisa, where are you?*

The uneven stones of the building loomed before her eyes as her attacker, with determined footsteps, dragged her away, apparently intent on the stable as a destination. Only the horses for witnesses. Still, no one around. No one to save her from—

And then, a familiar voice penetrated the roar in her ears, coming from behind the man who held her in his crushing grip. With clipped, precise diction, the owner of the voice issued a taut command that could not be mistaken. "Unhand her."

Her attacker stopped, caught by surprise. As he turned, his hold on Andi's mouth relaxed enough that she could force her teeth apart and then together, hard, to bite his finger. With a screech of pain, he released his hold, dropping her to the ground. She pursed her lips, spitting out the despicable taste of him, and looked up to see his face contorted with rage as he shook his hand.

Her eyes flew to the man standing next to him. Nathaniel's eyes were no longer sleepily sensual, but flashing, and his fist was drawn back and then forward, where it connected with the side of the man's head.

Andi covered her face with her hands, hearing first a startled shout and then a dull thud as the man landed on the ground beside her.

"Did he injure you?" Nathaniel's voice held a deep, rolling anger.

Andi dropped her hands and briefly squeezed her eyes shut, inwardly cursing the tears that filled them. "No, but he was about to."

She felt Nathaniel's arms close around her, gently lifting her up. When she reached a standing position, her knees shook so hard that she began to fall. He pulled her back and she buried her face in the smooth fabric of his jacket, inhaling the scent that was a mixture of horse, soap, and something musklike and imminently masculine. She couldn't look at him. For what seemed like forever, she could only hold on to him with a relief that made her want to sob and laugh, all at the same time.

Slowly, his strength and warmth seemed to meld into her body, and her thoughts began to arrange themselves in order once again. Did he know his prospective father-in-law had sent this dirty, smelly, inarticulate criminal to rape her into submission?

Because Nathaniel had dared to respond to an introduction to her with some interest?

Her breath began coming fast and furious. She stared into Nathaniel's jacket. "He was going to . . . I can't even think about what he intended to do."

The man made a low-throated growl and struggled to his feet. Clenching her fists, Andi turned away from Nathaniel and toward her would-be attacker. "He—" she began to choke out.

Before she could think about it, she brought her foot back and launched it forward, delivering a kick to the man's groin that landed even more accurately than the first one.

He sank back onto the ground with a high-pitched squeak.

She pursed her lips in satisfaction, rubbing shaky hands together. This guy would never see the George Washington side of a God dollar. "Should have kicked him that hard the first time."

Nathaniel turned toward her, his expression incredulous. Feeling a bit sheepish, she raised a finger to brush aside a stray hair. Her eyes rose to meet his as her cheeks grew warm. The women he knew wouldn't fell a man like that.

His mouth was open, but he appeared struck speechless. And there was the smallest bit of a cringe in his expression.

"I . . . um . . ." She wasn't sure what to say, but in a spurt of what she decided might be brilliance, she decided to fall back on cultural differences. "In America, women are taught to defend themselves," she said, her voice faltering in a way she was pretty sure belied her confident words.

Nathaniel's eyes widened. "America," he murmured. "I am quite certain I have no desire to journey there." He stroked a finger along his chin.

The man on the ground made choked noises, but at the same time tried to rise to his feet, sputtering foul curses in Andi's direction. He staggered upward, spittle on his lips and his thighs pressed into a tight line. One hand, with fingers splayed, protected his vulnerable area as he lurched toward Andi, seemingly sure that this time Nathaniel would be on his side.

Nathaniel glanced at him, frowned, and heaved a sigh. Then he delivered a punch to the other side of the man's head. This time, when the man stumbled back and fell flat on the ground, he didn't even attempt to move.

"You are not to venture near Miss Lofton-Hale at any time hence," Nathaniel warned. "Should you choose not to heed my words, I shall have no choice but to inflict permanent injury."

He looked at Andi and then back at the man, still lying prone on the ground. "You may be assured that your master will hear of this. You are to collect your things at once and be gone before he has the opportunity to find you."

Andi gave a sharp nod of her head toward the man, reinforcing Nathaniel's warning. "You don't want to mess with him *or* me," she said. "I've kicked you twice and I'll do it again. Harder next time." He didn't need to know that her leg could barely hold her up.

The man raised his head far enough to cast her a disgusted look. Andi glowered before her eyes swept past him and on to Nathaniel.

"Twice?" he asked.

She laid a hand on her heart and took a deep breath, searching for the appropriate words now that her panic had begun to subside somewhat. "My aim was not quite accurate on the first attempt."

His brows drew together. "Never again," he ordered, tight-lipped, "are you to venture out without an escort."

"Is your concern for me or for low, vile men such as this?" she asked lightly, hoping he'd take her up on the teasing banter. He didn't. "I do not require an escort," she added, but her voice was faint.

He moved closer. "Perhaps my instruction was not clear. You will not tread these grounds alone again, under any circumstances."

"Surely, sir, the danger will pass once this man is dismissed. And I do possess the ability to defend myself, to kick a common criminal right in the—" Her hand flew to her mouth. She'd almost said a word inappropriate to this setting. A twenty-first-century man might have blinked at it; a nineteenth-century man might have her locked up. "My apologies," she mumbled.

He jerked his head, acknowledging what he seemed to think of as her assent.

Okay, the chivalrous thing was wonderful, unique, really great, but also a little over the top. "I did not allow him to do me harm." Then the terror of being held by the man, the fact that she couldn't escape, returned, flooding her body in an instant. Who was she kidding? She couldn't have gotten away from him. "I must admit, however, to a great sense of . . ." Her voice wobbled. "Fear." To say the least. "I shall heed your warning."

And what about the man who had issued the

warning? His endearing concern and defense of her? Her eyes flew up. "But you saved me from him, from the vile things he would have done!" What a hero. She *knew* she had chosen well this time. Wrapping her arms around his neck, she held on tight. "Thank you."

His arms reached up, as if intent on disengaging hers. In response, she held on even tighter, turning her mouth to his ear. "When I dare to think what might have happened, how am I ever able to thank you? The words seem so inadequate."

He hesitated, before pulling her arms down gently, but firmly. "It is hardly necessary to thank me," he said, not looking at her. "Simply fortunate that I chose this moment to undertake a walk to the stables."

"Oh, no, you are wrong," Andi breathed. "You saved, if not my life, then surely my virtue." She pulled her lips together. He didn't have to know the term wasn't technically correct as it applied to her. It was appropriate to the setting. Although the unspoken thought she wanted to add, *but you're welcome to take it anytime,* might not be.

"Yes. Well." Nathaniel drew himself up. "I shall escort you back to the house." As he offered her his arm, he directed a steely gaze at the man still lying on the ground. "And I shall see your master regarding your immediate discharge."

A sudden, terrifying thought occurred to Andi. "No!" she said. "Please do not."

Nathaniel turned to her, surprise written across his face. The man on the ground again lifted his head, one eyebrow cocked.

"I do not wish Mr. Havington to be told of this."

Better to have Nathaniel threaten the stable hand into keeping far away from her, but have Horatio Havington think she'd been scared into submission. If the man was fired, Catherine's father would only think of another way to foil Andi's plans.

"It is wise to ensure," she said now, "that he will never come near me again. But please, sir, allow him to keep his job. For now." She aimed her most menacing gaze at the man, speaking between clenched teeth. "And his mouth shut about what happened here."

The man's lips parted, as if to respond, but he remained silent, contempt creased into his face. Nathaniel's cold gaze caught his and Andi's would-be attacker looked away. "Aye," he said grudgingly.

Andi took Nathaniel's arm with one hand, brushing at her skirt with the other. "Please, let us leave this place," she said, inwardly despising the trembling in her voice. The last thing she wanted to do was show any kind of weakness before her would-be attacker. "I no longer have a desire to visit the horses."

"As you wish." He delivered another terse warning to the man on the ground. "You shall not come near Miss Lofton-Hale again. Or there most assuredly shall be hell to pay."

Nathaniel led her from the stables, his boots ringing across the cobblestones on a path that she now saw led from the house. She had taken a little used back one, apparently. Last time that would happen, no matter how compellingly the lonesome call of a horse summoned her.

He was moving too fast. Andi barely had time to savor the brief moments when he had saved her from a horrible fate, from those horrible hands that had held her flesh in their grip. She shivered.

He slowed. "Have you a chill?"

She shook her head. "If you had not arrived at precisely that moment . . ."

"It shall not occur again."

Closing her fingers tighter around his arm, she gave voice to the thought that had begun to dance around the edges of her imagination. "I cannot believe it an accident that you were the one to save me from such a fate."

He continued to stare straight ahead, quiet for so long that she wasn't sure he'd heard. At last, he said, "Louisa is not writing at this moment. These events are not a part of the story."

"They could be," Andi whispered hopefully.

He didn't answer, instead pulling her fingers gently from his arm and turning toward her to give a slight bow. "You are safely returned," he said. "And I shall not see you again until we gather this evening in the parlor."

Andi looked up at the windows of the house. In one, she could see the white clothing of a scurrying servant flash by. "Why were you walking to the stables?" she asked.

He looked past her. "I was of a mind to look over the horses."

She swept her gaze back to his face. "Because it occurred to you to do so at precisely that time?"

He frowned. "It was the best time to do so." His tone was even, but he wouldn't meet her eyes. Andi had the distinct feeling that he had actually seen and followed her, wanting to talk with her, or maybe even knowing something sinister could be up. The thought sent a tingle of excitement up her spine.

He had come to save her, practically ridden there on a white horse. She knew it.

Impulsively, she reached up to land a kiss on his cheek. "Allow me, sir, to thank you for your brave actions. And for arriving in the right place at the right time."

Appearing at a loss for words, he raised his hand to his cheek. "I believe you misunderstand."

*Someone* might misunderstand, but it probably wasn't her. The wide smile faded from her face a moment later, when she heard the soft voice of Catherine, from somewhere not far away.

"Alexandra," Catherine said. "Pray, whatever has happened to you?"

Andi spun around, glancing down to discover her skirt was streaked with dirt. She hesitated for a moment, then said, "I am so clumsy. I stumbled and fell on the path. It is hard for me to believe I could be so awkward." Her eyes sent a quick flash of warning back to Nathaniel. "Fortunately, Mr. Chamberlain, by chance, arrived in time to help me to my feet."

He said nothing.

"That was fortunate, indeed," Catherine said in a voice that seemed to hold nothing but genuine warmth. "I am relieved you have suffered no injury."

"No," Andi confirmed. "No injury." *Go now, just go. Please.*

Aiming a shy smile at Nathaniel, Catherine extended a small, gloved hand. "The carriage awaits, sir."

She directed her next words at Andi. "Mr. Chamberlain has proposed a ride through the countryside today. Would you do us the honor of accompanying us?"

She couldn't. No, she *shouldn't*. Catherine had asked her, but that wouldn't be right. She was tempted, though. Really tempted. Andi put a fingertip to her mouth in contemplation and, as she did, caught an unmistakable glare in Nathaniel's eyes. Letting her breath out in exasperation, she said, "I am sorry, Catherine. It is not possible. This dress . . . I must change." She gestured downward. The nod from Nathaniel was slight, but she caught it. Unable to resist, she added, "But I will see you this evening?"

At Catherine's murmured assent, Andi smiled. So let them go on their carriage ride. She had things to do. Things that would ensure this was the last time Louisa ever sent them riding together.

# Chapter Seven

Nathaniel forced himself to concentrate his attention on Miss Havington, sitting quietly at his side in the carriage, instead of glancing back toward the house where the thoroughly baffling Miss Lofton-Hale had retreated.

The woman spoke somewhat strangely and behaved abominably, yet for some reason he could not fathom, she intrigued him. It was, perhaps, the flash of fire in her eyes, the passion with which she uttered every word, and her utter disregard for all that was proper. Kicking the stable hand. It had delivered a most certain message, yes, but the means of doing so . . . He could not think of another female who would dare attempt such an act, despite the danger in which she might find herself. And there was the issue of the soft, warm body he'd held in his grasp, however briefly. It had promised things he would do well not to consider, now or at any time hence.

She was absolutely unsuitable in all she did. He

could only hope Louisa would quickly bring the matter under control.

The carriage hit a rut in the road, causing both of its passengers to bounce against the seat. He reached a hand out to steady Catherine and she looked up at him, her gentle countenance a confirmation of proper womanhood. A small smile curved at her lips, giving him hope that the match would at least be a tolerable one. She was a handsome woman, with features pleasing enough to tempt any man, though the scandal that accompanied her had prompted others to end all thoughts of courtship.

He knew of scandal. And of the necessity to make a match, despite any wishes to the contrary. They were, in that, kindred souls, perhaps, which brought, at the very least, a certain understanding to the marriage. His hope renewed, Nathaniel looked again into her eyes, only to discover they revealed little more than a well-bred young woman performing her duty.

He silently cursed the sense of disappointment that stabbed at him. Preposterous. Catherine Havington was the perfect match for him. And he for her. Louisa had proclaimed it to be so.

He could awaken the fire that had to lie deep within her. Indeed, it was his duty.


Opening the door, Andi hoped she'd found the right bedroom. It looked like it. There was the same bed, made of a dark, forbidding wood, that had seemed to want to swallow her whole last night. The wash basin, close to where she now stood, with the tiny chip she'd noticed this morning. And the gilt-edged mirror she hadn't wanted to look in, afraid that it might turn out to be someone else's face looking back at her.

It was her room, all right.

A young woman in a crisp apron fussed with authority over a dress spread on the bed. The longed-for maid. *Yes*.

She cleared her throat and stepped inside, hoping the woman could shed some light on her role without Andi having to look like an idiot and ask. Or worse yet, have to wander the halls, hoping to run into the formidable Annabelle for a dose of stiff-lipped guidance.

"Oh, miss." The woman dropped what she was doing and, turning, bobbed a curtsey. "Begging your pardon, I did not believe you would awaken so early." Her face working with agitation, she clutched work-reddened hands in front of her.

"Please do not cause yourself distress," Andi said. "I did not see a need to disturb you."

Relief and then alarm flooded the woman's face. "Miss, what has happened?" Instantly, the woman was at her side, peering at Andi's mud-stained skirt, darting her hands toward it without touching the fabric. "Did you have a fall?"

"Fall." Sounded good. "Yes, I did," she said slowly, forcing herself not to think of what had actually happened. The last thing on her mind at the moment was a muddy dress. "And I need to change my clothing." She half hoped the maid would say it wasn't necessary, but instead, the woman made a move to help. Andi stopped her with a raised palm.

"I am able to do so myself." Then she added, "But thank you."

The maid murmured something unintelligible and turned back to the dress on the bed, all the while darting sidelong looks toward the door, as though contemplating escape.

Andi stood awkwardly. It was one thing to read all about servants, even lecture with no small degree of expertise on their role and social class in the Regency era, but it was another to see one appear before her, living, breathing, and caring for her clothing. Maybe she could slip out quietly so she wouldn't be called on for any sort of instruction. She could barely take care of herself, let alone tell someone else how to do it.

Of course, it would be handy to have a maid at her disposal. Servants, after all, knew everything that went on in a Regency-era household.

She willed her face into what she hoped would be a mask of composure and crossed the room. Composure. Not exactly her strong suit. One eye began to twitch. She did her best to ignore it. Great. Her uncooperative features weren't content with revealing every thought that ever passed through her head, now they'd decided to provide comic relief.

Stabbing a finger toward a small closet in the corner of the room, she said, "I shall change." The maid turned, bobbing her head in acknowledgment.

A few minutes later, she emerged from the closet, clothed in a pretty dress with sprigs of flowers against a pale background, but longing with every part of her being for the comfort of her well-worn jeans. And her Nikes. What she wouldn't give to have them on her feet right now. Funny what a

person missed, even one who had dreamt forever
of wearing this type of clothing.

She dropped onto an upholstered chair, her
mouth opening when her backside bounced on,
rather than sank into, the seat. Something crunched
beneath her and she reached down to pull out a
bent fan. As she stared at it, half her hairdo fell onto
her shoulder with an unceremonious plop. All that
and a twitching eye.

With a sigh, she set aside the fan, grabbed a fistful of hair, and held it out toward the maid. "Please.
I would like you to assist me," she said, her voice
quivering with frustration. Her straight hair was so
much easier to handle than this mass of thick curls.

"Oh, yes, miss," the woman said, scurrying to her
side. She tugged gently on Andi's arm, leading her to
a chair placed before a dressing table. Andi obeyed,
dropping into the chair with a tortured sigh.

The remaining pins were pulled out with quick
precision, allowing the rest of her hair to tumble to
her shoulders. Andi massaged her head with the tips
of her fingers, took a deep breath, and asked the
woman's reflection, "I am quite certain I know your
name, but I am sorry, I seem to have forgotten."

"Betsy, miss." The voice sounded puzzled.

"Betsy. Of course."

The maid worked quickly, pulling, poking, and
taming the hair into submission. Andi marveled at
the deftness of the fingers, but winced twice when
pins scraped against her scalp. She'd been right to
think of them as weapons.

The maid's face was earnest, young, and eager to
please. If Louisa's story held true with other novels
of the time, most people never even saw the girl as

she went about her duties, which meant she would know more about the people visiting this place than anyone would ever suspect. Andi pondered that thought for a few minutes before asking in a deliberately casual tone, "Are you from this area, Betsy?"

A small frown, then the maid nodded. "From Nevingfair, miss."

"Ah." Andi nodded gravely, as though that meant something to her. "And are you acquainted with Miss Havington's maid?"

"I am, miss. One of 'em. Me and Mary are friends. Knew each other since we was small."

Andi opened her mouth to correct the grammar, but immediately thought better of the idea. The habits of an English teacher were hard to suppress, but rarely welcome. A lesson she'd had to learn the hard way. More than once.

Instead, she asked another question. "What does Mary tell you about Miss Havington?" She took care to keep her tone only vaguely interested, in deference to an instinct that warned she might be overstepping her bounds. Could be time to start listening to her instincts.

She heard the woman's intake of air right as another pin stabbed her scalp. Looking up, she saw Betsy, eyes wide, ask, "Miss?"

Andi chewed on her bottom lip for a moment, wondering how best to phrase her next question. "I understand she is intended to wed Mr. Chamberlain," she said. "Does she hold that to be a happy prospect?"

"Oh, I couldn't know that, miss. Mary would never speak of such things."

"Of course," Andi agreed quickly. "She would think too highly of Miss Havington to speculate about such personal things. Just as you would." She gave the maid a reassuring smile. "I know that."

Betsy's head nodded in agreement before her eyes darted back to the hair challenge at hand.

Andi allowed the maid's fingers to continue working without interruption while she regrouped. True, getting the information this way might not be how things were done, but at the moment, it was the only hope she had. It wasn't like she could meet Catherine for a glass of wine and get her talking after two. Or pump Catherine's best friend, since it didn't look as though she had any. But Betsy would know a lot more than she might want to volunteer. Andi was sure of it.

She blurted, "I must confess, I am terribly worried about her."

When that didn't get a response, she sighed loudly, squinting up at Betsy. "There is someone else, I know it. She started to tell me today while we were out walking. She wanted to talk, I could tell, but she is ashamed for some reason. That doesn't make any sense. It is not as though anything untoward happened with the first man, is it? Why would it be so very difficult for her to talk about?"

Holding her breath, she waited. The answer didn't come for a moment or two. By then, Andi had exhaled noisily and weathered two more sharp pokes to the head. Much more of this and she was going to need a dose of aspirin. Oh, *of course.* It had not been invented yet.

Betsy clicked her tongue softly. Head bent, she

avoided meeting Andi's eyes in the mirror. "Miss Havington, she's had a rough time of it."

"But why would she be unhappy when she has, within her grasp, the opportunity to marry a man like Nathaniel Chamberlain. He is . . . You must have seen him. She should be—" *Ecstatic.* Andi waved her fingers in the air to restrain herself from giving voice to every one of Nathaniel's qualities. But how could anyone be so blind as to not see them? "I can only deduce that she must still be in love with the other man."

"Not for me to say, miss," Betsy said, this time pretty crisply. The maid patted the newly tamed, upswept hairdo with finality. "There we are."

Andi's heartbeat quickened. Not so fast. This woman had information she needed. She rose abruptly from the chair, her head dipping back with the unexpected weight of her hair, and reached for the maid's hand. "I want to help Miss Havington," she said, eager that Betsy understand. "She is so lonely. And if it's because she has lost someone she truly loved, that is a decided tragedy, don't you think?"

Betsy pressed her lips together.

After a few seconds, Andi let go of Betsy's hand and sat back against the chair, realizing with surprise that she meant the words, and that the desperation coursing through her veins to make the maid talk seemed fueled as much by empathy for Catherine as it was by Andi's own intentions.

It was a little unnerving, this feeling that someone else might be genuinely worse off than she. The few good friends she'd made were dramatically lucky in love and, because of that, took pleasure in focusing their less-than-perfect matchmaking skills on Andi. Every one of them was sure that before long, someone would succeed at turning her into a couple, instead of a single.

Maybe that's why she'd been avoiding them lately.

Something about the forlornly brave figure of Catherine had touched a part of Andi that wanted to help. Catherine reminded her, more than a little, of the doomed heroine by the same name in *Wuthering Heights*, a story that had reached into the very soul of a teenaged Andi and pulled out a fervent wish that, someday, she could find that kind of intensity and passion. Sure, Heathcliff had his flaws, but oh, how he could love.

It couldn't be easy, living in a time like this, when women had so few choices and their happiness often depended solely on the direction of authoritative men. How would she herself have reacted if marriage, even to a man as wonderful as Nathaniel, had been thrust upon her as a foregone conclusion?

Where was the romance, the passion, in that?

And maybe she had been wrong about Catherine not knowing enough to crave an all-consuming, abiding love. The "improper relationship" might have been the one true one for Catherine. Deep in her forbidden feelings, she might long for it as deeply as Andi longed for Nathaniel.

Andi put her hand to her heart. If that was the case, Catherine's father had committed a grave injustice. It was possible, she supposed, that the man would have no idea what he had done to his precious daughter. But that didn't make it any less of a crime. From what she'd seen of the man so far, he made sure he got what he wanted first, and asked questions later. If ever.

To help Catherine, she needed Betsy's intelligence-gathering. Again, she clutched the maid's hand. "Do you not believe Miss Havington deserves to be with the one she loves?"

Betsy dropped her gaze. A long moment passed before she spoke to the floor. "Mary says Miss Catherine does pine. Most dreadfully."

Andi realized that, yet again, every emotion must have shown plainly on her face for Betsy to confide this nugget of information. She gritted her teeth. Sometimes it worked to her advantage, sometimes it . . . She shook her head. No time to think about it now.

"But the puzzle is who she pines dreadfully for." Andi tried unsuccessfully to keep the urgency from her voice. "Betsy, what is his name?"

"Mary would not like me saying, miss."

"If we are going to help her, I must know." Andi made it a command this time. Though she didn't condone ordering people around, unless they were immature, unfocused, high school students, the situation left her little choice.

The maid shifted her weight from one foot to the other, still staring at the floor. "It's Mr. Evernham, from Fortis House," she said, her voice barely above a whisper. She clapped a hand over her mouth.

"Mr. Evernham," Andi repeated. "But why would Catherine's father be so opposed to her marrying him, if he is the gentleman who has claimed her affections?"

Betsy looked up at that and dropped her hand,

her eyes wide. "Mr. *Edland* Evernham, the youngest. The one that—" She stopped.

"The one that what, Betsy?" Andi shook her head. "I do not know him. What is it about him that makes the liaison unwanted?" *Out with it,* she wanted to screech. Instead, she tried to keep her face a mask of barely patient politeness.

Betsy's eyes creased, whether in sympathy for Catherine or in misery at her own predicament of having to spill what she knew, Andi couldn't tell. The words came out in a rush. "He's the only one of the three sons with the black hair, miss. And eyes as dark as you ever saw. The rest of 'ems fair as can be, and blue eyed. Includin' the mother and the poor father, God rest his soul."

Andi knit her brows, struggling to understand. "But genetics can be—" She stopped and tried again. "It is entirely possible that any one of the sons could have a different eye and hair color than his parents."

Betsy simply stared at her.

There had to be more to this story. "So, he is adopted . . . born of different parents. Is that it?" Had adoption amounted to a social branding in this era?

"No, miss. His mother gave birth to the young gentleman, that's for sure." Betsy's head moved up and down, reinforcing the gravity of this situation. "Just months after Master Evernham rode his horse off a cliff, God rest his soul. They say as how he might have seen . . ." Once again, Betsy clapped a hand over her mouth.

Andi might have found a kindred soul in speaking before thinking, she mused. Instead of saying

so, she murmured, "You must tell me, Betsy. In fact,
I insist. I shall see to it no consequence befalls you."
She turned her expression to imploring. "Catherine was not allowed to associate with him because
he looked different from his brothers?" Maybe she
was a little slow, but really . . . Oh! Mr. Evernham
had seen Mrs. Evernham with . . . someone else?
Possibly someone with dark, even black, hair?

Wouldn't be the first time that had ever happened. Common occurrence, at least once a week,
in the soap opera Andi scheduled her classes
around, though she'd rather die than admit that
fact to anyone but another die-hard soap fan.

Once released, Betsy's tongue took flight. "The
missus, she took to her bed a long time ago. Don't
anyone see her anymore, though she makes sure
her boy is taken care of." Betsy made a soft clucking
noise with her tongue. "And the young gentleman,
he's a fine-looking man, though there's some that
don't much like him. Mr. Havington, he didn't like
it when Mr. Edland started coming around. Said he
wasn't to step foot in the house. Wasn't fit for the
likes of his daughter."

"But Catherine fell in love with him," Andi said,
her voice sounding far away to her own ears.

Betsy nodded furiously. "And then," the maid continued, "before anyone could know it, Mr. Evernham
took off with her, said they were to be married!"

A gallant leap into the night, bound for freedom.
Andi could see it in her mind. Catherine's hair
flying behind her as the horse galloped faster and
faster, holding on to her handsome young lover's
waist, trusting he would shelter her, love her as no
one else. Together, they would take on the world,

show everyone they were meant to be as one. And her father would *have* to accept them, once they were married.

She sighed. The image was gone as fast as it had come, like a giant bubble that had popped. Blinking hard, she asked, "What happened?"

"Mr. Havington found them before the vows could be read." This time, Betsy nodded sagely. "But not before the night had passed. He brought Miss Catherine back with him and told her she would be married to the first gentleman as would have her. And she was never to see Mr. Evernham again. Not a soul was to know, but of course, there's them thatn . . ." Betsy shook her head.

Andi's chest tightened in sudden, heart-wrenching sympathy for the wounded Catherine. She drew up straight in the chair. "So anyone would be better than Edland Evernham, is that it? Even after they went through all that to show him how they felt about each other?" Her voice rose. "That is no better than treating her like a slave! Like an imbecile who cannot possibly know what is right for herself!" If she'd had a podium, she would have pounded it. Hard.

Betsy cast a quick glance behind her and laid a finger across her lips. "I shouldn't have said what I did, miss," she said urgently. "Please."

"No worries. Truly." Andi narrowed her eyes, chewing on her bottom lip. A wholly unpleasant thought occurred to her. "So, Betsy, what happened to Edland Evernham? Did he survive the fury of Catherine's father, or did he meet the wrong end of a gun?"

Bright spots of color suddenly stained Betsy's

cheeks. The maid dropped her chin, mumbling a response.

"What did you say? I didn't catch it." Andi ducked her head down to come up under Betsy's face.

"I do not know, miss!"

"I think you do, Betsy. And as long as you have told me this much, you may as well tell me the rest. I shall find out, with or without you." She probably wouldn't, but Betsy didn't have to know that.

Betsy crumpled the corner of her apron in one small white hand. "He . . . went away. To London."

Andi sat up, pressing her back into the chair as she considered possible reasons for the trembling in Betsy's voice. Sudden repentance for gossiping? Realization that she'd gone too far, said too much? Or maybe something more. The maid still would not look at her. "But he is not in London any longer," she ventured.

"I wouldn't know, miss."

"Betsy, look at me." She used her best, most brisk teacher voice.

When the woman raised her head, Andi saw all she needed to. "He is back, is he not? And you know that because . . . you have talked with him? That must be it. You are helping him try to see her." It was a stab in the dark. One that surprised her with the reaction it elicited.

Betsy's face went nearly purple. "Not me, miss! It wasn't me as helpin' him!"

Andi sat perfectly still. "Then who? Mary?"

The maid's response was a torrent of self-recrimination. "I shouldn't have said anything. Mary, she'd be in for it if anyone were to know. Only trying to help, she has been. She'd do anything for

Miss Catherine, that's for certain she would. Not that it's doin' any good. You worry too much for Miss Catherine, that's what I tell Mary, and you've got to watch out. But she don't listen. It was wrong for me to speak, miss. Please." Betsy stopped, gulping in air. "The master, he would be terrible angry."

"What is Mary doing, Betsy? Tell me. I will not have it any other way. Though I promise you most fervently the secret will go no further."

Betsy hesitated, wringing the apron in her hands. Her face made it clear that she was desperate to take back everything she'd revealed.

"I don't make promises lightly," Andi said gently. "And we have a duty to help Catherine. No one should find herself forced into marriage with a man she does not love."

Betsy's eyes widened as the plea hit its mark. "Mr. Edland has Mary carryin' messages to Miss Catherine," she said. "He wants her to meet him. But Miss Catherine won't even look at 'em. Tells Mary to take 'em away, even though Mary's takin' her chances bringin' 'em." Betsy paused. "But Mary says there's tears in her eyes."

Andi looked away, pondering this information. "She must be greatly frightened. Her father exerts a great hold over her." What could it be, she wondered. A threat of physical harm? Or guilt from the fact that Catherine's mother had died after giving birth? Louisa could have set things up a few different ways.

She turned her gaze back to the maid, who was nodding furious agreement. "You did the right thing in telling me, Betsy. We are going to help her."

"Please, miss, you mustn't say—"

"No one need know how I learned of this." Andi waved a hand in front of her face, nearly forgetting the maid as her sense of indignation built. She stood abruptly. "I need fresh air."

"Yes, miss." Betsy ducked her head, scurrying around Andi to redirect her attentions, and shaking hands, to the dress on the bed.

Andi walked the several steps to the door, turning back when she had her hand on the knob. "Betsy."

The maid turned slowly, apprehension in her eyes.

"Pray, tell me why I am here, on this visit? That my mother is here? It appears as though we do not live far away, so I am not certain why we are . . . lodging with the Havingtons."

Betsy's mouth opened with what looked to be surprise. "But you're invited guests, miss. For the ball."

The information was not all that helpful. Andi gave her head a little shake. "How long shall we stay?"

"Just until the morrow, miss, I believe."

If Betsy was right, that meant she'd have to work fast. Very fast. She nodded and then touched her hair. "My hair . . . it looks quite lovely. Thank you."

The maid nodded. "Yes, miss."

It was a good thing organization was one of Alexandra Lofton-Hale's greatest strengths. Her fellow teachers teased her often, saying that Andi could have a test graded and returned before her students had even had a chance to take it.

That skill might come in handy right about now.

# Chapter Eight

The best way to think, Andi had always found, was to walk briskly, with her head down and all of her attention on the matter at hand.

With so much vying for her attention, it wasn't until she'd put considerable distance between herself and the house that she'd cleared her mind enough to focus on the dilemma that had propelled her out the door and onto the road.

How to get Edland Evernham and Catherine Havington back together? To make them believe in themselves enough to relive the depth of feeling that had led them to take the phenomenal risk of eloping in the middle of the night. Could it be reclaimed despite Catherine's father?

So Edland's mother had fallen in love with someone else and given birth to his son. A movie plot so commonplace it was almost boring. Though she had to say, she hadn't often read it in a novel written during the Regency era. Not that the scenario wouldn't be understandable, given the number of arranged marriages that took place. Louisa might be more adventurous than Andi had first thought. She'd have to give her credit for that.

This time, her mind's eye imagined Catherine running in a field, her filmy dress rippling in waves behind her, with the heartbreakingly handsome, and inappropriately dark-haired, Edland running toward her, his strong arms outstretched. Andi smiled sadly, right before she frowned. He might have had the guts to spirit Catherine away and try to marry her, but when that plan went wrong, the guy's attempt to regain the love of his life seemed to be limited to scribbled notes delivered through a maid. And the notes weren't even getting to Catherine. The chances of that approach ultimately leading to a romantic reunion in the field weren't good. What about the idea of riding up to the house, sword gleaming and eyes flashing, ready to defy Catherine's father and reclaim her?

Well, okay. Edland probably hadn't read many romantic novels. He might need help from someone who had. Someone who *taught* romance literature. Or . . . Louisa needed help, or . . . You know, this whole thing was getting pretty confusing.

She glanced over her shoulder. The house had disappeared and no others were in sight. In the recesses of her mind, she dimly remembered turning from the main road onto another at least a time or two. Uttering a curse, she rolled her eyes in irritation. This was not a good time to become lost. If she took a wrong turn, would she end up in yet another manuscript? Her luck, it would be a tale of murder and she'd end up the victim.

Spinning in a slow circle, she took in her surroundings. The dirt road wound its way through the rolling hills with no visible signage and not the slightest indication of a main horse thoroughfare. Probably should retrace her footsteps and hope for the best, she decided.

She stood, searching for some kind of bearings, with the sun warming her face, the smell of horses and country air filling her nostrils, and the sound of birds twittering in the distance. She strove to remember each detail, to drink it in. Her lectures would ring with a realism that would have her colleagues filled with envy, her contract renewed, and even better, every one of her students enthralled—finally—even the basketball players who came in with the wrong impression of an easy A. That weaselly chemistry teacher would have to fold his working model of a spaceship and leave in the night.

Andi took a deep breath, squared her shoulders, and turned back in the direction she was fairly sure she had come.

What would Edland have to do to win Catherine back? She allowed her imagination to drift back to the fantasy of the two reunited, adding in herself and Nathaniel, blissfully locked in their own embrace, fondly watching from the sidelines, just before Nathaniel turned to her and—

The road began to shake beneath her, shattering her daydream, even as a pounding sounded in her ears. She stopped. An earthquake? But the sound was coming from behind her. Turning, she saw a horse appear at the top of the rise, his powerful body filling the sky, and heard the shout of his rider split the air.

*Run*, screamed the warning racing through her head, but her body wouldn't listen. She stood rooted to the ground, fear surging through her. Her legs were lead weights, her feet embedded in the ground as though concrete had swallowed them whole.

The horse swerved and then flew by her, in a blur of black, leaving Andi to stand helplessly in the road as he charged past, the wind from his wake sweeping over her, the sharp smell of him overtaking her, her heartbeat thudding in her ears. *Close. Too close.* Killed by a runaway animal on a deserted road in Regency England. How would anyone explain that to her department chair?

Wait a minute. That horse wasn't a runaway. She stood, taking uneven breaths and willing her pulse to slow to something less dangerous. When at last it did, she squeezed her eyes shut, concentrating on the impression the scene had imprinted on her mind. A rider, bent low, urging the horse on, each apparently as intent on speed as the other.

Racing. Within inches of her, an innocent bystander. That horse had barely had time to avoid her. She could have been left to die here in the road, the very life seeping out of her with no chance for a paramedic. At the thought, she pressed a hand to her chest, feeling faint.

Then she heard the sound of hooves again, slower this time. The reckless rider, returning to the scene of the crime, no doubt. She didn't want to open her eyes. If she did, and actually saw him, she might have to let loose with every swear word careening through her mind. And she'd already seen how well that went over here.

The horse snorted and reins jangled. Heavy steps that sounded like boots pounded toward her on the path, coming closer, and then stopping. She'd let him have it. Who cared if he couldn't handle a few choice words?

She opened her eyes to find herself staring directly into the burning ones of Nathaniel Chamberlain. He grabbed her shoulders, holding her so hard her bones telegraphed frantic messages of pain. She went as limp as a rag doll in his grasp.

"My God, woman, are you injured?" Even in her confused state of mind, she could hear the fear behind his harshly spoken words.

"No," she answered in a voice so small it came out no louder than a whisper. How could it have been him? He wouldn't be so irresponsible. Of course not. He'd probably been passing by, saw the whole thing and had come to make sure she wasn't hurt. Yes, that would be Nathaniel. After he saw to her, he'd chase down the other guy and make sure that kind of racing didn't happen again. Yes, he would.

"My horse did not strike you?" Chest heaving up and down, Nathaniel straightened to his full height. "I did not see you." He stopped, dropping his hold on her to take a step back, eyes wide as he raked a hand through his hair.

She shook her head in stunned disbelief. Apparently, he *was* that irresponsible.

Silence, for a moment. Only the sound of a bird, somewhere close by, calling out, and the horse, sputtering as he shook his head and reins. And then, Nathaniel, the man of her dreams, spoke again.

"Enlighten me," he nearly spat. "Why do you stand in the middle of the road? Without the most cursory look to determine what, or who, else might be venturing forth?" He paused, and then, as if it had just occurred to him, thundered, "Without an *escort?*"

She opened her mouth, then closed it again, exhaling sharply. Her heartbeat, after racing at breath-robbing speed, had now plummeted to a dull throb that made her dizzy. She blocked the urge to sway, fighting off the blackness that threatened to envelop her.

She refused to pass out, to play the part of an idiotic, weak female, wandering into harm's way unaware. Some tiny part of her brain began to chime in, *like you haven't already once today?* before she shut it down.

Louisa wasn't writing now, she had only her own body to fight. So why wouldn't it cooperate? The danger had passed. And after he had nearly killed her, Nathaniel Chamberlain had the nerve to talk to her this way? Let's talk definition of a hero here, shall we?

With effort, she drew her shoulders back, taking a deep breath. "I was not hurt. No thanks to you." Knowing her voice shook, she infused it with all the power she could summon. "What did you think you were doing, racing that horse on this road?"

He drew back. "I risked my own life, and that of my horse, to ensure you received no injury."

"You must have been doing sixty miles an hour! Who in the hell races a horse on a road where people walk?"

He looked confused for a fleeting second before his face darkened with anger. "Madam," he sputtered, a clear warning in his voice.

Madam! Of all the . . . Try and put her in her place, would he? She'd see about that. "Don't you call me madam," she snapped, surprised at the strength her voice had regained.

Nathaniel took a step forward, his eyes searing into her with such intensity that she backed up, her shoes sinking into soft dirt at the road's edge. She could have sworn she saw the green flecks in his dark eyes flash.

He looked away and then back at her, his jaw muscles working with a vengeance. "Did you not see that you were walking directly in the middle of the road? Just as I rode up over the crest of the hill, unable to see what lay ahead?"

Walking directly in the middle of the . . . As if she somehow were at fault. Andi hesitated and then glanced in the direction he seemed to be indicating. She'd been so lost in her own thoughts, she hadn't even noticed she'd been walking up a slope. When she turned, she saw the blind spot that he referred to. Okay, not so good for a horse and rider. She should have kept her eyes open.

But that didn't give him any right to come flying up a hill without regard for anything or anyone. He was the one who lived in this century and ought to know better. "Doesn't matter! Who are you, Top Gun? You've got a need for speed? A death wish? What?"

She watched as he blew out a breath, his eyes blinking hard. Then he frowned. "Your speech is most . . . I fail to understand . . ."

"Forget it!" She threw her hand in the air and then struggled to regain her teacher bearing and Regency speech. Both attempts failed. "The point is, you were not watching where you were going, Mr. Chamberlain."

"You could have been killed, or grievously

injured. You should not have been walking in the middle of the road."

Andi pulled her mouth into a tight line. Enough already. She got the point. And somehow, even though she was innocent and he was the reckless one, it wasn't coming down that way.

At the same time, his concern for her welfare wasn't that unpleasant. How long had it been since someone had risked injuring himself to save her? Once, let alone twice in one day? Wait a minute. She thought about it. Okay, never. She blinked, mulling that over, feeling her expression relax. "It appears," she said, looking up at him, "that your superb horsemanship meant neither of us came to harm."

His brows drew together, like two storm clouds banding. "Do you mock the gravity of the situation, Miss Lofton-Hale?"

God, no. If anyone ever saw the gravity of a situation, even when it wasn't actually there, it was her. She shook her head. "I remember reading how well you ride a horse, and now I was able to see it in person. Skillful. And heroic." Her voice caught on the last word as the truth of the statement sunk in.

Replaying the incident in her mind, and this time adding in sound effects, she had a mental glimpse of the effort it had taken him to control the frightened animal. To save her from injury. She'd known from the very beginning what kind of a man he was. Congratulating herself on finally recognizing a man with substance, she gave him a smile that trembled more than she would have liked.

Nathaniel looked unimpressed. "And you are yet again without an escort. Even though I quite clearly instructed you—"

She clenched her teeth and fists and curled every one of her toes in the flimsy shoes. No one instructed her to do anything unless he was carrying a title that meant her paycheck depended on it. With a deep breath, she willed herself to calm and her body to relax. It was not yet the time to raise the issue with Nathaniel.

Instead, she stared at the ground, forcing herself to count the pebbles within her range of vision. He was being protective. That's what any good hero would do in this time and place. Fourteen pebbles. Okay, then. She could trust herself to speak. "The only person who caused me concern in this instance was you," she said mildly. "And I know you had no such intent."

He pulled his cheek muscles tight in an obvious battle for self-control. "Come," he said. Taking her arm, he led her to the spot where the horse, fixing a wary eye on Andi, stood. *Don't look at me like that,* she silently told the animal. *I don't need a lecture from you too.*

"Why were you not accompanied on this walk?"

He would have to keep insisting on that, she thought with a flicker of impatience. Andi lifted her chin. "I do not require the services of . . . of . . . a minder. I have two legs, and they are quite capable of taking me where I wish to go."

She saw the annoyance in his eyes before he turned away. After a moment, he asked, "And pray, what is your intended destination?"

"I was in need of fresh air, had taken a short stroll, and turned back toward the house."

"You must learn to be more alert when undertaking such an activity."

Not unreasonable. Alert might not be the best

way to describe her mind at the moment. Except . . . exactly who could criticize her after all she'd been through? She exhaled in one noisy breath. "Should not have allowed my thoughts to dwell on you to the exclusion of all else, that much is clear." Uh-oh. Probably shouldn't have let that pop right out. Wouldn't earn any points for subtlety.

But it got his attention, she noted. He abruptly turned toward her, the reins dangling from his fingers. "Me," he said.

She raised her eyebrows. "You," she said. In spite of herself, she allowed a tentative smile. Let him chew on that for a minute.

Instead, he leaned in, searching her eyes. "You will explain that remark, I presume."

Gladly. Then a tiny peal of warning bells began to sound in her mind, accompanied by the feeling that he could read her every thought and blundering intention with those eyes of his. She didn't much like that feeling.

Not only that, but he had moved so close to her that, instead of country air, her nostrils were again drinking in an enticingly masculine aroma—soap, horse, leather—and scrambling her attempts to think rationally. She looked up at him through her lashes. What the hell, rational thinking hadn't done much for her so far.

His gloved hand cupped her chin with soft leather, his eyes never leaving her face, while her stomach spun in circles in reaction to his touch. He contemplated her, the shadow of a smile curving at his mouth.

He knew exactly what she was thinking, she was sure of it. Including the picture that had flashed

through her mind of being drawn into his arms
when he wasn't quite so encumbered by that jacket
and shirt. What would the warmth of his bare chest
feel like against—?

Her knees turned weak, causing her to dip. He held
tight to her shoulder, steadying her as she searched
his face. What did he see in her eyes to cause such a
self-satisfied expression? It wasn't fair. He could see
everything going through her mind while he so coldly
shielded his own thoughts? Not going to happen. If
she couldn't manage seductiveness, she'd have to
throw him off guard. If he kept the upper hand, she
had no chance. He'd already made it clear Louisa's
story would go off exactly as written.

Grabbing his arm, she blurted, "Catherine's in
love with someone else."

She caught her breath and held it; at the same
time, she railed inwardly at her blunt tongue. He
had feelings. Feelings that could be hurt. Something
she would never want to do to the love of her life.

He dropped his hand and moved closer, until
only a few inches separated his nose from hers. She
swallowed the lump that had suddenly materialized
in her throat, but didn't look away, fixating on his
face, the shadow of whiskers just beginning to show,
the sweep of thick eyelashes, the mouth, now
slightly open and so close to hers. She blinked hard.
As long as she'd had the nerve to say what needed
to be said, she'd stand her ground. And get an
answer.

A long, delicious shiver ran through her at the
nearness of him. At last, he spoke. "Do you really
think so little of me," his voice rumbled, "as to

assume I would marry a woman who would not be content as my wife?"

Thinking little of him wasn't the problem. Might be helpful if he didn't know that, though. "It appears to me as though you may have every such intent, although possibly now that you know . . ." She cleared her throat and attempted to straighten her shoulders. No luck. Like the rest of her, they had melted into submission.

"What would cause you to presume I would not have Miss Havington's best interests at heart?"

Not a word would come out of her uncooperative mouth. She shook her head. As she did, tendrils of hair brushed against her face, a discomforting reminder that even the hair on her head wasn't really hers.

His lashes swept down and then up as his lips again formed the shadow of a smile. "I see," was all he said before he turned away, again apparently intent on the needs of the horse.

Andi struggled to recover the sense that seemed to have deserted her. *He saw? Just what exactly had he seen?* Her fists, at her side, clenched. Damn. She hated that he could read her like—like a book. She choked out a strangled laugh.

He threw her a glance over his shoulder and then went back to the horse, running a gloved hand down its flank.

"*I* have seen the manner in which you look at her." There, she'd said it. Let him try to refute that.

He turned back. "While it is an uncertain flattery to find that you watch me, quite possibly your gaze has not been fixed upon me at the proper time." His voice was annoyingly calm.

"I have seen what is in your eyes. What is in hers. And what is not."

Nathaniel squared his shoulders with unmistakable purpose. "This conversation is at an end," he announced in a voice obviously accustomed to obedience. "I will escort you back to Barrington Manor, and then proceed on to my own destination."

"Escort me? On that horse? You would sooner leave me choking in the dust of his flying hooves. And you, Mr. Chamberlain, did not answer my query as to why you raced through here at such a speed. Most irresponsible, if you ask me."

"I do not recall such a request."

Very funny. If he would ask her a thing or two, he might not be making mad dashes along an occupied road. "And I do not recall requesting an escort. I have no such need." She said the last through clenched teeth. What was she, a child?

"I cannot allow you to risk your welfare further. Twice it has happened today that you have found yourself in precarious circumstances."

Try as she might, Andi couldn't come up with an answer to that before he spoke again.

"May I assist you in ascending my horse?"

Obviously, he wasn't giving up on this. And she'd had just about all she could take of him not grabbing her in his arms and kissing her unmercifully. She only had so much time, after all. She countered the words that threatened to escape her mouth with a prim, "I prefer to walk, sir. These two legs carry me quite admirably." She pointed.

He didn't miss a beat. "As you wish." His tone changed to brisk. "I will then as well."

Too late, she realized she might have made a

mistake. Behind him on the horse, she could have had a perfectly legitimate reason to grip that hard, lean body, giving fuel to her nighttime fantasies for weeks to come.

They began to walk, Andi taking two steps to each of his powerful boot-clad strides. The sounds they made on the road seemed the only ones for miles around. A strange, but soothing, scene. You couldn't find many places in Portland with this much quiet.

Was he planning to keep silent? She bit her lip for several seconds before breaking the stillness of the morning air. "You have little to say with regard to Miss Havington?"

"Entirely true," he said.

"It will not change the facts of the matter."

"That would assume you have knowledge of the facts."

"I—" Andi gave a frustrated jerk of her head. Knowledge she had. Facts were based on what Betsy had said, but the servant had no reason to lie.

It was several moments before Nathaniel spoke again. "You refer to reading of me," he said. The statement was flat, though it seemed to be posed as a question.

"In the book *Wedgfeld Hall.*" She tried to keep the eagerness from her voice. He'd remembered. "Though, as I said, I had only come to the third chapter."

"How did you happen upon this book?"

"Online, in a rare book auction," Andi supplied in a rush, before realizing how baffling the answer would sound to him. "That is, I purchased the book."

"As a finished volume," Nathaniel observed, "in bound form. Is that what you are proposing to say?"

Andi nodded.

"And pray tell me, how did it end?"

She heard more than mild interest in his tone. "I do not know the ending. I read only to the third chapter. But even then I knew Catherine was not the one for you." She frowned and shook her head, struck by the extraordinary strangeness of having this conversation with the hero of the book she was reading. Oregon to England, minus 200 years, with not a single frequent-flyer mile involved.

Even if she knew how the book ended, would she have told him? Something told her she would have had a moral obligation to the book's author to keep the ending quiet. Aagggh. She pressed fingers to her head.

"What would cause you to question the author's judgment and intention?" He stopped and turned to face her, bringing his horse to a halt.

She stopped walking. *One look from him. That's all it takes to send me reeling.* Some might think the angular planes of his face too severe or the slightly crooked nose not perfect. But to her, they only added to his mesmerizing appeal, as though the hard edges were there to protect and deflect attention from the deeply loyal, sensitive nature she knew lay within.

She scanned his face, hoping to find an inkling of his thoughts. He was, however, good at keeping them to himself, something she had yet to master. His face, with one brow lifted in question, revealed nothing. Her heart tottered right there on her sleeve, telling him anything he wanted to know. His, on the other hand, was firmly protected from view.

She looked down. Stalling for time, she kicked a rock, sending it skittering down the road. Ow.

Sturdy, these shoes were not. She halfheartedly muttered a choice word, stealing a look at him to see if he'd noticed. From the look of surprise that crossed his face, she would have to guess he had.

What *would* cause her to question the way Louisa wrote the story? Desire to snag the hero for herself, just because he was the most appealing man she'd fantasized about in a million years? Or because something about him tore through to the part of her heart that had been nearly ready to give up on the idea of love?

"I . . ." she began, looking back up at him, at a loss for words. It wasn't as though she had *asked* to be here, in the middle of the story. Unless you were being technical about it, in which case . . . But on what planet would someone think it could actually *happen*. "She—" Finally, she held her palms up and gave a small shrug.

"Precisely. You have no explanation for behavior that jeopardizes so much for so many. You offer only the demand that we abide by your notion of what should occur in the story of *Wedgfeld Hall.* Perhaps," he continued, dragging out the "s" in the word, "you would simply prefer to be the one authoring the book."

Andi's eyes widened as a hot anger shot through her body and her breathing escalated with alarming speed. As if this wasn't about her very survival. She, who had landed in this bizarre situation through no fault of her own and only, apparently, because she'd been desperate enough to make a wish to find a little love in her life. *How dare he make such a presumption?*

Worse yet, how could he know? She'd told no one about those rejection letters, so heartlessly worded, ripping her carefully crafted manuscript into virtual shreds. It had been five years since she'd indulged that particular dream and she'd promised herself, never again. No. He couldn't know. He'd made a lucky guess.

Her hands flew to her hips and she leaned toward him. "Perhaps," she said, making her own "s" hiss with authority, "this author does not know what she is doing. And you are intent upon covering that, selling yourself *and* Catherine short in the process by not fighting Louisa when she is clearly wrong. All for the sake of a guaranteed happy ending. So that you can go on about your life with a wife who stands dutifully by your side and is as little trouble as possible." She raised her arm, slicing it dramatically through the air. "If that is true, sir, you are not the hero I assumed you to be!"

That felt better. She could almost hear the orchestra building to a crescendo in the background. On a movie screen or in a book, this would be a great place to end a scene. Too bad Louisa wasn't hard at it right now.

"Indeed." One word from him, tersely spoken, said volumes more than she just had. Andi's heart plummeted.

When, she wondered yet again, would she ever learn to think before she spoke?

As it turned out, that was the last coherent thought she had before Nathaniel's body closed in and his mouth landed on hers, sending her senses into a startled, chaotic, and sensually terrified full alert.

# Chapter Nine

She melted into the warmth of his muscled body, her knees weak and sinking fast toward the ground. He held her upright with a powerful yet gentle grasp; his mouth moving over hers, commanding her every nerve ending with a slow-moving, confident seduction that rendered her unable to think. She wasn't even sure she was still breathing.

*This is more like it,* a small voice inside her screeched with glee.

Her arms floated upward to encircle Nathaniel's neck, fingers closing on the thick, soft hair curling around his collar. He drew back slightly, his lips clinging still to hers, his breath moist and warm, and then closed in again.

As her body began to regain enough strength to hold on, she pressed into his chest, relishing the sensation of his heart beating so close to hers. The heat, the very life of him, pulled her to him. His mouth brushed her nose and then across her flushed cheeks to the lobe of her ear, teasing the sensitive skin with his lips until she uttered a cry.

Just as her body opted for total and complete surrender to whatever his intentions might be, he pulled away and stepped back with the same abruptness he'd used to catch her unaware.

Knees wobbling, Andi struggled to recover her bearings. "No," she whispered, wanting to reclaim those last few seconds, unwilling to let them go. *What if this is the only chance I get?*

That kiss, she thought with a delirious abandon of all that made sense, had been one to hang on to and savor, one that made the other men she'd dated look like quivering, chest-puffing bullfrogs. With jelly lips.

She felt a wide, trembling grin spread across her face. *That kiss* had materialized as everything she'd dreamed of since she'd first picked up *Wedgfeld Hall* and lost her heart in its fragile pages. She raised her eyes to meet Nathaniel's, knowing they would reveal her every feeling and thought, laying them bare to his scrutiny. She didn't care. She wanted him to do it again. Longer, this time.

He pushed aside a lock of hair that had fallen across his forehead, the only visible sign he'd been in any way disturbed by what had taken place between them. "And what say you now?" he inquired calmly.

"Wha-aat?" Andi caught her breath in a painful gulp. "What say I?" she repeated, the words scraping against her throat.

"Have I regained my status in your eyes?"

So what she thought mattered to him. Her heart skipped a beat. She swallowed hard and drew her still-trembling shoulders up straight. "Not because you kissed me. Although I have to say . . . it was . . .

well, a great start." She gave a little nod of her head
and saw his eyes crinkle in response.

"It was but my humble aim," he said, giving a
courtly bow.

"Then I guess you could say, mission accomplished." Andi ducked her head, feeling the heat
radiate anew from her cheeks. Looking through
the tops of her lashes, she waited for his next move,
while concentrating furiously on mental telepathy.
*Just take me in your arms again. And don't let go this
time.* After what seemed like hours, she saw him gesture down the road with a sweep of his hand.

"We had best resume our journey," he said with a
finality that caused her heart to drop.

She lifted her head. "Why?"

He raised one boot-clad foot, setting it on a rock,
and folded his hands across his knee. Then he
dropped his chin, staring at the ground. But he
said nothing.

Andi rushed to fill the silence. "Something happened here. Unless I'm wrong and you kiss every
woman you meet like that." *Please, oh please, don't say
you do.*

No response.

The stillness seemed to close in on her from all
sides. *Try again. Get through to him this time.* Back to
nineteenth-century speech, shaking voice or not.
She cleared her throat, trying to keep the sound
delicate. "Does it not seem that we should . . . ?"
What, exactly. The nineteenth century and the
twenty-first century barreled through her mind at
the same time, colliding in a fury of conflicting
words and customs. "At the very least shouldn't we
sit down and talk or something?" She wrapped her

arms around her waist, pressing inward, to keep them from reaching out to grab him.

"Louisa will begin her day soon," he answered quietly. "And I must be at Barrington Manor when she does so."

No matter what, it always came back to Louisa. "Because Catherine will also be there?" she managed to ask.

He nodded gravely and turned his eyes to her. "The tale continues to unfold. Though you may know what is to happen, I do not."

"I told you, I read only the opening chapters." Andi exhaled, digging her fingers into her ribs. "I do not have the slightest idea what is to happen." Although the standard hero–heroine formula gave her a pretty good idea.

"Ah." He pointed in the direction of the Havington estate. "Then we shall both discover what is to lie ahead."

Andi moved her arms upward, folding them across her chest. "Discover. What Louisa chooses to pen."

He jerked his head in agreement.

"Does it not even matter to you what happens?" she choked out. "This is your life. How can you think it possible to merely wait to see what she decides to do with you? *Who* she decides you should marry? Because you *believe* you have no choice?"

He blinked slowly. Beside him, the horse gave an impatient snort. Nathaniel reached toward him with a steadying hand, his eyes never leaving Andi. "You believe you know something about me."

"I may not have read the complete volume, but I did get as far as chapter three." Her legs regaining at least a weak support, Andi began to pace back and forth, her steps quickening as emotion pitched her voice higher. "I know you see this as a way out of trouble for your family—possibly the only way out. But that does not remove your right to a life. Does not mean that there cannot be another for you. Another who would not represent a duty, an obligation, a loveless match."

Suddenly she had trouble looking in his eyes. He who could read everything in hers. So instead, she directed herself to the horse, who seemed a bit taken aback by her sense of outrage. "How does Louisa manage it, this great loyalty from all when she only sets out to create misery? Committed to happy endings, I don't think so. Unless this is the first draft, the one she plans to rip up and feed to the fire." She made a sound of derision and then braved turning back to Nathaniel. "Catherine longs for another." Andi threw her hands into the air. "Pray, tell me how that becomes a happy ending. Especially when you only moments ago kissed me. You would not do something like that for no reason. I cannot believe it of you." *This is a really good time to agree.*

No reaction in his face. He had dropped his leg from the rock and now stood with one foot ahead of the other, watching her, hands behind his back, appearing no more disturbed than if she had commented on the weather. She moved within inches of him. "I know you feel you must rely on this marriage to save your family home," she said, her eyes searching his. "Sacrifice your own contentment because of events you had no control over. Because your brother—"

"You know nothing of my brother." His voice remained steady and controlled but had the effect of thundering through the silence that surrounded them. His dark eyes blazed a warning, but Andi was certain she'd seen the smallest quiver at the corner of his mouth. A flash, then it was gone, replaced by a tight line of impatience.

After a brief hesitation, she took a chance. "Then tell me about him."

His eyes grew large. Andi couldn't decide whether he was appalled or caught off guard at the suggestion, but there it was again, that tiny wobble at the corner of his mouth. Her stomach contracted and moisture stung her eyes. He could bluster all he wanted to, but she'd seen the hint of vulnerability, probably caused by painful memory, at the mention of his brother. Oh yes, this was a hero, a man to love.

A man who needed to talk.

She squared her shoulders and thrust out her chin. "Come," she said, more gently now, as she turned to walk down the road. "We have a distance yet to go. Sufficient time for you to talk of your brother and your family." She was back using her teacher voice. People had a hard time saying no when she used it, she'd found.

"I hardly think it—"

"Appropriate? Indeed, you may be right. But you need to talk with someone. And once I have heard, I will be able to tell you if Louisa has it right so far. You devote such effort to these scenes, you must wish to know what she writes about you. What if, kind sir, she has portrayed you entirely wrong?" She tried, successfully, she was pretty sure, to keep the pleading from her voice. She could think of nothing she wanted more than to know everything inside his heart. Especially the parts Louisa hadn't shared in the opening chapters.

"That would presume that I . . ." His voice was tight.

"Have some control over what is written about you? You do." Andi started walking.

He caught up with her steps in two effortless strides, the horse following obediently behind. She stole a glance at Nathaniel, to see his jaw muscles working furiously as he stared straight ahead, down the road.

"You have a most direct manner of speaking."

"You are not, I fear, the first to make such an observation." She made a light scoffing sound and smiled at him. "Although not precisely in those words."

He didn't respond to the smile. He didn't answer at all.

After a few minutes of silence, she decided to plunge ahead without him. "I shall begin," she offered. "Your older brother possessed a . . . a . . ." She hesitated. "A love of gambling that perhaps went too far. When he disappeared, you discovered the money was also gone. You have a strong loyalty to your family home and are determined to do whatever it takes to save it."

He stared with great intent at a distant point she was sure he didn't see.

"Even if it means marrying Catherine Havington solely for the money she would bring."

He stopped suddenly. So did the horse, and Andi. She spun to face Nathaniel as he turned toward her, locking his gaze on hers. What she saw there made her take a small step backward.

"Miss Havington is a fine woman. I hold her in the highest regard and possess every intention of ensuring her happiness. Was that not clear in Louisa's telling of the story thus far?"

Again with the booming voice. Andi raised a palm upward, but a moment later, let it fall awkwardly against the skirt of her dress. "I am certain that is true, because you would only—" She began to sputter.

"Was it also not clear that I am quite certain I shall learn to love her, unequivocally and without reservation?"

The word "love," used by Nathaniel when talking about Catherine, stung with the pinprick of uncomfortable truth. He would do it, actually do everything within his power to learn to love her. Because he had to. If it didn't work, he wouldn't let on. "This is a marriage of convenience. Louisa has made that clear. You do not have to pretend—"

"Pretense is not a factor, I assure you. Miss Havington is a handsome, accomplished woman with a gentle and kind personality. How could a gentleman such as myself not be positively entranced?"

"Being entranced, positively or otherwise, does not last. Do not attempt to deceive me. Pretense is everything here."

"A most unflattering comment, Miss Lofton-Hale."

She paused, her mouth fluttering open and shut. "Do you wish to know what Louisa is writing about you? Do you not think it might help you to ensure that you and all concerned achieve the longed-for happy ending?"

He looked away and then back, conflicting emotions

crossing his face in rapid succession. Finally, he asked, "Has she then portrayed the upcoming engagement as only a means to an end?"

"She has." Andi pushed aside the unwelcome knowledge that Louisa was, no doubt, planning to force the two to fall in love along the way, a turn of events Nathaniel seemed not only to be prepared for, but ready to go right along with.

He appeared to contemplate her response for a moment before asking, "And has my niece been mentioned as yet?"

Andi shook her head.

Again, he looked away. "I thought not."

"There was only a vague mention of family."

"She is my brother's child." His eyes flicked back over her face. "Her mother died in childbirth, and now her father is gone as well. As her only remaining family member, I am responsible for her care and upbringing." He gestured ahead. "Shall we proceed?"

"No." Andi planted her shoes in the dirt.

"No?" He didn't sound pleased. "I believe we have addressed this subject adequately."

"We have not." She took a deep breath. "So, it is not only the family home you must save, but also your niece. At least until her father returns." Her voice softened as she continued, "It is so wonderful she has you to take care of her, that you would—"

"Her father will not return." He dug the heel of his boot into the road and then kicked at the dirt, sending up a cloud before he set off down the road, without a glance back.

Andi followed, half running to catch up with his purposeful strides, kicking with frustration at her cumbersome skirts. "How can you know?" she asked. "Louisa didn't make that clear. At least not in the beginning of the story." She glanced at the stubborn set of his chin and then back at the road. She had opened her mouth to speak again when he cut her off.

"He will not return. The *persons*," he spat the word out, "he owed money to saw to that with one shot, on a London street corner."

Andi sucked in a surprised breath. "I am so sorry," she whispered. "But can you trust the source of this information? Perhaps there is something to be gained by leading you to believe that—"

He stopped and turned, his face hard. "Since the source of this information, as you refer to it, is my own witness, I can believe it quite without reservation."

"Oh." Andi's voice faltered. Nathaniel had seen his own brother killed before his eyes. The mantle of family responsibility had passed to him in that second of horror, and he had claimed it as his own, whether he had wanted it or not. He was willing to sacrifice his own happiness to marry for money and save a family that now included his young, helpless niece.

"That must have been too terrible, to watch as they— Did he know you were there? I am certain he must have. While you were trying to help, to save him . . ." She gestured wildly as her thoughts scattered in different directions, trying to piece together the whole terrible scenario with sketchy information. Villains in dark coats, casting Nathaniel aside, firing one terrible shot at his brother who lay alone in a pool of dirty street water, his sad, irresponsible life slipping away.

Her heart clenched with sympathy for Nathaniel. His situation was so much worse than she had even imagined, and here he was, carrying on with such—

Just then his voice crashed through her reverie, tight with raw fury. "Indeed, he knew I was there, as I had spent the better part of the evening with him, gambling away the family fortunes. And while my brother lost his very life on that street, I was left with a mere gash on the head. Had I not consumed quite so much to drink, I may have been better able to defend him from such a fate. Indeed, it very likely should have been me to suffer that fatal injury."

He drew in a sharp breath, his eyes flashing. "And there you have it, Miss Lofton-Hale. Your exalted hero must now redeem himself by attempting to mend grave mistakes in judgment that cost a young girl not only her father, but an untarnished family name."

Though he didn't appear conscious of the movement, he raised a finger to touch a white scar that ran along the length of his eyebrow. Andi hadn't noticed it before, but now it seemed to stand out in his face, radiating the pain he must feel at remembering where it had come from. A lasting reminder of a fight to the bitter end?

Her forehead creased as she tried desperately to understand, to change her mental picture of that night's events. His burden of guilt had to weigh on him like a boulder. He couldn't have been responsible for his brother's death. There had to be more to the story. "No." She shook her head.

"Yes," he responded placidly. "And yet you would

seem to imply that I am the unlucky one to be wedding Miss Havington. As you can now most surely
understand, I am the one who is fortunate."

"You kissed me," she whispered. "Why would you
do that, unless . . . ?"

"An error in judgment," he said, his voice dropping. "Yet again, forgive me."

"There is nothing to forgive," she said, her chin
rising. "You would not have done so unless you
wanted to, unless you also knew Catherine was not
the one for you." The imprint of his lips remained
on hers.

Nathaniel's hand dropped to his side with the
sharpness of a blow. She jumped.

"You are mistaken, Miss Lofton-Hale," he said, his
voice deadly even, "in assuming I possess the manners of a gentleman."

"I'm not." She shook her head until the curls
flew. "I am not mistaken about you."

"Time grows tight," he announced. He bent from
the waist in a bow and, as he swept back up, added,
"We are entering the grounds of Barrington Manor.
I shall leave you now to return on your own. I
assure you, you will be quite safe." His expression,
tight with the words he didn't speak, did not invite
her response.

Andi watched him place his boot in the stirrup
and swing his leg easily over the horse. *Don't go*, she
wanted to plead. *Let's talk about this. I can help, I
know I can.* "Miss Lofton-Hale" was all he said with
a dip of his head before he rode away, spurring the
horse to a gallop.

She stood in the middle of the road, feeling
bereft, deserted, and confused by the new pictures

of Nathaniel she was trying to process. A gambler, as irresponsible as his brother? Caught in a street-corner brawl over bad debts? Less than a gentle-man? Slowly, she began to walk toward the house, kicking aside the unfamiliar length of her skirt with each step.

This was awful. Terrible. Nothing in this whole situation made any sense at all. Not only was she stuck in some kind of time warp/bizarre dream, now she didn't know if she could believe in Nathaniel, when that very belief had thrown her into the middle of this story in the first place.

And what about Catherine and Edland? Was she wrong in thinking she could get them back together, help them find the love they'd once had, but lost? If Nathaniel wasn't the man she thought, maybe *they* weren't the wounded lovers she'd thought.

If she'd landed in the middle of *Emma*, of *Pride and Prejudice*, she'd know what to do. But in the middle of *Wedgfeld Hall* . . . ? There might be a good reason why this author had never garnered the attention her peers had. She may have been related to a publisher, who put the book out as a favor, where it landed flat and died. Until Andi discovered it languishing as a rare book. Rare because no one had wanted it. Because the author was incompetent.

In the whole scheme of things, this could qualify as really bad luck.

She stared down at the tiny rocks pressing into her soles with each step. The sun washed over her with fingertips of warmth as Nathaniel's face drifted before her mind's eye. He'd been furious at the confession he'd had to make. Anger that had to have come from guilt that plagued him over his brother's death.

He'd made a mistake. A serious one. On the other hand, a man who would then rise to the occasion and do what he had to do to rectify the situation had clearly heroic qualities, with a touch of a dark side thrown in to spice things up. In a time when females were largely expendable, he was sacrificing himself to make a life for his orphaned niece. And he wouldn't have stood aside and let criminals take his brother's life, drunk or not. This man would have fought, tried to defend his brother, and then shouldered the remorse at his failure to do so. His ability to make the confession only endeared him to her further. Despite her choice of heroine, Louisa knew a little something about creating a hero.

A gentleman. He was one, every inch of him. There could only be one reason he'd kissed her. He felt the same thing she did and knew she was right about the mistake in marrying Catherine.

She wanted nothing more than to enfold him in her arms, stroke that scarred forehead, and convince him that everything would be okay. After all, she believed in the kind of love that could overcome every challenge, big or small.

But this did complicate things a little. Raising her face, she gazed at the blue sky, dotted with wisps of cloud. "What," she asked, "am I going to do now?"

Nathaniel Chamberlain rode fast and furious, reveling in the pounding of his horse's hooves. Possibly the sound could drown the regret, the confusion pushing at him from all directions. He could not say what had possessed him to take hold of Alexandra Lofton-Hale and kiss her in such a way. At first, it had been simply a wish to stop her from talking, to prove to her why Louisa had entrusted him as the hero of her tale. It was not a role he accepted lightly.

Then it had turned to something else entirely, and he had not let go of Alexandra until the sense that had deserted him made a sudden reappearance. The passion with which she demanded answers from him, the warm, willing lips on his were nothing less than intoxicating, and he had allowed himself a heady swallow.

All that he might forgive himself, attribute to an entirely understandable, though less than gentlemanly, lust for a desirable woman, but the act of confessing to her about what had occurred that terrible night? Deplorable. And certainly outside Louisa's plans.

If he demanded honesty of himself, he would be forced to confess that he had sought her understanding. It had mattered greatly to him that she know all. And still consider him a hero.

He bent lower in the saddle, urging the horse on. It appeared clear that he must not again place himself in circumstances leading him to speak with Alexandra. His tongue had loosened of its own accord.

Louisa had abandoned stories in the past, leaving her characters to dwell in their own sort of hell. He had vowed no similar fate would befall him, or those he bore responsibility for.

Nothing must endanger the conclusion of this tale.

\* \* \*

"Betsy!" Andi shouted for the maid before she had the door to the bedroom closed behind her. "Betsy, where may I find you?"

"Here, miss." Betsy emerged from a corner of the room, neatly piled clothing in her hands. She swung a leg in back of her to drop a quick curtsy, the clothes nearly toppling from her grasp.

Andi strode across the room until she stood in front of the girl. "Leave the clothing, Betsy. I must talk with you."

"Yes, miss." The maid laid the clothes down uncertainly, keeping one hand on them.

Andi took a deep breath and then said, in a rush of words that ran together, "I will be the one to give Edland Evernham's notes to Catherine."

Betsy's face turned bright pink. Turning and dropping her chin, she said to the clothes, "Oh, miss, please don't do that."

"It is the only way."

"But Mary would get in trouble, she would, then. Terrible trouble." Betsy's entire body shook at the idea.

"The only way," Andi repeated, her voice firm.

"But, miss—"

"We have no time to waste." There were advantages to an era where servants were required to obey. She might feel badly later about issuing orders, but right now, she didn't have the luxury of time to debate what should be done about the so-far-unsuccessful suitor. "Mary cannot convince Catherine to open his notes, much less read them. That leaves us little choice but to abandon one plan for another. You have my solemn vow I will ensure Catherine will read at least one note from him."

Betsy's eyes became as round as saucers. "I shouldn't have told," she whispered.

Andi ignored the comment and pushed on. "Does Mary have the notes still?"

Shaking her head, Betsy answered, "I don't know, miss."

"Then we must find out." Andi grabbed the smaller hand in hers and began leading the maid to the door.

"Miss Alexandra. Please."

"We need to talk with Mary."

"Ohhhh . . ." she heard Betsy say in a high-pitched plea as they left the room.


Mary, as it turned out, wasn't hard to find. But she was as shocked by her friend's betrayal as she was by the idea of turning over the letters Edland Evernham had entrusted to her stalwart care. "Mr. Edland said only Miss Catherine must see them," she said, pulling her lips tight, her round cheeks flushed and brown eyes flashing nervous accusation at a cowering Betsy.

"I endeavor to help him," Andi insisted. "With my encouragement, she will read them." She figured that, even if she had to hold Catherine down and read the letters to her, she was willing to do so.

How could Louisa have simply written off Edland? Had he been the first hero, but hadn't worked out? Grudgingly, she might see Louisa's point if all the guy could manage to do was send letters through a maid. Or had he always been a tertiary character from the very beginning, never intended as more than a means to an end? Hardly fair.

"Mr. Edland, he said—"

"He said that he wished for her to read his letters."

"But he told me—"

"To deliver them only to Catherine. I understand." With effort, Andi softened her tone. "But do you not see that all he wants is for her to read them, with no regard to the manner in which it happens? We must make sure of it."

Mary's eyes darted to Betsy and then back to Andi.

"Mary . . ." Andi said, struggling to keep the apology from her tone, "you are to hand me the letters. At once."

The maid opened her mouth, but closed it again before saying anything. "I don't think I should, miss," she whispered, her dark curls bobbing. But she reached into her pocket.

Andi watched as Mary's hand reappeared, clutching white papers tied together with ribbon. She extended her own hand. The stack landed on her palm with a soft thud, Mary's hand still attached to it.

Gently, she disengaged the maid's pudgy fingers. "Thank you," she said, trying her best to inject reassurance into her tone. "Through me, you will have fulfilled your promise."

"I don't know as how you can get her to read 'em, miss," Mary answered, her face crumpling. "'Never,' was what Miss Catherine said. 'Not for as long as I live, Mary,' was what she told me. 'I must forget I ever knew his name.'"

# Chapter Ten

Andi had no sooner stashed the packet of letters in her pocket than she felt a hush descend on the house, as though an invisible hand had closed over its occupants, startling them into silence. She looked up at the ceiling, blinking, not certain what to expect.

"Hurry," she heard Mary whisper to Betsy. "There is little time."

"Time?" Andi asked. But as her body began to take on its now familiar reticence, her shoulders curling inward, she understood. Louisa was writing again. She waited for her mouth to open, for words to come out that weren't hers, in a voice she would never use in a million years. Nothing. So far, so good. The plan she was beginning to form required her to operate under Louisa's radar for a while.

Mary and Betsy scattered in a rush of flying feet. Andi crossed the room to make her way to the hall, expecting to see Annabelle issuing instructions. She looked both ways, but saw no sign of her fictional mother figure. Good. An encouraging sign that she wasn't directly involved in the scene.

All the same, this was an inconvenient time for Louisa to begin a writing session, just when Andi's mission was beginning to take shape.

Tapping one shoe against the polished floor, she wound a tendril of hair around her finger, thinking. She needed to get to Edland Evernham. This could be exactly the right time, when Louisa was distracted elsewhere. If she could find Mary and tell her . . . Hold on. Louisa also had a mission: to finish the book. She likely had her attention focused on Nathaniel and Catherine right at this moment, with the intention of moving the developing romance along to its author-pleasing conclusion. The carriage ride earlier might have been a prelude to Louisa's sealing the deal between the two.

If Andi wasn't in the scene, she wouldn't be able to influence the outcome. Releasing her hair, she raised fingertips to her lips, closed her eyes, and remembered how Nathaniel's mouth had felt on hers, the rough gentleness that had taken over every rational part of her being and awakened a longing she hadn't even known existed. One that seemed to come from a place deep within, soaring to the surface to lay bare her every nerve. With one kiss. Just think what would happen if they were to share an interlude in one of those formidable beds in a cavernous room . . .

Forget Edland. She had to find Nathaniel. Now. Make him remember what they had shared, what more there could be. Exactly how could she be expected to lecture with real-life authority about the mores and customs of the day if she hadn't had a chance to push them?

Pressing her fingers to the wall, she made her way down the hallway, irritated to find herself stepping on the hem of her skirt with nearly every step. Not the most practical of outfits, these. Finally, she reached the broad staircase, then grasped its railing to peer over, her eyes searching every corner she could see of the floor, which was two flights down. The house appeared deserted, except for muffled voices coming from somewhere below. She squinted, but still could see no one.

She stretched a hand out and watched as she willed it to ball into a small white fist. Not easy, but she managed to do it. Louisa must be otherwise occupied and only exerting minimal control. With satisfaction, she pounded her fist once on the hard wood of the rail. *Ow.* It might be wise to watch the declarations of independence.

She crept down the stairs on the tips of her toes; the shoes she wore, which were little more than slippers, did not make a sound.

All around her, an eerie sense of quiet hung in the air. She imagined the house's occupants crouched behind its heavy doors, waiting until it was safe to emerge. That might work for them, but not for Alexandra. Wait . . . *Andi.*

As she grew closer to the bottom floor, the voices became more distinct. One masculine, the other feminine. The man spoke in low tones, and the woman's much higher voice seemed to punctuate his with agreement. Andi slowed her steps to lean against the banister, straining to hear, growing more and more certain, with a tightening of her every muscle, that the man's voice belonged to Nathaniel.

When she reached the final stair, she leaned forward to peer through the open door of a parlor on her left. There he stood, stiffly upright, his profile to her, his hand holding a much smaller, delicate one. As Andi watched, her mouth open, Nathaniel raised the woman's hand and bent his head toward it, lips apparently readying for touch. It was either Catherine's or Andi hadn't been called for the new heroine auditions. Despair flooded through her, weakening her knees. She grabbed the banister, holding on hard. He couldn't . . . he wouldn't—

*No!* The protest screamed through her head. Those lips had touched hers with a hell of a lot more than courtly contact, and she wasn't about to allow some other woman to—

Not without a fight, anyway.

Ignoring her unsteady legs, Andi lunged forward, off the stair and toward the floor. In the brief second she was airborne, she slammed into something that sent her sprawling backward, as though she'd thrown herself straight into an invisible glass wall. She fell against the stairway; head snapping back with the impact, and her skirt ending up bunched around her knees. Sharp bolts of pain shot through her as her body met the unforgiving wood of the stairs.

*But there's nothing there.* Dizzy, she lifted a hand to her head, covering her eyes. She tried to speak, but her mouth only moved in bewilderment, with no sound. She'd smacked head-on into something hard and unyielding. An invisible barrier. She lifted two fingers from her eyes and squinted, moving her head gingerly to find a reflection in glass or clear plastic. Nothing.

Sucking in a breath, she ignored her body's warning that, if she moved, the ache in her backside might reveal itself as something more. Letting her hand drop from her eyes, she stretched her arm out in front of her, attempting to touch her fingertips to whatever stood between her and reaching Nathaniel.

Still nothing. Her hand floated through the air, fingers waggling, as she watched. Whatever it was had gone. Or somehow, she'd had an incredibly bad moment of coordination and caused the spill herself. Certainly within the realm of possibility for her of the glass-spilling fame.

But even as she searched for reasonable excuses, she knew, in her heart, if not her head, exactly what had happened. Louisa, locked in her world of manipulation, had stopped her from interfering.

Andi drew herself far enough upward to lay her chin on the stair railing. "Merciless is not a great quality for an author," she whispered, wishing the stairs could have at least been semicushioned with carpet. As she watched what she could see of the scene in the parlor, she saw Nathaniel's mouth touch what she now saw was clearly Catherine's small white hand. Gently, gravely. He hadn't witnessed Andi's painful moment; Louisa had seen to it.

His eyes appeared locked on Catherine's face, though he said nothing. Andi caught her breath, imagining his look and what it would feel like to have it once again directed at her. People opened and closed their eyes all day, but no one did it like Nathaniel, with a raw, sleepy sensuality that caused a woman, at least *this* woman, to practically melt into a puddle of literary desire at his feet.

In the next instant, Andi heard Catherine's voice, sounding small and faraway, but carrying with what sounded like a newfound projection. "Sir," she said, "I confess that this declaration of your feelings is not unexpected." Even Andi, sitting spread-legged on the stair and unable to see Catherine's face, could hear the quivering in her voice.

*I'd be shaking myself if I was in her place,* she thought.

*In fact, I did.*

*Why does he have to declare his "feelings" already? Have we never heard of courtship?* Misery swept over Andi, tears welling to blur her vision. In the next minute, he was going to propose and Louisa would throw Andi into a scene as a simpering, empty-headed bridesmaid, smiling gamely in a dress guaranteed not to take attention from the gorgeous bride. Or worse, marry her off to some feeble-minded jerk.

While her heart broke inside, where no one could see. She shuddered with the injustice of it all. A girl should be able to get a break in *some* century.

She pulled away from the railing, drawing her knees together and burying her head in them, telling herself, as she did, that it was ridiculous, psychotic even, to be this disappointed in losing a man who had never been hers. A man who existed only in the pages of a book.

It didn't lessen the physical ache that seized her heart and squeezed tight at the thought of him, the sight of him. There was so much there that could have been, so much that could have made her forget she was a thirty-year-old woman, a high school teacher, a let's just say the word that fits the era, *spinster,* who had never actually fallen in pulse-racing, sense-robbing love. Who had never known—

*Hold on.* She hadn't lost her chance just yet. Raising her head, she rubbed fiercely at her eyes and narrowed them, staring straight ahead. Yes, he might be preparing to propose marriage to another woman, but if she could manage to get through to him, to somehow interject herself into the scene, Louisa might have to write it all over again. And if Andi could do it before Nathaniel proposed and Catherine accepted, all might not be lost. Make it hard for the writer and she could decide to take an easier track.

Andi could do easy. No problem.

"Right," she muttered, knowing, as she considered it, how idiotic the idea seemed. After all, she'd just encountered what could happen when Louisa wanted to keep people out of a scene. She rubbed the small of her back to make sure nothing was broken, contemplating her next move. Then, tentatively, she stretched her fingers out in front of her. It really did not feel as though anything was there.

She pursed her lips and blew out a noisy breath, ruffling the curls on her forehead. What did she have to lose? She hadn't grown up watching football games with her father not to have the experience come in handy at some point in her life. This could be it. Or even better, maybe Louisa wasn't watching at this particular moment and the invisible barrier, untended, was gone. And even if the barrier *was* still in place, Andi had already proved to herself that the author could, in some ways, be fought.

With slow, deliberate movement, she rose and climbed backward, halfway up the staircase, repeating *I'm crazy* again and again in her mind just in case there was any doubt. But even so, she bent over, thrusting her shoulder forward and curling her arms into her body, cradling an invisible ball. It had worked, on TV at least, for all those men who barreled through whole lines of huge, hulking opponents. How much harder could it be to break through Louisa's concentration?

She tore off her shoes and stockings, curled her bare toes against the wood, and drew a deep breath, concentrating on the spot at the end of the stairway. "I can do it," she told herself. "I can, I can."

And then, barefoot, she threw herself down the stairs at breakneck speed, an escalating cry building in her throat and flying out of her mouth, mimicking what she remembered hearing the football players yell as they ran onto the field, puncturing paper barriers to pump their fists defiantly in the air.

When she reached the end of the stair and leapt off, she met resistance, as though she'd run into a giant, tautly stretched rubber band. But in the next second, the force of her momentum broke through, sending her sailing into the wall that faced the stairs. Just before she would have hit face-first, she forced her body to turn so that her back instead hit the wall with a loud crack, dislodging a painting hung just inches away. From the corner of her eye, she saw a flash of its gilt edge shooting downward.

Andi groaned, her back sliding against the wall until she landed on her bottom. Next to her, the picture frame cracked sharply and splintered, sending gold spears across the polished floor. The face of someone's ancestor came to an abrupt rest faceup, staring his disapproval at the ceiling.

The dress had wrapped itself like a bandage around her legs, leaving her bare toes sticking out. But she'd apparently been successful at breaking through Louisa's barrier, though a dignified arrival, it wasn't. No broken bones. At least, she didn't think so.

She reached up to shove her hair aside, catching sight, as she did, of the startled faces of both Nathaniel and Catherine leaning over her.

"Alexandra," they said in unison, Catherine's softly baffled voice nearly drowned out by Nathaniel's much sharper one. He kicked aside a piece of splintered frame, sending it skittering across the floor.

"Yes—I," Andi began, but before she could finish, all three froze in place.

And it was over. Relief washed over Andi as she felt her body relax, limb by aching limb. Then she remembered the two standing over her and, reaching up wrapped a hand around her neck, reflecting, as she did, that this might not have been such a good idea, after all. "Hello," she ventured, for lack of something better to say. At the answering sight of Nathaniel's furious eyes, she demurely pulled her knees together.

"But pray, why are you here?" Catherine asked. "I do not understand." She turned to Nathaniel, her face puckering in polite confusion.

"It is most important I speak with you," Andi said to Catherine, scrambling to get up while still maintaining some sort of grace. It didn't work. Finally, she gave up and rolled onto her knees, pushing against the floor with her hands. Once she reached a standing position, she brushed her hands off and zeroed in on the other woman. "Please."

Nathaniel stepped between them. "No one will move from this spot," he commanded in a voice that carried through the long hall and echoed with authority. His eyes searched the air above, as though waiting for a cue visible only to him.

Andi hesitated, and then said quietly, "You have my word, sir, that it will take but a few moments." Her hand reached toward Catherine, who drew back. "Louisa . . ." she murmured.

"Is at a pause," Nathaniel finished. He glowered at Andi. "You will do nothing."

She tried again. "I *must* talk with Catherine—"

"Silence."

Well, she liked that. She'd already fought the law, in the form of a narrow-minded author, and she'd won. Couldn't he see that? Not likely she was going to allow someone to command her into silence now. She snapped her mouth shut, but pulled her shoulders back straight and leveled her most intimidating stare at him so that he would know it was her choice.

At last, he turned to her and said, "She has closed her desk." He didn't add the "Are you satisfied?" but Andi thought he might as well have, since she heard it so clearly in his voice.

"As it should be," she answered primly. "Because as I am certain I mentioned, I must, however briefly, claim the attention of Miss Havington."

Catherine looked at her with what appeared to

be well-bred suspicion. "Mr. Chamberlain and I were speaking," she began.

Speaking, true, but not talking. That was Louisa's way, but not Andi's.

"Louisa will resume in a few moments and I am certain your conversation shall as well. First, however, *I* need to speak with you." Grabbing Catherine's elbow, Andi pulled. The woman really could be infuriating. Any decent female acquaintance should see when there was something that had to be said privately—outside the hearing of a man.

She and her friends had used the time-honored tugging on one ear signal as a nonverbal sign for a quick escape to the ladies' room. She should teach it to Catherine.

Catherine turned to Nathaniel as Andi began to lead her away. "But I must—"

His expression could have been chiseled from granite.

"Let's go this way." Still holding fast to Catherine's elbow, Andi steered her along the vast hallway and into another parlor, this one decorated in soothing shades of blue and gold. Shutting the door behind them, she leaned against it, hands splayed, fairly certain that she might look as crazed as she felt. No matter. "Please take care to listen. What I have to say is critical to your future happiness."

"What," asked Catherine, an affected sigh escaping her lips, "can be so very pressing that you must spirit me away in this fashion, Alexandra?"

"I have in my possession Mr. Evernham's letters, which you have not yet been convinced to read. The ones he penned with all the love he continues to hold dear for you. I am told he is

*Take A Trip Into A Timeless World
of Passion and Adventure with
Kensington Choice Historical Romances!*

## —Absolutely FREE!

Enjoy the passion and adventure
of another time with Kensington
Choice Historical Romances.
They are the finest novels of
their kind, written by today's
best-selling romance authors.
Each Kensington Choice
Historical Romance transports
you to distant lands in a bygone
age. Experience the adventure
and share the delight as proud
men and spirited women
discover the wonder and
passion of true love.

# Get 4 FREE Books!

We created our convenient Home Subscription Service so you'll be sure to have the hottest new romances delivered each month right to your doorstep—usually before they are available in book stores. Just to show you how convenient the Zebra Home Subscription Service is, we would like to send you 4 FREE Kensington Choice Historical Romances. The books are worth up to $24.96, but you only pay $1.99 for shipping and handling. There's no obligation to buy additional books—ever!

## *Save Up To 30% With Home Delivery!*

Accept your FREE books and each month we'll deliver 4 brand new titles as soon as they are published. They'll be yours to examine FREE for 10 days. Then if you decide to keep the books, you'll pay the preferred subscriber's price (up to 30% off the cover price!), plus shipping and handling. Remember, you are under no obligation to buy any of these books at any time! If you are not delighted with them, simply return them and owe nothing. But if you enjoy Kensington Choice Historical Romances as much as we think you will, pay the special preferred subscriber rate and save over $8.00 off the cover price!

We have 4 FREE BOOKS for you as your introduction to
**KENSINGTON CHOICE!**
To get your FREE BOOKS, worth up to $24.96, mail
the card below or call TOLL-FREE 1-800-770-1963.
Visit our website at www.kensingtonbooks.com.

Zebra Book Club
P.O. Box 6314
Dover, DE 19905-6314

quite distraught." She watched as a look of panic spread across Catherine's face. Andi continued, "I know you hesitate greatly, possibly with reason, but you must at least look at them, Catherine. While I am here to be of aid. And before you accept another man's proposal."

"No!" Catherine began to bolt for the door at a faster sprint than Andi would have predicted possible, given the woman's fragile appearance. "I will not."

Andi shot one arm straight out in front of her, holding Catherine back, and with the other, she reached inside her pocket to slowly draw out the ribbon-tied packet. "But you must," she said, her voice even and determined. This was for the other woman's own good. If Catherine didn't know how fortunate she was to have someone love her so, Andi would have to point it out to her. Two men, *two men* were ready to marry her and Catherine didn't appreciate it in the least. "You are obligated to do at least that, would you not agree?"

"I am not obligated!" Catherine's shrill voice sailed upward. "You will stand aside and let me pass."

"I will not."

Catherine paused, looked down to brush something invisible from her skirt, and then looked back up at Andi. Her delicately sculpted chin thrust forward in seeming determination. "Then I shall demand it." Though the demand was spoken softly, Andi could tell she'd touched a nerve. Feelings for Edland. They were still there, all right.

Trying to inject a steely note into her tone, Andi answered, "And I shall wish you the greatest of luck with that. I fear I have had quite enough of being ordered to do things today." She nodded in her best "come on and try it" attempt, hoping, as she did, that Catherine would give up and back down. She could probably figure out how to tackle the woman, since she had, after all, remembered at least one football technique, but she wasn't laying odds on it. Dropping her voice to just under her breath, she muttered, "Besides, I face a roomful of bored students every day. Demands don't go far with me."

Catherine placed her hands on her hips, knuckles whitening as she dug her fingers into the forest green fabric of her dress. "I shall scream," she said, her voice edging toward hysterical, "requiring explanation that shall likely cause you much embarrassment. Your mother would be dismayed, I am certain, to discover you had caused such a stir."

Okay. Points for Catherine. Andi tipped her head, pressing her lips together. Then she asked, "What have you to fear in merely reading a few lines, Catherine?" She dangled the packet of letters in front of the other woman's face. "Once you have done so, I promise to take my leave." She snuck her free hand behind her back to cross her fingers.

Catherine, tapping her toe in quick little beats, didn't answer for a moment. Finally, she said, "Why must you involve yourself in affairs not of your concern?"

"It is but a small request," Andi implored. "And if you did not still harbor feelings for Mr. Evernham, it would matter little to you. Instead, you are angry. So angry you can hardly see straight. Does that not tell you something?" Hah. Those sessions with a psychologist last year had done something for her, after all. Look out, Dr. Phil.

Catherine spun around until her back was to Andi. She stood, head down, staring at the floor.

Andi held her breath, allowing a small amount of hope to creep into her heart. Catherine was thinking it over. She had to be. If she could just get her to calm down for a moment and . . .

But the next instant was a blur of forest green and flashing jewelry as the woman rushed at her, apparently intent on reaching the handle of the door. Andi made a grab for her and, in a flurry of tangled skirts, managed to wrestle Catherine away, both of them falling to the floor.

"This is ridiculous," she heard herself mutter as she held on to Catherine's arm to keep her from escaping. After a brief struggle that mostly involved ineffective little pushes, Andi turned around and sat on top of her, pinning Catherine's dress to the floor with her knees.

She blew out an exasperated breath, lifting hair she imagined was by now sticking out all over her head. Calmly holding her fingers in front of Catherine's face, she said, "Five moments. You shall listen for five moments, and then I will let you go." At the unladylike sound that came out of Catherine's mouth, she added, "I would not say that if I were you. Most unheroine-like."

Catherine tried to scowl, but looked as though she couldn't quite figure out how to do it. Failing that, she began to kick her feet. Andi took a deep breath and tore apart the ribbon that held the letters together. She removed one and opened it, placing the others back in her pocket.

"*My dearest Catherine,*" she began to read in a voice that wobbled slightly from the exertion of having to keep Catherine pinned to the floor. She paused and frowned, scanning the letter. Edland didn't have the power of words to help him here. Time for a change of tactics.

Andi cleared her throat and continued, "*It is with the heaviest of hearts that I write this letter to you* . . . Oh." Andi stopped, laying a hand across her heart. "Perhaps I was too rash, Catherine. You may *not* wish to read this." She pretended to pick and choose bits and pieces. ". . . *the loveliest face ever to be seen . . . the gentlest of women* . . . uh, oh. The gentleman may have relinquished his affections for you, after all."

Catherine's feet stilled. *Excellent*, Andi thought. *Got her attention.*

"The loveliest face ever to be seen," she repeated. She stopped reading, screwing up her face. "Not gifted with a turn of phrase, is he?" she asked Catherine, whose face was beginning to take on a fierce interest.

"Allow me to see the letter."

"Let us choose another one," Andi said, reaching back inside her pocket. "Perhaps a different letter will contain words more to your liking." She scanned the first few lines of the boldly drawn words. "Ah, an improvement. Listen to this." Quirking an eyebrow at Catherine, who pursed her lips, she began, "*Catherine, my love. You must allow my heart to speak with you.* Huh . . . .*became man and wife*—" Andi stopped abruptly.

"He has taken a *wife*?" Catherine screeched.

"Not quite clear. I fear only further reading will reveal that." Andi heaved a large sigh and continued to read, ". . . *loved me* . . . uh, huh. What is one to do, of course, when love enters in . . . *I must know* . . ." She watched from the corner of one eye as Catherine's small pale hand wavered upward toward the letter. *That's right*, Andi urged. *Keep going. Take it.*

But the hand dropped. Catherine fixed a surprisingly cold gaze on her, even as moisture began to fill her eyes. "He has not married. It is not possible."

Andi's heart squeezed tight in sympathy. The woman was trying so hard to be brave, but behind the tears she wouldn't let fall must be a hurt she couldn't allow herself to feel. Catherine's father was an ogre. That's all there was to it.

Clearing her throat, Andi answered, "I *might* have read a few of his phrases out of context. Not a difficult thing to do. The gentleman does not have the heart of a poet."

An understatement. He had written, *My very being longs for your gentle touch, aches in a pain that will not remove itself. We so very nearly became man and wife.* She would have to hope he spoke better than he wrote.

"I cannot believe it."

Andi turned a hand up. "I did not utter a word about the gentleman's character. Only that it may be necessary to look past his inability to turn a phrase."

"Please remove yourself from my person and allow me to sit up." The words were polite, the tone was not.

"If you would only take these missives in your hands, you would see, quite without question, that he loves you and wants you back. I have not even made the acquaintance of Mr. Evernham and it is apparent to me."

"It is of little consequence." The words caught on what sounded like a half sob.

"Forgive me, Catherine, but to the contrary, it appears as though you have suffered dreadful consequences," Andi said gently.

"You . . . will . . . let . . . me . . . go!"

Andi sighed and swung one leg around. She scooted over to sit beside Catherine, who pushed herself up from the floor to a sitting position, her face flushed and perfectly coiffed hair knocked askew. "I cannot fathom why you would behave in this manner," she said, haltingly. "My father would—"

Andi shrugged a shoulder. "His opinion of me is already lost. I worry little about impressing him." She leaned toward Catherine. "Tell me of Mr. Evernham."

"I shall not."

"But why? You cannot allow yourself to even think of him?"

"Nothing of the kind." Catherine brushed at her skirt with tiny flicks of her trembling fingers. "I do not think of him at all."

"That seems most ungenerous," Andi answered. "After running away to marry him. Not so long ago."

Catherine raised her head to stare at the wall, her profile to Andi. "I was foolish," she said in such a small voice that Andi wasn't sure Catherine even knew she was speaking.

"I see," she said, "and you were fortunate enough

to have your father correct the presumed error of your ways?"

The other woman didn't move.

"I can venture a guess. A disgrace to the family name?" Andi tried, but couldn't keep anger at the injustice from her voice. "How nice that your father would sacrifice your happiness to make sure he was not compromised in any way."

Catherine's head whipped around to face Andi. "My father thinks only of me. It has always been so. He prevented me from a fatal mistake in judgment." She scrambled to her feet in a flurry of forest green fabric, looking down her nose at Andi. "One must be careful, Miss Lofton-Hale, not to let the heart wander unchecked, as mine so very nearly did."

Staring, Andi watched as Catherine's mouth pulled into a tight white line of determination. "I have seen the folly of such behavior," she continued, "and shall now do what is best. For my family. And myself." She leaned down to deliver a parting command. "You will not interfere, Miss Lofton-Hale." With that, Catherine spun on one foot and headed for the door.

"That's what you think," Andi said mildly, but she said it low and to herself as she watched Catherine throw open the door and propel herself through it with what Andi thought was an admirable amount of self-righteousness.

And while she supposed it wasn't entirely appropriate to tackle the mistress of the house to the floor and sit on her, she hoped, really hoped, that Catherine did not find it necessary to carry that tale straight to her father.

# Chapter Eleven

"Mary!" Andi said in a loud whisper from the open door of Catherine's room, trying to attract the attention of the maid, who was hard at work.

The look that Mary threw her held suspicion in it, as though she knew she wouldn't like what Andi was about to say. She looked down at the clothes in her hands and then back at the door, obviously deciding she could not afford to ignore Andi entirely.

"Yes, miss?" She drew herself up straight, clasping pudgy work-worn hands in front of her crisp white apron.

"It did not turn out quite as well as I had hoped," Andi said. "Miss Havington refused to do more than listen to a few lines."

"I am not surprised, miss. She told me as much herself."

"I remember you mentioning that."

The maid started to nod, then stopped abruptly, ducking her head with obvious chagrin. In the nineteenth century, a servant could be fired for even appearing to venture close to an "I told you so." Not so different in the twenty-first century sometimes, Andi reflected. Her department head would become nearly apoplectic at being corrected in public by a subordinate. Unfortunately, Andi had once been the subordinate who dared to try. But never mind that now. She screwed up her mouth and said, "We shall simply have to take a different approach."

Mary drew back in horror. "Different?" she repeated in disbelief. "Miss Catherine knows what's best. I shouldn't have carried those letters at all, even spoken to him. No, I shouldn't have."

"Mary—"

"Miss Catherine will marry Mr. Chamberlain." Mary's head shook harder. "And have the life she is meant to. It's the way of it, miss."

Andi stepped inside the room, shutting the door behind her. "You cannot allow her to do that. *I* cannot allow her to do that."

"Beggin' your pardon, miss, but it's not for you or me to say." Mary clapped a hand over her mouth, struck by the magnitude of what she'd said.

"One thing I rarely do is shrink from saying what must be said." Andi began to pace up and down, growing more agitated with each step. Catherine wouldn't stand up to her father, even as she was forced into marriage with someone she didn't love and shoved away from the someone she did. Edland evidently feared doing anything more than writing a letter. Maids were drilled into not speaking their minds and standing up for what was right. A whole lot of intimidation was going on here. A romantic time to live in, but definitely not the easiest.

She wouldn't have lasted two minutes . . . wait. She rubbed her forehead.

The maid murmured, "I must get on with my work," and gave a deferential half curtsy.

"No, I must speak with Edland Evernham." There, it was out, in one bold rush of words. Did she really want to do this? Too late. She was. "You will tell me how to arrange it. Please."

Mary turned back, her face puckering in confusion. "Arrange it?" she asked.

Andi chewed on her bottom lip a moment, thinking. "How is it you see him?"

"Oh, miss," Mary whispered, "that would not be right."

"It is absolutely right." Andi's voice began to rise as a familiar devotion to correcting wrongs built within her. One year, her mother had bought her a cape not entirely as a joke. "In ten years, when Catherine is saddled with being mistress of an estate she has no wish to run, five kids she did not wish to bear, and a heart irreparably broken because she is married to a man she does not love, we shall see if you again shake your head. For a different reason."

The maid blinked, her mouth forming a small, round circle.

In. Count to four. Or five. Out. Never mind. "She must at least meet with him once. You know that as well as I. Before she marries Nathaniel, she must be sure it is not Edland she really wants."

"Wants?" The maid seemed to roll the word around on her tongue, as if it were foreign.

"It is possible for a woman to make such a choice."

Mary laid the clothes she'd been holding on the

snowy white cover of the bed, smoothing them with deliberate sweeps of her fingers. After a moment, she said, almost as if to herself, "Mr. Evernham, he'll be deliverin' one more note. Said this one was to be the last."

"When, Mary? Where?"

"I'll be meetin' him at the door to the servants' hall. He knows as how she'll soon be sayin' yes to Mr. Chamberlain. I was to do everything I could to get this one to her." She shook her head. "But I was givin' up because it's just no use with Miss Catherine. She wants none of it." She blinked hard, adding, "But I was tryin'. I was."

"Of course you tried. I could not believe otherwise." Andi clasped her hands in front of her. "I tried, as well, for all the good it did. That is why I say the time has come for a different approach. You and I will work together to make this happen." She nodded hard, hoping the maid would agree, but there was no response. "When were you going to meet him?"

"I was goin' to do that when I've finished here," Mary whispered, her eyes troubled.

"Then it is quite simple." Not hardly. "I shall take your place. Give me directions to the servants' hall. And I shall need to know how to recognize the gentleman."

"Please, miss."

"It is the only thing to do. The right thing."

The maid closed her eyes and moved her lips in an apparent silent prayer. Andi waited until the woman's mouth had stilled before she said, "I am quite set upon doing this, Mary. Nothing you can say shall sway me from it. Tell me how to get there."

* * *

The servants' hall smelled of strong soup, even stronger ointment, and unwashed bodies. Andi threaded her way along a narrow passageway and then into a room with sparse furniture and a painting of a stern Horatio Havington that hung on one wall. Inspiration for the below-stairs crowd, she supposed, slanting her eyes at Havington's image.

She passed the kitchen, where two female servants chatted noisily at one end of the room, banging dishes as they worked; at the other end, a plump cook, her gray hairs standing out beneath her white cap, slumped in a chair, fast asleep. The soup boiled unattended.

Andi reached the door that fit Mary's reluctant description. Good thing no one seemed to be going in or out at the moment. Just to be sure, she slipped back into a dusty, dark corner and watched. She would stand out in this part of the house, and all the scraping and bowing that the Havington servants did, with a watchful eye, made her nervous that someone would spot her as an imposter, as someone clearly not a character of Louisa's invention.

After a few minutes, satisfied that no one had seen her, she silently began to rehearse what she would say to Edland. Better to ease into it, she guessed, maybe offer a compliment on what she had heard about him from Catherine, which actually was next to nothing. But she could embellish a bit to start things off smoothly.

Andi practically had a master's in embellishment.

He would be kind and grateful for her help, and likely sheepish about his failure to reach Catherine.

So Andi would have to be gently reassuring and ply him with you-can-do-its that would have him flashing a sword to reclaim his love in no time. She could do that. Sometimes she became a little impatient with people, but she wouldn't with Edland. Anyone who wrote like he did needed a little extra, patient attention. Under her guidance, he would quickly go from shy lover to—

A knock close to her ear startled her from her reverie. Two sharp raps, a pause, and then three. This was it. Edland. Was he ready to fulfill his destiny?

Andi looked over both shoulders to make sure no one had seen, then opened the door, slipping through it and outside into the early evening air, closing it behind her.

The man's expression, at first expectant, hardened as soon as he saw her. He stepped back, opening his mouth, but Andi spoke before he could. "I am taking the place of Mary," she said.

Only an inch or so taller than Andi, Edland Evernham was slender, but athletically built, dressed in meticulous gray riding pants and jacket. He was an extraordinarily handsome man, with thick black wavy hair and a nose that looked as though it had been sculpted as an example of perfection. But it was his eyes, dark as midnight and startlingly cold, that caused her to catch her breath and second-guess the wisdom of stepping in to guide his love life. What happened to shy and grateful?

He was the first to break the accusing lock of his gaze, his eyes darting in the direction of his horse as he apparently contemplated a quick exit.

Summoning her courage, Andi laid a hand on

his jacket to reassure him. "I am here only to assist you, sir. There is no cause for alarm." Once he knew that, things would be fine. He'd be grateful for the assistance.

Instead, he removed her hand as though it were distasteful. "Assist me? You have not even deigned to offer so much as your name." Though she wouldn't have thought it possible, his voice was as cold as his eyes. This was the man who had swept the gentle Catherine off her feet? How? By scaring her to death?

"With all this secrecy, meeting at the back door and a special knock, I thought it best not to offer my name," she said, infusing each word with a sarcasm she hoped would cover her disappointed first impression of the man. She had pinned such hopes on him. "We have, after all, matters of higher consequence to discuss."

A tiny *you are so not ever going to get Nathaniel* nudged at her heart. She shoved it away, not willing to indulge in self-doubt at this particular moment.

"Mr. Evernham." She directed her best teacher glare at him. "At the moment, I must confess to a belief that a block of ice contains more personality than you do. Still, Miss Havington quite obviously sees something of merit in you, so I offer my services to help you win her back. I am in a far better position to do so than a servant."

For the briefest second, she thought she saw something melt a little in his eyes at the mention of Catherine's name. But she couldn't be sure. And then it was gone.

"Your manner of speaking is—"

"American," she answered abruptly. In her

dreams, the accent had come naturally, when her chance came, not so much.

His forehead creased into tight lines of annoyance, the nostrils in his perfect nose flaring as he stared back at her. "I, madam," he said in clipped tones, "have, within only moments of meeting you, become convinced that you are not entirely of sound mind. I suggest you return inside where someone will most certainly see to you."

Oh for . . . Here she was, risking everything to help this man get together with the woman he loved, and he had the nerve to question her sanity. Because she had the nerve to compare him to a block of ice. She was the *only* one who had the right to do that. "I do not have time for this," she shot back. "And neither do you."

That seemed to catch him off guard, if only for a moment. He stepped back, his eyes once again darting to his horse.

Andi put a hand to her forehead. "Of course," she said. "Run away. Is that not what you did last time? And yet it proved so beneficial."

His eyes left the waiting silhouette of his horse to zero in on her, not bothering to hide the fact that he was sizing her up. After a moment, he asked, "Why has Mary not come?"

"She wished to come," Andi answered. "But I convinced her I should be the one. Perhaps you did not hear me clearly at first, but as a guest at—"

"And whose employ might you be in?"

Somewhere in the question, Andi sensed, was an insult. She decided to ignore it. "I am a confidante of Miss Havington. One who does not wish to see her marry against her heart."

"Pray, your name?"

"Alexandra Lofton-Hale."

"For such an intimate friend of Miss Havington's, why is it I have never heard her speak your name?"

"Oh," she said, dragging out the word and loading it with sarcasm. "So you speak with her so often you know all that is in her life? I confess I did not realize *you* were any longer on such intimate terms with Catherine. I had the impression you were not seeing each other and that you had a desperation to do so. I have made an error." She waved a hand in the air. "But of course. What could I have been thinking? You have no need of my assistance."

She saw him wince the slightest bit. Enough to make her go back to feeling the smallest bit sorry for him. Pride, she knew about. She might have been a little harsh, but really, he had deserved it for being such a jerk.

He turned away.

She tapped a toe on the ground while she thought for a moment, then tried again. "Perhaps we should begin anew. May I call you Edland?" Without waiting for an answer, she plunged ahead. "It is not a wise idea to linger at the door. Someone is likely to step outside and become curious at the sight of you. It would take little to determine that you are not the most welcome of guests." Grabbing his arm, she led him away from the house and toward a stand of trees that offered cover from prying eyes.

He resisted at first, but then followed her, with sturdy, determined strides that seemed bent on proving the change in location to be his idea. At least he might potentially be a match for Catherine's bristly father, Andi reflected. Maybe that's what Catherine had seen in him.

When they had reached the cover of the trees, Edland took a few quick paces back and forth, then turned to face Andi, his face set. "Tell me of Catherine," he demanded in a low voice. "Is she well?"

"She is well physically, if that is what you mean."

"And is it true she is to be married soon?"

Andi rested her steady gaze on Edland, hoping he understood the gravity of the situation. "Very likely. Unless you find it within yourself to stop her."

He clasped his hands behind his back and drew himself up to full height. "I would never attempt to stand in the way of her happiness."

Great. He'd decided to be noble. Letting a sharp, irritated breath escape, Andi shook her head. "It is because you are *not* standing in the way that she will be unhappy."

His brow furrowed as he tipped his head to one side. "I have attempted all that is acceptable within a gentleman's behavior." He drew his lips in tight, appearing to think this over. "If she chooses not to speak with or see me, there is little more to be done."

Excuses. He was full of them, Andi decided with more than a little exasperation. "Sir, you are indeed the one who ran off with her, by all accounts ruining her reputation. That very act has led her to the prospect of this union. Yet you refuse thus far to fight for her." She glared at him. "To stand up to her zealous father and proclaim your love and willingness to ensure her happiness. Has that not occurred to you?"

She began to pace back and forth now, punctuating

her words by stabbing at the air with her fingers. "You commanded the bravery, the determination to ride away with her once, to make her yours. Could you not summon the courage to do so again? In this instance, you might well succeed in marrying her before her father can arrive. Then, no matter what others might say, you and she could settle down to raise little Evernhams, spending a lifetime together in perfect bliss. And she would always have the knowledge that you loved her enough to stand up to her father, whose only wish seems to be saving the family name, instead of ensuring his daughter is marrying the one man she truly wants."

Andi stopped her pacing to aim a piercing look at Edland.

He was staring straight ahead, blinking, as though trying to take in her words. Then he said, in an authoritative tone that reminded Andi of Catherine's on much the same subject, "I shall not impose my wishes upon her. I have made attempts to convey my . . ." He hesitated. "My . . . feelings to Miss Havington. And as you say," he said, directing another cold gaze at Andi, "my rash actions earlier have caused her great pain. I could not do such a thing again."

"Yet you are here. With a letter in your hand."

"Even returning to this place has meant taking liberties that were unwise. I was to have remained in London, and should have done so."

"Were you banished from this place, sir?"

"It was thought best."

"And you do not protest at the decisions made *for* the two of you?" Andi kicked her toe at the ground. So Edland was as stubborn as Catherine.

She thought for a minute, tapping one finger on her chin, and then said, "You loved her enough to spirit her off in the middle of the night to marry her. One nasty old man blocked your way. And now you would give up and allow him to win, yet again?"

His mouth was set in a hard line, and the perfect nose had a decidedly angry crease at its top. "Your insinuations are most inappropriate."

"The truth can be difficult to swallow," Andi murmured. "But let us leave that and turn our attention to the matter at hand." With effort, she gave him a bright smile. "You must speak with Catherine, not simply confine yourself to letters she will not read. You will never determine how she feels until you ask her yourself." *And Heaven help us if you can't manage to put feeling into those eyes when you do it*, she added silently.

He pondered that before he responded, "That would not appear to be a possibility." Though he seemed intent on sounding as though he had little interest or faith in such a plan, she could hear the spark of hope that lifted his voice on the last word.

Balling her hands into fists, she moved to stand directly in front of him. "Enough sparring," she announced pleasantly. "This is how it is going to be." Spotting the question marks his eyebrows formed, she decided to rephrase. "I have already devised a plan for bringing Catherine to you. When I do so, it will be up to you to convince her of your best intentions."

His gaze dropped, eyes searching the ground for a long moment, as though he would find an answer there. Andi stayed perfectly still, not daring to move, her pulse sounding in her ears. He had to go along with her plan. He couldn't say no.

Finally, he raised his eyes, sweeping them over Andi in what looked to be grudging agreement. "I have no reason to believe you," he said quietly. "Yet I may well do so, even against my better judgment."

Andi rolled her eyes. It wasn't easy to attempt a heroine coup around here. "And though I find your lack of confidence quite vexing, I will believe you." As his eyes darkened, she hastily added, "It shall all work to the benefit of you and Catherine, you shall see." She paused, her mind working faster than her ability to articulate the words. "Any time now, we shall be gathering in the parlor for some kind of activity. Before long, I am going to—" She broke off as a familiar feeling began to steal over her, drawing her shoulders together in the hunched, defeatist stance she'd grown to hate. "No!" she choked out. "Edland, you must listen to me! Stay right here. Do not leave. I will get her to you."

There was no time to hear his answer before everything around her went black. It felt as though the giant hand once again squeezed her body together and then relaxed its grip, until she opened her eyes to find herself in a large, ornately furnished room lit by the glow of candles mounted in sconces on the walls.

She was seated, stiffly upright, on a sofa so tightly upholstered a quarter would have bounced up to the ceiling. Shoulders hunched and chin obediently tucked, Andi knew she was once again relegated to the role of secondary character in the tale of the blossoming romance she was determined to cut off at the roots.

She lifted her head, looking around her with a timidity Louisa seemed to be dictating. Though tastefully done, the room had an oppressive, stifled air to it that had her feeling, for the first time in her life, claustrophobic, as though the walls could begin moving at any time, smashing the occupants flat. Couldn't someone at least open those curtains that hung from ceiling to floor?

In another corner of the room, someone played tinkling notes on an instrument that sounded like a . . . pianoforte! At last she could hear the music, *feel* it. A lighter, happier sound than a piano, it helped to set the mood of genteel sophistication. She squinted for a better look and made out the rigid posture of Amelia, her face pinched with tight determination as she plodded through the notes.

A few moments later, Amelia finished her piece, casting her gaze downward as polite, appreciative murmurs rippled through the room. Andi felt and heard them coming from her own lips in an almost childlike voice.

Rising from her seat, Amelia crossed the room, rushing her steps as though she couldn't wait to escape. She sank into a chair next to her mother, who turned to her, beaming with approval. Mrs. Dolson next turned to Annabelle, who sat in a neighboring chair. "My Amelia is so often requested to play," she confided loudly. "I fear that her fingers will tire; but she is such an accommodating girl, she would never decline a request."

"Someone so well brought up certainly could not decline such a request for her talents," Annabelle responded dryly.

Miranda Dolson nodded vigorously, pleased with the perceived compliment. "So true, so true."

Andi leaned forward, anticipating some sort of retort from a more confident Amelia. None came. Maybe it had been too much to hope for this early. Or maybe she ought to go over there and get Amelia started. To do anything like that, she'd have to hope for Louisa's attention to wander. From beneath the cover of her lashes, Andi's eyes swept the room.

Horatio Havington stood against one wall, looking every bit the country gentleman and master of the house. The memory of what he'd ordered the stable hand to do made a cold anger rise within her, but she knew her face remained bland. She couldn't even work up a semihaughty look to aim in his direction. Apparently, that didn't fit with Louisa's plans.

She had a sudden, irrational urge to run to the invisible author, spilling the tale as though, by tattling, she could somehow change things. Louisa had to have a heart or she couldn't write romance literature. Could she?

Catherine stood several feet away, the center of attention in a creamy light blue dress with delicate layers of fabric that seemed to float as she walked toward Amelia, words of praise bubbling from her mouth. Andi cast a quick glance down at her own dress—pretty, but ordinary by comparison. Self-consciously, she reached a hand up to touch her hair—curled and tamed, no tendrils this time.

She laid her hands in her lap, watching with fascination as they shook. Had to be Louisa's doing. The only emotion running through her mind at the moment was the fervent hope that Edland had heard her plea and would stay long enough for Andi to get Catherine to him.

A door opened and Nathaniel walked into the room. She watched his entrance, a tentative smile on her face. Also Louisa's doing. If she'd been left to her own devices, it would be a huge, relieved grin.

Catherine glided toward him. "Mr. Chamberlain," she said, "how very lovely you could join us."

"Miss Havington." He gave a slight bow and reached a hand behind him, pulling forth a small child. A girl of eight or nine, with eyes wide with curiosity and hair carefully curled, her cheeks a rosy pink. "May I present my niece, Miss Julia Chamberlain." Faces turned her way one by one and she shrank back against Nathaniel. His hand moved to rest on her thin shoulder.

Catherine stopped midglide, her mouth opening and closing, as though she didn't know what to do next. Andi leaned forward, forcing her chin up, to watch with interest. At last, Catherine extended one hand to lay it lightly on the child's curls. "Miss Julia Chamberlain. This is indeed a wonderful surprise."

"I sent for my niece yesterday," Nathaniel offered. To Andi's inquiring ears, he sounded uncertain. "It seemed a fine time for her to meet . . . everyone."

"And so it is," Catherine answered. "Please do sit down," she said to Julia. "I am so pleased Mr. Chamberlain sent for you."

The girl was deposited on a sofa not far from Andi, where she sat primly, feet dangling, while a general fuss was made over her. Mrs. Dolson could be heard encouraging Amelia to show interest in the child, presumably to demonstrate maternal tendencies. Amelia tried, to no avail, to quiet her mother.

Catherine, in the meantime, was asked to play the pianoforte, which she did with both modesty and, it sounded to Andi's untrained ears, skill. The guests applauded politely at the end and Nathaniel walked over to stand beside her, bathing her in the warmth of his approving gaze.

Feeling began to creep back into her shoulders as Andi felt Louisa's hold on her lessen. She rose and walked over to sit by Julia, who, apparently forgotten, was watching the grown-ups with well-mannered excitement. Andi took care to skirt the edge of the room, but almost immediately felt the searing gaze of Catherine's father on her. She tossed him a stony glance. The nerve of the man. After the low he had sunk to, she wasn't about to let him intimidate her.

She lowered herself to the hard seat. "Hello," she said in a stage whisper. With relief, she realized her tongue worked easily. For the moment, Louisa's attention was elsewhere. "I am Alexandra."

"Hello," Julia answered, her voice small.

"Are you enjoying yourself?"

"Yes." She looked down and then up again with a shy smile. "It is most agreeable. And I have a new frock to wear." She smoothed the skirt and scrunched her face at Andi. "Do you like it?"

"Why, my dear, you are the very belle of the ball," Andi replied with a mincing, old lady voice. She was rewarded with a giggle from the little girl and happily joined in, hiding her mouth behind her hand. Their eyes smiled at each other.

"Did the new frock come from your uncle? As a present, perhaps?"

Julia nodded, swinging her feet. "My uncle is most kind." Her nose wrinkled. "And we had cherry ices. I did not allow a drop to fall," she said proudly.

Andi considered the mental picture of Nathaniel sharing, or sneaking, cherry ices with his niece before inflicting a roomful of adults on her. The thought of the two of them together, huddled over the treat, made her chest go warm all over. A carefree uncle now turned into a fiercely protective father figure.

"That is an accomplishment, indeed," Andi said softly. "I do not believe I could eat a cherry ice without dripping." Taking Julia's hand, she gave it a gentle squeeze. "And you do look very lovely."

Julia thanked her with a tremulous smile. Then she asked in a whisper, "Who is that lady, please?" She lifted a finger just a few inches from the sofa to aim it toward Mrs. Dolson, whose round face beamed at the child, even as she poked her daughter in the side and hissed at her to walk over.

Leaning down, Andi whispered in the girl's ear, "That is Mrs. Dolson. Loud but harmless. Simply smile and pay her little heed."

Julia gave the smallest of nods to show she understood, aimed a quick, innocent smile in the older woman's direction, and turned her attention back to smoothing the folds of her new dress. Social grace beyond her years, Andi noted. Julia could teach *her* a few things.

Catherine again began to play. Andi turned to see Nathaniel watching the woman's face intently as he turned the sheet music. He looked from Andi to his niece and back again, with a small, but courtly, dip of his head. For half a second, Andi's heart stopped beating.

And then, everything froze. All around, she heard frustrated sighs. Mrs. Dolson sniffed loudly, and someone tapped a boot against the hearth. From somewhere to Andi's right she could hear the clicking of a tongue.

For the first time, Nathaniel seemed to have to jolt himself into the role of spokesperson. He blinked hard for a few moments, then swallowed hard, as if reorienting. Those assembled in the room waited. At last his voice cut through the silence. "She is once again at a pause," he announced.

"How fortunate," Andi said to no one in particular. A break would work just fine with what she had planned, as long as Louisa didn't resume too quickly. Hopefully, the author had enough to chew on that she wouldn't pick up that pen again right away.

She looked down to see Julia give her a puzzled look. Andi returned one that was meant to be reassuring. And then she grasped her middle. "I am feeling a bit unwell," she whispered by way of apology.

The little girl looked sympathetic. "Perhaps you ate too heartily."

"That could be it." Andi rose, making her way across the room to where Catherine still sat, her fingers poised and ready to continue playing. One characteristic of a successful Louisa heroine, Andi mused, seemed to be the ability to follow directions. Obediently and without so much as a squeak of protest. More like the military than the creative process. *That could be why your books ended up rare, instead of widely published, Louisa.*

Not Andi's style. Never had been. She skirted her way along the wall, moving behind people and taking care to attract as little attention as possible. When she reached the point where Catherine's father stood directly across the room, she cast him a sidelong glance. Horatio Havington was talking quietly with another gentleman, no doubt bemoaning the delay. But at least he was too occupied to notice a character illegally skirt the edges of the scene.

By the time Andi reached Catherine, she was gripping her stomach harder. She bent down to whisper in the other woman's ear. "Forgive me," she said in what she hoped was a pathetic plea, "but I do not feel well. Could you help me find my bedroom so that I may lie down until it passes?"

Catherine's mouth opened in alarm. "Oh, Alexandra, I do so hope you are not dreadfully ill."

Interesting response, Andi reflected. Worthy of a conclusion she herself might leap to. She cocked her head, indicating with her eyes that she couldn't be at all sure she wasn't seriously ill. Then she winced, pressing her fingers harder against her middle.

Catherine rose, putting her hands on Andi's shoulders. "Come with me. I shall see to you."

A glance at Nathaniel revealed a dawning suspicion in his eyes. He took a step forward. "May I be of assistance." It didn't sound like a question.

"No," Andi said a little too fast. She fluttered a hand, trying her best to appear pale and worthy of sympathy. "I only need to return to my room." She hesitated, then added, "But could you help me ensure my departure goes unnoticed? Louisa must have determined I am not to be a part of this scene. It is somewhat embarrassing, I find."

He hesitated and then gave a firm nod, manners overtaking what must have been his better judgment. "Make your exit behind me," he said. "You will not be noticed."

Andi looked pitiably at Catherine. "Please, go with me."

She felt a stab of guilt at the look of compassion that spread across the other woman's face. "Of course," the other woman murmured. "You must put yourself in my hands."

When they arrived safely in the corridor, Andi pointed weakly in the direction opposite the one Catherine tried to lead her in. "Might we go this way, please?"

"But Alexandra—"

Andi cut her off. "We must"—she clutched at her stomach—"go this way."

Her brow furrowed with concern, Catherine followed, her hands on Andi's arms, all the way down to the corridor that led to the servants' hall. Just as Andi was congratulating herself on having learned her way around the huge house, Catherine stopped. "I do not understand."

Andi straightened. "You will," she said firmly. This time, she put her arms on Catherine's shoulders, propelling her straight ahead, ever mindful of the fit of strength the woman had shown the last time Andi had tried to make her do something. But she couldn't think of that. She could only hope Edland Evernham had heeded her plea to stay.

Fortunately, they didn't encounter anyone in the hallway, or Andi might have had to explain Catherine's startled exclamations and dragging feet. That scenario likely would not go Andi's way.

When they at last reached the door that led outside, she told Catherine, "Trust me. I have only your best interests at heart." With that, she pushed her outside and grabbed a lantern. She shut the door behind them and grabbed the woman's hand, pulling her across to the designated meeting place while holding the lantern high. The flame leapt, causing the trees to cast long, wild shadows in the cool night air.

At the sight of Edland, standing with his back to them, Andi pulled to an abrupt halt, nearly sinking to the ground in relief. Then he turned, and she saw a ferocious expression directed straight at her. It might be semi sort of possible that he'd had second thoughts while she was gone. Catherine, hidden from view behind her, made ineffective noises of protest.

Right before she pulled Catherine out from behind her and toward Edland, Andi had a fleeting moment of self-recrimination, wondering what in the world she had gotten herself, not to mention the innocent Catherine, into. It could be, as much as she hated to consider it, that Louisa knew best in this particular case.

Or at least that's what she thought until she saw what happened when Edland laid eyes on Catherine.

# Chapter Twelve

"Catherine," Edland mouthed in a disbelieving whisper.

Andi watched Catherine go rigid, her face draining of color, as though she'd seen a ghost.

Edland, on the other hand, came to life. The chilly, dark eyes that seemed capable of shooting icicle daggers straight into an unsuspecting heart melted immediately, and the hard lines of his face relaxed visibly. His mouth twitched into a tentative smile.

He held out his arms. She didn't move into them.

Instead, she stood woodenly, turning her gaze to Andi. "How could you do such a thing?" she asked, her voice trembling.

"Because it needed to be done," Andi answered. "Only cast your gaze upon him, Catherine. Do you not see how he cares for you?"

Edland flashed Andi a quick look of what might actually have been thanks before his eyes again settled on Catherine. "It is true," he said softly. "We have not spoken since the night you so very nearly became my wife. Since the night my heart was broken into pieces and scattered to the winds."

From her spot on the sidelines, Andi grimaced slightly, wondering if she should volunteer to act as interpreter. *Let's get this straight,* she wanted to shout. *It's not about you.* But in the breathless moment that followed, he seemed to rebound, laying his fingers lightly on Catherine's arm. Then he said, "You are the sun, the moon, the stars in my life. The very gentleness that teaches me life can be a thing of pleasure. Of happiness." He inhaled sharply and blinked. "But my own happiness is secondary to yours." His fingers pressed harder into Catherine's arms, urgency roughening his voice. "I love you, Catherine, with every breath I take. But it is for precisely that reason I would never allow myself to stand in the way of your marriage to another, if that is what your heart truly desires."

Andi shook her head, trying to signal that was the wrong move. He should stand squarely in the way of her marrying someone else. Catherine was far too much under the domination of her father to assert herself. Edland should know that. If she wouldn't fight for her own happiness, then he would have to do it. She crossed her hands in front of her and waved them, palms toward him, in a desperate "no play" motion.

The movement must have caught his eye as he looked up and over at her, narrowing his eyes as if he'd just remembered she was there. And wasn't all that happy about it.

Andi jammed her hands on her hips. After all she'd done to get the two of them together again . . . Then she heard the delicate voice of Catherine say, "But I was left quite alone. To face my father and what I . . . we had done."

"Your father sent me away. Threatened to ruin my family's fortunes if I did not leave at once for London. I am not proud to admit such a failing of heart to you, but I could not allow my family to suffer for my deeds." He laid both hands on Catherine's arms now, holding her.

"As I could not," she answered in a near whisper. Silence fell. Then Catherine asked, "My father? He would never have done such a thing. His intent would only have been to frighten you."

Edland corrected her quickly, "He clearly intended to do such a thing. In fact, he was quite determined."

Andi could not see Catherine's face, but imagined, from the tone of her voice, that she had moved to imploring Edland to understand. "He is not an evil man. He simply acted out of his love for me. Our plans, dear Edland, were flawed from the beginning. Do you not see?"

"No, I am afraid I do not." He lifted his chin into the air, looking wildly at the trees before pulling her into his hard embrace. "I am able only to see that I love you with my entire heart and soul," he said. "And I believe that you love me as well. Nothing you say to the contrary will convince me."

Pushing her gently from him so he could look into her eyes, he continued, "It is why I have returned, though most emphatically instructed never to do so. I have to know that this marriage to another is what you truly desire. If you do not . . ." He stopped, again folding her in his arms, and caught sight of Andi, starting violently as though she had suddenly materialized.

Talk about single-minded focus, she thought. While in Catherine's presence, Edland seemed to forget the rest of the world existed. She gave a little sigh. Not an altogether bad thing, she guessed.

Catherine pulled away and also turned back to look at Andi. She dropped her eyes, then said, "Already once I have unwisely put my wishes ahead of my duty. I cannot do so again." In the waning light, Andi could see a tear glistening in the corner of Catherine's eye. "You must understand . . ." And then she straightened abruptly.

As she did so, Andi felt her own shoulders begin to curve in what she immediately recognized as a case of the worst timing she could remember. "No-oo!" she said, her words falling uselessly into the air. All of her hard work to get the two of them together and now this happened. It was beyond unfair, bordering on cruel.

She saw Catherine lift one hand into the air, extending her fingers toward Edland before all turned to black; the invisible hand squeezed at Andi, and she and Catherine landed once again in the drawing room, a place no less stifling than it had been only minutes before.

Catherine again began to play, as though nothing had happened, with Nathaniel turning the pages of music for her with great chivalry. Aside from a slightly wild look in her eyes, nothing seemed to have disturbed her.

"Great," Andi muttered in her mind, since by now she knew that Louisa wouldn't let the words come out of her mouth. "Just great."

* * *

The scene ended on the high, mincing notes of the pianoforte. After Catherine finished her piece, she invited, in an elaborate show of hostessness, another female guest to demonstrate her musical talents. Then she moved to stand before Julia, smilingly offering her a pretty cake on a thin, fragile plate. "I hope we shall become fast friends," Catherine whispered to the girl, but her face wavered between pleasure and uncertainty. The broad smile of Nathaniel, looking on, seemed to hold a similar incongruity. A chink in Louisa's armor? Andi could only hope so.

The music, as played by the other guest, continued on.

A few minutes later, all characters paused and Nathaniel held his finger up, signaling quiet. When at last he dropped it, saying, "She has closed her desk," it wasn't with the satisfaction Andi had seen earlier. The murmurs of "well done" spread all around even seemed to have a slight reticence, as though their speakers weren't entirely convinced of the sentiment. A general feeling of disquiet seemed to settle over the room.

Andi remained seated, her hands folded in her lap, as people milled around and then left the room, until she found herself the only one still there. In the distance, doors closed and voices lifted, but in the drawing room, there was only silence.

She should tell Nathaniel. Let him know she had arranged for Catherine and Edland to meet again, under the cover of darkness outside. Admit that was the reason Catherine had acted so strangely, that the scene hadn't gone well.

While a tiny thrill of excitement traveled up her spine at the small success she'd had so far in influencing Louisa's story, she also had a fear, churning in the pit of her stomach, that she'd stuck her nose in where it didn't belong. That she had somehow cut a few of the master puppeteer's strings. Seemed a good thing on the surface, but what if . . .

Pressing her fingers together tightly, she forced herself to concentrate on mustering the courage to leave the room and talk to Nathaniel. What could he say, after all? She had all the justification she needed for what she'd done. Just look what had happened when Catherine and Edland saw each other. Louisa wouldn't have been able to keep that kind of emotion under wraps for the entire book. She would *have* to address it sooner or later. Andi had only helped it occur sooner.

Okay, that sounded pretty good. An act of charity, not solely self-interest. She was as ready as she'd ever be.

She rose slowly and crossed the room, her way lit by candles flickering on the walls, their dancing flames echoing the uncertain pounding of her heart. Opening the door, she looked into the hall, but drew back when she saw Nathaniel a few feet away, crouching down, his niece facing him.

After a moment of hesitation, Andi peered around the edge of the doorway. Julia's back was to her, but she could see the little girl spreading the skirt of her dress, holding up the sides with small fingers. Nathaniel was smiling, the warmth of his eyes washing over the child with gentle affection. "It is most lovely," he said. "A color that suits you well."

The girl's response was too soft for Andi to hear. Nathaniel, however, laughed quietly. "Yes, my dear," he said, and reached out to fold the child in his embrace. He closed his eyes for a moment as he did, then pulled away to grasp both of her hands in his. Julia said something else to him and he listened intently, his smile fading.

"You must not worry so," he told the child. "You shall not be alone. I am here now." He reached to ruffle her hair, saying as he did, "And one day you will be a fine lady, with all the young men of the county bowing before your feet, wishing only to claim your attention." His forehead creased as he watched her, his expression holding both concern and reassurance.

Julia murmured a response and lifted her head as a woman swept into the hallway behind Nathaniel, her subservient yet authoritative bearing suggesting she might be a governess. He turned, and as he rose, the woman acknowledged him with a small curtsy, "Mr. Chamberlain."

"To sleep you must go, poppet," he said to Julia, releasing her hands to lay one lightly on her back. The little girl pulled his hand back to press her lips against it. "Good night, Uncle," Andi heard her say as she followed the woman down the hall.

"Good night," he answered, standing to watch after her. Even when she had disappeared from sight, he didn't move, standing with his profile to Andi, but he dropped his chin, as though deep in thought.

Andi's heart swelled. This man, so strong and take-charge in all other situations, had been rendered helpless, his heart in the hands of a child who now saw him as her whole world. He would do anything for Julia. She'd seen it in his eyes.

As it should be.

But if he sacrificed his own happiness to end up miserably locked into a marriage to Catherine, what would that do for Julia? And what about the thought of thrusting an anxious, heartbroken Catherine into the role of stepmother?

Andi took a deep breath, screwed up every available ounce of courage, and left the shelter of the doorway to ask Nathaniel, "Does something trouble you, sir?"

He started visibly and turned, sweeping her with an appraising gaze before he answered, "Not every day is a productive one for a writer."

A writer? He'd been thinking about the scene they'd just left. "Louisa." Andi nodded to show she understood, though she wasn't at all sure she did.

"Yes."

This didn't tell her a lot. Andi tried again. "But she finished the scene. Or at least it appeared so."

He was the one to nod this time, looking at a point over her head, the straight line of his lips and set of his jaw making it apparent his thoughts were elsewhere.

"Then how can you believe it not productive?"

"Perhaps I spoke too soon. But it is of great concern when the writer pauses several times during a scene. It is quite possibly a sign she is not enamored of it, that we may find it eliminated and another direction followed."

He blew out a noisy breath. "Or it may be an indication we shall find characters disappearing, in favor of others." The last was said in an unconvincingly mild tone that raised the hairs on the back of Andi's neck. He was worried. About Julia? Himself?

"What occurs if a character . . . if someone is, as you say, written out?" She pulled her mouth together tight, afraid to believe in what she'd asked and even more afraid to hear his answer. That act of charity was looking pretty high on the self-interest meter about now.

"There is nothing that 'occurs,'" he replied. "That person simply does not enjoy an existence, a life, unless summoned for another manuscript the author may choose to pen." He paused. "In most circumstances, that will not be the situation. A character once discarded is seldom called upon again."

Not . . . called upon. The person didn't have a life. It couldn't be. Nathaniel was standing right in front of her, living and breathing. He wouldn't disappear in some kind of a poof.

Andi tried desperately to sort out the panic this idea was beginning to cause her. "I cannot believe she would leave everyone . . . hanging. Even if the story caused her trouble of some kind, she would continue on until she finished it. One cannot breathe life and then snatch it away." She attempted a smile, despite her hammering heart. "She might only have to listen harder to the characters."

"If she possesses the strength." His voice sounded far away. "It is entirely possible," he went on, "this will be the last manuscript Louisa will undertake. Her eyes give her much trouble. She grows weary, I fear."

Where was an organic food store when you needed it? A supply of vitamins? Give Andi five minutes with the woman, and she'd have her feeling better in no time. "Oh!" She tapped her fingers against Nathaniel's shirt. "But she *did* finish it. Of course she did! I have a copy. I was reading it when I . . . Uh, when circumstances dictated I would find myself here."

"Ah, yes." He looked down at her hand, then back up to meet her eyes. "Up to chapter three. So you said."

"Exactly. So I have knowledge that all will be well." What a relief.

"But with what characters. Since you did not finish the book, you are not able to answer that question."

She'd had a book in her hand; she'd started reading it. It couldn't be that—no, he was right. She didn't know how it would end up. Right then, in that moment, she wasn't sure she liked writers at all, though she'd devoted a career, even a lifetime, to reading and appreciating their work. And teaching others to appreciate it as well. Who knew they held so much power? That the people they invented really did exist? Was Stephen King on this at all?

Oh. A writer.

Andi only knew for certain that her time had to be running out. And she had to somehow make Nathaniel see that. Screwing up every ounce of her courage, and infusing her voice with all the earnestness she felt coursing through her body, she said, "Nathaniel, we must talk." Her heart took a bounce, so that even the tips of her fingers felt shaky. She looked to her right and to her left. "Somewhere private. Where no one else will hear."

He rolled his head back and shut his eyes, seeming to debate whether it was a lost cause to deny her. Not waiting for him to decide, she grabbed his hand and started to pull him away. He was the second person she'd forced to follow her today. "Come on."

He remained firmly in his spot and said, "We are alone."

Andi gave the hallway a quick scan. He was right, but then Catherine's father had been in the room just behind, only moments ago, and chances were good that he might decide to return. "Not here," she said. "Somewhere else."

He began to stride away. He tried to release his hand, but Andi held on to it with determination, hurrying to keep up with his long strides.

One door opened into another hallway, into yet another, and then into another room, much smaller and with brighter colors, though still furnished with an uncomfortable formality. All these rooms and only two people lived here.

Nathaniel paced back and forth along one wall.

Time for her to launch into it, for better or worse. "Louisa makes a grave error."

"An error," he repeated. "Pray, tell me how you arrived at this conclusion."

"First of all, you must promise to listen without judgment."

He stopped pacing and gestured impatiently for her to go on.

"Are you aware there is a particular gentleman who loves Catherine very much? Who very much wishes to spend the rest of his life with her?"

Nathaniel coughed and looked away. When he spoke again, he directed his words to the painting of yet another Havington ancestor. "As you have ascertained, I intend to marry Miss Havington. Which would, I believe, mean spending the rest of my life with her. What would cause you to believe I do not wish to do so?"

"But you—as wonderful a man as you are, and believe me, I do not say so lightly, I mean it with all my heart—are not the one Catherine desires to wed. She loves this man as much as he loves her. Louisa is doing a cruel thing by keeping them apart. I fail to understand how she can wish this to be a tale of love, when love is the very thing she rejects so soundly."

She paused for breath. Then despite the fact that Nathaniel's face was growing somewhat red, she continued, "I confess I do not know why I even purchased the book except that I am utterly passionate about old books, especially romances. The title of this one beckoned to me. I was, you know"—she clasped her hands together, struck by the irony of it all—"very likely born in the wrong time period."

This observation seemed to have little effect on Nathaniel, who bristled visibly as he prepared to respond. Andi jumped in before he could, lifting her chin high and letting her voice soar with emotion. "Louisa is not allowing the story of Edland and Catherine to be told. She uses him only, sir, as a means to an end. The fact that they ran away together appears merely as a vehicle for the ruin of Catherine's reputation, making her available for you as a wounded, vulnerable heroine. But Louisa looks not at *why* they ran away together, at the passion, the desperation that caused them to take such a drastic step." Her hands swept the room. "Think of all they risked to be together. When they both knew how much they had to lose."

Silence. She let her hands fall awkwardly to her side. Nathaniel stood rigidly next to the wall, his features taut.

"It is possible Louisa is planning for you to defy Horatio Havington and save his daughter," Andi went on. "But would it not be better for Edland to do that? He is the one who has been wronged. And he is the one Catherine loves." Now Andi began to pace. With each step, her sense of injustice grew. There could be no reason to trust that an aging author with bad eyes, trying to finish her last manuscript, would do the right thing. No. She'd do the easy thing. Now Andi waved an outraged finger in the air. "Did you know that Havington threatened to ruin Edland's family financially if he did not abandon all hope of securing Catherine's hand and leave town?" She nodded her head. "I have it on good authority. I even—"

"Miss Lofton-Hale."

"Call me by my—"

"Alexandra," he barked, cutting her off.

"Andi," she murmured. Not that this was a good time to insist on use of her nickname, some part of her, way back in her brain, notified her mouth.

"You demonstrate little regard for others' feelings in this matter," he said, his voice tight. "And you are engaging in a most dangerous game. Attempting to change an author's mind is to risk a person's existence. Characters are the invention of an author's mind. She has given them life. A life they may continue on with quite happily, should the manuscript be completed."

Enough, already. They'd been over that. If he didn't exist, he could hardly be standing here trying to put her in her place, could he? A small scream of frustration built in her throat. She wasted only a second or two trying to suppress it. "You stand there, looking drop-dead gorgeous, and I'm supposed to believe you're only a figment of Louisa's imagination?" She began to walk, up and down, back and forth, her slippers making small, hushed noises.

She heard a small choking sound before he asked, "Drop-dead . . . ?"

"Oh. Um . . ." Distress caused her to slip into speech patterns familiar to her, but not to Nathaniel. She waved a hand. "It is an American term. Pay it little heed."

He opened his mouth, closed it, then opened it again. "You must understand what occurs when characters become troublesome. They are eliminated. Replaced." He paused, as if giving time for the words to sink in. Then he grasped her firmly by the shoulders. "That means, Alexandra, that I could well disappear should I not be revealed as the hero, and that you, as a secondary character, could find yourself in precisely the same predicament, should you continue to torment our author."

"But I, you will remember, possess the wishing stone. I wished myself here, I can wish myself back." Not worrying about that right now, thank you. More research to be done, including the state of intimate relations in the Regency era. Only one way to find out . . . She felt the corner of her mouth turn up.

Nathaniel watched her face, his expression unreadable. He released his hold on her and took a step back.

"And," Andi continued, "I attempt to do only what is right." But was she? She wanted Nathaniel for herself, no question about that. And she would take that desire as far as this dream would go. Did that make her equally as guilty of using Edland and Catherine as a means to an end?

Nathaniel's voice broke through her reverie. "What you are asserting is, you must most assuredly admit, your interpretation of what is right. Yet you are not the one with the inkwell."

*Tell me something I don't know. In. Count to four. Out. Count to four. Oh, forget it.*

"You may say these things," she said slowly, "but I have read . . . No, I have *seen* your character, sir. And I shall have no belief you would wish to marry Catherine when you have learned her heart is held by another." She paused, holding his gaze. "Is that not so?"

He turned to stare out a window with his back to her. "You know nothing of what has passed between Catherine and me. And I have no reason to explain my intentions or actions."

"I have seen her look at you. And you at her." She swallowed hard. "But perhaps more to the point, I have seen her look at Edland Evernham."

He rapped one hand against the window frame; the sharp noise echoed throughout the room. "Edland Evernham," he repeated in seeming disgust. "A suitor who stole away with her in the night, caring not that such disgraceful behavior would force her into a marriage most ill-advised."

"And that appalls you."

"It was a cowardly act."

"But who told you of the details, Catherine or her father?"

"It matters not," he said abruptly, but Andi thought she might have heard a note of doubt.

"She is indeed a victim of disgraceful behavior," Andi said softly. "Inflicted upon her by a tyrannical, egotistical father who has likely dictated all to her since the age of two. This time she stood up for herself, though it was brief. Her only crime was falling in love. With someone *her father* determined was ill-advised as a match for her." Then she remembered something. "This is the very same person who arranged to have me assaulted by a stable hand because you dared to look at me with some interest!"

"That is an accusation clearly without proof."

"He's pond scum."

Nathaniel turned so quickly that Andi took a step back at the same moment his fist landed with a thump on the table. She held her breath.

"Preposterous. I cannot risk grievous consequences for so many simply because . . . of a look you purport to have seen pass between—" He broke off, raking a hand through his hair.

Andi let her breath out slowly, waiting. And waiting some more. For the first time in as long as she could remember, her mouth obeyed her cease and desist order.

"I shall talk with her," he said at last.

"While that is admirable, I do not think it the best way to . . . approach it." Seeing his eyes widen, she rushed to explain. "Catherine would only be humiliated by the conversation. And she would deny all, not wishing to ruin the evil plans of her father nor the story Louisa pens. If you will allow me the observation, she is entirely too much like you in that regard."

Nathaniel's chin lifted dangerously high.

"Do not suffer undue concern," Andi told him. "The story shall not be ruined. Far from it. It shall turn out better. I give my word." True enough, she thought. If things worked out right, she and Catherine could both be happy. *But Catherine will be the only one who actually stays here. I'll take my happy ending and leave, thanks.*

She let her eyes sweep up to rest on Nathaniel's dark ones, drinking in his face, that small scar, irresistible now that she knew where it came from, those lips that had felt so right on hers and promised far more than they had delivered so far. She gave a small shake of her head, trying to clear it. "There is but one way for the story to resolve itself," she said slowly, "and that is for Louisa to be convinced it must change. If Edland becomes a part of it and Catherine is not able to deny how she feels when he is present, Louisa will be forced to change the direction."

A struggle played out across his face as he pondered that.

"I understand that would leave you in an unenviable position, without a clear means of saving your family estate, but I have every belief that Louisa shall then call upon her talents to become more creative. You are a hero who leaps from the pages to . . ." Andi felt her voice stumble, "land in the heart of a reader, quite without reservation. She will simply find you another heroine. Someone from the cast of secondary characters, possibly?" She attempted a flirtatious smile but gave it up when she failed miserably. At this moment in time, she would have gladly swapped cleavage for witty, seductive lines.

Glaring at her, he said, "I shall not resolve my situation at the expense of another. Yet, there is my niece . . ." He lifted his palms upward in a gesture of helplessness. "I cannot think only of myself."

"Julia." Her voice softened. "You're right. You have to think about her." She screwed up her face, thinking. "Catherine did not seem to know what to do with her. Perhaps that gave Louisa trouble." She snapped her mouth shut. Probably going a little too far to offer up that observation, though it had been the truth.

Nathaniel gripped the corner of the table with one hand, his lips barely moving. "My niece is my concern."

"As is the fact that your intended does not appear to know what to do with her." It would help, really, if she knew when to stay quiet.

He made a sharp sound of exasperation and loosened his hold on the table. "Enough." He walked to the window. "Might I presume you have thought through how Mr. Evernham would insert himself into a scene? Without meeting Havington's wrath?"

She only wished she had. "Not exactly. Although I did at last arrange for them to see each other, outside the time when Louisa was writing."

His features tightened. "You? Arranged a meeting?" he thundered.

"It was the only thing to do." Unreasonably, she found herself feeling like Lucy explaining things to Ricky in the old reruns she loved to watch late at night. Too bad she wasn't a redhead, it seemed to work for Lucy. Of course, so did twin beds. Maybe it hadn't worked *that* well. "To determine that, indeed, her feelings for him had not wavered."

"And?" The word seemed to be spoken with great effort.

"She could not deny that she loves him still. Yet Louisa whisked her away before any further events could transpire."

He rubbed the back of his neck. Hard. "I must be mad," he said. "Utterly mad, to be listening to you."

"You are listening to your heart. And it, sir, is listening to me."

"I shall not discuss this further."

"You assert your existence could well depend on following Louisa's wishes. What if it actually depends on *not* following her wishes, but instead helping to make the story work?"

He folded his arms across his chest. "And what do you imagine I shall be, if not the hero?"

Andi opened her mouth, then closed it. He— She— Wait a minute.

"I thought as much," he replied dryly. Nathaniel strode past her to the door.

He couldn't leave like this. "I have not devoted a life to the study of literature for naught," she said in a voice that carried through the room. "I shall determine a way for all to end happily."

"Do you not find," Nathaniel asked, each word precisely formed for emphasis, "that you have done quite enough already?"

"Oh, no," Andi breathed, anxious that he understand. "Not nearly enough at all."

Nathaniel's breath seemed to leave his body at that, a feeling that left him suddenly quite spent. He opened the door and closed it behind him with a heavy click. The woman had the audacity to attempt reversing the author's course, and when asked, allowed that she intended only to do more. It was beyond belief.

She had not the first idea of the pure folly of what she set out to do. Of the many lives she would alter. Even end.

He pushed down the hallway, boots ringing on the wood floor, and out into a back garden, where a deserted stone bench beckoned invitingly in the waning sunlight. He ignored it, choosing instead to stand in the shadow of the house.

He should have simply ordered her to obey. Vowed he would see her relegated to an even lesser role. In truth, he could not conceive of why he had not yet done so. With a sharp exhale, he narrowed his eyes, allowing his gaze to fall some measure in the distance. Instead of the bed of flowers, he saw beguiling blue-green eyes, flashing sparks of fire. A small, perfect mouth below a delicately sculpted nose. The face of a hundred transparent emotions that carried a sense of worldliness as baffling as it was . . . alluring. Alexandra Lofton-Hale. What name had she insisted upon? Andi—

"Uncle?"

He whirled around to see his niece gazing innocently up at him, her face alight with childish delight. "Julia." His voice scraped against his heart. She looked so very like her father.

"Miss Moore says I may visit the stables, Uncle." She clasped her hands together.

The governess glided up behind the child. "With your permission, Mr. Chamberlain, Miss Julia has expressed a desire to see the horses before she retires for the evening."

The woman appeared at a loss to counter that desire. He himself had been the object of his niece's charms more than once. At times it had proved impossible to say no when the child's eyes were fixed upon him as they were now. Behind their innocence, there was, always, a reminder of the devastating loss she had suffered.

Clearly, he should order her back into the house and to bed. Instead, he said with a smile, "Then she shall most certainly see the horses."

He was rewarded with a hug as Julia buried her head in his knees, clasping her arms fast around him. It served to remind him that his brother would never again feel the warmth of the child's love. A father's life unjustly taken, because—

What was done was done. He leaned down to pat the child's back awkwardly, catching as he did a whiff of Julia's hair. Sweet. Clean. Her care, her very future, entrusted to an uncle who had never before proved himself capable of such responsibility.

"Come," he said, taking his niece's hand. "I shall escort you to the stables, and then you must go straight to sleep, poppet."

He could not allow himself to become distracted by a woman whose eyes, and curious words, carried the hint of a promise she could not possibly fulfill. He had one path for redeeming his actions, and he intended to take it.

"Uncle?"

"Yes?"

The child chewed her bottom lip and fingered

the fabric of her small frock before finally she asked, "You will not allow the horses to venture close?"

The beasts were large. She was quite small. Julia was fascinated by horses, indeed drawn to them, but obviously reluctant to admit their size gave her somewhat of a fright. A Chamberlain was not meant for such weakness. He'd heard his brother convey that exact sentiment to Julia on the occasion of her scream at the sight of a spider. Nathaniel had thought it preposterous then and even more so now. She was a child.

He understood the trust implied by her admitting the fear to him now and asking for his protection. "I will not," he promised solemnly.

Relief sped across her face and she clutched his hand tighter, free now to enjoy the horses because of her uncle's promised intervention. Warmth surged through him. She could be confident that he would forever ensure her safety, her well-being.

Alexandra's words rushed back at him, as the face of Catherine flashed by in his mind. Would he one day require that Julia do her duty by the family and marry well? What action would he take if she made the grave error of fancying herself in love with a man not suited for her?

He glanced down again, certain only that he would never be able to force her to go against her own wishes. In this short time as his niece's sole caretaker, he had come to find her happiness more important than his own.

His shoulders sagged with the weight of that responsibility.

# Chapter Thirteen

For the first time in as long as she could remember, Andi had a good night's rest. It had been the most wonderful dream, with her and Nathaniel on horses, riding off into a blazing sunset, their hands locked together. The sunlit strands of her hair flowed behind as his eyes washed over her in that way that said he couldn't tear his gaze away. The smile on his lips said there would never be another, that he would never leave her. *The Notebook* had nothing on their love story the way Andi had scripted it.

And then, as she began to slowly open her eyes, the blackness and the invisible hand closed in yet again. She had only enough time to let a small moan escape before she resumed her position on the sofa, the small of her back pressed diligently into it and her shoulders hunched, surrounded by the same drawing room scene she had been a part of only hours ago.

*Writer's block,* she decided in frustration. *She doesn't get it right the first time, so she has to put us*

*through it again. And again. What gives her the right to
yank us around like pawns in her chess game?*

Louisa's control over her, and everyone else in
the room, was nothing short of deplorable. What if
Andi were to organize the others and they all
trooped into wherever this author's desk might be
to demand their rights to a fair life? She'd like to
discover what Louisa would have to say then. Hah.
Just see if she ever again went to so much trouble to
dig up any of Louisa's out-of-print books. *Out of
print, out of mind.* For a fleeting second, she wished
it were true. But then . . . she wouldn't be here with
Nathaniel.

She looked up through her lashes, watching as
he again turned music for Catherine, with a smile
that seemed to say she was already the focal point
of his life. *Doesn't he remember what we talked about?
How can he continue to practically seduce her, when he
now knows that her heart belongs to someone else? How
can he?*

Andi's hands were folded demurely in her lap,
her body language in total opposition to the
thoughts racing through her mind. *I have to get
Edland here. Somehow. At a time when Louisa has finished writing for the day, so she won't whisk Catherine
away again.*

With effort, she pulled her chin up to scan the
room. No sign of Nathaniel's niece this time. That
was an interesting turn of events. Had Louisa decided it didn't help the developing romance to introduce Julia to Catherine at this point? *Julia is an
important part of Nathaniel's life. If it doesn't work to
have her in a scene with Catherine, change heroines.*

Her shoulders, already curved into their don't-come-near-me position, tightened. Andi's eyes drifted closed, but she forced them to open. She could not allow Louisa to take over every part of her. To have the best chance of influencing the action, she had to remain acutely tuned into it.

Her eyes landed on Amelia, who was seated on a sofa close by and looked stiffly miserable. Beside the young woman, Amelia's mother perched upright, smiling with a steely determination. And there, just across from her, sat Annabelle, who turned to shoot an inquiring glance at Andi.

Andi dropped her eyes. She needed a way to talk with Amelia, out of the pin-drop hearing of their mothers. Someone had to help her carry out the plan she was sure to come up with anytime now. That someone might have to be Amelia. No doubt she knew how to get to the Evernham estate or, at the very least, how to reach a certain person hiding out there. Then what? *Think, Andi. Think.*

Lilting notes came from the pianoforte, culling murmurs of pleasure from the assembled guests, until Catherine's hands unexpectedly stumbled, making a jarring sound. Andi watched the other woman direct a trembling smile at Nathaniel and whisper words that looked to be an apology. She resumed her playing. A few seconds later, she tripped over the keys again.

Catherine froze and, for a moment, all movement and sound in the room suspended. Louisa's pen was lifted and not yet put to paper again. A collective breath was held, waiting.

The door to the drawing room opened and a servant, her cheeks pink with distress, curtsied and scraped before Horatio Havington, murmuring something to him in low tones. As he listened, Havington's own face flushed. He clenched his fist and opened his mouth to respond, but before he could, a man entered the room to stand defiantly before the assembled guests, hat clenched in one hand, his *GQ*-worthy chin high.

Edland Evernham.

Andi's mouth opened in surprise and she whipped her head around to Nathaniel and Catherine. A squeal of panic came from Catherine, who laid her hands on the sides of her face, eyes wide.

Nathaniel remained calm; his dark eyes narrowed in contemplation as he turned in slow motion toward Edland. Cary Grant couldn't have done it any better.

Havington, however, looked as though he might burst a blood vessel. He took a step toward the uninvited guest. "Evernham—" He spat out the name.

As he did, Andi felt her shoulders, which she had begun to lift, curl. *Louisa's writing.* The realization, coupled with the action taking place before her, sent a thrill up her spine. Louisa was going with this. Taking a chance, for once. Good for her!

Edland, ignoring Nathaniel and every person in the room but one, strode toward Catherine. Her hands left her face and she pressed them together in front of her in a prayer-like pose, her luminous gaze fixed on him. Andi tore her own eyes away from the two to steal a glance at Nathaniel, who stood watching them, his expression unreadable.

"I must speak with Miss Havington," Edland said. Though it sounded as though he meant to state the request firmly, it came out with an audible note of desperation. Catherine swayed slightly on her seat before the pianoforte. Then her expression began to crumple. "Oh, Edland," she said, with a nearly imperceptible shake of her head.

He took her hand and held it up. Appearing locked into an almost comical struggle with his mouth, he used his free hand to wipe his brow before finally forcing out the words, "My dear." And then he took a great gulping breath.

*Wait a minute.* Andi knew that kind of a battle with body parts. Was Edland . . . ? Could he possibly be defying Louisa? She wanted to break into applause at even the remote possibility of the idea. *Go, Edland, go.*

Havington, having found his voice, now began to use it to excess. "You will leave here at once!" he shouted, startling most occupants of the room. "You are most certainly not welcome at Barrington Manor. I would have thought that clear enough the last time we met."

Edland turned to face the furious father. "It was made perfectly clear," he said calmly, "along with threats to myself and to my family if I did not accommodate your wishes. However, I have at last come to the realization there is little in life I hold dear . . ." Again, he stopped while his mouth worked furiously, until at last he forced out, ". . . including my own person, if I cannot be with the lady I love." He seemed nearly exhausted with the effort of the words, but no less determined.

The responding mutual gasp from the Havingtons, and their guests, was audible. Andi's eyes shot back over to Nathaniel. His brow creased dangerously and his chin thrust forward. She could have sworn she saw a glimmer of approval in his eyes, but it was gone so quickly, she decided she must have been mistaken.

Havington crossed the room to stand directly in front of Edland, his nose inches from the younger man's face. His mouth curled in rage, he announced to the room at large, "Sir, you will leave this house at once."

"And if I should refuse to do so?" Edland challenged, stiffening until he looked like a poster child for perfect posture.

Havington didn't flinch. "If this is how you would insult my family, we shall have no choice but to meet at dawn."

"No!" Catherine's frightened voice cut into his words. All color drained from her face, and she once again began to sway in her seat.

Andi felt her legs, of their own accord, quickly scramble into action. Rising from the sofa, she rushed to stand by Catherine's side, laying an arm around the woman's shoulders. Imbecilic expressions of comfort tumbled out over her lips, even as her mind veered in a different direction. *Turn him down, Edland. Get out of here. Now! I'll figure out how to get Catherine to you.*

"No." The one word Nathaniel spoke seemed to reverberate through the room. But though he opened his mouth, it took him a moment to speak again. "If anyone is to challenge this gentleman to a duel, it shall be me. It is, after all, I who have been wronged by his profession of love to the woman I shall marry."

Havington turned to Nathaniel. "You?" he demanded.

Nathaniel gave one sharp nod.

"Very well, sir," Edland said to Nathaniel, his mouth so taut that his upper lip had all but disappeared. "I shall see you at dawn."

Andi's heart turned a somersault and dropped. A duel. Not possible. It wasn't happening. Surely Louisa would never go for a— *Omigod, who would she have killed?*

Havington wasn't about to wait for the details of the arrangement. "You will leave this instant," he bellowed, his cheeks puffing with the effort, "or I shall have you thrown out like the dog you are."

Edland turned to Catherine, lifted her hand for a swift, urgent kiss, and bolted through the door, his furiously determined face enough to make the servants in his path run for cover. Catherine covered her face and dissolved into tears, her shoulders shaking.

Andi, still poised in the role of comforter, continued to murmur unhelpful words, her hand now moving to hover above the other woman's shoulder. Before she knew it, Amelia had moved in, guiding Catherine up and toward the door. "Come with me," Amelia whispered, to Andi's great relief. She'd never been one of those people who knew exactly what to say.

Once Catherine left, the others moved to also disperse, whispering as they did. "A most unlikely turn of events," Annabelle said to Amelia's mother, who responded with, "Shocking, indeed. And such a dreadful thing to do. They cannot be truly intending to carry it out. I quite refuse to believe it."

In the next instant, everything stopped. And then came the by now familiar signal from Nathaniel. "We are at an end," he said, his cool gaze appearing as unfazed as if they had just finished an evening of polite, boring conversation.

Andi felt her shoulders relax, but instead of her usual reaction of drawing up straight in relief, she sank onto the seat Catherine had vacated, shaking her head. "What is she doing?" Raising her palms, she implored the ceiling, "How can one story get so out of control?" No answer.

The room emptied, except for Nathaniel, Andi, and the blustering Havington, who came to stand by Nathaniel, his broad chest still heaving with the insult. "Inopportune," he barked.

Nathaniel remained unmoved. "We shall see," he said, "what the dawn holds."

"There is no alternative but for you to shoot him through the heart."

"He shall choose the weapons."

"Nevertheless. Surely pistols shall be the choice. And I offer mine."

Pist— Did he say pist—? Gunshots ringing out at dawn, with someone falling to the ground— Huh-uh. Not going there. Not even going to think about it. The hero didn't die. That would suck all romance straight out of the book. Wait. Creating a great hero seemed to be the *only* thing Louisa could do well. She might not even know the basic rules of fiction. Great. Andi couldn't end up in a Jane Austen book, it just had to be Louisa's.

"Your offer is generous," Nathaniel said, "but unnecessary. I am prepared."

Thank God for that.

Havington took a step forward and aimed his forefinger at Nathaniel's nose. "My daughter is to marry you. We agreed upon this." His breath was coming in rapid bursts. He paused and then spoke again, shaking his finger, "I gave my oath to her poor mother, upon her deathbed, that I would see her married well. She will not live out her days as the wife of a man outcast from all decent society. I shall see to it."

Andi watched Nathaniel's eyes narrow as he fixed the other man in his gaze. "I am quite aware of our agreement."

Havington blinked rapidly and let his finger fall. Then, drawing himself up sharply, he said, "When dawn comes, be so good as to ensure Evernham is the one left on the field." Turning on his heel, he left the room.

And it was just Nathaniel and Andi, alone. Her mind raced, trying to make sense of all she had just witnessed. Catherine's father was trying to keep a promise he'd made to his wife to ensure the security of their daughter, but he was going about it in all the wrong ways.

Married well could mean all sorts of things, but should, more than anything, mean *happily*. Because of his blind determination to carry out his narrow interpretation of a promise, he would keep his only child from the man she loved. He was narrow-minded and hard, no matter what intentions drove him.

"Mr. Havington takes no rest from the author's pen," Andi observed. "Though the others . . ." Hmm. How to say "take a break"? ". . . find opportunity for leisure, he does not waver from his cause. I find him as thoroughly hateful when Louisa is not writing as when she is."

"I am beginning to suspect," Nathaniel said thoughtfully, looking at the door, "that Havington is a man of lower character than Louisa is capable of accurately portraying."

Andi couldn't help it, the snort escaped before she knew it was gone. "A keen observation, with one flaw. She created the gentleman."

"That is true. However, he seems to have taken on characteristics of his own design."

"Ha!" She shook a finger at him. "That can only be because he challenges her. Is steadfast in what he wishes to do, rather than what she wishes him to do. And *he* has not been written out." She crossed the room to stand before him, grasping the lapels of his jacket. "You will remember how firmly I believe that can be done. And what have you to say about Edland? He fought Louisa to be in this room, professing his love for Catherine." She clutched the fabric harder. "And she wrote it. She did."

He glanced down at her hands on his jacket and then back to her face, his eyes half closed. "You were perhaps accurate in your assumptions." The deadly quiet with which he said the words caused her gaze to shoot up, meeting his. His eyes were troubled.

She released her grip and forced herself to swallow, no easy action in a throat that had gone bone-dry. *Easy, Andi. This could be it. Don't blow it.* "About Catherine?"

"He claims her affections." He leaned against the pianoforte.

Andi sank onto the seat and turned the corner of her mouth up in rueful agreement. "I do not understand what she sees in the gentleman. And I use that term generously. It certainly cannot be the warm, endearing personality he offers." Again, she shook her head, saying to herself, *When she could have* you, *she picks* him. *Unbelievable.*

He smiled. It began slowly, but then it spread across his face until his eyes crinkled. Andi's heart took a cautious leap forward and she clenched her stomach muscles in anticipation. That smile—the real thing, not the one he'd been giving Catherine —was directed at her. *Her.*

"Not only do you have a distinctly odd manner of expressing yourself," he said in a rumbling voice that sent a shiver shooting straight up her spine, "but there is a spark to your words that is most unusual."

"And you have the courage to see things as they really are," she said earnestly. "So many do not."

His smile faded. "Ah, but in this instance, it will mean a meeting at dawn."

The duel. She'd shoved the archaic ritual to the back of her mind. If Nathaniel were to die on that field, she'd lose the man of her dreams. If Edland were to die, she'd still lose the man of her dreams because Nathaniel would marry Catherine. Besides that, why did anyone have to die at all?

She had to nip this whole thing in the bud. Now.

"You cannot fight a duel. It must not happen." She quivered from head to toe with indignation and moral outrage.

"As you must surely know, Alexandra, it is a matter of honor and entirely out of your hands. I have challenged Mr. Evernham. Fear not. Louisa has seen to it that I am a skilled marksman."

She shot to her feet, kicking the bench seat with her leg to send it crashing backward. "Then you shall be good enough to miss."

"Ah, and allow him to instead hit his mark?"

She shuddered. "What kind of a marksman is he?"

"That, sadly, I do not know." He shrugged one shoulder, a gesture Andi would have found endearing if she didn't have to focus so hard on making him understand this was a matter of life and death. "Pray, enlighten me, Alexandra," he said thoughtfully, "as to why it is so important to you the story take a different turn."

If he couldn't figure that out . . . She pulled her mouth in tight. "We must determine a course of action that will mean a duel does not become necessary." She made a move to start pacing back and forth, but stopped when he laid both hands on her arms and drew her close. Every muscle in her body melted at his touch, and the brain that had just begun to kick into planning mode shut down, able to think of nothing but the warmth of his hands on the flimsy fabric of her dress and the eyes that held hers and muddled every sensible thought.

"A man who may die on the dueling field tomorrow could wish for a last kiss." His voice teased its way through her senses as his warm breath tickled her nose. She heard herself make a choked sound as his lips brushed her cheek on their way to her mouth. Then she drank in the sensations shooting through her body as he cupped her face with his hands and began to kiss her with a gentle insistence.

A last kiss. Might die on the dueling . . .

"No!" She shoved him from her. The force of the sudden movement sent him stumbling backward. "Last kiss?" She pushed her hand through her hair, blinking hard. She was flushed, her forehead damp, cheeks burning. "I refuse to believe it." Slapping her fingers against her palm, she said, "You are not going to die tomorrow. And neither is Edland."

His eyes flared. "The author chooses the result."

"Not without you. So you exert your influence. Choose what you will or will not do. Not arrive at the field, not fire your gun. Something, anything not to cooperate with this." She couldn't lose what they might have, brief though it would be. If she did, her life would return to miserable, a dried-up teacher who taught because she'd never been any good at living. They'd all have been right, her "colleagues" who never believed she belonged in their league. And worse . . . worse than anything, Tristan would have been right when he left her standing at the altar, smiling brightly in pink lip gloss and clutching pink roses, to make his escape with—

*No.* She was not going to give Tristan and his Bitchy Becca one more inch of space in her thoughts. It was over. *Over.* Five years ago. And he'd been wrong. Andi *was* good for more than— She was.

Nathaniel didn't answer.

"Edland did it. And the scene went on. She allowed events to proceed; she wrote them." Andi pounded her fist into her palm. "You will have to do that."

"I have done enough."

Though some part of her heard him, she barreled on, convinced he wasn't listening. "You can't stand back and take what she writes for you. You—" She paused for breath and blinked at him, his comment beginning to sink in. "Explain. Please."

He walked toward the window, turning his back to her and resting a hand against the frame, his powerful body outlined by the candlelight. "It was not Evernham's own thought to arrive here this evening."

She thought that over for a minute. Edland had come because she'd set him up with Catherine. When he'd seen her again, it had only shown him how much he still loved her and he'd known then, finally, that he had to do something. Nathaniel must have found out about her interference. Wouldn't go over well with a by-the-book guy like him. Oh. Funny. She reined in a vaguely hysterical laugh to instead clear her throat. "What do you mean?"

"I thought it best to lay to rest your concern that Catherine's affections had been claimed by another." He gave her a quick, wry glance before turning back to the window. "Perhaps I discovered my pride challenged by your words. I preferred to think of her situation as her father had portrayed it, as simply an error in judgment that meant the lady was misled, though not so far as to ruin her."

His pride. So he was gorgeous, principled, *and* self-aware. It just kept getting better. "So you went to see him." Wait just one minute. Was Nathaniel saying that he, who warned her against such actions nearly every minute she spent with him, had done something behind Louisa's back? Influenced the story?

Hope began to dawn, spreading its way through her chest on fluttering wings.

He stared straight ahead and said to the darkness outside, "It is, therefore, my actions that have precipitated the duel. I can hardly thwart it, as you would suggest."

And there he stood, every inch the gallant hero, not only confessing to his doubts that the woman he was to marry would actually want to have him, but also to the fact he had listened to Andi and tried to do what he thought right for Catherine. Her heart swelled.

She took a step toward him, but folded her arms tight across her chest to restrain herself from reaching for him. All his body language said, "Keep your distance." For once, she listened to herself and stopped moving, struggling for the right words before finally, she said, "Perhaps you found yourself *hoping* she was still in love with Edland, which would then leave your course of action quite apparent."

His gaze zeroed in on her. "You, my dear, persist in viewing all as decidedly one way or another. Rarely does life give us such a clear path."

So she saw things as they were! What was wrong with black and white? Right or wrong. You did it, or you didn't. His thick-lashed eyes held hers. Waiting. For what? A debate over the finer points of dying, or not dying, on the dueling field wouldn't serve any purpose. Or, would it? Suddenly, she was having a hard time with being sure of anything anymore.

He folded his arms across his chest. "As her husband, I will afford Catherine the greatest of kindness. Assure her of a contented life."

Big change from what she had now living with her father. "I am certain of it," Andi agreed, nodding her head slowly. "You could not do anything less. But it appears you were not sure yourself it would be enough, or you would not have had Edland . . ." She paused. "What did you encourage him to do?"

"It is of little consequence." Even he didn't sound as though he believed that.

"On the contrary, it is of great consequence." She let her voice drop. "Tell me. Please."

He looked up to stare at the ceiling and exhaled sharply. "He received word that she was to be forced to marry against her will. I presumed that would be enough to cause Mr. Evernham to act. And Catherine would either accept or deny his professions of love." His voice held a resigned finality.

She gave him a tentative half smile. "So you stirred the embers enough to give him the courage to fight Louisa."

He contemplated her words. "That may be true."

Interference. From Nathaniel, this time. Every part of her body ached for him, longed for his touch on her; the feeling swept through her with the ferocity of adrenaline. She took another step toward him, but clenched her fists and dug her toes into her shoes in an attempt to stave off leaping into his arms, which were clearly not inviting her. *Not now, Andi,* she warned herself. *He's still reeling from the events of this evening. Everything is going south, and he doesn't know what to do. He could even be,* she shuddered at the thought, *killed tomorrow.*

The duel. It wasn't going to happen. She wouldn't let it. If Edland, a character who was supposed to hover around the edges, could actually influence Louisa, then so could she.

Nathaniel raised one eyebrow, questioning.

Of course. She might have succeeded in holding herself back physically, but the internal struggle had to be written across her face. Like always. She'd give anything for a poker face about now. A Scrabble face. *Anything* that hid her every thought. She tried arranging her features into a bland, nonreactive expression, which lasted exactly five seconds before she burst out with, "We will put an end to this idea of a duel tomorrow morning. You will be ill, horribly ill. Too ill to go out. Not actually, but we will make people believe it. Or . . . possibly your pistol is not ready. Has met with a tragic accident that requires its repair." She tapped her finger against her chin. "You cannot locate your second. Yes, that might do. Send him away and then he will not be here. No one will be able to find him. No gentleman could fight a duel without a second." She frowned. At least, she didn't think he could. With a snap of her fingers, she added, "I have thought of something better. We bandage your shooting arm. Claim it to be sprained, broken. Something." She waved a hand in the air. "No one could expect you on the dueling field, then." So simple, really. Her shoulders sagged in relief.

"Have you quite finished, Alexandra?" he asked, something close to laughter in his voice.

*Alexandra.* She loved the way he said her name. While other people pronounced it with a thinly veiled annoyance that it required so much effort to say, her name rolled off his tongue effortlessly, caressing each of the syllables. "I have," she answered, reveling in the way her name lingered on his lips. "Unless you have a different thought?"

"Evernham and I will meet at dawn. And nothing will be done to make it otherwise. Do you understand?" His words were clipped, crisp.

Andi pulled herself back with a jolt. "But—"

"This story, and indeed our fate, is in the hands of the author. She alone shall decide what will take place tomorrow morning."

She wanted to scream. She settled for a screech. "What if she decides you will die on that field?"

"Then it is as it should be. I will simply no longer continue as a part of the story."

So what did that mean? He'd be floating somewhere in the universe, out of her reach forever? Andi's heart pounded so hard she was sure he must be able to hear it. She laid a hand across her chest, hoping to still her racing pulse before it knocked her flat and she couldn't make him see reason. "That can't be true. Do you understand me? It can't."

He shrugged, but the gesture wasn't casual. "It is the way of it."

"How can you accept—?" She gestured wildly. "What if she decides to kill Edland? Where does that leave you? You cannot marry Catherine."

"And why, pray, would you make such a statement?"

"You know she doesn't love you."

"She will need the protection of a husband. There will be much that will be said, and rumored to be said, about her." He shook his head. "After this evening, I daresay it has already begun in earnest."

"She requires protection. And you require her money." The hurt that squeezed at her heart rolled into her voice as a stinging sarcasm.

He evaluated her from behind a gaze that had slipped back into unreadable. "That has been evident from the very beginning. I made no pretense otherwise."

Andi couldn't remember a time when she'd felt more miserable. She stared at her feet, regretting with all her heart that she'd ever had the thought to introduce Edland behind the scenes. Obviously, this whole story, and its characters, would have been better off if she could have kept her well-intentioned, but slightly screwed-up, soul out of things.

This era was not as clear-cut as it appeared when reading books. The often simpler rules of behavior both bound and chafed, while a sea of emotion and unmet need raged behind. She loved and hated it, all at once, wishing for something better, afraid to find it. If she couldn't find refuge here, where could she find it?

After a moment, she felt his finger on her chin, tilting it upward. Her eyes, wet with unshed tears, met his.

"This you must promise me," he said, his voice low and determined. "You are not to interfere with what takes place tomorrow. You must remain in your room, unless Louisa summons you elsewhere." Locking her into his burning gaze, he continued, "If there is to be another story, we must allow Louisa to make it so."

She squeezed her eyes shut, refusing to let the tears fall. When she opened them again, he had not moved. "You must promise," he said again, more urgently this time.

"I cannot," she whispered, "because I cannot lie to you. And I'll be damned if I'll sit quietly in my room and wait for this to happen."

His eyes blazed. "You will," he responded in a voice that left no room for a person to disagree.

Unless, of course, that person was Andi.

# Chapter Fourteen

In her haste to leave the house without being spotted, Andi grabbed the first shoes she saw. Unfortunately, they proved to be the flimsiest of the flimsy. Though she wasn't even halfway to the spot where Amelia had told her the duel would take place, her shoes were already soaked with dew.

Not only that, but the shawl-like wrap she'd picked up to throw around her shoulders had to have been intended only for show. She began to shiver in the early morning chill, not sure her inappropriate clothing and footwear were entirely to blame. But she had no time to lose.

The dawn began to show signs of breaking through the darkness with pink fingers of light, a beautiful beginning to a day that could be fraught with tragedy. Andi quickened her steps. Arriving too late to help would be the only thing worse than staying safely shut in her room. A vision of Nathaniel lying in the field, blood spattered across his white shirt, his face deathly pale, veered before her at freeway speed. She shook it off with a tearful jerk of her head.

Men. Honor. Whatever happened to talking things out? Instead, they chose to fire loaded pistols at each other, with the intent of eliminating the other person so they wouldn't have to have a discussion.

Just when she'd managed to shove the picture of a bleeding Nathaniel out of the way, another one intervened—Edland, in much the same state, with a thoroughly healthy and contrite Nathaniel leaning over him, now forced to marry Catherine, no matter what. He could hardly abandon her once he'd shot and killed the only man she loved. Besides, there was still that pesky problem of money. Catherine had it. Nathaniel didn't.

It occurred to Andi that she should be frightened, plodding through the near darkness in sodden shoes. The stable hand, or anyone else recruited by Horatio Havington to scare her away from Nathaniel, could be lurking nearby. Havington was determined that Nathaniel marry his daughter, no matter what. And Andi was clearly a "what."

But she wasn't scared, not for herself. Maybe it had something to do with the surreal quality of the whole situation, or maybe . . . it had to do with the object safely tucked into her newfound cleavage. An object she'd been startled to find poking her in the toes this morning when she'd first slipped on this pair of shoes. She reached a finger up to touch the spot on her dress where it rested safely, hidden from view.

The wishing stone. That which may well have been the vehicle to bring her here when she'd made her desperate wish. It seemed so long ago now, though with the way Louisa kept reinventing time, it was difficult to tell how much had actually passed.

*Louisa.* She had to get there before the author awoke and picked up her pen. Andi pushed on, stumbling over the grass, her dress becoming heavier as the hem grew increasingly wet. When at last she reached the clearing Amelia had told her about, the light was breaking through. A beautiful morning. For disaster.

In a corner of the field, she spotted something. A movement, a flash. It might be an animal, might be a person. Andi squinted for a better look but still couldn't tell. Worst case, it was the disgusting, menacing stable hand. On the other hand, it could very well be one of the two men's seconds, and her plan, thought not yet fully formed, involved somehow getting rid of one or both of them. Surely, two decent men of honor wouldn't be able to carry on a duel without their trusty assistants?

Andi searched the ground for a stick, just in case it was the stable hand or another of Havington's emissaries. She found one, a pitiful branch that would probably snap in two at the first blow, and gripped it in her hand. It would have to do.

Taking a deep breath, she skirted along the side of the field, hiding behind trees until she reached a place not far from where she'd seen the movement. The light became stronger, making it easier to see. She strained her eyes. Nothing.

She stepped into the open field, brandishing her stick as a sign of readiness to defend herself. "Is . . . anyone there?" Her voice quavered in the stillness.

"Oh!"

Andi heard the female voice before she saw

whom it belonged to. She blinked at the trees. "Who is there?"

A woman slipped into the clearing, dressed from head to toe in black, blond hair flowing across her shoulders. "It is I," Catherine said simply. "And I must presume your intent in being here to be similar to mine."

Andi nodded, weak with relief. Catherine was an unlikely ally in this situation, but an ally all the same. Neither of them wanted to see this duel happen. She moved quickly to Catherine's side, asking in a conspiratorial whisper, "Have you seen anyone arrive?"

Catherine shook her head. "I have not. But I must think they will at any moment. Unless—?" She grabbed Andi's arm. "Is it too much to hope they will have come to their senses and abandoned this foolish endeavor?"

Andi bit her lip and shook her own head. "Yes," she said, "I fear it is too much to hope. I myself endeavored to persuade Mr. Chamberlain, to no avail." She felt a surge of sympathy as Catherine hung her head.

Catherine buried her face in her hands. "I am entirely to blame," she said, the words muffled. She pulled her hands back, dragging them through her hair. "If only I had refused Edland's attentions, had told him quite adamantly that we must never see one another again, it would not have come to this."

"Perhaps you were simply unable," Andi pointed out gently. "Which may reveal the depth of your feelings for the man."

"It reveals only that I am too weak, when in his presence, to do what must be done."

"He does appear to be somewhat . . ." Andi racked her brain for the right, diplomatic word before finally settling on, "intimidating."

Catherine raised her head, her face illuminated in the breaking dawn. "He is at times brusque with his manner. But you do not know him as I do. His upbringing, his family. It has not been easy for him to bear. Being treated as though he were somehow less in the eyes of all but his mother."

Andi cocked her head to one side, listening. Sounded like excuses for bad behavior to her, but she let Catherine continue.

With her face beginning to take on a glow all its own, Catherine cast her gaze upon the empty field, almost as though she had forgotten Andi's presence. "With so many paying little heed to his feelings for all of his life, I find it perplexing that he was able to discover and name mine so easily. And understand about me what even I cannot understand. He is much kinder to me than he is to himself." She sighed, a soft, wistful sound. "At times, when he speaks, his words are those I would have spoken, had I been able to form them."

"A soul mate," Andi whispered in appreciation.

Catherine turned back to her. "Soul mate," she repeated, appearing to mull the word over. "Yes, that may be an exceedingly good way to characterize him." She smiled gently. "There is a side of him that I believe is shown only to me."

Andi turned away. "Good thing he shows it to someone," she said under her breath. She looked around, growing nervous about the lack of activity. "Possibly we are not in the correct location. Might they have traveled to another place?"

"This is the only place a duel would take place on my father's land," Catherine said sadly. Then she brightened. "Unless they have determined—"

She was interrupted by the sudden appearance of a horse riding into the field, followed by another. Both animals moved slowly, their riders sitting tall in their saddles, surveying the field with a cool detachment. They guided the horses toward the corner opposite to the one where Catherine and Andi stood.

As if on a simultaneous cue, both women moved back into the hedges, with Andi grateful for the fact that, even though she'd chosen the completely wrong dress for an early morning rendezvous, it was at least a very dark green.

"Nathaniel," she breathed, watching him. He dismounted with ease and, taking the reins in his hands, stood. Waiting. Above him, a bird trilled.

She glanced over at Catherine, whose white-knuckled fingers clutched the branches of the hedge that hid them. "Perhaps Mr. Evernham will choose not to arrive," Andi suggested hopefully.

"You do not understand," Catherine said into the hedge. "With Mr. Chamberlain at the ready, he could not allow himself not to come."

True to Catherine's words, the next horse and rider appeared in the clearing. Edland, alone. "He is not accompanied by a second?" Andi said. Could this possibly be a default? Like too many men on the field in football, or not enough?

Catherine shook her head slowly. "So very like him," she said. "He will meet this challenge alone." And she began to cry, in big, splashing tears.

"Oh, Catherine." Once again, Andi's heart welled

in sympathy and she reached out to draw Catherine's head in close to her. "We must not cry. We have to keep our heads clear, so we can determine what to do." Then her voice rose. "They are going to go through with it. The idiots!"

Edland dismounted and walked to the middle of the field, where Nathaniel had laid an open case. Edland's eyes never left Nathaniel's as he reached down to select a pistol and hold it up. He gave a nod, answered by one from Nathaniel.

"You must act! Make haste!" Catherine urged.

"I know, I know." Andi clutched her thin wrap. She couldn't think straight, her instincts to rush headlong into the situation colliding with a newfound hesitation to act so rashly. *This is the time for me to learn to behave rationally?* She rapped her knuckles against the side of her head, hoping for an answer. None came.

And then she felt it, the hand of Louisa closing in, drawing her inward. Great. *Now* she picks up the pen. With effort, she looked at Catherine, who had gone very still and pale as she watched the two men.

"You are not accompanied by a second," Andi heard Nathaniel say to Edland.

*Oh, no, please,* Andi pleaded silently to Louisa. *Don't kill either one of them.* She'd never felt so helpless in her entire life.

Edland gave a jerk of his head to acknowledge the correctness of the observation. And then the two men began to walk off their paces, Nathaniel's stride broad and powerful, Edland's shorter, but equally determined.

Right here in front of her. A duel. Louisa wasn't doing a thing to let either one of the men back out.

What? Did she have to have a body count in her
book? Did the victims have to be people other
people were in love with? Andi's inner voice hit a
furious high pitch. She had everything at stake.
Everything she'd ever wanted, all wrapped up in
that one man.

Forget calm, cool, and rational. There was nothing to do but fight.

She tried flexing her arms and mouth to gauge
the level of Louisa's attention on her. Not bad. Just
a little resistance. So the author knew she and
Catherine hovered in the hedges, but had her focus
on the duel about to take place. That gave Andi
enough wiggle room to make something happen
before Louisa could stop her. Before the invisible,
but lethal, barrier went up to keep her away. Even
if it did, Andi was prepared for the fight of her life.
Louisa had no idea whom she was dealing with.

"Stay here," she instructed Catherine in a low whisper. "And keep out of sight." Hmm. Her own words,
in her own voice. Louisa really *must* be distracted.

Catherine's wet eyes turned huge, but she
nodded. "Proceed with care."

Little did Catherine know that Andi's whole life
could be a *proceed with care* sign with a bold slash
through it. But then, what did she have to lose? She
couldn't be hurt or killed, unless Louisa wanted it
to be so . . . right? She shivered. She wasn't, of
course, Louisa's favorite character at this moment.
And an author did have the power to do something
about that, with a page torn to shreds.

Duly noted. And ignored.

She ran behind the cover of hedges and trees,
their branches stabbing at her arms and legs. One

or two snapped quietly. The hem of her dress made slapping noises against her skin as the wet fabric tried to wrap itself around her ankles. She kept her breathing shallow, afraid even that might give her away. She had to get to those men. Before Louisa had a chance to write the outcome of this duel.

Nathaniel completed his paces. She stopped abruptly when she drew level with the spot where he stood. Though he faced directly into her hiding spot behind the hedge, he didn't see her. But she could see him. In his eyes she saw a steely focus. And something else—a stubborn sense of honor. He would carry this out to the end. That much she could tell without question.

*Nathaniel, you cannot die!*

He turned to face Edland, who now also stood waiting across the field. In Andi's mind, what came next happened in vivid Tarantino-like stills. At the same moment Nathaniel made his turn, she flung herself through an opening in the hedge, directly at him, the yell that pierced the morning sky coming from somewhere deep within her, a cry that had been building, it seemed, for all of her life.

Her chest burned, her vision blurred, and just before she got to Nathaniel's back, she launched into the air, arms straight out in front of her, to tackle him from behind. He spun at the noise and put his hands up as she came down on top of him, knocking him to the ground. Another sound, loud and cracking, shot through her consciousness, but this one hadn't come from her.

As she fell, she noticed with a dull clarity that her shoulder stung. A lot. And it seemed to be growing wet. She allowed her eyes to close, and stay closed. Nathaniel was breathing underneath her, and she noted, with a confused sense of relief, the warmth of his chest moving up and down.

Then she noted the expletives spewing from him with some degree of force right next to her ear. They weren't all ones she'd heard in the twenty-first century, but she could be pretty certain they meant the same thing. That shoulder was really beginning to hurt.

"Alexandra!" His terrified voice penetrated her consciousness with a hint of an echo to it. Interesting turn of events, she thought, not quite convinced it represented concern for her well-being. He could just as easily be preparing to throw her out of the field on her ear while he gunned down Edland Evernham.

She could have a little trouble preventing that, since her body wouldn't seem to move. Then she heard words come out of her mouth. "I believe I have suffered a shot, sir," she said in that funny, high-pitched voice. *Whaa-at? I have?* As her thoughts played a frantic game of bumper cars, she waited for what would happen next. Did Louisa get to write Heaven for her as well? Or maybe someplace a little hotter, since she wasn't exactly high on Louisa's list? *Please don't send me away. Not yet.* She lobbied the unseen author, pleading with her eyes mentally squeezed shut. Physically, they fluttered in seeming helplessness, allowing her no clear look, and then closed again.

Terrific, she thought. This damned character had better have enough pluck to persevere through a gunshot wound and not just lay here, waiting to pass on in a tragic, flowery death on the dueling field. That was so . . . well, 1800s.

"Alexandra." Nathaniel moved out from under her to gently turn her over, laying his hand underneath her head and rolling her onto the grass.

"Oh." She gave a little cry.

From somewhere close to her head, she heard pounding feet and then a sharp voice. "My God, what has happened?" The frantic voice belonged to Edland. She pictured him to match his voice, running a hand through his hair, eyes wild, desperate at the thought he might have killed her. Still, her eyes would not open.

Not even when she heard the lighter steps running and Catherine's frightened voice in her ear. "Oh, my poor, poor Alexandra. Nathaniel, is she very hurt?"

Fingers probed at her shoulder. *Ow.* A hesitation. Louisa deciding what to do?

Finally, Nathaniel said, relief apparent in his voice, "It appears that the bullet only grazed her skin. It has thankfully not lodged there." His next words crackled in command. "The bleeding must be stopped."

"Use this." Catherine's voice was muffled; then something soft was stuffed onto Andi's shoulder and pressure applied.

*Ow, again.* Hurt more than a little. *Thanks, Louisa.*

For a long moment, she could feel only the push against her shoulder and hear what sounded like collective breaths held. At last, Andi's eyes opened. "I meant only to save you, sir," she said, a smile trembling at her lips. *Oh, drop it, Louisa. Isn't it time for a walk? Or for you to take to your bed?* She tried to move, but found her shoulder held tight by Nathaniel.

Another pause, and then . . . "She will not die!" Catherine exclaimed. Andi saw her rise and collapse into Edland's arms. At least from Andi's vantage point on the ground, he seemed to be holding her, or she was holding him. Either way, they both seemed pretty shaken up, but were in each other's arms. That much was good.

"She must have the attention of a surgeon," Nathaniel said to the ground, though his words appeared directed at Edland.

"I shall return to the house and send a servant for the surgeon," Catherine said, the distance of her voice signaling that she had already broken away from Edland and was on her way.

Another voice, an unfamiliar one. "Sir?"

"Round up the pistols," Nathaniel barked. "And see to Mr. Evernham."

"I have suffered no injury, sir," was Edland's desperate response. "Think only of Miss Lofton-Hale. She must be seen to."

Nathaniel seemed to hesitate for a moment before responding, "Then you shall see to Miss Havington. And you," he said, apparently to his second, "may be on your way as well. Leave my horse."

Again, pounding feet, this time leaving. And a pause, which in Andi's current state seemed endless. But after what seemed like forever, Nathaniel exhaled and sat back, though his hand remained firmly pressed to Andi's wound.

"What in the *hell* would cause you to do such a thing?" were the first words out of his mouth. "Do you have even the slightest idea how dangerous it was for you to thrust yourself into the line of fire? Was it your thought that we were simply pretending? Or did you have no thought at all?" The anger built with each word.

Andi tried out her mouth. It was working reasonably well, though she could still feel the presence of the invisible hand. "May I . . . stand?" She asked in her own voice. Interesting. She tried shifting her body as the cold, damp grass seeped through the oh-so-thin fabric of her dress.

"No!" The words thundered so loudly the ground seemed to shake in response.

"It is but a flesh wound." She suppressed a giggle. Not bad. Monty Python appearing at a time like this, and Louisa, of all things, allowing it. Then she pulled her mouth straight. "You admitted as much yourself. There is a bit of pain, but it is not overwhelming." She puckered her face, not liking the slightly petulant note she heard in her voice. But at least it was back to being hers. Just then, relief flooded through her body. "Nathaniel, you were not killed! And neither was Edland!"

"You nearly were," he groused, his eyes darkening. "What in the deuces were you—" He broke off, shaking his head.

"I could not allow you to do it," she said. "One or both of you lying on the ground. Dy—" She couldn't say the word.

"Instead, you are the one who lies upon the ground. Unforgivable." He bent closer, until his face was just inches away from hers. "And at this moment"—he looked around wildly, raking his free hand through his hair—"I should be the one who is shot, for the thoughts that occupy my mind."

"Thoughts? Why?" Andi's heart began to beat faster. Had she driven him to the brink of doing her in, just to save himself the pain of all the trouble she caused?

His agonized gaze drifted above and then landed back on her, the dark, smoldering eyes causing her to catch her breath. In the next instant, his mouth closed in on hers, at first questioning, as if begging permission to continue, and then with a fire that bruised her lips and emptied her mind of anything but the sensation of his touch. She was only vaguely aware of bringing her free arm up to close her hand around his neck. From a part of her body that seemed very far away, her injured shoulder was throbbing, though it was no match for the burning anticipation that had begun in a much lower part of her.

He pulled away, his eyes searching her face. "You are a most bedeviling woman."

She arched her chin upward, unwilling to let his mouth leave hers. "I could not stand by and see you shot." Her throat was scratchy, her eyes misty with tears, and her stomach playing leapfrog in anticipation. All that, combined with the part of her that wanted to rip the shirt from his body and throw all caution to the wind in an empty field on the Havington estate, had her generally turned into a state of confused, rapidly escalating lust.

He'd better cooperate.

But instead, he talked. She forced herself to listen, no easy task in her state of mind and body. "I would not have been shot," he said, brushing a piece of hair from her face. "Evernham has a decidedly miserable aim."

She blinked, trying to understand. "You would have shot him, then?"

"Quite to the contrary. *I* have excellent aim." He smiled and Andi's heart fell to pieces, scattering with wild, thrilled abandon. She lifted her head, struggling to a sitting position, doing her best to ignore the pain that made her bite her lip. Placing a hand on her back, he helped her. She reveled in the feeling of his warm hand against the skin beneath her damp dress.

His eyes narrowed. "We cannot linger. Your wound must be attended to."

"*No!*" She wanted more. And she wanted it now.

Raking a hand through his hair, his eyes searched hers.

She raised a hand to his cheek. It felt warm and newly shaven.

He reached up to take her hand, enclosing it in his much larger, rougher one. "I must ask your forgiveness," he said. "I do not know what possessed me."

"Forgive you?" Her voice had a little shake in it that made her sound half unhinged. Probably not that far a stretch, she thought, all things considered. "I don't want to forgive you. I just want more." She grasped his shirt with the hand of her good arm and leaned in. "I came all this way to find you. We're not stopping now."

# Chapter Fifteen

She could hear her breathing and his, even the pulsing of her heart, as they stared into each other's eyes. After a moment, her hand began to ache with the effort of her grip on his shirt. She forced it to relax.

"I am to marry Catherine," he said.

"Possibly," she answered.

He made a sound of frustration. "Why did you place yourself directly in the path of a bullet?"

"Because it was meant for you."

Now he really shook his head, looking down and then back up at her, his eyes raw with vulnerability. "I do not understand. It could well have killed you."

"Have you not ever had someone want to protect you?" She gave a watery smile.

"No." His voice was scratchy, but there was wonder in it.

"You protect people you care about. That is all I sought to do."

He moved closer slowly, and with every inch Andi lost her heart further in the depths of his dark eyes.

Their lips had nearly touched when she became aware of a pounding sound thudding into her consciousness. As it grew steadily louder, she gradually became aware it was coming from the ground and shaking her body. Nathaniel bolted upright, his hands pushing the tails of his shirt into his pants. *Why?* she wondered groggily, still locked into the tingling memory of his lips on hers. It had been about to happen again, but something had interfered.

The pounding stopped only a couple of feet from Andi. She turned to see a horse standing overhead; it cast an ominously long shadow, as well as a jolt of discomforting and unwelcome reality, across her. She lifted her suddenly heavy head upward, but pain shooting from her shoulder stopped her, causing her to remember with some surprise that she had been shot. Or at least grazed.

The rider was not visible from her position, but his voice, booming at Nathaniel, made seeing him unnecessary.

"My daughter has just now flown in the door, greatly agitated by what she claims to be a grave injury to Miss Lofton-Hale," Havington announced. His voice took on a verbal sneer. "I see no evidence of such an injury. Perhaps the profession of such was merely a ploy to send my daughter away, leaving you to enjoy other pursuits."

Nathaniel stood his ground. "The lady has suffered a bullet wound to her shoulder."

"And precisely what have you done to care for the wound?" Havington's words dripped with innuendo.

Andi glanced down to surreptitiously make sure all parts of her dress were tugged into place. Catherine's shawl fell forward and onto the ground, caked with blood. She stared at it. Her blood. More of it than she would have thought. Maybe she *had* been pretty lucky. But even as a mild panic shot through her at the close call, she knew she would do exactly the same thing all over again.

After all, the bullet had been aimed at Nathaniel.

She saw Nathaniel wrench his attention from Havington and back to her. Retrieving the shawl, he placed it again on her shoulder. "This must remain pressed tightly," he said in an undertone, "until the surgeon is able to attend to you."

"I shall not inquire," Havington said dryly, "how the events of this morning transpired, since I have seen with my own eyes that Evernham is able to walk this ground still. But I must know, was he so fine a marksman as to hit the young woman with the shot he intended for you? And where, pray, did your shot land, if not directly through his heart?"

Andi tried to climb to her feet, shoving, pushing against the ground and toward Nathaniel.

"No," he instructed her in a voice both low and steady. "Do not move." He readdressed himself to the rider. "The shot fired was an accidental one."

"And from such a result I am to choose my daughter's suitor."

Nathaniel's jaw muscles tightened and he reached down to scoop Andi, and the shawl serving as a compress, into his arms. "As you can see, Miss Lofton-Hale requires a surgeon."

Havington made a scoffing sound. "This creature is no longer welcome in my home once her wound has been seen to. It was only an ill-placed loyalty to the memory of my departed friend that prevented my turning her out earlier."

A muttered swear word escaped Andi's lips. So she would be sent on her way. Kicked out. Horatio Havington would have no reluctance in crafting his own story behind the scenes. He'd have her, and Annabelle, out the door before Louisa had a chance to pick up her pen again.

Insufferable idiot.

Nathaniel cast her a quick glance. The shallow but rapid rise and fall of his chest told her he was also seething inside, possibly only containing his response because of her presence.

"I shall leave you to see to her, then," Havington said tersely. "But know, sir, that I have determined the wedding between you and my daughter is to take place in two days' time." He picked up his reins.

*Say he's wrong,* she pleaded silently with Nathaniel. *Tell him you have no intention of doing any such thing.*

"The bargain, Havington, has been struck only between you and myself," Nathaniel said, his tone controlled with what sounded like a frightening effort. "Your daughter has not agreed to become my wife, nor, it appears, is she likely to do so now."

Andi squeezed her eyes shut and buried her head in Nathaniel's chest. *Yes. Now just let the tyrant see that his daughter will never become Mrs. Chamberlain. Ride off into the wind, Havington, and crumble into dust, never to be seen again. Or at the very least, just take off and leave us alone.*

"If it is necessary to repeat myself," Havington answered, anger surging forth in each word, "I am perfectly willing to do so. The wedding will take place in two days' time. My daughter shall marry you. Her wishes are of no consequence."

Andi's chin flew up. *How could a parent be so cal-*

*culating, dictating who his daughter would marry? How could Catherine go along with it?* It defied belief. It— Oh God. It felt familiar, though her own mother had been more subtle. And no one had been waiting in the wings, ready to fight to the death for Andi.

Havington turned his horse's head but added one parting shot. "Whatever inconsequential dalliance you may be indulging in, sir, shall end before the ceremony. I shall not have you breaking the heart of my daughter once you have become her husband." With a harshly delivered command to his horse, he rode away, his back rigid, the hooves of the animal he rode clattering across the ground.

"Inconseq—dalli—?" Had Havington just insinuated she was no more than a slut? Her mind spun with the implication. In one smoothly spoken sentence, he had declared her to be of little importance. A nothing. But Nathaniel didn't believe that. He couldn't. She tried to speak but succeeded only in stuttering out portions of the words.

The smell of roses stung her memory. The feel of her hand on Tristan's arm, clutching, pleading with him not to leave. He'd whispered again, *"Becca is the one I'm supposed to be with, Andi. I know that now. You and me, it was really only the"*—he'd glanced over his shoulder at her bridesmaids, hovering at the edges of the foyer, and covered his mouth with one hand— *sex."*

How nice of him not to embarrass her.

An inconsequential dalliance. That's what Tristan might have called their relationship, except that he'd slipped an engagement ring on her finger. Promised to . . . She, at the urging of her mother, had been willing to believe him. Her stomach folded itself into one giant knot.

Nathaniel shifted her in his arms and began walking in the direction of the Havington estate, each stride of his boots hard and purposeful, his eyes focused straight ahead. He wasn't Tristan, heir to a seafood fortune as large as his ego. She had to remember that.

"Talk to me." Her teeth actually chattered.

No response. His mouth pulled into one tight, thin line.

She watched him anxiously. "Put me down. Please. I can walk."

"I shall carry you."

"I am not hurt badly."

"You are bleeding."

"Not anymore. It has dried." She tried pulling the shawl away to demonstrate. The injury to her shoulder was the last thing she wanted to talk about with him.

"Alexandra." A roughly spoken warning.

"As you wish. I will leave it," she said, trying to stifle the hurt as she pressed the shawl into her shoulder.

She stayed silent for a few more minutes, the sound of his boots hitting the ground ringing in her ears. Then she couldn't stand it any longer. Every worry that she'd misunderstood, that the interlude in the field hadn't meant anything to him, that he agreed with Havington on the nothingness of it all, came out in her voice, laid painfully bare for him to hear. "*Do* you intend to marry her in two days?"

"Calm yourself," he growled. "You make it most difficult to carry you."

"Calm myself?" Nice thing to say when she felt like Mount Saint Helens, right before the volcano blew. "That man ordered you to marry his daughter in two days and you"—she gulped for air—"did not contradict him! Did not say it will not happen. Not now, not ever. Why is that, Nathaniel?"

He made a sound of exasperation and stopped moving, still staring straight ahead. Eyes narrowed, he said, "I have not yet determined the best course of action."

"The best course of action? I cannot believe this." She kicked her legs. "Let me down. I am able to walk."

"As you wish." He opened his arms and she sank toward the ground.

She stumbled a few steps, holding the shawl against her shoulder, then grabbed his arm. "I may require some assistance, after all," she admitted faintly.

Again, he scooped her into his powerful grasp. She clung to him with her good arm, never wanting to let go. He was everything she wanted, everything she'd dreamed of for so long. She could lay her head on him forever. Forget her job, her classes. They could find someone else to teach restless teenagers.

He stopped. Andi looked up to see Nathaniel's horse waiting. "I shall lay you atop my horse," Nathaniel said, "and lead you back."

Just as he began to lift her up, Andi whispered urgently, "Nathaniel."

He stopped midlift, but didn't look at her.

"Catherine longs for Edland and must be able to find her happiness with him. If we work together, we may be able to convince Louisa to give them their own story." Her voice trembling, she added, "And make the necessary changes to this one."

He exhaled slowly, then turned, sweeping his eyes up to hers. "There is much at stake in battling Louisa," he said, sounding as though the words hurt him to say. "I must think of Julia, of what could befall her if I were to . . . if I did not . . ."

"If we could convince Louisa that something exists between us, she could give me the background, the money. It is within her power. She could arrange it so that my mother and I were here to offer you another legitimate marriage prospect. Julia included." Tears hovered close behind her eyes, she could tell, and it must have been them making her voice shake so badly. She couldn't get this close and then have to let go of him forever. The universe could not be that cruel.

"It is unlikely she would do so," Nathaniel answered, his words cutting right through her heart. "Louisa seldom makes such a significant change once a character has been created, and she has proceeded far into her manuscript." Now he looked genuinely sorry. "It has been her practice to simply cut the character and begin again."

She blinked hard, trying to keep the tears at bay. They would help nothing here. "So, you will be left with no choice but to marry her, then?" she croaked. "If that is what Louisa wishes to happen?"

His eyes closed in one dramatic sweep of his lashes, then opened again. He refused to look at her.

"Nathaniel?" Her voice was little more than a whisper.

"Yes" was all he said before lifting her gently up and onto the horse. Then he took the reins and, with a clucking of his tongue, began to lead the animal toward the Havington estate.

While he could vow never to inflict the same fate on Julia, it appeared as though his own was sealed. Once wed, his first order of business would be to ensure the lovely Miss Lofton-Hale was dispatched far from this place, to ensure he would no longer be tempted to recklessly take her in his arms.

He glanced at the still body on the horse, her eyes closed now, long, thick lashes resting against ivory skin, a teardrop glistening on one cheek. She had suffered an injury that could well have been far worse. At the thought, a part of his chest clutched at him hard. Yet it would prove pure folly to defy the author whose very pen held so many fates in the balance.

She had claimed not to belong in the story. Unlikely as the tale seemed, he was inclined to believe it. How else to explain her manner of speech, and her actions that had confounded his best attempts at understanding? If she was truly not meant to be here, the path for her to leave must be made clear.

No easy task. Although perhaps his gravest error lay in not conveying to Alexandra the fact that, were she to succeed in her quest to take on a larger role, the fates would never again hold even the possibility of return.

A minor character might go on elsewhere. The hero and heroine would dwell in the story forever.

* * *

The surgeon summoned to attend to her injury went about his business with a stoic air, saying not a word to Andi as she lay on the bed in misery, unwilling to move and unable even to look at Catherine, who hovered nearby. Andi didn't make a sound as the white-haired man cleaned the wound, not even when his fingers examined it less than gently. It hurt far less than the dull, throbbing ache in her heart.

Finally, after pressing a bandage into service and making her drink something that tasted like wine with a disgusting kick, the man gave a brisk nod and left the room. Catherine followed closely behind him, her brow furrowed with worry. And Andi was alone.

*Nineteenth-century medicine. All that poking and probing, without antibiotics, will probably lead to an infection the old guy won't know how to treat.* Andi sighed so hard it hurt. But she couldn't work up a good case of anxiety over the thought.

She closed her eyes, reliving those last few moments with Nathaniel until the memory consumed her and tears began to spill from the corners of her eyes, shut tight against an upside-down world.

She could hardly bear to think what she would see when she opened them again. Or maybe she didn't have to wonder. It was fairly easy to visualize. Louisa would place her in the crowd of onlookers at the wedding of Nathaniel and Catherine, whispering good wishes with only the faintest hint of regret in her insincere smile. The foolish girl who tried to steal the hero from the oh-so-deserving heroine. A secondary character. Meaningless, really, except for a few contributions to moving the plot along. Funny how those inconsequential dalliances could end up like that.

Her stand-in mother, Annabelle, would carry the burden of a rejected daughter with a stalwart air, all the while surveying the men in the crowd for the next potential victim. Andi wouldn't stand for it. She couldn't bear anything without Nathaniel. It wasn't just the blissful, passionate night anymore that she wanted. She wanted this man for a lifetime.

She choked back a sob, imagining herself waving from the door of a convent, her hand pressed piously to her breast. If she left this place without, at the very least, the promise of something intense and heated with Nathaniel, she might as well look for a convent willing to accept her brokenhearted self.

She wasn't Catholic, but maybe it wouldn't make a difference on the application. They must provide on-the-job training. And she'd be stalwart and focused, that much was for sure. The perfect candidate for a chaste life. She'd never be able to look at another man. Who else could possibly measure up?

With single-minded deliberateness, she pushed aside the thought that terrified her most. What if she never, ever, in her life found another man who mattered, one who cherished her as she cherished him?

But she couldn't keep the fear suppressed for long. When it began to creep in again, pressing at her consciousness for attention, Andi kicked her leg toward the edge of the bed and began to scoot herself over, until she was able to raise herself up to sit on its edge. Dizzy again. Really dizzy. Not a good sign. And then she had to try and remember why it was she wanted to get up in the first place. Funny. Her thoughts seemed to blur. Still, she must have had a perfectly good reason for getting on her feet, so she'd better go ahead with it.

The air in the room felt heavy and stifling. It was depressing, the fact that someone insisted on keeping every pair of curtains in this house closed, day or night. She rose unsteadily to her feet, crossing the floor to the windows. Using her good arm, she pushed aside the curtains to let in the light, wondering as she did whether what's-her-name was writing at the moment. *What in the heck was in that wine slash medicine?*

The door made a squeaking sound and then pushed open. Andi's stomach responded with a quick somersault of anticipation. *Nathaniel?* Would this be a replay of the 1970 version of *Wuthering Heights* with Heathcliff at the door, the music crashing and thundering as he rushed to crush her into his fierce embrace and scoop her out of bed and into his arms? God, she loved that scene. Oh, hold on a minute. Catherine Earnshaw died a few minutes later. Never mind.

But the agitated, flushed face that showed itself around the door belonged to someone else. Beads of sweat stood out on Mary's round face as her mouth worked desperately to speak. She stepped inside the room and reached behind her to close the door.

"What is it?" Andi asked, leaning against the window. Something awful must have happened.

Laying a hand across her heart, she ignored the stings of pain that traveled from her shoulder on down.

"Mr. Evernham," Mary choked out. "He's here, miss." Her voice faltered on the last words. "You must make him go before the master finds him. Please, miss."

"Me?" Andi straightened, letting her hand fall to her side. She blinked hard, trying to understand, even as Mary's image wavered before her. Right. Edland. "He's not going to listen to me."

"The master will kill him. And that would kill poor Miss Catherine." Mary began to cry softly, wiping at the tears with the chubby fingers of a reddened hand.

The scene flashed before Andi's eyes. Horatio Havington likely would shoot Edland Evernham this time. Discovering him hiding in the house would incite the miserable man to murder. He'd already tried, and failed, to get Nathaniel to do his dirty work for him. The explosion of the shot and Edland's body hitting the floor with a thump played over and over again in her mind.

It would be her fault, of course. She was the one who made sure Edland inserted himself into the story when . . . the writer had planned he be nothing more than backstory. "You're a bull in a china shop, Andi," her father had warned her more than once. "So determined to get your own way that you never see what's crashing down behind you." At the time, she'd been outraged by the comparison. Now, she wasn't so sure.

Hands on her throbbing head, she exhaled slowly, looking toward the window, then back at Mary. "Where is he? Hiding on the grounds?"

"No, miss, he's—" Mary stopped.

"Where, Mary?" Andi tried her best to focus. It would help if her legs would quit shaking. "Tell me." *Before Havington takes the story into his own hands or Louisa starts writing again and decides that killing Edland off would be a good thing.*

Mary's eyes dropped. "He's in Miss Catherine's chambers," she whispered, as though unable to believe it herself.

Andi frowned. Even in her semialtered state, she could appreciate how morally outrageous it would be for Horatio Havington to find a man in Catherine's bedroom. With any action he took, he would be guilty only of guarding his daughter's chastity. A free ticket to take justice into his own hands. "I cannot imagine what Mr. Evernham can be thinking, making such a bold move."

"Oh, miss." Mary dissolved into tears. "Miss Catherine is so frightened. And Mr. Evernham says he will not leave her side."

Edland didn't have, from Andi's point of view, the very best sense of timing. "I understand, Mary. And you did the right thing by coming to tell me. We shall determine how to work out this grievous situation." Andi wished she sounded anywhere near convincing. "Does anyone else know?"

"No, miss. But they soon will."

Despite her fuzziness, a chill ran through Andi.

# Chapter Sixteen

Andi leaned against Mary's sturdy shoulder as the maid led her through dim hallways to Catherine's chambers. She heard the maid whisper a prayer that they meet no one along the way.

Apparently someone was listening. Except for the two women on an urgent mission, the hallways remained quiet.

Mary knocked on Catherine's door, her knuckles barely making contact with the wood. No answer. She tried again, saying through the lock in a voice hushed with urgency, "It's me, Miss Catherine. Mary." They waited; the servant crouched at the door, Andi leaning against the wall for support.

She tried her best to look nonchalant, as if she had every reason and no reason to be at Catherine's door. But at the same time, she couldn't suppress the mental picture of Horatio Havington racing down the hall to his daughter's room, brandishing a gun and looking forward to a great excuse to use it. She shuddered, a movement that seemed to continue reverberating through her body. The smell of polished wood, sweat from the maid, and candle wax mingled together and drifted up to her nostrils. Somewhere in the distance, she could swear she heard someone humming. She pressed her head into the wall. Again, she wondered, *what was in that wine?*

Then came a padding of footsteps and the creaking sound of the lock being undone. Andi turned. The door opened a couple of inches, revealing Catherine's anguished eye. When she saw the two other women, Catherine opened it farther, beckoning them in. She said to Andi, "I am so relieved you have come."

Andi straightened, allowing Mary to gently push her into the room. She had to get her thoughts in working order again. Catherine needed her. She couldn't pass out. She wouldn't.

When they were inside the room, Catherine closed the door again, hard, spreading her hand across the wood. The expression on her face told Andi all she needed to know.

She drew herself up as straight as she could manage, though her shoulder screamed its protest. "Where is he?"

There was a brief silence before Edland stepped from a shadowy corner and strode over to Catherine, wrapping one arm around her waist.

Straight to the point. Only way to go. "This is crazy," Andi said, but not without sympathy. "You must know that."

"Father will have him sent away again." Catherine sounded near tears. "He is determined that I am to marry Mr. Chamberlain in two days' time."

*In two days' time.* The words seared into her soul.

Andi turned her attention to Edland, concentrating hard. "I must believe you arrived with a plan, Mr. Evernham. You, of course, know what is to be done." She kept her tone as brisk as it could be, considering it felt as though she had Jell-O for a brain and her tongue had expanded to twice its size. As long as no one came to the door, as long as no one interfered, she might get through to the guy. She was sure she could. Pretty sure, anyway.

He furrowed his brow. "I fear I——"

How in the world could he be confused by this. He was in Catherine's room, risking her reputation again, after he'd thrown it to hell once by running away with her in the dead of night. Now he didn't know what course to take? She pressed the tip of her finger to her forehead. "You must marry her. At once."

"But my father——" Catherine broke in.

"He stopped you once before. That means this time you make sure you're married before he catches up with you." Really. This was not hard.

Catherine cast her gaze at the floor, her voice brimming with sadness. "My father would never forgive me. I . . . disappointed him once. I cannot do so again. Though Edland has been trying to convince me that we indeed could . . ." Her words trailed off.

Score one for Edland. He had at least been trying. Andi dropped her hand and leveled a look of qualified approval on him before turning her attention back to Catherine.

"Let's ponder this for a moment," Andi said. With effort, she made herself follow her own instruction. "You allowed Edland into your room to hide while you tried to . . . to . . ." What was the nineteenth-century term? Oh, just say it. "Figure things out, which is pretty dangerous, given the circumstances. If you're that willing to jeopardize his safety, you must at least be considering defying your father." Her head listed to the left.

From the corner of her eye, Andi saw Edland bristle at the word "hide." Too bad. Whether he was on the right track or not, that's exactly what he was doing.

Catherine turned and gazed up into Edland's eyes. Again, Andi was struck by the immediate transformation she saw in the man. He seemed to melt in her presence, turning into a buttery version of his bristling self. Could be that's why he had such trouble standing up to Havington, she thought. Catherine turns his head, and his heart, to mush.

"But I do not know how it is possible," Catherine whispered.

"This is not your father's life. It's yours." Andi was running out of patience, and damn it all, her head was still doing some sort of a spin.

Catherine looked up quickly, her expression as shocked as if Andi had just proclaimed the sky to be green.

Emboldened, Andi continued, "He thinks he's keeping a deathbed promise to your mother by seeing you married to Nathaniel. But is that truly what your mother would have wanted for you? Wouldn't she have told you to marry the man you love?" A chance statement, since Andi had no idea what Catherine's mother had been like, but it was fairly safe that mothers usually took their daughters' sides in affairs of the heart.

Except her own mother, she thought suddenly.

Hattie pushed and pushed for her to marry. That would be bad enough, if her mother wanted love for her, but her goal was her daughter's security. The heart never entered into it. And had Andi ever called her on it? Not exactly. Instead, she had tried her best to find someone who would satisfy both. And came up empty. She jerked herself back to what was happening before her, but not before she tucked that thought into a working part of her brain to revisit later.

Edland bent his head down, laying his cheek against Catherine's. "It is the truth of it, Catherine," he said. "It is your life. Our life together."

"But where is it we would live? My father would most certainly not allow us to remain here." Catherine's face puckered with worry.

"Then we shall go to London." Placing a finger under her chin, he drew her face to look at his. "We shall begin our life there. And one day, your father may even come to see how very much I love and care for you."

Andi was impressed. Too bad Catherine couldn't seem to make this kinder side of Edland surface more often. He could turn into a pretty likable guy.

The two appeared oblivious to her presence. "Will you marry me, my love?" Edland asked Catherine, his voice throaty with emotion. "Say that you will and I shall be the happiest man ever to tread upon this earth."

Catherine closed her eyes for a very long moment, as the other three in the room held their collective breath. When she opened her eyes again, they were filled with tears. She gave a delicate sniff and answered in a surprisingly steady voice, "I do

not see how I can refuse. I am truly happy only
when I am at your side."

A wistful sigh escaped from Andi before she knew
it. Would that it were her, with Nathaniel. *Wait. If
this plan works* . . .

Edland turned his eyes on Andi and, slowly, they
took on the defiant look she'd seen before. On several occasions now. "We may require your assistance."

"In creating a diversion?" she guessed. "I seem to
have a gift for it."

"Yes, Alexandra will know what to do," Catherine
said. "We must listen to her."

Edland's gaze swept from Andi to Catherine and
back again. He appeared to struggle with what he
would say, but at last allowed, "I am willing to . . .
listen."

"What about Louisa?" Andi hated to bring her
into it, but the author could easily spoil everything,
just when they had it all figured out.

"Louisa has taken to her bed," Catherine volun-
teered. "Mr. Chamberlain spoke of it earlier. She is
most distraught over the course the story has
taken." She looked at Edland, as though begging
for reassurance. "Mr. Chamberlain was uncertain
what would occur once she arose."

"Then we do not have much time." Andi hurled
herself into planning mode with all the strength she
could muster while slightly tipsy. It was, at least, a
fairly comfortable way to operate. "First, Edland." He
whipped his head back around to her. "When you set
out to be married last time, where did you go?"

He didn't look as though he appreciated the ref-
erence to the previous failed attempt, but after a

few seconds of aiming a narrow-eyed gaze at her, he conceded, "We were journeying to Scotland."

"Oh-hh," Catherine began to wail. "We are being foolish, I fear."

Andi wrapped her arm around the other woman's shoulders in a fierce, quick hug. "Come on," she said. "Remembering back on it would frighten anyone. But things will be different this time. They will. You have to believe that. He is the one you want to be with, is that not true?"

Catherine nodded mutely, her lip trembling. "Yes," she said.

Relief showed on Edland's face and he moved toward her, his arms out to embrace her.

"Then we shall have to determine how to make it work." Andi removed her arm, putting a hand out to stop Edland in his tracks. He blinked. "Scotland is too far a journey," she announced. "Louisa will be up from her bed and back to her old self by then. Or Catherine's father will realize she is missing and have time to follow you right to the place you went before." Almost to herself, she added, "Won't work. Only an idiot would try the same tactic twice in a row."

Edland puffed out his chest before grudgingly acknowledging, with a nod, that she could be right. And then he glared at her. He might have heard something of her last comment.

"Now that we have agreed upon that," Andi said, "we need a friendly, but discreet, rector who is fairly close by." She pointed a finger at Edland. She was in delegation mode. "Do you know of one?"

Not a man who reacted favorably to a finger being pointed at him, she observed, or maybe it was that *she* was now planning the wedding, instead of obediently taking on the distraction assignment he had graced her with. Storm clouds gathered on his face, but subsided when Catherine laid a hand lightly on his arm. "I may have knowledge of a rector," he allowed with a chin thrust to the heavens before turning to Catherine and melting into butter again.

Andi put a hand on her hip, trying hard not to sway. He either knew one or he didn't. "Where is he?" she asked.

"In a village not far from here. Wickston."

"And do you already have the license, or whatever it is you need?" Andi was beginning to take on the familiar teacher feeling of drilling a reluctant student. That worked. She was pretty good at it.

He gave his jacket a short, brisk pat. "Yes."

"Very good." She tapped a finger against her chin. "Now. The distraction. We must get the groom out of here alive. No reason for a ceremony if we cannot." The room fell silent.

When Edland spoke, breaking into her thoughts, Andi jumped, startled. Ow. A bullet grazing hurt worse than she might have thought. Not that she ever had actually thought about it.

"The back stairs that lead to the servants' hall," Edland was saying. "I will simply make my way down them quickly. If my horse is brought to the door, I shall be off and on to Wickston before anyone is the wiser." His voice softened as he turned to Catherine. "And you will join me there, my love."

Both Catherine and Mary turned their eyes to Andi. Okay, she thought. Servant stairs. Could work. Seemed too easy, though. And really, Edland needed to show a few guts here, a little something to demonstrate to Catherine how far he would go for her.

"A nearly sound idea," she said slowly, her finger still on her chin, "but lacking something."

The other two women waited expectantly. Edland's expression changed to one of suspicion.

"A disguise," Andi announced. "That is what is needed. Otherwise, someone might see you slipping away down the back stairs. If they recognize you, you're toast."

Catherine looked puzzled. *Damn*, Andi thought. *I have to keep from reverting to "Americanisms." I've been doing so well, despite the vaguely drunk feeling.*

"Simply an expression we use in America," Andi said. "I meant only to say that if someone were to see him on the back stairs and alert the master of the house, Mr. Evernham will never be allowed to reach his destination. The gun, the shots—" She cut off her words abruptly when she saw the look of horror that began to spread across Catherine's face. She'd move on to the part of the plan that Edland would, without a doubt, resist. That had some entertainment factor to it, after all.

"We shall dress the gentleman as a servant," she said, knowing that the wicked sense of fun she felt at the idea had to be apparent for all to see.

"A servant?" Catherine repeated. "I confess I do not understand."

"It is the only way to ensure he will not be spotted." Three pairs of eyes zoomed in on her. "And shot."

"I—I suppose that Mary would be able to secure clothing from one of the men, if you feel that such an act is necessary, Alexandra," Catherine said, her voice faltering. "But truly, Edland, it does seem an impossible thing to do."

Spoken like a true pampered member of the upper crust, Andi mused. She'd known more than a few in her life.

Mary murmured something. Andi leaned closer to hear.

"I shall do it," Edland pronounced with a gallant air, unexpectedly seizing the opportunity for good PR. "For you, my love, I profess that I shall not mind. I devote my life only to ensuring your happiness. No matter the sacrifice." He leaned down to kiss Catherine's hand in a grand, sweeping gesture. *Ah, but you, Mr. Evernham, are no Heathcliff,* Andi thought. *And you're not even coming close to Cary Grant.*

"Very good," Andi said with a smile that she had to struggle hard with to keep from breaking into a full-out grin. "Because it is not the clothing of a manservant we shall need. It is that of a maid."

Jaws dropped. It was perfect, really, Andi decided. Most fun she'd had since she arrived. She put a hand to her head. "Does anyone else feel as though the room is . . . moving?" She scanned their faces, wondering if she dared ask what was in the drink she'd been given. "Guess not."

"Surely, Alexandra, you cannot be suggesting that Edland—" Catherine stopped, struck speechless.

"It is the only way, I fear." Andi shrugged her shoulders in feigned helplessness. "We must ensure no one will recognize and stop him. And as Mary pointed out to me, the back stairs closest to this room are the ones used by the women servants." She thought she saw a small twinkle in Mary's red-rimmed eyes right before the servant averted her gaze.

Edland's jaw muscles worked furiously. "Dress as a servant woman?" he rasped. "You most assuredly cannot expect me to . . . to . . ." He raked a hand through his hair, indignant eyes boring into Andi.

"But you said you would do anything for Catherine," Andi said innocently. "So, Mr. Evernham, which is it to be? Ensuring you leave this house safely is as much for her as it is for you. Surely, a gentleman of your fine character would not think anything of a simple ruse that would, in the end, allow you to marry the woman you love?" She waited half a beat before adding, "It is not as though you are *choosing* to dress in women's clothing. But now that you have entered Miss Havington's chambers, we are left with little choice for your departure."

There. Let's see what he would have to say to that.

He muttered under his breath. Andi thought she might have detected the word "American" said in a derogatory sense, along with any number of other words that had nothing to do with her being American. She clasped her hands in front of her, wincing at the pain the movement prompted, and waited for his answer.

Catherine recovered herself enough to urge, "If Alexandra considers it imperative, I fear you must do it, Edland. It is entirely true that you would not, dressed as such, be likely to attract attention."

"Not likely?" He turned an incredulous gaze on her. "No one could possibly believe me to be a woman."

"When we have finished, not a question will arise," Andi said, keeping her voice light. "I assure you."

Edland looked as though he wanted to do anything in the entire world *except* take Andi's assurance. "This course of action is unacceptable. We shall proceed with mine." He bobbed his chin with authority.

Andi's patience, already in short supply, was about to reach its expiration date. "And being shot off your horse *is* acceptable?"

"Please, Edland," Catherine breathed. "You must do as Alexandra asks. I could not bear it if you were to . . . if . . ." Tears began to spill down her pale pink cheeks.

His expression softened immediately and concern filled his eyes. "I am sorry, my love," he whispered, folding her to his chest.

Andi tensed and held her breath, as did Mary who was beside her. Had they come this far only to have him blow it now? If he did, he didn't have the stuff of a potential hero. And Louisa would instantly nail him on that.

"For you, no sacrifice is too great." When he continued, it sounded as though he choked on the words, "I shall do it."

"Thank you, Edland," Catherine sniffed into his jacket.

The face he turned on Andi was less kind. "However, I say to you, once again, that no one shall believe me to be a woman."

"I understand, sir," she replied, feeling almost cheerful that the dizziness seemed to be making a retreat. That wine concoction wasn't bad, once a person got used to it. "And yet we must make our best attempt." She turned to Mary. "Bring me some

of your clothing," she instructed, "and take care
that no one sees you."

Mary nodded, looking both ready and glad to flee.

Edland held up a hand. "Once done, bring my
horse around to the door of the servants' hall."

Again, Mary nodded. But at the same time, Andi
shook her head. "It cannot be your hope that is
how you shall make your escape."

"It is." Edland kept his voice even, but there was
an audible edge to it.

"A female servant charging off the property on a
thoroughbred would most assuredly attract attention you would not wish, sir." She paused to let the
words sink in. "You could be shot at once."

His mouth opened and then closed again.

"It is true," Catherine whispered urgently. "Oh,
Edland. What are we to do?"

Edland cast his eyes at her and back at Andi.
"How then shall I reach my horse?"

"You will be required to walk to your horse.
Slowly. As if nothing is amiss. Mary can ensure that
the horse is still hidden in the trees."

Impatiently, Edland dismissed Mary with a wave of
his hand. Head bowed in deference, she curtsied
and shuffled out of the room, skirts swishing. For the
few minutes she was gone, no one moved or spoke.
Somewhere outside, the muffled noises of the day
continued. Horses, voices, the sounds of people
going about their chores.

The dull pain in Andi's shoulder became a reminder, not of the bullet and how close she'd come to
severe injury or death, but of Nathaniel. Of throwing
herself at his body, of feeling his arms wrapped
around her. Of how close they'd come to—

The door creaked open and Andi started guiltily, looking over to see that Mary had returned. She held the clothing, folded in piles in her arms, with near reverence. "No one saw me, miss," she said to Andi.

"Very good, Mary. Thank you." Andi took the clothing and, with a grateful smile, beckoned the maid to leave. "We shall proceed from here."

Edland, taking a step back, stared at the clothing as though it might attack him. Catherine regained her voice to make a faint gesture toward one corner. "My dressing closet," she said, her voice shaking. "You must dress in there, Edland." Then her eyes widened in alarm.

The thought of Edland taking his clothes off in her personal closet *would* shake Catherine up a bit. An intensely personal sort of occurrence in the Regency era. If it was Nathaniel, Andi thought, she herself would only be hoping he'd leave the door open. She wondered if that thought had crossed Catherine's mind. What began as a giggle ended as something closer to a snort. Blame it on that whatever it was she'd been made to drink.

Edland grabbed the pile of clothing, striding powerfully toward the small room Catherine had indicated and closing the door. Too bad for Catherine, who could have had a prewedding preview.

She looked at the other woman with a grin. "There can be no doubt of the gentleman's affection for you," she said.

"I cannot believe Mr. Evernham would allow himself to do such a thing," she confessed, looking in the direction of the dressing closet. "I am convinced it must cause him—" She stopped, apparently not sure how to finish the sentence.

"You must not cause yourself distress. It is, after all, another adventure in love."

"Your manner of speech is most extraordinary, Alexandra."

"It is quite different where I come from. And men there would have no such hesitation." So what if most were drag queens? Minor detail.

The other woman tipped her head to one side. "I do not believe you."

"Only think, Catherine, of the stories you will be able to tell your grandchildren."

Catherine's amusement dissolved into an embarrassed blush at the prospect of the act that would eventually lead to grandchildren. Andi decided to change the subject. "We shall have to put . . . or stuff . . . something into . . . the top of his dress," Andi said. She looked away, pretending to scan the room for something suitable. Now even she was becoming reluctant to offend Catherine's delicate sensibilities.

But Catherine, not seeming bothered in the least by that idea, murmured her agreement and focused on the task. She walked through the room, laying her hand lightly on different pieces of fabric, until she spied a small wrap, folded on a chair by the window. "This, perhaps?" She held it up for Andi's inspection.

"A good possibility." Andi took it from her and folded it a few different ways until she found the bulk she was looking for. "Perhaps if we were to push it into the top of the dress like this . . ."

Catherine gave it an appraising eye. "Yes," she said, "I believe it would do admirably."

At that point, Edland emerged, his arms stuck out at straight angles to his sides, the print dress hovering inches too short above his boots and gapping horribly in the bodice. His face was a mix of fury and humiliation.

Andi stared. Catherine put a hand to her mouth.

"For you," he said to Catherine, his voice rolling to the point of a low boil, "I have attempted to do as Alexandra wished. However, you can clearly see the foolishness of the idea."

"While it is true you do not make an entirely believable woman," Andi agreed, though he wasn't talking to her, "we can make this outfit passable enough to allow you a safe escape."

He shook his head with vehemence. "I have done as you wished. Now I shall take my leave. Dressed in my own clothing." He took a step backward.

"No!" Catherine cried.

A knock sounded at the door, startling all three. "Miss Catherine?" said a young female voice. "The master is asking for you."

Catherine started, emitting a small squeal of panic.

"Answer," Andi hissed. "Say that you will be there in a moment."

Catherine cleared her throat, managing to make even that sound gentle and well-bred. "Please tell my father I shall see him in a moment," she said, raising her voice enough to carry through the locked door.

"Yes, miss," came the reply. Then they heard footsteps in the hallway as the servant left.

"There is little time," Andi said, grabbing one of Edland's arms to keep him from escaping back into the dressing closet. "Make haste." Pain stabbed at her, but she refused to give in to it. Whatever the doctor had given her must be wearing off. Catherine took his other arm and both women held fast.

"This is a thoroughly foolish undertaking," he sputtered. "I shall be identified at once."

Andi let go of his arm long enough to grab the wrap she and Catherine had picked up moments ago. She pulled open the top of the dress, thanking the fates that Edland had a smooth chest, and began to stuff the fabric inside. "You would give me a woman's—" He stopped, twisting his mouth, apparently so stunned by the thought that he couldn't continue.

"You are not going to appear close to a woman if you cannot fill out the top." They had almost, but not quite, succeeded in endowing Edland with a bust size to rival Mary's ample one.

Catherine looked less certain, but she made no move to stop Andi. Even as she held tight to Edland's arm, she gave him a look of encouragement. "You must," she said softly.

He looked at her and hesitated, before grabbing the fabric to pull it out and throw it to the floor. "If there is nothing to be done about this," he said, "pray use my shirt so that I may put it back on and discard this women's clothing once I have left the grounds." Reaching behind him, he produced the shirt and held it up like a shield into battle.

Andi shook her head. This man could rival her when it came to throwing in some drama, but at least he was coming up with workable ideas of his own instead of resisting hers. Definitely progress. He might make it as a hero yet. "A sound idea," Andi agreed.

Catherine didn't look as though she had the courage to take the shirt and stuff it into the dress,

although Andi suspected that she might enjoy the
chance to try. Andi took the shirt from Edland,
folded it, and stuffed it into the bodice, wincing as
pain again shot from her shoulder. Once she had
finished, she gave it a little pat and stepped back to
survey the result with a critical eye. Edland gave a
wince of his own, she noticed, but his had nothing
to do with injury.

Next, she carefully folded a white triangular-
shaped wrap around him, covering as much as she
could of his chest, and turned her attention to his
head. Gesturing toward the dressing closet, she told
Catherine, "Mary must have brought a bonnet."

Scurrying into action, Catherine disappeared
into the small room, to emerge a moment later
with the desired object in her hand. She stopped
several feet away from Edland, her mouth open.

She couldn't take the final step to put it on his
head, probably fearing his perception of her part
in this whole scheme. But there wasn't any time to
waste. "Please," Andi said, stabbing toward it with
her finger. "You must hurry, Catherine."

Edland closed his eyes, lifting his chin upward, as
though he just couldn't take any more.

Oh, for Heaven's sake, Andi thought, is that what
I look like sometimes? She hoped not. It wasn't that
attractive.

When the bonnet had been placed on his head
and his stray hairs tucked beneath it, Andi took a
final step back to view the effect. The boots would
have to stay, there was nothing she could do about
that, but the breeches he had insisted on keeping
on gave the skirt a fullness that did help, since Mary
was plump and Edland wasn't.

She desperately wanted to giggle, but knew he was too close to the edge. One misstep from her and she imagined he would hurl himself back into the dressing closet, tearing apart the servant effect they had worked so hard to create and rocketing down the stairs, out the door, and onto his horse, certain to take a shot through the heart before he'd made it off the grounds. That wouldn't help anyone.

And then, the soft sound of semihysterical laughter was coming from Catherine, who put a hand in front of her mouth but could not suppress it. "Forgive me," she managed to say, "but you do look most amusing."

Andi's eyes shot to Edland. This could be a tricky time to laugh at a man, even for Catherine.

He appeared startled, just for a moment, before his eyes warmed. "To hear your laughter again." He stopped, seeming at a loss for words, and then smiled at both Catherine and Andi.

The softer side of Edland Evernham. A Hallmark moment. But they couldn't continue to stand here. It was too dangerous. "It is time," Andi said, suddenly less sure of herself. "You must take your leave and so must Catherine." Had her sole reason for doing this been to stick a pin in Edland's arrogant bubble? She hoped not. She believed Mary's statement that the closest route of escape was used only by the female servants. Edland would stick out like a sore thumb in men's clothing.

And if this whole scenario provided a little entertainment, it would be a side benefit. Besides, it had been somewhat of a revelation to see how much fun a drama queen, or in this case, drama king, might not be. She might have to mull that one over a bit more.

Now was the time for action, not contemplation. "Take care to slow your steps when approaching your horse," she said, infusing the instruction with urgency. "Or you will raise suspicion. And with that caution, you must take your leave."

Catherine nodded, her eyes shining. "I shall meet you," she said to Edland, "in Wickston. Before the sun sets."

He nodded, the bonnet bobbing on his head. "I shall be there. Waiting," he promised solemnly. They gazed into each other's eyes.

Andi crossed the room to the door, opening it to stick her head out and survey the hallway. She turned back. "The way is clear. Go!"

Edland hesitated briefly before going through the door and into the hallway. The glance he threw at Andi over his shoulder as he reached the stairs told her he would not forget what she had done. Not that it warmed her heart; rather, it seemed to be more of a warning than thanks.

"He will thank me when they are happily married," she told herself after he'd gone. Fervently, she hoped she was right. If she wasn't, and he had to meet an ungracious end while in women's clothing . . . He thought being the only dark-haired one in a family of blondes was bad. She turned her attention back to Catherine. "In speaking with your father, it will be necessary to appear as though you acknowledge the error of your ways and are resigned to his wishes," she advised.

"You would wish me to lie to my father?"

Andi shook her head in disbelief. Just when she

thought Catherine had taken a giant step forward, she retreated back two. "It is necessary. Tell a lie or *live* a lie. And kinder, when you consider it, because your father seeks only what is best for you, yet is unable to see what that is."

Catherine nodded slowly. "Yes."

Andi dropped her gaze to the floor, searching it for a moment before she asked, "Catherine? You are absolutely convinced Edland is the one you love? The one you want to be with forever?" Slowly, she brought her eyes back up to peer anxiously into the face of the other woman. She had to know she wasn't pushing Catherine into Edland's arms just because it would further her own goal. Things might have started out that way, but she couldn't let them continue unless she knew, beyond a doubt, that the two belonged together.

"I am." Catherine's tone, which until now had largely sounded shaky and tentative, turned firm. "I see now that I so desperately attempted to push him away only because of how very much I love him. But I did not believe I deserved him."

"*You* did not deserve *him?*"

"He is the gentleman who lives in my dreams," Catherine said softly, a smile playing at the corners of her mouth. She toyed with the sleeve of her dress, rolling the fabric between her fingers. "When I close my eyes and until I again open them, it is he who dwells there. He knows me better than I know myself. That is why he chose to stay away, to reach me only by letter. To wait until the time was right. Until I was ready to claim my life. With him."

He would have stayed away until it was too late, Andi wanted to interject, if not for her interference. But instead, she pulled her mouth in tight and nodded her head. "I had to be sure."

"Mr. Evernham may seem . . . abruptly natured at times," Catherine conceded. "But truly, he has the kindest of hearts. He has been grievously hurt and keeps that part of himself concealed."

Andi contemplated that for a moment. She could see it, she supposed. It did seem the man had been treated badly, solely because of speculation he was the product of his mother's affair with another man. Could be enough to make a person develop a few thorns.

"From him," Catherine went on, sounding as though she marveled at the words as they came out, "I acquire strength I did not know I possessed."

Andi nodded. "Strength of purpose is indeed desirable. As it would be good," she suggested, "if you could encourage him to show the kind side of himself to other people. At every opportunity."

"They would be most surprised to discover it."

The two women smiled at each other for a moment. Then Andi's smile died on her face, and she screwed up her courage enough to force herself to ask, "Do you know much of Nathaniel Chamberlain? Has he told you the story of his niece? His brother?" She paused. "Or, have you asked?"

Catherine drew her brows together in a delicate furrow. "His niece seems a charming child. His brother?" She shook her head. "I confess I do not understand . . ." Her voice trailed off.

"His niece is, sadly, an orphan. Nathaniel has taken the responsibility for her care upon himself. He is a gentleman who puts the needs of others above his own."

Andi held her breath while Catherine appeared to think about this. Would it make a difference for her to know that about him? Andi had to take that risk, or she couldn't live with her actions to change the storyline. Then, the other woman said with a small smile, "I understood there to be certain rumors about the gentleman, ones that suggested he could have somewhat of a rakish side."

"A rakish side. While that is true, I believe the generous, devoted side of him to be vastly more important." Andi looked at Catherine long and hard. "His sacrifices are of no consequence to you?"

Catherine eyed her with slight suspicion. "Each of us makes sacrifices, Alexandra. Mr. Evernham himself has long sacrificed the good opinion he is due."

It didn't matter to Catherine. It really didn't. Edland was the only person she wanted. And Andi didn't have to wonder anymore if she was doing the right thing. "Of course. Absolutely, he has." She clapped her hands together. "Now, on to the wedding," she said. "Your task is to convince your father that you are willing to do all that he asks, no matter how misguided."

Catherine nodded.

"And then," said Andi, her confidence suddenly waning, "we will be required to hope that Louisa keeps to her bed and does not begin writing until events have progressed too far for her to turn them back."

Piece of cake.

# Chapter Seventeen

Andi stood at Catherine's window, watching, as Edland, the fabric of his dress flapping and the white bonnet sailing off his head in midflight, became smaller and then disappeared. It wasn't until she could no longer see him that she allowed herself to relax enough to draw a full breath. He'd made it. Undetected. And now was off on his way to Wickston and a marriage to Catherine.

What would Louisa do with this turn of events? Andi couldn't be sure. Maybe once the author discovered what had happened, she would fling herself on her bed for good this time, permanently discouraged by characters who had the nerve to seize control of their own destinies.

But if Louisa *did* refuse to finish the book, that could mean, according to Nathaniel, that all of the people in this story, including . . . she swallowed hard . . . even herself, might end up flailing around in the universe without ever really existing. No happy ending. Not even the prospect of one.

Nathaniel. No matter what he would think of her

now, she had to tell him, warn him. The story was about to change dramatically, and he needed to be prepared for it. Never mind that she would be forced to confess to interfering. Again. He would have to understand why.

Turning from the window, she crossed the room and slipped into the hallway, hoping with every bone in her body that she could manage to escape detection by anyone but the man she sought. All around her, the house appeared deserted, not even a servant in sight. Through the halls she walked, her shoes padding lightly on the floor, past the framed pictures of disapproving Havington ancestors, until she came to the main staircase and began to descend it on tiptoe.

She wondered how Horatio Havington would handle rattling around in this gigantic house alone, now that Catherine would be gone. People in this era didn't sell and move to a condo. And they didn't exactly rent out a wing. Could be best for the blustery old man to waste away here by himself. Might make him appreciate what he'd had in the daughter whose happiness he'd thrown away so callously.

She reached the bottom of the stairs and made her way toward the drawing room, intent on seeking out Nathaniel. He couldn't be far away. She stopped short when she heard a voice coming from inside the room.

It was Havington's, speaking in a gentle, affectionate tone Andi had never before heard him use. She hesitated, then stopped to flatten herself against the wall and listen.

"My dearest daughter," Havington was saying, "I know this courtship has at times caused you concern, and for that I express my sympathy. But you must know that I carry out the wishes of your departed mother in arranging this fortuitous marriage between you and Chamberlain."

A pause, and then it sounded as though he sighed deeply. A sense of foreboding began to steal over Andi as she heard his self-pitying, pious tone. She moved closer, until she stood just outside the door. How far would he take this? Catherine didn't come close to being strong willed when it came to dealing with her father. Or anyone else, for that matter.

"Ensure that she is well married, Mr. Havington, your mother said to me before she took her last breath. You were but an infant. Too young to know that as your mother lay dying, she thought only of her daughter. And that I gave my solemn vow to carry forth her wishes, no matter the difficulty."

Catherine made a muffled sound. Andi couldn't tell whether it was one of protest or sorrow. Havington was playing hardball by trading on Catherine's perceived obligation to her deceased mother.

He continued, "Your mother was of an excellent family. She knew that making a good marriage for you would be the only way to secure your happiness. It was, of course, just such an arrangement, made for her, that brought her a fine life, though far too short."

Andi strained her ears. There was no detectable response from Catherine. She stuffed her fingers in her mouth and bit down to keep herself from shouting at the two in the drawing room. How could the man do this to his own daughter?

"Evernham is not a match for you," Havington

went on. "His situation is such that even his own family shuns him. Unfortunate, perhaps, but the fact of the matter all the same. And not without cause."

"His mother—" Catherine's voice was very small.

"Is as great an empty-headed fool as ever she was." Andi's ears perked up at the obvious distaste in Havington's voice. She frowned. Sounded to her like more than neighborly judgment in his words. There was something else there.

Catherine must have wondered the same thing. "Have you made her acquaintance, Father?" Andi heard her ask. "If not, I must ask how you would presume to offer such an opinion about a son she cherishes? And about the lady herself?"

Andi relaxed. Catherine seemed to be veering close to downright spunkiness.

Her sense of relief didn't last as long as the long silence that followed. She put a hand to her heart. What would Havington do, fly into a rage? Now that she thought about it, this late entry of spunkiness wasn't a good thing when she had specifically instructed Catherine to give her father the impression she was going along with his plan for her to marry Nathaniel. In fact, spunkiness could pretty well work against them right about now. She took a step closer.

Finally, Horatio Havington's footsteps sounded, signaling he had likely risen to cross to another side of the room. And then he spoke, "It may surprise you, daughter, to find that I am indeed acquainted with Lucretia Evernham." He cleared his throat. "I presented her, when her son Edland was yet quite small, with an offer of marriage."

Catherine's sudden intake of breath, luckily, matched Andi's. Horrible things began to race through her mind, things she didn't even want to put words to, but did, anyway. Could Havington have been the mysterious man who fathered Edland and then cast him aside? *No.* That would be too awful. Too—

Had Andi actually—she began to choke. Set . . . Catherine . . . up . . . to . . . marry . . . her . . . half brother? She pulled the fingers she'd been biting away from her mouth, laying both hands and her forehead against the wall. It couldn't be. Not possible. Let a heart attack do her in now. She might as well go quietly. If she was going to have to undo this whole thing now, life in this era, or any other, might not be worth it. At least in this time zone, sex wouldn't have yet entered into the relationship. *Eewww.* She shuddered.

In the next moment, her fears were, thankfully, laid to rest. "I had made her acquaintance," Havington said mildly, "in earlier days. She and her husband often attended balls here when your mother was alive. We found them both to be pleasurable company, and she and your mother called upon each other with some regularity. Once her husband died in an accident so tragic, and the child was born, however, she was rightfully excluded from all proper society."

Andi pulled away from the wall and put a hand to her temple. She had definitely not seen this one coming. She had to think.

But Havington didn't give her much time to regroup. After a brief pause, he continued, "I found myself with a motherless child and no mistress of this household. It was my hope that, in offering marriage to Mrs. Evernham, I could fulfill both needs, while also assisting her in regaining her name. It seemed a highly generous thing to do, but I did know her to be a kind person."

"Oh, Father," Catherine said. Was she shocked? Appalled? Andi couldn't tell.

"It was a rash proposal, one not carefully considered. And Mrs. Evernham rejected it quite thoroughly."

When Catherine spoke, it was with tears in her voice. "Father, I had no idea. It must have been a most difficult time for you. To have offered marriage and to have been rejected . . ." Her voice trailed off.

Andi, listening, balled her hands into fists. So Edland's mother had shown sense *and* taste. Good for her. *Don't let him get to you, Catherine.*

Havington spoke again, a martyr's pity filling his voice. "It was an insult to your mother's memory and an act I did not repeat."

There was a scraping of a chair and then Catherine's voice, too faint to hear. Andi envisioned her hugging her father. *A father–daughter reconciliation is good,* she thought anxiously, *but don't get too wrapped up in feeling sorry for him, Catherine, or all of our plans are going to go down the tubes.*

Think how he's treated Edland. How callous he is about Edland's mother. And how he sent a stable hand after me who tried to hurt me in a horrible way. Regency-era and cultural differences aside, Havington was a pretty despicable person, to Andi's way of thinking.

"So you see that I could never allow you to marry Edland Evernham," he said. "Your dear mother would have had her heart broken to know you would have no hope of being accepted in the best homes." He sighed, long and loud. "I think only of you, the daughter I have raised. On my own, without the benefit of a woman's care."

Catherine said something Andi couldn't hear. Unable to stand it any longer, she poked her head around the edge of the door. There she saw Catherine in her father's bearlike embrace.

"With Chamberlain," he said, "you will have the best of everything and, along with it, the respect of the entire county. His family name is a fine one and your children will bear it proudly. A bit of trouble recently, but nothing worthy of long memory."

He pushed her out to arm's length, searching her face with a grave expression. "You must always think of your future children, Catherine. I nearly did not do so in making a proposal to Lucretia Evernham, and she most certainly did not do so in producing a child who would never know the benefit of society's approval." He gave a loud sigh. "Not giving thought to the well-being of a child is indeed the cruelest of crimes."

*You hypocrite,* Andi wanted to scream. *How can you even say that with a straight face? You are not putting your own child's happiness first. If you did, you would give her your blessing, your best wishes, and throw her and Edland a huge wedding!* She pressed both fists against her temples now, trying to stifle the agonized cry that was ready to escape. She had to let Catherine handle this and call her father for the fool he was.

*Come on, Catherine. Let him have it.*

But instead there was silence. Oh, please, don't have that mean . . . Not when we're so close. Not when the plans are in motion, when Catherine will marry Edland in just an hour or so. On legs that felt wooden, Andi moved from the door to walk into the room. She put a hand up to lean against the wall, but neither of the two inside noticed her.

Her instincts had been right, the sense of foreboding accurate. She watched as Catherine's head dropped, her thin shoulders crumpled, and she began shaking with sobs. "Oh, Father," she cried, "I have so very nearly deceived you yet again."

Andi groaned. Havington looked up at her, but only for a second. "Don't, Catherine," she pleaded, her throat raw, but to no avail. And then, she felt her shoulders begin to hunch and her chest curve inward as the invisible hand closed in. *Not now. Please, not now.*

Everything in the room suspended for a few seconds; then Catherine's tearful voice continued, "I am to meet Mr. Evernham in Wickston, Father, where I have agreed to become his wife. He waits for me even now."

Andi's heart, and along with it, every hope she'd harbored of a happily ever after with Nathaniel, tumbled and crashed, even as her character's body registered shock at Catherine's words. "Oh, but this is dreadful," the high-pitched voice that came from her mouth trilled.

*Damn right it's dreadful, you twit that has control of my voice. Horrible, devastating, tragic, inhuman even.* That Catherine spilled her guts and ruined all chance for her happiness. Threw away a guy who loved her because of a father who worked her over with a guilt no parent should ever be allowed to inflict on a child.

Horatio Havington drew up straight. "This cannot be true."

"It is, Father." Catherine, her eyes filled with tears, nodded. "I am so very sorry to have caused you such disappointment."

Havington's eyes veered first one way, then the other. "I can see that I may have given Evernham too little credit," he said fiercely. "He seems to be most persistent in attempting to claim your affections."

"But I—" Catherine began, but closed her mouth and fell silent.

Andi wrestled with the author but couldn't work up the concentration needed to make it a real battle. She heard herself clucking her tongue in recrimination, while inside her thoughts raged. *Go on. Tell your father that you love Edland. That it's beyond ridiculous to blame a man for the circumstances of his birth. As though he could do anything about it. Tell him!*

Catherine stood with her head bowed, a vision of daughterly obedience, awaiting her father's next move. The room echoed with an ominous stillness.

Inside her body, not visible to anyone who looked at her, Andi cried. Huge, wracking tears. For Catherine. For Edland. For Nathaniel. For Julia. And for herself.

"Then married you shall be," Havington said at last, with a bite to his tone that belied the seeming graciousness of the words.

Catherine raised her head. "Father?"

"To Mr. Chamberlain, of course," her father continued pleasantly. "I have this day secured a special license, though I could not have imagined it would be needed so quickly."

"But Mr. Evernham—"

"Will see you properly married," her father finished. "I shall summon Mr. Chamberlain." His eyes took on a steely glint. "If Wickston is where you wish to marry, then Wickston it shall certainly be."

He gestured impatiently at Andi. "You there shall serve as attendant. Yes, that is most fitting." His eyes glittered as he cast them back at Catherine. "Have no concern, my daughter. You shall become a wife today." Then he strode toward the doors, leaving a stunned Andi and Catherine in his wake.

Right before sweeping through the open doors, he turned back. "Come," he commanded. Andi began to follow him, her head down, staring at the tips of her shoes as they moved out from under her dress with each mincing step. Catherine tried to mount a protest. "But, Father, surely my dress . . ." Her voice carried down the hallway.

His boomed back at her. "Will do nicely. This is to be a small wedding. Not the one you had perhaps wished for, but Mr. Evernham has seen to it that it must take place sooner than we had thought."

"Yes, Father," came Catherine's dutiful response as she and Andi hurried to keep up with him. Andi inwardly cursed the feet that were carrying her after Havington, despite her intentions to the contrary.

Once in the entryway, he snapped his fingers, calling for his servant. He barked out instructions to have his carriage brought around, sending the servant scampering away, before turning back to the two women.

"I shall instruct Mary to bring the flowers I saw her gathering only this morning. Though they will pale next to her beauty, my daughter must have flowers at her wedding." He gave a tight smile.

Catherine trembled, Andi saw, though her father appeared to be making a great effort not to notice. "This is the only course of action," he said gruffly. "We shall not chance another misguided effort from Mr. Evernham. Now go and get your wrap and your bonnet. There's a good girl."

*Just say no!* Andi tried frantically to telepath the message to Catherine, who stood miserably at her side. *Tell him this is not the wedding you have dreamed of, that you need time to plan it, to have all of your friends there. Time for us to figure out another way out of this.*

But the message didn't make it through a telepathic service provider. Instead, as if in a daze, Catherine headed for the stairway. Andi's legs also began to move, once again following obediently behind. Her mouth opened, but she bit down hard on her lip to keep from speaking. Whatever words Louisa thought should come out of her, Andi would do her level best to make sure they didn't.

The two women proceeded up the stairs; Andi struggled desperately against the invisible hold, trying to get Louisa to let her talk to Catherine. To say something that wasn't empty-headed and incredibly unhelpful.

Okay, if Catherine wasn't going to stand up to her father, to tell him she wouldn't be married today, then they could go out the window, steal a horse, do *anything* in their power to make it to Wickston before Catherine's father did. A rope out of bed sheets. Disguise themselves in servant clothing. Have Mary sabotage the carriage. *Something.*

A mental image of Nathaniel and Catherine passed in front of her, both of them utterly miserable, with children crowding, wailing at their feet.

Locked into a marriage that neither wanted, but the mores of the time dictated. Catherine would become Lucretia Evernham all over again, forced into affairs as she looked for the love she'd lost forever, trying to mend her broken heart until she finally lost hope and retreated from the world in despair.

Andi couldn't let that happen. It was as much about Catherine now as it was Nathaniel. The woman might have trouble standing up for herself, but she didn't deserve this. It wasn't fair.

She willed herself to concentrate. Hard. Though her tongue felt as though it were swollen to twice its size, she forced out the words, "You cannot let him do this," in her funny, high-pitched voice, just as they reached Catherine's bedroom.

Catherine turned to her, eyes luminous. And empty. "I shall marry Mr. Chamberlain. And learn to love him. He is a fine gentleman. My mother was a wise woman, I am told. She could not have been wrong."

Andi stared. Louisa's words. But the author was having trouble writing the expression on Catherine's face, which didn't match the words she spoke.

After a deep breath, Andi forced out the words she wanted to say. "How can you be certain this is what your mother would have wished?"

Catherine tipped her head, looking at Andi as if she were dense in the head. "I must trust my father."

"Has he offered you reason to do so?" Treasonous words. It surprised even Andi that Louisa would have let them emerge.

"He is my father. He has suffered her loss most

terribly." Catherine's eyes filled with tears. "She died after bearing me."

Andi's eyes stung with tears of empathy. "You bear no blame for your mother's death."

The other woman's gaze veered away. "Nevertheless," she whispered.

"Then I shall find Mr. Chamberlain and talk with him. He must know that . . ." Andi gulped and tried again, ". . . that your father has thrust this upon you."

Catherine looked at her in alarm. "Father awaits us in the carriage. We must not delay."

"Let him wait." To Andi's surprise, Louisa released her hold long enough to allow Andi to say the words with at least some of the disgust she truly felt. She imagined the author sitting up straight, a puzzled expression on her face as she tried to figure out where the words had come from.

*To you from me, Louisa.*

Though the author had allowed her to say the words, it turned out that Andi had to fight Louisa every minute and every step as she fled down the hallway and the back stairs, looking frantically for Nathaniel. Servants scattered out of her way as she passed, sweeping aside their skirts and shaking their heads. After several minutes, on the verge of despair, she threw a side door open and found him standing just steps beyond it, next to his horse.

Inexplicably, the author's hold on her eased when she stepped into the outside air. She could even straighten her shoulders. Almost. But she had no time to think about why that might be. She'd have to be grateful for it and hope Louisa had instead decided to occupy herself with Catherine's preparations for the fateful ride into Wickston.

If she startled Nathaniel with her sudden out-of-breath appearance at his side, he didn't let it show. Turning slowly toward her, he fixed her with a calm gaze, the horse's reins tossed casually across one palm. The black jacket he wore accentuated the long, lean lines of his body, while the light-colored breeches, tucked into tall riding boots, clearly outlined his powerfully muscular legs. In his other hand, he held a black hat by its brim, seeming ready to toss it on his head at any moment in a fine display of what the well-dressed Regency hero would wear.

The man of her dreams, inside and out. Ready to do what he considered the right thing, no matter what it cost him personally.

"You cannot go through with this," Andi said. Relief washed through her at the sound of her own voice. There was still a chance.

His dark eyes held hers. In them, she could see both resignation and determination. But he said nothing.

She wasn't about to wait until he did. "You *can* fight her," Andi said, her voice cracking on the last word. "I should know. I had to fight her to be able to leave Catherine and find you. Would you believe that to be Louisa's idea?"

"Her health is waning, as is her vision." He paused and she knew it wasn't just for effect. He wanted the words to sink in, no matter how much she didn't want to hear them. "This is the last manuscript she will undertake." Raising a hand, the cuff of his shirt a stark white against the black of his jacket, he touched her cheek with strong, sun-browned fingers. "We have had too short a time together, but I confess I find myself reluctant to leave you, Alexandra." He made a small sound of regret, his eyes crinkling. "The fire that burns within you is something Louisa disregards at her peril."

"Then don't leave. Don't marry her. All you have to do is say 'I do not' instead of 'I do.' It's easy. Try it with me now."

He dropped his hand. "I must ensure a life beyond the book for my niece, for Catherine . . ." Again, he paused. "And for you."

"Me?" She would have shrieked the word, but somehow, it had turned into a whisper.

"If Louisa is not vexed by your character, you will be allowed to continue on, to one day marry in this world she has created. Or perhaps return to the place from whence you have come."

"I don't exist to please Louisa," Andi said miserably. "I'm the one character she did *not* invent, and I can leave when I want to." She raised a hand to touch the stone securely tucked into the bodice of her dress. "At least, I think I can."

"Ah," he said, "then leave you should."

"But I don't want that. I want things to turn out right, for you, for Catherine. Amelia. Julia." With a soft gasp of surprise, she realized she meant it. She'd come to believe in these people, in more ways than one. She worked her way around a sudden lump in her throat. "It can happen if we stand up to her."

"That is simply not to be." He straightened. "I am the hero of Louisa's book. With that comes a certain responsibility. I cannot be responsible for you meeting an uncertain fate."

"Don't you get it? You don't have to defend me, protect me." Tears stung the backs of her eyes. The very things that had drawn her to him—his sense of loyalty, honor, and unshakable sense of right and wrong—would prevent him from sweeping her into his arms and riding away on his horse. Away from the Havingtons, Annabelle, Louisa . . .

Even in a fantasy life, Andi couldn't get a hero. Hello convent. Sister Andi, devoting her days to ministering to the perpetually lovelorn.

"In this life," he said, "we are not always free to do as we wish. But perhaps in another . . ." He took her hand; then his mouth moved close to hers, so slowly that her eyes widened and her heart leapt in anticipation. But just before their lips touched, he stopped and abruptly changed direction, instead landing the kiss on her forehead, beneath the soft curls that didn't belong on her head. She felt disappointment rush through every part of her, her stomach wrapping itself tightly into yet another knot.

He didn't have to say good-bye. She knew it as clearly as if he had shouted it. And there would be no point in her protests, in her trying desperately to make him see things her way and not Louisa's. Nathaniel would do what he thought right.

She dropped her chin to focus at a spot of grass on the ground, unable to look at him, to see in his eyes what she knew he had to do. "Good-bye," she whispered. Against her better judgment, she looked up at him. "If this is the only way it can be, then I hope you and Catherine will be happy." A little arrow pierced her every hope and fervent wish.

He pulled her to him in one swift embrace, pressing her so hard against him that she could hear the beating of his heart through his shirt. She loved that heart. It didn't let people down, didn't veer from its course. Because of the steady heartbeat pounding against her ear, Julia would have a heritage, a social standing, and an uncle who adored her. She closed her eyes and listened.

Then he released her and, with another kiss to the top of her head, turned to his horse. "I must be off to Wickston," he said, facing the animal. "And I believe the carriage awaits you."

"Yes." Andi's mouth formed the word without sound. This time, her shoulders curled in a defeat all on their own. She'd never felt so completely and utterly alone in her entire life.

# Chapter Eighteen

The carriage, as befitting Horatio Havington's station in life, was both a lovely and imposing one, polished to a sheen that reflected in the waning sun, with two beautifully matched horses standing at attention to carry its occupants along the dirt road and away from the house.

The three females making the journey were folded inside, while Havington and Nathaniel mounted their horses to accompany them. Julia, a baffled expression on her pinched white face and her feet dangling uncertainly from her perch on the leather seat, sat quietly next to the woman who was to become her mother figure. Catherine sat very still and stiffly upright, a brave smile pushing its way onto her lips.

Andi sat across from the two, her eyes flitting from Catherine to the scene rolling by outside her window. Hills, some green, some brown, for miles ahead and behind. No telephones, cell towers, or freeways.

She wondered if Nathaniel had insisted on Julia

riding along to test Catherine as a stepmother. If the heroine didn't work well in a mother role, how could the three be happy ever after? But with a small sigh that Louisa didn't allow her to breathe out, she told herself it was only wishful thinking on her part.

She looked back as Catherine bent her head toward Julia, murmuring something Andi couldn't hear. The little girl nodded, pressing the fingers in her lap together tightly, and Catherine turned away, still with that tremulous smile. She appeared resigned to becoming Nathaniel's wife, as though she had pushed Edland to the back of her mind, where he would firmly remain.

"It is so very exciting," Andi said, her voice the high-pitched one of Louisa's doing. "You shall be married to a fine gentleman today." *Oh, for God's sake, Louisa, do you have to rub it in?*

Catherine's smile stretched further, but her eyes, blank and haunted, did not match it. At the same time, Andi's heart swelled with sympathy for the woman; she wanted to congratulate her on not making it easy for the author. The realization struck Andi with a sudden force. In her own way, Catherine was trying to put her own mark on the story.

The carriage bounced along the road, the wheels hitting one rut after another. Andi's arm shot across to make sure Julia didn't fall from her seat and onto the floor. At the same time, Catherine's hand moved in the same direction, pausing, fingers splayed, until she dropped it again into her lap. Then she settled for a raised eyebrow, which lowered again as she apparently became satisfied the danger had passed.

Motherly concern? Not nearly enough shown. Louisa must have had trouble with that one.

The road became smooth and Catherine turned away to gaze out the window. Andi watched as her eyes landed on Nathaniel. The path had widened enough for him to ride next to the carriage.

Chin high and thrust forward, Nathaniel stared straight ahead. *Make a run for it,* Andi wanted to lean out the window and urge him. *I've seen that horse in action. No one will catch him. Or you.* Her thoughts shot back to that day, to his fear he had injured her, to walking beside him.

Catherine spoke. "Yes, I shall be married to a fine gentleman today," she said, repeating the words that had tripped out of Andi's mouth, even as she stared at Nathaniel. Her eyes swept back to Andi. "I owe him much, you understand. Once we are safely married, my life shall begin once again. I fear I have not been thinking rationally of late."

Not thinking rationally. Louisa's words.

Another mental picture. Catherine on the floor in her bedroom at the Chamberlain house, wrists slashed, the blood leaking from her still, white body, a victim of the ultimate realization that she had only once been truly loved. *Louisa be damned,* Andi thought viciously, fighting again for control of her body. But the author held her tight.

Louisa, failing health and all, was apparently determined to finish this story exactly as she wished and was not about to let one unruly character get in her way.

On the other side of the carriage, Horatio Havington rode up on his own horse, peering in the windows intently. What was he doing, taking a head count? The enforcer. *Guess who's the bull in the china shop now. Everything is crashing and breaking in his wake and he doesn't have a clue. Worse yet, he doesn't care.*

As they rolled into town with clattering hooves and creaking wheels, Nathaniel and Havington rode ahead, in clouds of dust, to lead the way. Andi stared dully out the window. From what she could see, everything and everyone in the village seemed shriveled and deathly pale, and the odor that wafted from the village wasn't an attractive one. Children, dressed in little more than rags, hovered in doorways, darting furtive glances at the fine carriage.

A romantic setting, indeed. Why in the world had Edland chosen Wickston? *Edland.* Oh my God, he would be at the chapel, waiting.

They pulled to a stop before a small, inauspicious building, all three passengers waiting until Havington opened the door. He held his hand up to the women. Catherine and Julia took it as they stepped lightly down to the ground. Andi's hand extended as well, but before he could take it, she reached over with her other hand to slap it down, leaving his hanging awkwardly in the air. Surprise flickered in his eyes.

*Take that, Louisa,* she thought.

He recovered quickly, insisting that Catherine enter the chapel first, with Andi right behind her. Under the author's direction, they did as they were told. It was small, cold, and dark inside, the sanctuary lit only by a few flickering candles on the walls and small windows that let in what little was left of the setting sun.

An accurate reflection, Andi decided, of the emptiness of Louisa's plot. And the light in

Nathaniel's eyes, which was about to leave the story for good.

Edland waited in the front row, his head bowed and his fingers pressed against his temples. At the sound their shoes made on the stone floor, he turned and leapt to his feet, his expression exploding with joy at the sight of the woman who was to be his bride. He held out his arms. "At last you have come."

Once again Andi found herself struck by the incredible change that came over the man when he was in the presence of Catherine. All of the haughtiness, the too perfectly chiseled features, and the brusque manner seemed to fade away, leaving a man who wanted nothing in life but the woman he loved. She stepped away from the two of them and turned toward the side of the chapel, hating what she would see next. Should she warn him? Couldn't he tell something was wrong by Catherine's stiffness? By her face?

And then the sound of boots rang out on the stone. Edland looked up as Havington strode into the chapel, every inch of him radiating the fact that he was enjoying each second of the pain he was about to inflict on the man whose only crime was loving his daughter.

Edland's expression hardened immediately. "Sir," he began, in something close to a growl.

Nathaniel entered next, his bearing regal and his expression a carefully composed and unreadable mask. Julia trailed behind him, darting uncertain glances up at her uncle. As Andi watched, Julia's tiny hand reached for his much larger one. He paused and then took the child's fingers, holding them firmly in his own. Nathaniel nodded once, sharply, at Edland, whose features had changed to a dark, thunderous warning.

Andi clutched the freshly picked red flowers that had been wrenched from Mary's startled grasp, crushing the stems between her gloved fingers. Her shoulders curled in submission, telling her that she was still subject to someone else's power. Ill health or not, Louisa was running this show.

She moved to hover against the wall of the chapel, watching as the rector entered from a side door, his weary face lined and shadows of fatigue under his eyes. He drew up short when he saw the people who had assembled in his chapel.

"I intend to be the man marrying your daughter today, Havington," Edland proclaimed boldly; but Andi, peering through her lashes, could see that his hands shook. *Courage, Edland,* she wanted to shout.

"My daughter shall indeed be married today." Havington directed himself to Edland, cold steel underlying the words. "But it shall not be to you." He reached a hand backward, trying to draw Nathaniel forward. Instead, Nathaniel eyed him with what looked to be a cold mistrust, sidestepped his arm, and moved ahead on his own.

"This is the man who is to become her husband," Havington announced. "Stand aside, Evernham. The matter shall at last be settled."

Andi watched as Edland's mouth worked furiously. *Yes!* He was fighting. She held her breath.

And then, inexplicably, he seemed to give up the battle, looking at Catherine with a raw longing in his eyes. "If it is he whom she loves, I shall stand aside, sir," he said quietly, then took a step to his left.

Louisa won, Andi realized with an outrage she wasn't allowed to express. Edland couldn't, or wouldn't, stand up to her. And now, she'd made him out to be a wimp, one who will not even fight for the woman he loves.

The next thing she knew, she was shoved ahead to the altar, the remaining petals from her now pitiful bouquet scattering to the floor, like drops of blood on the stone floor. Havington's boot came down firmly, crushing them.

The befuddled rector frowned at the group that did not include Edland. "Am I to understand . . . ?" His voice trailed off as he seemed to realize that he did not understand in the least.

Havington shoved a piece of paper before the rector's face. "A special license," he bellowed. The echo of his voice seemed to bounce off all four chapel walls.

In the silence that followed, the door at the back of the chapel creaked open and, a moment later, crashed shut. All eyes turned to see a petite woman, hair piled high on her head, sweep inside with a crush of skirts and cape, and then stop, surveying the scene before her. No one moved, not even Horatio Havington, whose jaw, Andi saw when she stole a look at him, had dropped open.

The woman began marching toward them, her skirt swaying elegantly, shoes tapping a brisk rhythm on the stone. When she drew closer, Andi saw that her features were tight with anger.

Edland spoke first, saying simply, "Mother."

The shoe tapping continued until the woman reached the altar. Her demeanor told Andi that Edland's mother had more than a few things to say, which could work to Andi's advantage. If Louisa was so busy writing the action this woman with the red hair promised, she might not notice Andi hovering at the edge of the scene. And that usually meant that she could regain some control. On tiptoe, Andi tried to back away, but found herself hemmed in by the stunned group at the altar.

Blue eyes flashing, the woman turned to Horatio Havington, every inch of her body seeming to shake with fury. "My son is to be married today. I have come to witness the occasion."

"That may well be, madam, but it is not my daughter he shall marry." Havington's eyes narrowed as he glared down at the woman standing before him, whose level of ire seemed to match her fiery hair, but Andi, standing at close range to him, thought she could see at least a hint of uncertainty in his eyes. She tried to lean forward for an even better look, to see if she could dare to hope for a turn of events. No luck. Louisa kept her firmly in place.

The woman placed both hands on her hips. "He shall marry the woman he loves. I intend to ensure it."

"Lucretia Evernham," Havington spat, "you will leave this place at once. I shall not allow you to stand in the way of my daughter's happiness. Which, I would remind you once again, is most certainly not with your son." He twisted the last word until it came out sounding close to something obscene.

Lucretia, gloved hands still on her hips, turned from Havington to his daughter. "My dear," she said, her voice shaking with what sounded like barely contained rage, "my son professes himself most assuredly in love with you. Tell me, who is it you shall marry?"

Catherine dropped her gaze to the floor. "My father wishes—"

"I did not inquire as to what your father wishes," Lucretia said, sounding as though the words came through gritted teeth. "I am all too well versed with the methods your father uses to bend another's will toward his."

"Lucretia." Havington's voice seemed to hold a clear warning.

"It is the truth. It is only because I did not permit your threats to sway me that you did not force *me* into marriage. Had I been so foolish as to do so, I would have lived a life of intolerable misery as did your wife, but this girl"—she pointed a finger at Catherine—"would not have today found herself in such a position. I would never have allowed it."

"You are to leave! Now!" Havington shouted.

Lucretia turned back to him. "I will not," she answered, contempt clearly edging her words. "I have remained quiet far too long. Allowed you and others like you to mark my son. It will happen no longer. I have at last found my voice and I intend to use it."

Beads of sweat began to stand out on Havington's forehead, his lips turning white as his jaw muscles tensed. "My daughter shall marry Mr. Chamberlain. As her mother would have wished." His hands gestured wildly. "Your outburst, Mrs. Evernham, will not change that."

"Her mother would have vigorously protested such an event." Lucretia's words rang out in the chapel. "I am here to also serve as *her* voice."

From the corner of her eye, Andi looked at the faces around her. Every member of the assembled group, including the rector, stood in what appeared to be a shocked silence.

Havington recovered himself first. "How dare you say such a thing?" he hissed. "I, and only I, will speak for the wishes of my wife."

"Jane Havington was my friend. How dare you suppose that she would have approved of her daughter being denied marriage to the man she loves, only to be married to another, against her will?"

As Havington sputtered in indignation, Lucretia shot him a cutting look and turned back to Catherine, trying again. "You must not allow him to do this to you, child. A life without the one you love is no life at all!"

"I—I—" A mixture of confusion and shock contorting her face, Catherine looked from Lucretia to her father, then turned away from both and toward the rector. "Please proceed," she directed him, choking back a sob.

"And you will be silent, woman," Havington commanded Lucretia. He gestured at the rector. "My daughter has spoken. Proceed with the ceremony."

Catherine was going ahead with it. In spite of everything Lucretia had said to her. *She wouldn't if she knew what kind of a man her father really is. She'd have no choice but to stop and listen.*

With every bit of strength she could muster and all the mental determination she could find, Andi concentrated on one goal: breaking Louisa's hold. When at last she did, her words sailed into the air on a shout, bouncing off the stone walls. "Your father tried to have me raped!" she cried. "Because Mr. Chamberlain dared to look at me. Your father believed a filthy stable hand, laying his hands upon me, could frighten me away!" Gulping for breath, she wrenched herself toward Catherine. "Your father did such a thing to ensure you would marry Mr. Chamberlain and not Mr. Evernham."

Catherine drew in a breath and stared at Andi, her eyes wide. Then she whirled on her father. "Father, can this be true? Would you stoop so low to attempt to injure Alexandra?"

Something was happening to the left of Havington. Andi tore her eyes away from Catherine and saw Lucretia's hand, rearing back and up to connect with Horatio Havington's face in a stinging slap that reverberated around the assembled group. "You are a vile man, sir!" Lucretia said in a high-pitched shriek.

Havington's face twisted alarmingly. He raised his own hand above the head of the small woman.

Andi couldn't let him strike Lucretia. "Noooo!" She cried, throwing herself toward the smaller woman. But both Nathaniel and Edland were there even more quickly, pushing Andi out of harm's way. She toppled backward, catching herself against the altar. Ow. Her shoulder. She'd nearly forgotten how much it still hurt.

"Father!" Catherine's voice pierced the stillness. He turned toward her, hesitating, his arm still held high.

"You shall not hurt her," Catherine said with a newfound strength. "I will not allow it."

Havington appeared confused. He looked up at his arm, as if just realizing it was there, and dropped it slowly. Edland's fist then connected squarely with his face, sending the older man reeling. He staggered back until he hit a pew and then gripped it with his hands.

It took Catherine only a few steps to reach him, but instead of rendering assistance, she glared down at him, hands on her hips. Andi watched as, knuckles white, she crushed the bouquet of flowers between her fingers. The petals shook and scattered to the floor.

"You have proved to me, Father, just how little one's parentage can mean," Catherine said, her voice shaking with anger. "I have always believed you to be a gentleman. Only now do I see that I have had to rise above you to become a lady."

"Daughter," Havington protested, "I thought only of you—"

"Silence!" All in the chapel were shocked into ceasing any and all motion. Catherine's finger aimed at her father, pointing straight at his nose.

"You gave little thought to me. It is now time for me to think of myself." She drew her shoulders straight and dropped the hand she'd used to make her point clear. "I shall marry Edland Evernham. And I shall do so now." With a dismissive gesture, she said, "You may stay, if you wish, to witness the event. But only if you will vow to accept him as my husband and hold him in the highest regard."

Edland stepped in next to her, tentatively slipping one hand around Catherine's waist. Together, they faced down her father.

Havington fumbled for words, at last saying in a faint voice, "As you wish, daughter." Suddenly, Horatio Havington looked very, very old.

Andi felt something begin to steal over her. A crushing sense of defeat that made her knees so weak she had to reach for the altar and hold on. It wasn't coming from within her, it was as if it came from the outside, transmitted somehow through her body. *Louisa.*

Andi's eyes flew to Nathaniel. He, always the monitor of the author's emotional state, seemed to feel it as well. She saw the sadness in his expression as his gaze swept down to Julia, the wide-eyed figure standing bravely at his side. Then he looked at Andi. The pain and regret she saw in his eyes made her want to weep. She pressed a clenched fist to her heart.

Edland and Catherine, hand in hand, moved slowly toward the rector. Catherine turned toward Nathaniel and smiled at him with the determined strength of a woman who had at last made up her mind. "You will release me from my obligation?"

He let his gaze linger a moment on Andi before he turned back to Catherine. "I must be granted one request in return."

"Yes?" Catherine arched an eyebrow. Edland took a step toward Nathaniel, suspicion written on his face.

"If your father is unwilling to do you the service, I would be most honored to present the bride."

Relief flooded Catherine's face and she reached out to give Nathaniel a quick hug. Edland stuck his hand out to pump Nathaniel's vigorously. Andi's eyes filled with tears as the author's sense of futility consumed her body, from her head to her toes.

Louisa had given up. She would finish this scene and end the book, with no happy ending for Nathaniel or Julia. Catherine had become a heroine with her own intentions, and Edland had now stepped into the role of hero.

All because Andi, hoping for a Heathcliff and Cathy scene, couldn't stop interfering.

Her only hope was to leave. If she wasn't here, Louisa might find the strength to do something with the story, to tie up loose ends for Nathaniel or move him back into the hero role by having him declare an undying love for Catherine. It could be that a happy life might still await him, without the complication of Alexandra Lofton-Hale. But if the story proceeded on its current track and he gave away the bride, he would be giving away his life as well.

She couldn't do that to him. Or to anyone else. She'd done enough already.

Forcing her shaking hand to move upward, she found the place in the bodice of her dress where she had hidden the wishing stone. As Edland and Catherine faced the rector, who opened his book and began to read, Andi reached inside and pulled out the stone. She clutched it in her palm, feeling its smooth, odd comfort against her skin.

Her only other choice would be to continue on as self-centered as she had been since this dream, or whatever it really was, had begun. She'd thought she had tremendous, earth-shattering problems not finding a man to spend the rest of her life with. But she hadn't known what knee-crumpling heartbreak meant until she found, and then couldn't have, him.

This was it. Time to be the bigger person she'd never known she could. Andi concentrated hard, pushing against Louisa with every drop of energy she had, with every breath she could hold in tight. Would it work? Finally, gasping and with tears welling in her eyes, she whispered the words that would bring both her and Nathaniel the freedom to meet their destinies.

Eyes turned toward her in curiosity. She found and held only his, her mouth forming the word "Good-bye," as she clutched the warmth of the stone in her palm and began to rub it with her finger. His eyes widened, as if in warning. Then she again began to whisper the Latin words that had appeared, with surprising clarity, in her mind.

*Next, form a wish.* This time, it wasn't as easy. *Concentrate,* Andi told herself. *Allowing him, and the others, to have a life is more important than the miserable state of mine.*

And then she had her wish. *Please take me home. And let Louisa's health hold out long enough for her to finish the book, with a happy ending for Nathaniel, Julia, Catherine, and Edland. Amelia, too. Without me.*

She had one last, lingering look at him as his dark eyes began to comprehend what she had done. The whir of light and dark overtook her, and Andi again was hurled through empty space.

Dully, she thought that she should probably hope she ended up back in her apartment and not caught in some other window of time midjourney. Maybe she had even been supposed to put that into the wish, to ensure her landing spot.

But she couldn't work up enough energy to really care. If all she had left was the imprint he'd left on her soul, so be it. At least she would have the memory of the touch of a man who would live forever in her heart, if nowhere else.

At last, she landed, with a small bump against soft padding. She sat very still for several minutes. When she finally opened her eyes, which were still stinging with unshed tears, she found herself sitting on her couch in her apartment, in the bathrobe she had worn the fateful night that had started it all. A copy of *Wedgfeld Hall* lay in her lap.

Open to the third chapter.

# Chapter Nineteen

The book. Finished. It would tell her what she couldn't bear to know, but had to find out.

She took a deep breath and, with trembling fingers, flipped through the fragile pages until she came to the final chapter. She stared at the opening line for what seemed like hours, then closed the book. "I don't want to know," she said to the empty room.

It occurred to her that for the first time in what seemed like centuries, she hadn't had to worry whose voice would come out.

She squeezed her eyes shut for a few seconds and opened them again. If she didn't force herself to read the last chapter in the book, she would never know if what she'd done had been worth it. If the people she now thought of with fondness, Catherine and Edland, had ever found happiness together. If Horatio Havington had actually allowed the wedding to take place. If Lucretia Evernham had seen her son happily married.

Andi placed a hand over a heart that beat so hard

it seemed to be crowding into her throat, making it hard to swallow. She opened the book again slowly, until her fingers found the last few pages. And then, she began to read.

*Horatio Havington stepped back, reeling from the blow the small woman had inflicted upon his cheek. The strength of it was somewhat surprising, he reflected, though he should have likely remembered its sting from the one she had similarly struck him with those many years ago. He drew his shoulders up, determined that no one should be aware of either the physical pain or the surprise Lucretia Evernham had effected. The woman was, after all, no one of consequence.*

*"Madam, you shall take your leave of this place,"* *he said calmly enough. "As you must certainly be able to see, a wedding is to happen."*

*"A wedding, indeed,"* *the irritating woman replied. "However, I intend to see that it shall not be the one you have so deviously arranged. As you are exceedingly aware, Horatio Havington, I am not one to accommodate your will."*

*He took a step toward her. It was too much for a man to bear, this infuriating person daring to contradict him yet again, to attempt to foil the plans he carried forth in memory of his dearly departed wife. There was nothing to do but to put a stop to it at once. His arm rose of its own accord, fueled by the anger burning deep within his gut and the red blazing before his eyes. This woman would not force a stop to the ceremony, not when he was so close to seeing his daughter well married, as he had faithfully promised.*

"Father!" His daughter's piercing cry broke through the stillness, echoing against the stone walls that surrounded them. He turned toward her, for the moment taken aback.

"You shall not harm her!" It was Catherine's voice.

In confusion, he looked at the arm he had raised, at the defiant, but frightened, look Lucretia Evernham cast at him, and finally, at his beloved daughter, whose furious, injured expression he had never previously been unfortunate enough to find cast upon him.

Catherine moved to his side swiftly, beaten to the place only by Edland Evernham, who had the look of the devil in his eye. Havington lowered his arm with a discomforting awkwardness, seeing as he did the eyes that had all turned to him. For the first time in many years, words appeared to elude him.

"Nonsense," he said, though none too clearly. It may have seemed, he realized, that he intended to strike the woman. Preposterous. He never would have done so. The thought gave him, however, a certain pause.

"Stand away, Mother," Evernham instructed crisply. "I shall not allow him to do you harm."

Havington snorted. The upstart.

But Evernham wasn't finished. "And you, Catherine," he said, "must at this moment tell me whom your heart proclaims you shall marry. If it is Westcott, here"—he gestured in the gentleman's direction—"I shall move aside. But I do believe it is me you love, and if you confirm that to me now, we shall stand before this rector and become man and wife. I shall not have it any other way."

He stopped speaking, his chest heaving, his eyes fixed on Catherine, awaiting her answer.

Andi caught her breath. Edland had stood up to
Havington. And Louisa had allowed it. Wait a
minute. Westcott? She'd been reading so fast she'd
nearly missed seeing the name. What had happened to Nathaniel?

Dread beginning to build in the small of her
stomach, she forced her attention back to the page.

*"You, sir, are the one I love," Catherine said in low,
clear tones that rose to penetrate the length of the
room. "I tell you, Father, that I shall marry Mr.
Evernham. You may leave us now or stay to see the
ceremony performed."*

*Havington stood, disbelieving, his gaze moving
from his daughter's face to that of the hapless Westcott,
who stood rooted to his place, unable to speak. Though
an Earl had seemed the finest choice by far for his
daughter, Havington saw him, for the first time, as a
mealy, sweaty man who had only his title to offer. If the
gentleman had any character at all, surely he would
have taken a stand against Evernham, called him out
or pounded him with his fists. Instead, he stood shaking, his brow disturbingly damp.*

*At times, a man had to face the consequences when
he found himself bested. Though he would have had
difficulty accepting such a result from the man glowering before him, there was little he found he could do
when it was his faithful daughter, her hand clenched
in the dank air of the chapel. Quite suddenly, he felt
overly fatigued, unbearably old, and alone.*

*"As you wish," Havington heard himself say;
though had he been asked to repeat it, he would have
had to profess an inability to do so.*

*His daughter would be married. To a man of less*

*than gentle birth. He lifted his gaze to the ceiling,
calling upon the soul of his departed wife to forgive
him. He had, after all, attempted to do as she had
asked. Their daughter had simply shown a determination he could not surmount.*

Andi, her anxiety rising until her pulse skipped
and the words seemed to blur together as one,
stopped reading. She scanned the final pages, her
heart pounding. No mention of Nathaniel. Amelia
appeared as a bridesmaid. Catherine and Edland
had married triumphantly, and Lucretia Evernham
had flounced out of the chapel behind them, show-
ering good wishes, satisfied that Horatio Havington
had finally met his match.

Louisa had completely rewritten the end of the
scene.

So someone named Westcott had taken the part
of the unsuccessful suitor, carrying not one of the
qualities of Nathaniel Chamberlain. No doubt
easier to write, Andi thought bitterly. Westcott was
clearly no hero. Which left only Edland.

She leafed through the rest of the pages. Nathaniel's
name did not appear anywhere. Neither did that of
Alexandra Lofton-Hale. He'd been right. When characters became too troublesome, they were written out,
never to have existed.

It couldn't be. She kept telling herself that even
as the tears stung her eyes and then began to flow
freely, splashing onto the page open in front of her
until its thin paper became wet. She leaned forward to lay the book on the table, then sat back and
buried her face in her hands. He had existed and
he still did, in her heart.

But Nathaniel hadn't been able to live on. Her interference in the author's thoughts and plans had, just as he had said it would, meant he could not end up with a life that would continue on in happiness. He'd been written out, and she as heedless of warnings as ever, was squarely to blame.

She had single-handedly killed him. Destroyed his happy ending. And that of innocent little Julia as well.

"I'm sorry, Nathaniel," she whispered, grabbing a tissue to swipe at the tears. *So very sorry. How could I have known how much that bull's crash through the china shop could cost innocent people?*

Images of Nathaniel and Julia sailing through space, calling to her, drifted before her mind's eye. His face as she'd left him. He would have been so much better off if she'd never barreled into his life, doing everything she could to manipulate an ending all her own.

Her shoulders shook and her stomach knotted painfully as she cried on, silently pleading for another chance to make things right, until a thought occurred to her. The stone. It had been a wish, one simple, but desperate, wish that had done the damage. Another wish might be able to undo it all.

All she had to do was find the wishing stone.

She looked down at her robe and jumped to her feet, hopping up and down. Nothing fell out. Falling to her knees, she began to search the carpet. A piece of popcorn. A penny. A forgotten parking ticket. No wishing stone anywhere. She shook out the contents of her purse, knowing even as she did how ridiculous it was. It would have been nice to have her purse on the . . . trip she'd taken. First time she'd traveled without breath mints.

An hour later, knees stinging with rug burn, she had to stop. She sat back and pulled her legs up to her chin, burying her face in the terrycloth of her robe and inwardly cursing whatever thoughtlessness had led her to not keep track of the stone. Her one chance to try and make things right.

Finally, after what seemed like hours, she dragged herself to bed, laying a hot cheek against the cool satin of the pillowcase, helped to a restless sleep by the effects of a glass of wine. It had been sitting on the table, still cold, right where she'd left it. Minutes ago. Forever ago.

In the dreams that came and went, she saw his face and heard his voice, always a fingertip away from her touch, and an ocean away from the sound of her own desperate voice, pleading to know if happiness had found him.

If she had to read every one of Louisa's books she could get her hands on, she would do it, on the slim hope that his character would have resurfaced. She'd search to the ends of the earth to find them, in rare bookstores, or over the Internet. But even as she made that promise to herself, she remembered what she'd seen on eBay about the book *Wedgfeld Hall*. It had been Louisa's last, written in the final days of an illness that had claimed her life.

No doubt about it. She'd killed him. Possibly Louisa, too.

When the sunlight streaked through her bedroom window in the morning, Andi awoke from a groggy near-sleep, deriding herself for the depths of despair she'd fallen into over a man like Tristan, and the series of bad dates that had followed him.

For the first time since that day five years ago, she allowed herself to think back, to really remember. To breathe in the roses, feel the smooth, shiny satin of the gown against her skin, take in the upturned faces smiling in expectation. He had been ready to say, "I do." They were almost to that part, her heart thudding against her chest so hard she'd been sure the guests could hear it.

She'd tried to smile, tried hard. Her mother would be happy. Her father, in his distracted way, would be as happy as he could be. Andi would be happy. Who wouldn't? Tristan was smooth, handsome, loaded with money. They'd picked out a great house. Half of her things had been moved in already. The fact that she hadn't moved them, or even known they were going, hadn't bothered her *too* much.

Other things had, though, if she allowed herself to finally admit it. The fact that her mother had insisted her bridesmaids be women she knew from the private school where she'd always felt out of place. Not friends she'd made since, like Rita, who loved books the way she did and favored long, faded skirts and an easygoing guy named Chet, who smoked a pipe for no reason they could fathom.

And the fact that Tristan didn't have the time to read, or even the interest in it. He'd ruffle her hair and tease her about burying her head in books. Then he'd lead her to bed. Sure, he made her feel attractive, alluring even. And they'd had a great time together. Everyone wanted them to get married, even his parents, who had said something about "academic genes," apparently wanting grand-children who could make it into college without the benefit of the building they'd paid to erect.

An almost perfect life had awaited her, she'd thought. No relationship had everything, but this one had security, just like her mother had said.

Until she found out he'd had drinks with Becca, his old girlfriend, she of the perfect tan and golden hair. It was nothing, he'd said, and then he'd met Becca for drinks again. Andi had tried to ignore it, told herself it didn't matter. But he'd whispered in her ear, on their wedding day, halting the ceremony before they got to "I do." She still remembered the rustle of his tux, and its new-fabric smell, the squeak of one of his shiny shoes when he turned to leave. The way her mother's cheeks, pink with humilia-tion, matched the pink of the bridesmaids' dresses.

Worst of all, she remembered his whispered words, saying that all they'd really had was great sex. In other words, that's all she was good for.

She let herself hold on to that memory now, let it burn through her, flame her cheeks, and pierce a hole in her heart. She'd never told anyone, afraid they'd look at her with disbelief and ask, "You didn't know? You thought he loved *you?*"

Yes. She'd thought he loved her. Although now that she allowed herself to dwell on it, to revel in the awful hurt of that day, she realized that *she* hadn't loved *him*. She would have been as miser-able married to Tristan as Catherine would have been if she had married Nathaniel.

And, you know . . . it might have been mostly about the sex for her, too.

From across the room, her cat, Mr. Rochester,

blinked with the wise eyes of an animal that knows everything but says nothing. Her cat. While she'd been gone, she hadn't even thought about how he would fare, who would feed him.

But it seemed she'd been gone only minutes, if that. "Come here, Mr. Rochester." He padded toward her and she gave him a good head scratching, her entire body feeling too heavy to move. Exhausted.

Epiphanies were, apparently, physically draining.

With effort, she stood, moving toward the bathroom. A few minutes later, she stepped into the shower, her eyes closed, letting the hot water wash down over her and adjusting the showerhead so that it pounded in pulsating drops that stung and reddened her skin. Somehow, she had to push aside the deep, aching sense of loss that lingered yet. It wasn't as though he had been a *real* person. But even as she said the words sternly to herself, over and over, they just didn't . . . take, somehow.

Absently, she rubbed soap over her body, hoping for a clean beginning that was more than physical, but stopped when her fingers glided across something she'd never felt before. She stopped and then let her hand go over it again.

A scar. She opened her eyes and wrenched her shoulder around until she could see it. Fully healed, but a raised white scar, nonetheless. One that came from the bullet that had grazed across her, on a nearly deserted field at dawn.

Andi sank against the shower stall and let the water pour down around her. She laid a hand across the scar to protect it, to keep it from washing away. A badge of honor, in some way, for her wounded soul.

As she watched the water swirl and disappear down the drain, her heart took a tiny leap of joy in the fact that she had been left with a lasting physical reminder of the one she held close in her heart. But just as quickly, she reminded herself that the scar was also indisputable proof that by falling for him and inserting herself where she didn't belong, she had cost Nathaniel his life.

Would she ever be able to look herself in the eye again? Did she, with all her drama-queen selfishness, deserve to live on as if nothing had happened? She stood up and moved back into the center of the stream of water, squeezing her eyes shut and raising her head to let the water cover her face. It poured in streams over her eyes, her nose, her ears, as she clung to the hope it would drown out the self-doubt she couldn't suppress.

At last, she found the strength to turn the water off and drag herself out of the shower. She dried off with a fluffy towel that she raked with a vengeance across the freshly healed scar, as if pain in that tender spot might somehow help her to atone.

Next, she woodenly stepped into jeans and pulled on a white T-shirt, pulling a comb through the hair that had returned to normal. No curls or tendrils. Nothing else that would serve as a reminder of what had happened, except the tremendous hole inside that only seemed to be growing larger.

A sneaker pushed against the green linoleum of the classroom floor, making a squeaking sound.

Pages rustled impatiently. A throat cleared and a high-pitched whisper came from the back, followed by a short guffaw. Through an open window, a single bird twittered from the branch of a tree outside. Andi's students waited for her to begin class. But she couldn't seem to tear her eyes from the cover of John Steinbeck's novel. Required reading. Required teaching.

"Uh, Ms. Lofton-Hale?" The question came from John, the budding football star sitting in the second row, right behind Brittany, his not-so-secret crush.

Andi took a long moment to close and open her eyes, then raised them to meet those of her class, some of them bored already, some leery, others thinking about prom. Still others with problems at home bigger than their narrow shoulders should have to carry.

And they were waiting for her to deliver the required lecture about John Steinbeck's work, followed by homework that would make them groan. It was her life.

Well, with apologies to Mr. Steinbeck, a gifted author, indeed, Andi had something else on her mind to talk about. Her wooden chair squeaked against the floor as she pushed it back to rise and take a few steps to stand before her students. "As you know, we are to begin studying *Of Mice and Men* today," she said. "And while I am relatively certain you have all diligently completed your reading assignment . . ." It didn't take long for the gazes to be averted, the muted rumbling of excuses to begin. ". . . I would like to instead revisit the last book we read, *Pride and Prejudice*. The beginnings of a protest came from the back row. She ignored it. "We were not quite finished with the work."

A pause and then some scurrying to find the book. Three or four, "But Ms. Lofton-Hale, we don't—" began to bubble toward the front.

"It's okay," she reassured them, her gaze moving row to row. "You don't need to have the book in front of you just now." Visible relaxation from her audience, as more than a few long male legs stretched out into the aisles, settling in for a snooze behind open eyes. She'd once overheard two basketball players saying her class was great for a nap.

"Today we're going to talk about the times in which Jane Austen wrote." The wonderful, confusing, rigidly structured and breathtaking times in which she wrote. "Jane Austen could be considered an early feminist. Any ideas why?"

A female hand raised, even as John, wrenching his eyes away from Brittany's blond head, snorted, "All she wrote about was marriage. She was obsessed."

"But not about marriage," ventured Alison, a studious girl with lively blue eyes, from a row over. "It was more about what *having* to be married did to women."

"Good point," Andi said. "And what it did to men."

"Huh?" John frowned.

"Let's talk about the complexity of life during that time period. *Really* talk about it." Andi began to walk, up one row and down the other, where feet quickly shuffled to move out of her way. Her words spilled over each other, describing the emotions of the Regency era, the societal constrictions, the importance of a woman's reputation, even the smells of the village and of the stables at Barrington Manor. Living by candlelight, without cell phones or DVDs. The horses, the raw feeling of living close to the earth, without barriers like sidewalks, planned developments, satellite TV. Then she tied it all in to the story of Elizabeth and her Mr. Darcy.

She was aware, on some level, of the passing of time as she thumped her fingers in her palm, punctuating her points, and called on students with rapid-fire precision. But when the bell rang that signaled the end of class, she stopped midsentence, surprised.

Three students still had their hands in the air.

"Well," she said. "Good, um . . . class. Tomorrow, Steinbeck. Get your reading done."

The usual scraping of chairs, groaning of desks, and thumping of books followed. John followed close on Brittany's heels as she passed Andi, and said, "That was fun." Behind her, Kim nodded vigorous agreement as her boyfriend, Nick, mumbled, "Yeah, well, don't be thinking I'm any Darcy."

"You wish," perky Kim responded, beaming up at him.

Andi's spirit soared straight up to the ceiling tiles. Her students. Talking about the book. Remembering character names, using them in conversation.

She raised a hand to touch the spot beneath her shirt where the new scar marked her skin with lasting memory. No, she'd never tell anyone what she'd had to go through to get from here to there.

But it had been worth it, in more ways than one.


The day was unexpectedly beautiful, one of those rare ones with the sun shining and Mt. Hood looming large and white against a blue sky. At the espresso shop, Andi gave her order with the quietly confident smile that seemed to now be her constant companion. Carlos, the gay barista she'd tried to seduce, so long ago that it now seemed like years instead of days, greeted her with an answering grin. "Hey, Andi. How's everything?"

"Good, thanks." The response he likely heard from everyone, but in her case, it might even be true. The world she'd viewed in shades of gray seemed a little clearer, sharper these days. She'd even told her mother last night to go adopt a puppy if she needed a grandchild so bad. The startled gasp on the other end of the line had been flat-out fun.

So . . . not everything she could hope and wish for, but it was a start.

Around her, she heard voices, some animated, some grumpy, along with the high whistle of milk steaming, the rustle of a newspaper, change being dropped into a tip jar. Sounds so familiar they always gave her a sense of comfort.

When she heard her order called, she reached toward the bar, but as she reached for the cup, another hand closed around her fingers. Startled, Andi tried to pull back, but her hand, held by the other, stayed put. A couple of drops spilled from the hole in the lid of the cup, splashing onto the gleaming counter.

The person stood behind her, so close that she could feel the warmth of another body brushing against her back. "Hey, sorry," she began to say, thinking that, in her desperation for caffeine, her hand must have shot out too quickly, unintentionally grabbing someone else's drink.

"It's all right," said a low voice in her ear. A familiar voice. Dear God, too familiar.

She was imagining Nathaniel's voice in a Starbucks. That part of her heart hadn't healed yet, but she'd imagined herself to be dealing with it in *some* way that worked. Apparently not. "I, um, okay, let *go.*" The frantic fluttering in her chest had her feet wanting to make a break for the door.

But, first . . . She had to see him.

The man opened his hand to release her fingers and she forced herself to turn and look at him through the slits that were the widest she would allow her eyes to open. *No.* It *couldn't* be. Not— How? Her mouth opened at the same time her knees buckled. He had to reach out and catch her.

Same black, curling hair. Same dark eyes that held hers and would not let go. Same proud thrust to his chin. But something different now, he was relaxed and smiling. And he wasn't wearing those impossible, wonderful, muscle-defining breeches. Instead, a T-shirt in royal blue, showing strong, tanned arms and jeans. Just tight enough that she wouldn't have to mourn the loss of those riding breeches.

"My mistake," he said with a British accent. "I thought it was mine."

She couldn't say it. Couldn't ask . . . could she? "Nathaniel?" she whispered, heart in her throat. Would he look at her askance and give the barista a look that meant, *Call the police, there's something wrong with this woman. She's not in her right mind. Has mistaken me for someone else. Happens all the time, I'm so incredibly good-looking that every woman thinks she knows me.*

"Actually," he said, with a wink and a conspiratorial whisper, "it's Nate."

"Are you who I think you are?" And then she squeezed her eyes shut and tensed the muscles in her body, afraid with every fiber of her being to hear the word "no."

She felt a gentle chucking under her chin. "It was our destiny, you know, Alexandra," he said, peppermint breath tickling her nose. Oh God! She felt dizzy, delirious. Feverish even. It couldn't be him. It couldn't. Could it?

From somewhere very far away, Andi heard the barista say, "tall mocha," in a voice that sounded amused by the goings-on at his counter. And then the sound of another cup hitting the surface.

"This one is mine," Nate said. He must have reached for it before he began to lead her away from the counter, but Andi was too afraid to open her eyes to tell. "You may look at me," he said, laughter in his voice, when he'd brought them both to a stop.

Did she trust herself to do that? Slowly and carefully, she did. It was him. It really was. Relief flooded through her until she dipped her knees halfway to the ground and had to grab the edge of the counter and hold on. Again, he reached out to steady her. She could not believe her eyes. Head shaking, she asked, "How can this happen? You weren't in the book. Louisa wrote you out. I'm so sorry, Nathaniel, that I didn't listen to you." She choked on the last.

"Ah, that," he said, giving her a look both deadly serious and tinged with something that looked like amusement. "You left something behind."

She didn't understand. There hadn't been anything to leave. "I couldn't have."

"The wishing stone."

The stone. It hadn't made the journey back with her. *That's* why she couldn't find it.

"I heard it drop, and because you had told me about it earlier, I knew what it could do. And I knew where I was meant to be."

"You made a wish?" she whispered.

"For me and Julia. I wished with every bit of energy I could find that the two of us would be written out of *Wedgfeld Hall* and into another story."

"Another story," she repeated slowly, trying to take it in.

"It worked, I am very glad to report," he said, the green flecks in his dark eyes twinkling. And now, *someone,*" he said, dragging the word out meaningfully, "has decided to give us a story of our own."

"Our own," she repeated.

"And you'll be glad to know," he said, with a wink that matched the gleam in his eye, "that this writer is much more inclined to listen to her characters. She'll give us banks of room to help her write the story, which I hear," he dropped his voice even lower, until it was a rumble that lit every one of Andi's nerves on fire, "is to be quite a sensual one."

Andi stayed perfectly still, not daring to move or breathe. Then a thought occurred to her. A horrible one. "But . . . Julia?" she whispered.

"Quite happily installed in school here," he answered. "I am again a bachelor uncle, as it turns out."

Andi exhaled suddenly, sagging in relief and reaching out to clutch the fabric of his T-shirt with her hands. Both of them were fine. She hadn't killed either one, after all.

"She is, however," he said, drawing a finger down her cheek and prompting every nerve in her body to leap in delight, "at a slumber party for the evening. Leaving me quite at loose ends."

"You are?" She still couldn't believe this.

Then Nathaniel, the man of her dreams, said, "This writer is perfectly willing to listen to how we would like this story to begin. So, what say you?" His arm swept the room in dramatic fashion. "Espresso? Or, dinner this evening, over a bottle of the finest wine?"

Andi's heart soared until she thought it would burst from her chest. Nathaniel had risked everything to find her. He wanted *her* as much as she wanted *him*. This time, she could say it with conviction, *Louisa be damned*. They had a writer who wanted to know who they were, who would let them write their own story.

And maybe . . . just maybe . . . she was ready for that story, for the first time in five years.

Hold on. She was stuck again in the pages of a book? An idea to wonder about, worry about, maybe even call the psychiatrist about . . . But then she threw back her head, tossing her hair with abandon. Who cared?

When she raised her head again, she grinned with every part of her, giddy with the sense of pure happiness washing over her. She was with Nathaniel. No, Nate. In a Starbucks. Coffee and love, could there be a more potent combination? Toss in chocolate and she was good.

"Just one bit of unfinished business first," he said

in a lazily sensuous voice that lit a flame that began to burn deep inside her.

The heat rose to her cheeks in a flash. She managed to find her hand to wave it in front of her face. "Yes?" she croaked.

"Your middle name. I find that I must know it. It's terribly important to me."

"Oh." The word came out in a tiny, breathless sound. "Ethel," she said.

"Alexandra Ethel?" He made a face of amused horror.

"My grandmother's name. My father insisted."

"Then, Alexandra Ethel, we must be off, I believe." He cupped her elbow with his palm. "We have a story to begin."